ABOUT THIS BOOK

MARA, DAUGHTER OF THE NILE
Eloise Jarvis McGraw

Mara is a proud and beautiful slave girl who yearns for freedom. But her escape from her cruel master only places her at the mercy of not one, but two rival masters who each support contenders to the throne of Egypt—and who would kill Mara instantly if they suspected her role as double spy. Although distrustful of both at first, Mara begins to believe in one of them, Sheftu, and his plan to restore Thutmose III to the throne. And as her belief grows stronger, Mara finds herself, against her will, falling in love with him. But before she can reveal that love and pledge her aid to Sheftu, her duplicity is discovered, and a battle ensues in which both Mara's life and the fate of Egypt are at stake.

"The characters are solid flesh and blood beneath their ancient costumes, and the vigor of their thoughts, emotions, and actions lend an appeal beyond that of historical fiction. This is a good, full-bodied story."—*The New York Times*

MARA

DAUGHTER OF THE NILE

by

Eloise Jarvis McGraw

PUFFIN BOOKS

PUFFIN BOOKS

Published by the Penguin Group

Penguin Putnam Inc., 375 Hudson Street, New York, New York 10014, U.S.A.

Penguin Books Ltd, 27 Wrights Lane, London W8 5TZ, England

Penguin Books Australia Ltd, Ringwood, Victoria, Australia

Penguin Books Canada Ltd, 10 Alcorn Avenue, Toronto, Ontario, Canada M4V 3B2

Penguin Books (N.Z.) Ltd, 182–190 Wairau Road, Auckland 10, New Zealand

First published by Coward McCann 1953
Published in Puffin Books 1985

23 25 27 29 30 28 26 24 22

Printed in the United States of America

Set in Lino Bodoni Book

Library of Congress Cataloging in Publication Data
McGraw, Eloise Jarvis.
Mara, daughter of the Nile.
Originally published: New York : Coward McCann, 1953.
Summary: The adventures of an ingenious Egyptian
slave girl who undertakes a dangerous assignment as
a spy in the royal palace of Thebes, in the days
when Queen Hatshepsut ruled.
[1. Egypt—History—To 332 B.C.—Fiction]
I. Title.
PZ7.M1696Mar   1985   [Fic]   85-567   ISBN 0 14 03.1929 8

TO ALICE TORREY

who is my idea of all an editor should be

Contents

PART V—THE RING

PART VI—THE TRAP

Part I—Menfe

CHAPTER 1

The Mysterious Passenger

NEKONKH, captain of the Nile boat *Silver Beetle*, paused for the fiftieth time beside his vessel's high beaked prow and shaded his eyes to peer anxiously across the wharfs.

The city that rose beyond them shimmered, almost drained of color, in the glare of Egyptian noon. Doorways were blue-black in white buildings, alleys were plunged in shadow; the gay colors of the sails and hulls that crowded the harbor seemed faded and indistinct, and even the green of the Nile was overlaid by a blinding surface glitter. Only the sky was vivid, curving in a high blue arch over ancient Menfe.

The wharf itself seethed with activity. Sweating porters hurried in and out among groups of merchants haggling over stacks of cargo yet to be loaded; sailors, both foreign and Egyptian, swarmed everywhere, talking in a babble of tongues. A donkey drover pushed through a cluster of pale-faced Libyans, shouting at his laden beasts; three Mitanni traders in the fringed garments of Babel laid wagers on a dogfight at one end of the wharf, while a ring of yelling urchins surrounded a cage of monkeys at the other. Over all rose the rank smell of the river—an odor compounded of fish, mud, water-soaked rope, pitch and crocodiles.

1

But nowhere in that tangle was the one tall figure for which the captain searched.

Nekonkh chewed his lip and drummed upon the gunwale with his big, blunt fingers. An hour ago he had been uneasy; now he was so tense that when his helmsman strolled across the deck and touched his elbow, he leaped as if he had been burned.

"By Set and all the devils!" he roared, whirling about savagely. "Fool! Coming upon me from behind like that! What do you want?"

The helmsman took a hasty step back. "The cargo," he mumbled. "Everything is stowed, master. We're ready to sail."

"Well?"

"The—er—we await orders."

"Then await them!"

The helmsman laid his right hand on his left shoulder in the attitude of submission, and escaped, casting puzzled glances backward as he did so.

Nekonkh sighed explosively and mopped the sweat off his upper lip with a hairy wrist. He was a burly man with a fierce jaw contradicted by mild brown eyes, and just now he looked and felt a good deal older than his forty years. For a moment he leaned wearily against the gunwale, staring upriver, where the luxurious barge of some noble moved over the sparkling water like a gigantic water bug, twelve oars on each side dipping rhythmically. Then he straightened, shoved his square-cut black wig askew in order to scratch under it, and adjusted it again with an irritable slap.

Automatically his eye checked the *Silver Beetle*, moving about her trim scrubbed confines from the two great sweeps at the stern to the tall masts with their horizontally furled sails; past the tiny cabin to the bales of wool and hides stacked on the deck, the oarsmen lounging at their posts.

Yes, all was ready to sail, so far as cargo and crew were

2

concerned. But the passenger? The puzzling, unpredictable, portentous passenger whose very charm set alarm bells ringing loudly in Nekonkh's mind—what of him?

Nekonkh swore under his breath, wishing fervently that cargo and crew were all he had to worry about—wishing he knew either more or less. It was dangerous to have brains these days in the land of Kemt.

He took a restless turn about the deck, his joined hands flapping impatiently at his back, and reviewed once more his brief acquaintance with the missing passenger. It was an acquaintance only ten days old; he had seen the young man for the first time the morning he set sail from Thebes on this trip to Menfe. Since the youth—Sheftu; he had said his name was—had paid his passage promptly, there seemed no reason to give him a second thought. He was pleasant but unobtrusive—tall, somewhere around twenty years old, with an attractively homely face and a common white *shenti* and headcloth like a thousand others. Except for a certain odd, lazy grace in the way he moved, the captain found nothing unusual about him.

That was at first.

Later, during the long, sun-drenched days of the *Beetle's* journey down the river, Nekonkh had good reason to study his passenger more attentively. Only then did he become aware of other details—for instance, the areas of slightly paler skin on Sheftu's upper arms, which indicated that he habitually wore bracelets, though his sole ornament now was a curious amulet on his left wrist; also the absent, brooding expression which sat so often and so oddly on his young face, and the suave charm which covered this instantly if he knew he was being watched. The charm itself was a little odd, once you thought of it. Since when did a scribe's apprentice—for so Sheftu had described himself—possess the smooth and subtle manners of a courtier? The captain grew surer and surer that his passenger was no ordinary nobody. Breeding was written in every line of his long, well-

3

muscled body, and his voice had the careless authority of one accustomed to being obeyed.

However, Nekonkh might have noticed none of this, had it not been for a conversation which suddenly focused his attention on the young man. It took place early one morning, about five days out of Thebes. The *Silver Beetle* was sailing past an ancient temple surrounded by scaffolding and piles of stone, around which workmen swarmed busily. Nekonkh, standing alone at the door of his cabin, scowled across the river and shook his head.

"*Ai!* There it is again!" he muttered sourly to himself.

"What do you mean, Captain?"

Nekonkh jumped. He had not heard his passenger come up beside him. "Why, the rebuilding of the old temple yonder," he answered, pointing. "If I've seen that sight once I've seen it forty times in the past few years. Our good queen Hatshepsut evidently thinks gold grows on papyrus stalks! Does she mean to restore every ancient building up and down the Nile?" Nekonkh grunted as scaffolds and workmen slipped upstream past the *Beetle's* stern sweeps. "It's not only the old ruins. Amon himself knows what her new temple at Thebes is costing poor folk like me in sweat and taxes!"

"The new temple is a beautiful one, though," remarked Sheftu. "They say every wall of the inner room is covered with handsomely carved reliefs."

"Reliefs depicting Her Majesty's sacred birth, no doubt?" inquired the captain sardonically.

"Of course. What better subject could there be? Hatshepsut was fathered by the Sun himself, nursed by goddesses, and named Pharaoh in her cradle."

"Aye, so she claims, so she claims!" snorted Nekonkh incautiously. "As for me, I would rather see a man on the throne of Egypt! That young Thutmose, her half-brother—when is he to grow up? For fifteen years now she's been acting as his regent, spending gold and silver like water,

4

sending ships—mine among them!—to the edge of the world for her own amusement, letting the empire foul its rudder for want of trained soldiers. And still the king does not come of age! Why? It's obvious, friend! He's not allowed to, nor will he ever be! Hatshepsut is pharaoh, and Egypt must put up with it!"

"You do not admire the queen, Captain?"

It was the very blandness of the voice that caused the alarm bells to clang suddenly in Nekonkh's mind. He swung around and really looked at his passenger for the first time; noted the cleverness of the irregular dark face, the odd little smile hovering about the mouth, the dangerous alertness of the long black eyes. Nekonkh went cold all over. What had he been saying! It was treason to speak against the queen—near treason even to mention the young king's name above a whisper, much less actually complain . . .

Full of a sudden clear picture of himself impaled on the torturer's stake in the midst of some desert, he sagged back against the cabin door. "May the queen live forever!" he exclaimed. "May my tongue be clipped if it utters a word against Hatshepsut, the Daughter of the Sun!"

"Pray rest easy, Captain." Sheftu's voice was like a purr. "You but stated an opinion. But you are somewhat indiscreet. There are those who might haul you off to the palace dungeons at once if they heard what I just heard." He gave Nekonkh a moment to absorb that thought, then added casually, "So you would overthrow the queen?"

"By the Feather of Truth, I said no such thing!" gasped Nekonkh. He darted an agonized glance up and down the deck, then strode to a deserted spot in the bows.

Sheftu followed, his face amused. "A wise precaution," he commented, arranging himself comfortably against the gunwale. "They say the queen's spies are everywhere."

"No doubt!" Nekonkh was convinced he was talking to one that minute. He wiped the sweat from his forehead and attempted to change the subject, but Sheftu overrode him.

5

"She has grounds for her constant suspicions. There's a group of reckless fools in Thebes—no doubt you've heard of them—who have organized in secret to topple Hatshepsut off her throne and set young Thutmose there instead."

"I know nothing of them, nothing! Such movements have started before, and been squashed like beetles. They must be fools indeed who would try again!"

"Perhaps." Sheftu shrugged expressively. He had lowered his voice, moving a little closer to Nekonkh. "But one must give them credit, Captain: they have courage. And they insist they are fighting for what all Egypt really wants. They say it's monstrous that a woman should wear the double crown, and call herself not Royal Wife and Consort, but King and Pharaoh. They say the backs of the people are breaking under her taxes, that the children's ribs show plainer with every statue of herself she erects in the new temple, while Count Senmut the Architect, the favorite, the Lord-High-Everything-In-Egypt, grows mysteriously richer each time a porch is built or a terrace paved. . . . Captain, they say—I but quote, you understand—they say she grows so arrogant that the gods themselves will soon rise up to strike her down, and Egypt with her! Should we permit . . ."

Nekonkh's brain was spinning. What was this young rogue up to, talking like a spy one minute, a firebrand the next? But no, of course he was but quoting. Yet the captain found himself responding fiercely to the forbidden words. Aye, it was true, it was all true, and everyone knew it! Count Senmut had a finger in every pot in Egypt, and as for the queen, that usurper . . . *Beware,* clanged the alarm bells. *You're walking into a trap.*

Sheftu was still talking, softly, insistently. "Should we permit these crimes, they ask? Can we risk the anger of the gods? Is not this woman a peril to all the Black Land?"

Nekonkh grasped blindly at a safe question, whose answer tradition had taught him. "The First Thutmose—he who was pharaoh in my youth—he lives with the gods now. He will protect Egypt from their anger."

"For Hatshepsut's sake?" came the mocking whisper. "For the sake of the daughter who snatched his throne without waiting for him to die? Captain, he disowned her himself, he chiseled her name off all his monuments."

"I know not for whose sake, I know nothing!" snarled Nekonkh. "You'll not trick me into speaking treason, I tell you! Hatshepsut is pharaoh. So be it! Maybe young Thutmose is not fit to rule. Aye, that's it! Only a weakling could be held down so long by a woman—like a rabbit in a snare!"

There was no answer for a moment. When Sheftu spoke again his voice was grim and quiet, without a trace of mockery. "You are mistaken, Captain," he said. "Thutmose is no rabbit, he is a lion. And the snare is not made that will hold a lion forever."

Nekonkh turned slowly. "By the Blessed Son!" he exclaimed. "Which camp are you in, young man? Who speaks treason now?"

Sheftu eased back against the gunwale, his face bland and expressionless. "Why, no one, my friend," he murmured. "We spoke only of snares and rabbits."

Suddenly he smiled. It had an astonishing effect, that smile. It lighted up his dark irregular features with a charm that seemed to warm the world. The nervous sweat dried on Nekonkh's brow, and his throat relaxed. He was even conscious of an obscure exhilaration, a sense of well-being. He found himself grinning genially.

"Aye, aye, you're quite right, mate," he agreed. "Snares and rabbits. Nothing more."

Sheftu bowed and took himself off to the other end of the ship, and there was no more conversation that day. But Nekonkh watched his passenger with feverish interest from that hour on. By the time the *Silver Beetle* docked at Menfe he was convinced that Sheftu was not and never had been a scribe's apprentice; in fact he strongly suspected that the youth was one of those very fools—or heroes—who had secretly rallied about the king.

Furthermore he realized with a reckless sort of excitement that he, too, would be glad to offer his life to such a cause, for the sake of this extraordinary young man, his fettered king, and the Egypt they both loved.

Now, two days after docking, the new cargo was stowed and all was ready to sail. But still there was no sign of Sheftu. He had left the vessel as soon as it tied up, having arranged to return with it to Thebes when the time came. Then he had vanished into the tangle of mud-brick buildings, twisting streets, and hurrying, shouting, sweating humanity that was Menfe. He had not come back.

Restlessly Nekonkh paced his scrubbed acacia deck, from gunwale to cabin, from cabin to sweeps, back again to gunwale. Ominous pictures rose in his mind—Sheftu seized by some spy of the queen, Sheftu questioned by torture, Sheftu hanging head downward from the city walls.

What a fool I am, thought Nekonkh desperately. Why do I fret over the young rogue? For all I know he's reporting *me* to the queen's men this instant! . . . No, by Amon, when he spoke of the king he spoke his heart, I'd stake my last copper on it! If I had told him—if I had offered myself and my ship to him and the king—then he would have let me know his plans, what to do if he did not come back. *Hai!* That I knew more—or else nothing at all! What a fool I am! Why doesn't he come?

Eastward from the wharfs, in another part of the city, a young slave girl of about seventeen years sat in a sunny corner between her master's storerooms and his garden wall. She was bending over a papyrus roll held carefully in her lap, and her lips moved as she read.

Spend the day merrily.
Put unguent and fine oil together to thy nostrils,

8

Set singing and music before thy face.
Cast all evil behind thee, and bethink thee only of joy,
Till comes that day of mooring in the land that loveth
silence.
Spend the day merrily . . .

"Mara!" The harsh voice shattered the quiet of the garden. The girl snatched up the papyrus and stuffed it into her sash, half turning away from the grim-faced woman who had appeared in the storeroom door. "So there you are, Miss Blue-Eyed Good-For-Nothing!" the woman said angrily. "Idling away your time while the rest of us work like the slaves we are! Up with you! The master's *shentis* must be starched and pleated!"

"I wish they clothed his corpse," muttered Mara, flashing a venomous look over her shoulder.

"Aye, aye, so wish we all," retorted the other. "But Zasha's far from in his tomb, and his stick's livelier than he is, as you'll know if he comes home from his jewel trading and finds you skulking here. Come, now, up with you!"

"I come. Go away, Teta."

"Nay, I'll not go until I see you on your feet, and starting for the pressing rooms. Move, now!" Teta leaned farther out the door and peered suspiciously over Mara's shoulder. "What's that you're hiding, you thieving wretch? One of the master's scrolls again, I'll take my oath! *Hai-ai!* Remember the last time! He all but took the flesh off your shoulders, stupid, isn't once enough? Put it back, make haste, or I won't answer for your life. . . . Reading!" she grumbled, turning back into the house as Mara scrambled to her feet and ran in the direction of the Room of Books. "Idle as the mistress herself, when there's ironing to be done, and a thrashing is all she'll get for her high-and-mighty airs!"

May the *kheft*-things take that Zasha and all his kin! fumed Mara as she ran up the red-graveled path. Better not

9

to live at all than to live like this! I swear the dogs in the market place have a better life!

She pulled open the heavy door and slipped across the cool clay pavements of the Room of Books, to shove the papyrus to its place among the others on the shelves. For a moment she stood, letting her envious gaze rest on one neat roll after another—*The Proverbs of Ptah-hotep, The Prophecies of Neferrohu, The Book of Surgery, The Eloquent Peasant, Baufra's Tale*—forbidden treasure houses of wisdom and poetry and ancient fable which it was a crime for her to touch. Yet Zasha could read no more of it than could his vain and empty-headed lady, who spent most of her time before a mirror. He could write no more than his name, but must call in a scribe on every occasion. Mara's lip curled. Beast! Slave though she was, she could both read and write, thanks to a former master. And she spoke Babylonian as well as her own tongue.

But what good did it do her? Zasha was rich, and that was what counted. He was rich and he was free.

She turned to look wistfully about the room, and as she did so the old memory returned to haunt her. It was all so long ago and vague now that she never knew whether it was real or imagined, but somehow, somewhere, maybe only in a dream, she had known a room like this; like this only finer —high-ceilinged and luxurious, with rich furnishings and shelves of scrolls.

There were times when her conviction was strong that she had once lived a different life. Sometimes—very seldom now that she had grown older—there had even come the fleeting vision of a face, a beautiful smiling face with blue eyes, like her own, and the dim recollection of someone bending over her and laughing. . . .

A dismal rumbling from her stomach brought her back to the present. Someone will be bending over me with a stick soon, she thought. I had best be gone from here.

Her stomach protested its emptiness once again, making her feel lightheaded and dizzy, as she hurried out of the room and across the garden. She clenched her teeth and pulled her sash tighter. One thing she could never remember was a time when she had not been hungry.

"Well, Teta, the scroll is returned," she remarked as she entered the storeroom. "Where are the precious *shentis* of that swineherd, that son of wretched Kush, beloved of crocodiles—"

"*Ast!* Behold them in their usual place!" rasped Teta, pointing. "That tongue of yours will flap once too often, Reckless One! Be silent and useful, for once!"

Teta turned back to her task of sealing wine jars, and the earthy smell of the clay she was using mingled with that of the hot starch as the two worked for a while in silence. Presently a new fragrance drifted in through the open door, from the direction of the kitchen nearby—the fragrance of roasting waterfowl.

"Ahhhhh!" groaned Mara, stopping in the midst of wringing out one of the linen kilts. "Great Amon, is there anything at all to eat in this place?"

Teta tamped down a pottery bung, tied it firmly with linen, capped it with clay and pressed down Zasha's seal before she answered. Then she half turned, gesturing toward the shelves that lined the walls. "Plenty," she said sarcastically. "Help yourself."

Mara's eyes traveled over the shelves, stacked with jars and kegs, and sacks of dried fish—all sealed and untouchable, save at the order of the mistress. Then she finished wringing out the *shenti*, flung it in the basket, and gave another yank to her sash.

"Someday," she said through her teeth, "I'm going to have gold. So much gold that I could eat roasted waterfowl every day. So much that I could buy Zasha and his simpering wife and all his relatives, and toss them to the crocodiles!"

Teta laughed shrilly. "*Hai,* tell me another, stupid! A slave

11

you are and a slave you'll be, if you don't die before your time from the beatings you get for your impudence. Gold! *Hai!* Gold!"

Yes, gold! thought Mara. And jewels, and linen so sheer you can see through it, and little alabaster pots like the mistress' to hold the paint for my eyelids, and freedom, freedom! A slave I'll *not* be all my life! Someday there'll be a chance—and though it cost my neck I'll take it, snatch it!

She hurled the last kilt into the basket and swung the basket to her head. "Farewell, Teta," she muttered, starting for the pressing rooms. "Take care you don't faint of emptiness where the mistress can see you—it might offend her!"

"Gold!" retorted Teta, still chuckling under her breath. "*Hai!* Gold!"

Mara slammed the door behind her. She crossed the courtyard to the pressing rooms with the smooth, swinging stride made second nature to those who habitually carry burdens on the head. Setting the basket on a stool beside the narrow table she went to poke up the fire that was to heat the irons.

Spend the day merrily, echoed the *Song of the Harper* ironically in her mind. *Bethink thee only of joy, till comes that day of mooring in the land that loveth silence . . . Lo, none that hath gone may come again.*

Aye, and who knew when that day of mooring would be upon one, swift and final? Here were the hateful fluting irons, the steaming *shentis* of that son of crocodiles, Zasha; outside the air was soft, the sky blue as the eye of heaven.

Suddenly Mara flung the poker into the fire with all her strength. She whirled out of the room and across the red-graveled path to a dom palm that grew beside the garden wall. Up she scrambled like a squirrel, her bare toes clinging to the rough bark. At the top of the wall she glanced once over her shoulder toward the closed storeroom door, then leaped down on the other side.

Freedom, brief and costly though it might be, was hers for a little while. She was laughing aloud as she plunged into the nearest alleyway and through the next street, in the direction of the market place.

CHAPTER 2

The Sale of a Slave

ON THE SHADOWED side of one of the mud-brick buildings that edged Menfe's thriving market place, Sheftu stood quietly, with folded arms. His position commanded a good view of the entire area—merchants' and bakers' stalls, shops of silver-workers, weavers, glassblowers and makers of sandals. Here a potter spun his wheel and shaped the clay, chanting supplications to Khnum, ram-headed deity of all potters, who had once shaped man himself on a divine wheel. There, in a shady corner, a barber plied his trade, jostled by roving fishmongers. The square was thronged with shoppers—the white-clad, copper-skinned, black-wigged inhabitants of Menfe with their baskets and their squabbling voices and their long, painted eyes.

They took no notice whatever of Sheftu, whose ordinary white *shenti* and headcloth made him inconspicuous, and whose immobility made him seem merely part of the shadow in which he stood. Outwardly casual, he was inwardly as alert as a cat at a mousehole. His eyes, the only

13

part of him that moved, flashed restlessly over the crowd, searching, probing, overlooking nothing. He had been waiting a long time.

Presently his attention was drawn to a little commotion in a far corner of the square. A group of soldiers, pushing officiously through the crowd, had shoved a ragged girl against a passing litter, so that she collided with one of the Nubian bearers. He in turn lost his balance, staggered and almost dropped his corner of the litter; whereupon the bejeweled great lady inside thrust her head between the curtains and began to scold furiously.

"Begone, rabble!" shouted the servant in attendance behind the litter. He sprang forward, yelling imprecations, and began to lay about him with his stick, his blows falling impartially upon the bearer and the unfortunate girl, who screamed back at him with equal fury, in both Egyptian and Babylonian. Suddenly she dodged out of his reach, ducked with remarkable agility between the legs of an ass and vanished into the crowd. An instant later, however, she reappeared some distance behind the litter, strutting along in the wake of the self-important attendant in a perfect imitation of his pompous swagger. The bystanders roared and slapped their thighs.

Sheftu was grinning too. He was sorry when with a final mocking impudence, the girl melted once more into the crowd.

Her lithe image still in his mind, Sheftu returned to his vigilant scanning of the market place. The messenger was late. A glance at the sun told him that he dared not wait much longer, that if the promised signal did not come soon, it would never come, and all his arguments and pleas of yesterday had failed. He stirred restlessly in his shadowed corner, and gnawed his lip.

Suddenly he caught sight of the girl again. This time she was quite near him, strolling with apparent aimlessness among the stalls. She stopped to watch a potter at work,

14

and Sheftu studied her curiously, unable to fit her into any
of the usual categories. Her face was mobile, alert and
vivid, broad across the cheekbones, smudged with dirt—a
gamin's face. But it was set with eyes as blue as the noon
sky—a rare sight in Egypt. She was far too ragged to be
the daughter of even the poorest merchant, yet she must
have some education, for she had spoken Babylonian; and
her slim, wild grace had nothing whatever in common with
the stunted brutishness of serfs or porters. What was she?

She wandered a few steps farther, and Sheftu's eyes followed her. Had he not been watching closely he would
never have seen the swift glance she threw into a side
street, where a baker's apprentice was hurrying along bal-
ancing his great flat basket of breadstuffs on his head, waving a palm branch over them to keep off the crows.

Tongue in cheek, Sheftu continued to watch. He was not
surprised when the girl stepped innocently into the street
at the precise moment that the baker's apprentice darted
around the corner of the stall. There was a shout, the inevitable sharp collision, and bread, basket, palm leaf scattered in all directions.

Instantly the girl was all remorse. She was everywhere
at once, snatching up the loaves and dusting them, soothing
the apprentice with smiles and sympathy that caused his
frown to give way to a flattered smirk. Only Sheftu, shaking
with silent merriment, observed the good half-dozen
honey cakes that found their way into her sash instead of
the basket. His enjoyment increased as she began to nibble
one absently under the baker's very nose, chattering to him
meanwhile; it passed all bounds when she actually took
another from her sash, offered it prettily to the bedazzled
youth, and strolled off down the street leaving him blushing
and gaping happily after her.

By Amon! thought Sheftu, nearly choking with laughter.
There is as witty a piece of deviltry as I've ever seen! What
a girl this is!

Suddenly he stiffened, and the girl vanished from his mind as if she had never been. There, across the market place, lowering his earthen jar into the public well, was a Nubian in a red headcloth.

Sheftu waited tensely as the jar went down once, twice, and after a pause, a third time. It was the signal. With a long sigh of relief he stepped at last out of his shadowy corner. The Nubian shouldered his water jar and departed; Sheftu, mingling inconspicuously with the crowd, followed in the same general direction, keeping the red headcloth always in sight.

Once out of the market place, the black man moved swiftly through a maze of alleys and side streets, Sheftu following at a discreet distance. Presently the guide vanished abruptly into a doorway.

There was a porter coming toward Sheftu down the street; behind he could hear other footsteps, and quarreling voices. Continuing his same unhurried stride he passed the doorway without a glance, strolling on until the porter had disappeared around a corner, and the quarrelers were abreast of him. He glanced at them casually as they passed, and was surprised to see the same girl whose antics had amused him in the square. She was being dragged along roughly by a scowling man with a cruel face, who wore gold arm bands and appeared to be a person of some consequence. It was he who was doing most of the talking. He muttered imprecations under his breath, exploding now and then into angry curses and giving another jerk on the girl's arm. She responded sometimes with a protest or a whispered Babylonian phrase, but for the most part accepted the abuse passively—or so Sheftu thought until she flashed a look in his direction and he saw her eyes, blazing like blue jewels in her tanned face. There was no submission there, and not a trace of fear, only fury. But Sheftu realized with a sudden shock that she was a slave. She must be; otherwise, angry as she was, she would openly rebel against this man, who was evidently her master. Now the contradictions in her appearance were no longer baffling. Probably she had been well born, stolen as a child from her family, sold and resold until there was no one left who could possibly know who she once had been.

As the two disappeared into a side street Sheftu turned back toward the doorway, feeling spiritless and depressed. It was a crass and ugly world where such a girl could be kept a slave.

So occupied was he with this notion that only habit caused him to conceal his face from the other figure who appeared at that moment on the street—a man swathed to the ears in a woolen cloak, though it was warm noonday. This man strode along in the direction the girl and her master had taken, and like them, turned the corner.

It was Destiny that passed, but Sheftu could not know that. He knew only that the street was now empty, and he walked swiftly toward the doorway through which the Nubian had disappeared.

Two streets away, the girl and her master were nearing home.

"Goat! Barbarian! *Swineherd!*" raged Mara under her breath, in Babylonian. She far preferred to rage in Egyptian, since its heavy gutturals lent themselves perfectly to invective. But she was too wise to indulge her preference at the moment. With her arm in her master's harsh grasp, and his other hand reaching for his stick, she confined herself to a tongue he did not know. Even so, it was satisfying, since she knew it infuriated Zasha to be reminded that his slave was better educated than himself.

"Son of three pigs! Know-nothing!" she spat at him.

"Cease that babble!" he roared. They had reached the front courtyard of his house and he gave her a fling that sent her staggering across the paving to land painfully upon the broad stone steps.

"Crocodile!" she added.

"Stop it, I say!" Zasha had his stick out of his belt now. "*Hai!* Unhappy day that I bought you, miserable one! Sister of the serpent you are, always sneaking away from your work to go mischief-making in the square! What have you stolen today? Well? What?"

"Bread," Mara answered him. "Feed your slaves like humans instead of dogs and they'll not steal."

"Silence!" bellowed Zasha. He strode across the court and the stick whistled across her bare shoulders. "Hold that tongue of yours, girl, or I'll have it out! Now, what else? Bread and what else?"

"Naught else!"

The stick whistled again. "The truth!" Zasha demanded.

"It is the truth! I took only a loaf or two from a fat baker who had more than he needed."

"Pah, you lie!" Zasha raised the stick again, and she decided to cringe, knowing that as long as she defied him he would continue to beat her. When she shrank against the column he grinned. "What, do you fear me then?"

Mara said nothing. Immediately the stick came down with savage force. "*Hai!* You *shall* fear me, though I wear my arm out teaching you!" All at once he drew back, gulping. "Turn away your eyes, you *kheft*-maiden! Look away, I say!"

His free hand groped for the amulet he wore at his throat, and a mocking smile deepened the corners of Mara's mouth. She knew what the amulet was—an *ouzait,* a little enameled model of the Sacred Eye of Horus. He had got it from a magician soon after he had bought her from her former master. Zasha was afraid of her blue eyes.

"What, do you fear me?" she could not help taunting.

She leaned forward, fastened her eyes upon him and widened them deliberately. When he stumbled back another pace she laughed aloud—then he was upon her again, his blows falling as fast as his curses, his voice shaking with

18

rage, while she wrapped her arms about her head and endured the punishment.

Both were too absorbed to notice the stranger, still wrapped from head to toe in his woolen cloak, who had that moment entered the courtyard. He stopped just inside the gate, watched the scene impassively a moment, then strode forward and dropped a heavy hand upon Zasha's shoulder, whirling him halfway around.

"Let be," he ordered. "Put away your stick."

Zasha gasped and blinked. "By Amon!" he puffed. "Who are you to walk into my own courtyard and tell me—"

"Be quiet, fool. I'm buying this slave of you. How much do you want?"

The jewel trader gaped. Then he straightened, massaging his hands craftily. "She's a valuable property," he grunted. "I've said naught about selling. What makes you think I'd part with a girl like this? Look at her—young, strong, quick as a cat. She's no common drudge, but can read and write, and she speaks Babylonian as well as our own tongue. Moreover she eats little and is docile as a— Stand up, you!" he hissed angrily at Mara. "Smile!"

Mara stayed where she was, merely regarding him scornfully. The stranger's laugh was brief and not altogether amused. "Yes, I see how docile she is! Come, cease this chatter, fellow. Name your price or you'll have to take what you get."

"Not so fast," retorted Zasha. "Who are you? I'll not sell until I know with whom I'm doing business. I'll not sell at all unless I get my price."

The stranger growled impatiently, brushed past the bridling jewel merchant and leaning down, seized Mara's wrist and pulled her to her feet. "You'll sell, right enough! I'm here to buy a clever slave and this is the one I want. Name your price or I'll simply take her."

"In whose name?" shouted Zasha.

"In the queen's name." The stranger reached inside his

19

cloak and brought out a purse, which he flung contemptuously at Zasha's feet. Then he led Mara out of the courtyard without another word, leaving the merchant white faced and staring behind him.

The whole thing had happened so fast that Mara felt giddy. In astonished silence she followed her new owner through the crooked streets, stealing curious glances at what she could see of his face. But he was an eye, a jutting nose, and a length of white wool, nothing more. She shrugged and gave it up. No doubt he would show himself in time. Meanwhile—she felt a glorious lightness grow within her at the thought—meanwhile, she was rid of Zasha! Of all the masters she had had, he was the worst. Perhaps this new one would feed her.

Her hand went to her sash, where a few of the honey cakes were still tucked away safe. She frowned. She had meant to give one to Teta, poor soul, who would now have to iron those hateful *shentis* still lying neglected in their basket. It was too bad. She had never resented Teta's scolding, knowing that most of her ill temper stemmed from hunger.

No matter, Mara thought, and her face cleared. Teta is gone from your life as others have come and gone, and their fate is no concern of yours. Look after yourself, my girl! Nobody else will.

After some minutes of walking they came to an inn surrounded by a high mud-brick wall. The man turned through the gate, ignored the lower-floor entrance and led the way up a flight of stairs set against the outside of the building. When they reached the room at the top he secured the door and turned to face Mara, throwing off his cloak at last.

She had to make an effort to conceal her surprise. He was dressed in the finest linen, with arm bands of chased gold and a broad jeweled collar of remarkable beauty. A man of great wealth! But his face filled her with misgivings. It was cold and stony as the Sphinx itself.

"Your name, girl?"

"Mara. Daughter of Nobody and his wife Nothing."

His granite face showed no flicker of expression, but his voice grew icy. "Take care! Wit becomes impudence in a slave's mouth." He sat down in the room's one chair and regarded her impassively. "I watched you in the market place. You are both daring and unscrupulous, and you think fast. I have been looking for a person with those particular characteristics. Also I noticed you speak Babylonian. I presume your command of the language goes somewhat beyond mere invective?"

"I speak the tongue well," murmured the girl. This conversation astonished her even more than the suddenness of her sale. She could not imagine its purpose.

"Good. Now look you. I have bought you for no ordinary purpose, as you may be guessing. I have a very special duty for you. But—" he leaned forward to emphasize his words, "it is so dangerous a duty that I will give you free choice whether or not you will attempt it. If your choice be 'nay,' you have only to say so, and I will sell you at once to some other master. I've no need for more household slaves."

"And if my choice be aye?"

"It may bring you sudden death, or worse. But you will find the danger has its compensations. So long as you obey my orders you will be quite free from the usual slave's life, and if you carry them out successfully, I will free you altogether."

Mara gripped the edge of the table that separated them. There was no hesitation in her mind, but it took a moment to control the wild excitement that filled her. "Aye! My choice is aye!" she whispered.

"Think well. You may be choosing destruction."

"No matter! I would rather be dead than a slave!"

He gave a faint smile. "So I thought. Now listen closely. One reason I picked you is that you have the appearance of a girl of the upper classes—or you would have if your hair

21

were clipped and dressed and your rags exchanged for decent clothing. If these things were done, do you think you could live up to your fine garments?"

"Why, yes, I suppose I could act the part of a human being."

He chose to ignore the sarcasm. "So be it. As you heard, I bought you in the queen's name. You will serve the queen as well as myself, though no one will know this. No one will realize you are a purchased slave at all, for you will masquerade as a free maiden, the daughter of a priest of Abydos, now dead. *If anyone should find out differently, you will die at once.* Do you understand thus far?"

Mara tingled with fresh astonishment. His eyes were cold, his mouth implacable. He meant exactly what he said. "I understand," she said slowly. "What service am I to do?"

"A princess of Canaan, one Inanni, is on her way to Thebes at this moment to become the wife of the young pretender Thutmose. She has her own train of servants and waiting women, but she will need an interpreter." The man leaned forward, jabbing his finger at Mara. "You are to be that interpreter. You will go at once to the city of Abydos, where the princess is spending a week in the usual ceremonies of purification. You will seek out an Egyptian called Saankh-Wen, who is in charge of the ships, and give him this."

He drew from his girdle a tiny green scarab, inscribed with the name of Hatshepsut. Mara took it in a hand cold with excitement. So far this man had not really told her anything. What was behind all these strange instructions?

"The clothes? The hair?" she murmured.

"Saankh-Wen will arrange for all that," returned her master, gesturing impatiently. "When you leave Abydos attached as interpreter to Inanni's train, you will be suitably adorned, and entirely above suspicion of any kind. Now."

He paused, fixing her with narrowed eyes, and Mara stiffened.

"Once in Thebes," the man went on softly, "you will accompany the princess to her quarters in the palace and remain there for an indefinite period. You will be present at all her interviews with the king, naturally, since she does not speak a word of our language, and he will not deign to speak hers. *Keep your ears open.* Listen to whatever goes on between the king and those who surround him—his servants, his scribes, his musicians. I want to know which of these people carries his orders to others outside the palace walls. Somehow he is sending and receiving messages. I want to know how."

Mara stared at him, breathing hard. "In short, I am a spy."

"Exactly. If you are as clever as I think you are, you should have no trouble obtaining this information. If you succeed, you will not be dissatisfied with your reward. But if you fail, whether by accident *or design*—"

He did not finish the sentence. He did not need to. He was smiling in a way that sent a little trickle of fear down Mara's spine.

She took a deep breath. "How am I to report to you?"

"Leave that to me."

"Is it permitted to know your name?"

"It is not. The less you know, the less you will be tempted to let your wits run away with you." The man stood up, taking a heavy gold chain from his neck. "Take this. It will pay your passage to Abydos. Get on the next boat that leaves." Again the thin smile. "Remember I am no stupid baker's apprentice. Should the chain—and you—disappear somehow between here and the wharves it would be . . . regrettable. Do we understand each other?"

"Perfectly," said Mara.

"Then go. Enjoy your freedom and your fine clothes and your acquaintance with royalty—while you can. It may not last long."

He leaned back, gesturing toward the door, and Mara

realized that she was dismissed. She was free, free to walk out that door, make her way unchallenged to the wharf, and set sail for Abydos, Thebes—adventure. No more rags. No more beatings or loaf snatching. No more hunger! Instead there would be luxury and royal intrigue and excitement; and once she was in the palace, whatever this man's threats might be, there would be endless opportunities for a girl who knew how to use her wits!

The future opened up before her in a vista radiant with possibilities, each more entrancing than the last. Without knowing it, she laughed aloud for joy.

The man's dry voice rasped suddenly across her daydreams. "Be careful, Mara. You are still a slave."

She shrugged and grinned. "I'll try to remember."

"I will be there to remind you," he remarked acidly. He jerked his head toward the door and this time she went, without even looking back.

CHAPTER 3

The War Hawk

WHEN Sheftu had assured himself that the street was finally empty, he opened the door in the wall and quickly slipped through it. The Nubian was waiting for him.

"This way, my lord," he murmured.

"Well, Ebi, what think you? Is there good news for me?"

Sheftu asked in a low voice, following the servant across the courtyard.

"I cannot say, master. This garden is green and pleasant. Khofra is an old man now. To be truthful, he is tired of both wars and pharaohs, having seen too much of both in his life. I think he will decide to stay here."

Sheftu's heart sank. But he said only, "Perhaps he may yet be persuaded."

"The old are sometimes stubborn, master," said Ebi.

Sheftu smiled grimly. "The young are sometimes even more so! He'll come to Thebes if I have to carry him there in chains."

"I wish you good fortune, then." Ebi stopped before a door. "He is here. Enter, if you will."

Drawing a long breath to calm his nerves, Sheftu opened the door and stepped into a quiet, sunny room. It was of familiar design, spacious, rectangular, windowless. But the two outside walls stopped some feet short of the ceiling, and through this open space, which was divided by graceful columns, light and air poured down into the room. In its center, in a chair beside a low table, sat the man Sheftu had come to see—Khofra, the warrior hero of all Egypt. Veteran of countless foreign campaigns, leader of men and for many years chief general of all the armies under the First Thutmose, Hatshepsut's father, Khofra was now, at sixty, enjoying a peaceful old age. But he was far from feeble. His eyes still flashed dark fire under his white eyebrows, and the hand he stretched out to Sheftu was vigorous and firm.

"Well, my boy. Were you observed?"

He laughed soundlessly at the expression on Sheftu's face, and waved his visitor to a seat. "No, no, naturally not. You are discretion itself, as skilled in mummery as you are in guile. One would never recognize the gold-hung son of Lord Menkau in those simple rags. I must congratulate you. You look neither more nor less distinguished than every

25

third man one meets in the street, and so are practically invisible."

"That was my aim, Honored One." Sheftu forced himself to sit down unhurriedly, place relaxed hands on the arms of his chair and smile with a confidence he was far from feeling. "When you come to Thebes to offer your services to the queen as head of her armies, I promise none but you and Ebi and the king will ever have known of my connection with the affair."

"*When* I come?" said the old man drily. "I did not know I had made the decision."

"A mere formality! Yesterday I spread the facts before you, revealed our plans and begged your assistance, without which we must fail. Today I come to hear your answer."

"And you have not the slightest doubt what that answer will be?" inquired Khofra, even more drily.

"Not the slightest," said Sheftu.

For a moment their eyes met, the old man's ironic and a little sad, Sheftu's dark and steady. Khofra gave a laugh that was half a sigh, and moved restlessly on his cushioned chair.

"Look you, my boy," he said. "I was young once, I know what you are feeling. I, too, loved my pharaoh; I rode in my chariot against his enemies and was fearless, and smote them down in great numbers and brought their severed hands and ears to his tent and was happy when he smiled. Together we subjugated the whole southern land of Nubia, even beyond the third cataract of the Nile. Together we rode northward against the Keftyews and the Canaanites and gazed at last on the strange Euphrates, the river which flows the wrong way. Together we returned to the Black Land with prisoners by the thousand—with an empire! But we were not together after that, not ever again, my friend. Pharaoh knew me not, once the empire was gained. He valued me not, loved me not, wanted me not. I was for-

26

gotten as though I had never been." The old general broke off, looking down at his hands.

"*Haut meryt*, you are mistaken!" protested Sheftu. "There is no name better remembered or more honored than yours in all the Black Land."

"Honor I never cared for—nor fame nor riches—then or now. 'Beloved General,' you call me—" Khofra raised his head. "That was what I wanted, to be pharaoh's friend at home as well as on the battlefield. But pharaohs do not love men, they use them. No, Lord Sheftu, I have seen enough of pharaohs. Serve yours if you will—I will stay comfortably at home. And when young Thutmose tosses you aside like a worn sandal, come to me. Perhaps I can comfort you."

There was a pause. Then Sheftu said gravely, "You do not understand, *Haut Khofra*."

"Understand?" The old man frowned in surprise. "Certainly I understand. You wish me to come to Thebes as head of Hatshepsut's troops, especially the two thousand of the bodyguard, who are sadly in need of training. You wish me to train them, inspire them, discipline them to blind obedience to me personally, so that at my word of command they will rise against the queen herself. I understand all this perfectly. What you do not understand, my boy, is that I have finished with pharaohs."

"But I do not ask it for pharaoh. I ask it for Egypt."

Khofra's fingers stopped drumming upon the table. "Egypt?" he echoed.

"Aye, my general! Have you never known that it was Egypt you served?" Sheftu left his chair to stand over the old man. "That empire you conquered—was that pharaoh's? No, pharaoh is dead. It is Egypt's! But by all the gods, how long can we keep it, with this pampered woman on the throne? All Syria is growing restive. The Kadesh, the Keftyew, they have not felt the point of an Egyptian spear since their graybeards were young, and they need to be taught respect. You think Hatshepsut will do it? Pah! She cares for nothing except building more temples—at whatever cost!"

Sheftu broke off, breathing hard. Khofra's still profile told him nothing, and he had a sudden terrible vision of returning to Thutmose empty handed. He leaned closer, gripping Khofra's chair. "But Egypt cares! Egypt groans under taxes, while the empire slips away, bit by bit! With you in control of the Army, Hatshepsut can be overthrown, and Thutmose, who is a man and a warrior, can set things to rights. *Hai*, think, Khofra! Pharaohs come and go—what matter if one used you and tossed you aside and loved you not? Egypt loved you, and she needs you worse than ever before. She is sick! Will you let her die?"

Still the old man sat motionless. Sheftu had done all he could, and he knew it. He straightened slowly, in a silence only intensified by the humming of bees in the acacia blossoms outside, and the shrill, far-off scream of an eagle. Khofra was looking at his hands, where they lay palm-down on the polished table. They were powerful hands still— blunt fingered and scarred and sinewy—and once they had gripped the mightiest sword in all Egypt.

The general rose suddenly and walked to the open door, where he stood looking out at the sunny courtyard.

"You are a remarkable young man, Lord Sheftu," he murmured at last. "Remarkable and wise, for you have shown me a thing I never knew. So Egypt loved me!" He paused, and for a moment longer remained motionless, leaning against the doorframe. Then he turned back into the room. "Egypt needs me? So be it. I will come."

"Blessed of Amon!" breathed Sheftu. He crossed the room and bowed low. "In pharaoh's name, in Egypt's name, I thank you, *Haut meryt*."

"I want no thanks. Up, my lord. It is I who thank you. You've cured an ache of twenty years' standing—and at last made my life seem a reasonable thing."

28

"Reasonable? By all the gods, it's glorious! Now, more than ever. This news—" Sheftu stopped, then suddenly laughed. "This news will cheer my prince so that he may even smile upon the Canaanite princess!"

"Thutmose has sent for a Canaanite princess?" exclaimed Khofra.

"Can you think so, my general? Nay, it is Hatshepsut who has sent for her. Thutmose wants no barbarian for a wife! He rages like the leopard of Upper Egypt at the very idea. It is just one more arrogant insult from that most arrogant of women, his sister. She holds him fast in a snare of politics and spies, and when he struggles, offers him this princess as one offers a toy to a fretful child. *Ai*, Khofra! She underestimates him!"

Khofra gave his soundless laugh. "A pretty scene it will be, the arrival of this unfortunate Canaanite! When does she come?"

"Soon. Her barge is at Abydos now. I may reach Thebes before her—unless my good river captain has set sail already, fearing me dead. I must take leave." Sheftu turned, placing his hand on his shoulder as he bowed once again. "Live forever, *Haut Khofra!* Till we meet again in Thebes."

Five minutes later he was hurrying through the side streets toward the wharf and the *Silver Beetle*. Thanks be to all the gods, his mission to Khofra had been successful. But there was one great obstacle in his path before it was finished. Word must be sent to the king as soon as possible. Since Sheftu's own carefully maintained position at court was that of a trusted favorite of the queen, it was unthinkable that he give Thutmose the message himself. And the old palace servant who used to act as go-between had been murdered in his bed two weeks before.

Sheftu's jaw set. It was dangerous business, to have anything to do with the king. So dangerous that it was highly uncertain where he would find another trustworthy messenger who was daring enough to serve him well. Yet find one he must, and soon.

He was still pondering the problem as he came out onto the wharves a few moments later, perceiving to his relief that the *Silver Beetle* was still waiting for him. It was the only southbound ship in the harbor; he would have been in a sorry plight had it sailed without him. A figure on its deck straightened suddenly and flung up an arm in greeting; Sheftu grinned as he waved back. Nekonkh must have been having a bad time of it the past hour. Well, so had he—but now all was done and they could be on their way. He moved swiftly toward the ship.

At the other end of the wharf, the slave girl Mara was picking her way through a tangle of fishing nets and up-ended reed boats. She shaded her eyes to scan the line of vessels which bobbed along the quay, their masts swaying and weaving with the motion of the water. Far down toward the southern end of the wharf she saw what she was looking for—a stout-timbered Theban craft with an embroidered sail.

For a moment she stood motionless, grinning triumphantly. Then she started to run.

A few minutes later she was on the deck of the *Silver Beetle,* looking coolly into the face of the fierce-jawed riverman who was its captain.

"Passage to Abydos?" he roared. "We're a cargo ship, Mistress High-and-Mighty! We've hides and sheep's wool on board, so many there's scarce room enough for the oarsmen to dip their paddles! Think you we can set up some dainty pavilion in the middle of—"

He stopped abruptly. From her outstretched fingers dangled a massive gold chain.

The captain grunted. "Hmmmm. *Hai,* what a trinket that is, to be sure. Is it not too heavy for you, little one? Pray let me bear the burden." He took the chain into his own square-fingered hand, flashed an appraising look into her face, then jerked his head toward a stack of hides at that end of the deck farthest from the spot where Sheftu had climbed aboard three minutes before. "You can sleep there," ho muttored. "We weigh anchor in five minutes."

Part II—The River

CHAPTER 4

Young Man with an Amulet

MENFE'S three great pyramids dwindled into sharp triangles of sun and shadow as the *Silver Beetle* left the harbor behind her. She pushed south against the current, her embroidered sail bellying in the north wind like a winged thing freed at last from ropes and trappings. Mara, curled upon her pile of hides near the stern of the ship, was luxuriating in a freedom far more glorious.

To be rid of Zasha was bliss enough! But to be rid of all masters for a time, to walk where she would, say what she chose, above all to plunge straight into a new life full of exhilarating danger—Blessed Osiris! Could it all be true?

She felt in her sash for the little scarab, and its hard reality sent a tingling along her spine. It was true, right enough. Now what came next? Sail to Abydos, find a man called Saankh-Wen, give him the scarab and leave the rest to him. Meanwhile she had only to delight in the cool breeze on her face, the gentle, leaping motion of the ship—seven sparkling, lazy, soothing days of it. She snuggled deeper into the pile of skins and drifted blissfully to sleep.

It was some time later that she opened her eyes to find a tall young man staring down at her. At once she was wide awake. Who was this? She gathered her feet under her, every muscle tensed for quick movement.

For a moment they remained thus, gripped by mutual surprise. Sheftu was so amazed at seeing the same slave girl for the fourth time that day—and here on this ship, of all unlikely places—that at first he could say nothing at all. Then he noticed her strong, deep breathing, her narrowed eyes and her quivering readiness for flight, and realized that he had startled her badly. What a wild thing she was! Her whole attitude spoke more clearly than words of the life she must have led.

"Do not fear me," he said gently.

She did not relax. "I fear no one. Who are you? Why do you gape at me?"

"I am a passenger on this boat, like yourself. My name is Sheftu. I was gaping because I am surprised to see you here."

"Why shouldn't I be here, if I choose?"

"Nay, wait a bit! I'm not questioning your rights. But it's very strange—" He hesitated. It had suddenly occurred to him that her repeated appearances in his life that day might be something more than coincidence. Had the queen set spies upon him? His own attitude became guarded; but with him, suspicion took the outward appearance of guileless charm. He flashed her his disarming smile and gestured smoothly.

"Please. It was very rude of me to gape. I crave pardon. Suppose we begin our acquaintance all over again."

She would not have been human had she not reacted to that smile. "If you like," she murmured. To herself she thought, I must get over my slave's ways! I have every right to be on this ship and I need fear no one on it.

Sheftu sat down beside her and at once began to talk about a great stone image they were passing, telling the legends of the ancient king who had built it there on the shore. His manner was perfect; it contained just the mixture

34

of friendliness and reserve best calculated to reassure her. Meanwhile, he was thinking fast, checking back on his movements of the day and examining the few facts he knew about her. He concluded finally that she could have no possible connection with the queen's followers, and thus was not dangerous to him. But what was she doing here? The answer leaped suddenly to his relieved mind. She had fled from that man who had dragged her along the street. She was a runaway!

He smiled now more engagingly than before, realizing that he had a powerful weapon to hold over her if need be. He finished his story softly: "And they say that the *ba* of the old king himself flutters about the statue at night in the form of a bat, looking at the face and the inscriptions, making sure his image and his name have not been forgotten in the land of Kemt."

She shaded her eyes for a last glimpse of the great, craggy, granite face disappearing downriver. "A strange tale that is," she said. "And well told. I've never heard better, even from the old yarn spinners who sun themselves in the temple courtyard."

He sketched a little bow of acknowledgment. "Perhaps I have followed the wrong trade," he remarked with a grin.

"And what is your trade?"

"I am apprentice to a scribe in Thebes," he lied glibly. "One Huaa. A fine old man, but with a tendency to overeat—a tendency his apprentices would gladly imitate, had they the chance."

She smiled. "You scarce look underfed."

"Nor am I. But no credit to Huaa."

This time she laughed outright. "I see we have experience in common. Are you hungry now? Here."

She reached into her sash and produced the last two honey cakes she had filched from the baker's boy earlier that day. She offered one to Sheftu, who took it with thanks, hiding his mirth. "So you are a scribe," she went on, biting

35

into her own flaky morsel. "I once had a—I once knew a man who followed that trade."

"So?" murmured Sheftu. Her quick retreat from the word "master" had not escaped him.

"He was in the service of a district chief, on the northern border of Egypt. There were many foreigners there."

"Foreigners flock to Egypt as birds to a marsh," observed Sheftu. That is how she learned Babylonian, he thought.

She pointed suddenly. "Look. There on the sandbank."

He turned. The sand bar was nearly hidden by long, brownish-green, sinister forms. His flesh crawled a little in spite of himself. Crocodiles! They lay sluggish and motionless, all facing north, with their great pale mouths wide open to the prevailing wind. He thought of the crocodile-headed god, Sebek, and felt for the amulet at his wrist.

Then he turned back to the girl. "That is why I have no fear of death," he remarked.

"The crocodiles? What have they to do with it?"

"Everything. I was born on the 23rd day of the third month of the Season of Growing."

Swift comprehension crossed her face. Everyone knew that the fate of those born on that day was to be eaten by crocodiles. They both looked back at the sandbank, but it was she who shuddered.

"They will have me in the end," murmured Sheftu. "But meanwhile I need fear nothing else." He turned to her with a shrug. "I shall cheat them as long as possible, until I am an old, old man. See!"

He extended the wrist from which his amulet dangled. It was a twist of flax thread strung with seven green glazed beads, and knotted seven times. One large flat bead, of carnelian, was inscribed on both sides. Her lips moved as she read the hieroglyphs.

"Oh, thou, who art in the water, behold! It is Osiris who is in the water, and the eye of Horus and the great scarab protect him. . . . Get ye back, beasts of the waters! Do not

36

show your face, for Osiris is floating toward you. . . . Beasts of the waters, your mouth is closed by Ra, your throat is closed by Sechmet, your teeth are broken by Thoth, your eyes are blinded by the great magician. Those four gods protect Osiris and all those who are in the water."

So she can read, and perhaps write, too! thought Sheftu, again surprised "You see, I am well protected," he said aloud.

"Perhaps." She raised her vivid eyes to his face. They were skeptical.

"You have no faith in magic?"

"I have little faith in anything," she said carelessly. "But I am glad I do not know how, or when, I am to die."

"What was the day of your birth?"

"I know not, nor does anyone else. Perhaps I was not born at all, but am a *kheft*-maiden, as Zasha used to say!"

"Zasha?"

She laughed. "A man I knew once. A stupid fellow. He was convinced I had the Evil Eye."

"*Hai!* Stupid he was, indeed! How could evil come from anything so beautiful? Blue is the color of the sky, the lotus, the turquoise. These things are all good."

She flushed a little; evidently compliments were new in her experience. "You are very trusting on short acquaintance," she said drily.

"In your case I have good reason," he assured her, smiling to cover any hidden meaning the remark might have. "But you seem not to trust me. You've not even told me your name."

"My name is Mara."

"Mara! 'Truth of Ra.' You see? Who could distrust one with such a name?"

She laughed, tilting her head to squint up at Ra, the sun god, whose golden bark sailed far westward now toward Libya and the Land of Darkness. Sheftu made use of the moment to study her profile intently. A gamin's face, he had

37

thought as he watched her in the market place. Yes, it was that. Her cheeks were sloping and shadowed, thin with years of hunger; her chin was obstinate and her mouth had a sardonic curve, as though it had learned well to lie. It was a skeptical face, a clever and unscrupulous one. But there was an elusive quality of wistfulness about it that fascinated Sheftu.

He found himself wishing that this Mara, this waif, this runaway, did not have to pass so soon out of his life. Next instant he turned away from her impatiently, wondering if he had lost his mind. The life he had chosen as the king's henchman had no room in it for bright-eyed maidens. Nor did the life he was born to—that of Lord Sheftu, son of the late wealthy noble Menkau—have any place in it for a common slave girl, save to iron his snow-white *shentis*.

And despite the amulet on his wrist, he doubted whether either life would permit him to cheat for long the crocodiles who were his destiny. He walked these days with death at his elbow.

Frowning, he studied once more the unsolved problem of finding a messenger to send to the king. It was a knotty one. Since the discovery and swift murder of the old palace servant he had used before, the queen's innumerable spies would be wary of everyone who came within hailing distance of Thutmose. No one would be above suspicion.

Except, he mused, someone from the outside, unknown to king and queen alike and therefore apparently a partisan of neither. . . .

He chewed his lip, playing with the notion. A foreigner? It was an unlikely idea, but he was desperate. What foreigner, then? He thought suddenly of the Canaanite princess. It was possible—but only just. He knew nothing of her, except that her welcome from Thutmose, who would never dream of marrying her, would be chilly indeed. Such a snub would hardly arouse in her undying loyalty toward the king! She might even turn vindictive and bring all his

38

followers' careful plans tumbling down about their ears. No, thought Sheftu, not the Canaanite princess.

"Your thoughts are not pleasing to you, friend Sheftu?"

He turned quickly. Mara had been watching him, and he was certain at once that no slightest change in his expression had escaped her. She was no fool, this girl.

He smiled and began talking easily of the voyage, of where they would tie up for the night, of the wonders yet to be seen tomorrow. But at the back of his mind an idea was beginning to take form—an idea so startling that he did not even stop to examine it at present. Time enough for that when he was alone to think it out clearly, to test and try it, to make quite sure it was not mad.

For seven days the *Silver Beetle* beat her way southward, her sails fat with the breeze off the Great Green—the Mediterranean. On either side of her gently dipping prow the long land of Egypt slipped by like an unwinding scroll, revealing fields and marshes, mud-walled villages, fishermen straining at their nets. Often the high chanting of priests drifted out from shore as a procession filed into some painted temple; the water's soft hiss blended with the occasional scream of a kite far overhead. Green bee-eaters flashed over greener meadows, farmers worked beside the creaking water wheels and little boys ran shouting along the banks. And always there was the sense of gliding motion, the song of wind in the rigging, the bright, clean air.

Mara wished the voyage would never end. Each morning she woke fresh to the miracle of her freedom; each night she lay in the moonlight speculating about the new life awaiting her in Thebes. Between times there was food in plenty— good food—and long, lazy hours of companionship with the young man she knew only as Sheftu.

They were much together, for there was small chance to avoid each other in the narrow confines of the ship, even had they wanted to. They strolled the scrubbed deck,

39

watched the crew at work, or lounged side by side on the stacked hides, each busy with his own thoughts. What Sheftu's were Mara would have given much to know. He tended to grow preoccupied, almost remote; now and then she caught him studying her with an expression she could not understand at all. But he could side-step her deftest question with an ease that exasperated as much as it amused her.

She soon shrugged aside her curiosity. What did it matter? She liked his company, she loved to lean beside him at the gunwale listening to his stories of the ancient ones, while the sails slapped overhead and the sparkling water threw little gold reflections over his dark face. And when he chose to be alone she could always amuse herself otherwise.

It was interesting to wonder about the captain, for instance. Mara had known plenty of rivermen in her seventeen years, but never one so nervous. When she and Sheftu were together, he was always somewhere in the background, standing about aimlessly or absorbed in unconvincing duties which invariably happened to lead him within watching distance of his passengers. She wondered if he feared they planned to swim ashore with some of his precious cargo. It was curious; he seemed always to be seeking a chance to find Sheftu alone, yet each time such an opportunity arose, he shied off as if he could not make up his mind to seize it.

One afternoon, to Mara's surprise, he sought her out privately. She was sitting, alone and somewhat sulky, in the shade cast by the cabin amidships. There remained only two days before they reached Abydos, yet Sheftu had elected to spend the morning in solitary preoccupation down by the stern sweeps. When Nekonkh strolled toward her to inquire after her health, she answered him almost irritably.

"I'm well enough, I suppose."

"But somewhat out of temper? Where is that constant companion of yours?"

"*Ast!* He's no company today! He broods, Captain. I wonder what about."

"Aye, so do I wonder!" grunted Nekonkh, so vehemently that it surprised her. He hesitated, glancing at the crew members working here and there around them, then jerked his head toward the cabin. "Suppose I try your skill at a game of draughts. I've a board and counters in there somewhere."

"As you like." Puzzled, Mara followed him into the cabin, which was dim and cool after the glare of sun on deck. "You're well acquainted with Sheftu, Captain? I thought he was a stranger to you, like myself."

"Aye, he is, he is!" said Nekonkh hastily—too hastily, she thought. "Here, which will you have, girl, the red or the black?"

He set the game on the table—it was a narrow wooden box on graceful legs, checkered with carved squares on its upper surface, and with a drawer beneath in which the "dogs" or counters were stored. Mara was busy arranging the red ones on her side of the board when the captain spoke again, his voice gruff.

"To tell the truth, it's you I wonder about, little one! I trust you know what you're doing, taking up with a chance acquaintance on a river boat. He may be a rogue."

Mara looked up in surprise. "Rogues are nothing new in my life, Captain. But I see no reason to think Sheftu one."

"Don't you, by all the gods! Come, what do you know of him?"

"Nothing," she admitted, "save what he wants me to know. But then he knows nothing of me, either."

"Aye, true enough! Nor do I, for that matter. Perhaps it's he I should be warning!" Irritably Nekonkh shoved a dog into the next square and sat back, scowling out into the sunshine.

Now I've offended him, she thought in amusement. But

41

great Amon! He acts as if I were some sheltered maid who'd never ventured from her father's court!

Automatically she countered his move, wondering what other game he might be playing. It had been a long day indeed since anyone had troubled about her welfare. That this burly riverman should do so struck her as curious indeed—so curious that she never thought of believing it. Was he going to say what he meant?

"Your move, Captain," she murmured.

But he only shoved forward another counter without speaking. For a time the dogs progressed from square to square in silence, but Nekonkh's ill humor wore off as they both became absorbed in the game. He played unimaginatively but well, and he knew the gambits thoroughly. Mara, having had little experience with any game in her slave's life, was forced to use all her wits to counter his moves and at the same time strike out for the other side of the board. In the end it was by sheer audacity that she inveigled his three last dogs into a position where she could capture them all and jump her sole remaining one into the "royal" square.

She sat back, laughing, as Nekonkh's eyebrows soared. "By all that's sacred!" he exploded. "Now how did you trick me into that?"

"Trick? I used no trick! Could you think so harsh of me?"

"I could and do! Ai, little one, you should have been a general!" Nekonkh chuckled as he swept the dogs into their drawer. "Or perhaps I'm getting old."

"Not so, friend captain," said a dry voice behind them. "That maid's a hard opponent. She plays to win."

They swung around. Sheftu was lounging in the doorway, his arms folded comfortably.

"Aye—well, now, who doesn't?" muttered Nekonkh. He busied himself putting away the game. Mara rose, on the defensive herself, though she could not have told why. "How long have you been standing there?" she demanded.

42

"Long enough," said Sheftu, "to make several interesting observations."

"Indeed! I suppose I've few secrets left now."

"Oh, none at all."

He grinned down at her. In spite of herself she felt an overpowering curiosity—which she had no intention of admitting—as to just what those observations had been. Brushing past him, out the cabin door, she strolled across the deck to the port rail. The sun, dropping into Libya, had set river and sky aflame, but she was less aware of it than of the fact that he had followed and was leaning on the gunwale beside her.

"Ra dies by fire tonight," she commented. "That's a lovely sky."

"Aye, so it is."

His tone finished that subject. She groped hastily for another. "I vow it's hard to believe another day is ending. Only two more and we'll dock at Abydos. Is it not amazing how—"

"Aye, aye, it's amazing. Come, I'm convinced you're quite indifferent to my opinion. Now go ahead and ask me what I was talking about in there."

She whirled to find his face alight with laughter. "The devil take you! Why do you plague me? What do you want of me?"

"I haven't decided yet," he told her imperturbably.

"Oh, haven't you! Haven't you indeed? By Set and all his demons, you're a cool one! I'll wager the captain was right— he said you were a rogue!"

There was a tiny silence. "Now that's interesting," remarked Sheftu. He was still smiling, but all at once his eyes were dangerous. "And what else did the captain say?"

Ast, watch your tongue, my girl! thought Mara. There's something here you don't know about. . . .

"What else?" prodded Sheftu.

43

"Why—naught else."

He waited. His smile had hardened into something so implacable that she felt a tremor of fear. Why should he probe so? Perhaps she'd better come out with the whole thing. "The captain did naught but caution me about stray young men on river boats. Aside from the fact that he fluttered like a hen with one chick, is there anything startling about that?"

He subjected her to that cold scrutiny a moment longer, then slowly relaxed, easing one elbow against the rail. "Nay, I'm not startled, only interested in the captain's opinion. So he said I was a rogue?"

"He said you might be."

"Aye, and so I might. Or something even worse."

He seemed amused now, and Mara's self-confidence rushed back, along with her usual impudence. "Doubtless! You've secrets you don't tell, that's certain. Ai, so be it. Guard your tongue if you will. I'll find you out in time, in spite of it."

"You're sure that's wise?" he answered lazily.

"Does it matter? I'm sure I mean to try."

She turned away, but he reached out suddenly and spun her back against him. "Are you *quite* sure, my—" He broke off, his eyes traveling over her upturned face. He gave a short laugh and tightened his arms deliberately. "By all the gods! I'd rather kiss than threaten you. I wonder if it wouldn't be more effective."

"*Hai!* Conceited pig! You'll do neither! Let me go!"

She squirmed violently, but he only laughed and continued to hold her fast. Then his smile faded. "Look you, my pretty guttersnipe!" he said. "You're too curious for your own good. Behave yourself, and stay out of my affairs."

Loosing her so suddenly that she half fell against the railing, he turned and strode off down the deck.

After a moment of speechless outrage, Mara fled in the other direction. Guttersnipe! Why, that son of seven croco-

44

diles! The rogue, the scoundrel! She'd pay him out for this! She flung herself onto the stack of hides that served her as bed and glared into space. Had she lost her wits completely? *How* had he managed to tease her, frighten her, make love to her and snub her, all in the same five minutes? Always she had been able to snap her fingers under the nose of any man! Yet this one—

Aye, this one was different.

She scowled, remembering unwillingly the strength of his arms about her. And why hadn't he kissed her, pray? Was she so repulsive? So ill favored? So shrewish? The devil take him!

An hour later she was still lying there, moodily watching the *Silver Beetle's* high black prow trace circles against the moon. Guttersnipe! All right, suppose she was. Tomorrow, by Amon, she would have revenge. She would treat him with a smiling indifference he wouldn't be able to break through no matter how hard he tried. She would be gay— aye, charming—but oh, how remote! It was the part of wisdom, as well as revenge; if she did not take care, he'd be surprising a real secret out of her!

She patted the queen's little scarab thoughtfully. How cold his eyes had been as he questioned her about Nekonkh! As if he could toss a girl to the crocodiles without thinking twice about it. For all she knew, he could. And who would there be to know or care if he chose to do just that?

The captain had been right to warn her about Sheftu. He was a dangerous young man.

CHAPTER 5

Dangerous Bargain

MARA FOUND Sheftu's manner next morning just as gay, just as impersonal, and so much more convincing than her own that she was out of sorts before an hour had passed. There was no outdoing him at irony, that was clear. She would have to find some other means of punishing him.

Resentfully, she allowed herself to be entertained by his tales of the ancient monuments they passed, which she had to admit were more interesting than anything she had found in Zasha's scrolls. Sheftu talked well, and he was in high spirits this morning, which spurred him to new flights in his storytelling. This was especially true when he related happenings of more recent years—fables of the present, they seemed to Mara, though he said they were true. Such a one was the story of Queen Hatshepsut's expedition to Godsland, the fabulous country of Punt, which was said to lie far, far south of Egypt across an inland sea. Mara had always thought that land a myth, and told him so.

"Such a voyage is impossible!" she scoffed. "There is no such place. You're too credulous!"

"Not so! Would you like proof? Our captain sailed on that journey, and so did this very ship. Ho, there! Nekonkh!"

At his hail the burly riverman crossed the deck to regard Sheftu warily.

"I pray you, Captain, give this maid proof that I'm no liar. She won't believe that the queen's ships sailed to Godsland."

"*Hail* That's easy!" grunted Nekonkh. He turned to her, then. "We found that land, right enough, so far to the south that we all but turned back before we reached it. It lies on a strange sea, and dwarfish little black men live there. We set up the queen's image in their village. And we brought back some of them. Apes, too, and greyhounds, and a live panther for the queen, and myrrh and cinnamon, Khesit wood, ivory, the green gold of Emu— By Amon, we had a cargo that time! Look you, little one, there in the scuppers. Do you see the dark spots? There stood the little incense trees we brought for the queen's temple, watered and tended like babies, each with its ball of earth."

"Trees?" echoed Mara incredulously. "You brought back trees?"

"Indeed, yes!" Sheftu broke in. He exchanged an odd glance with the captain, who immediately grew wary again. "The trees were the whole purpose of the voyage, Blue-Eyed One. Don't you remember the old tales of Godsland, and the gardens filled with incense trees, terraced down to the sea? The queen's aim was to build such a garden in Thebes for the god Amon. She sent to the end of the world to find what she needed."

"Indeed!" murmured Mara. She was suddenly less interested in the story than in the strange tension that seemed to have taken hold of Nekonkh.

"And did the queen build her temple?" she probed.

"Most magnificently," Sheftu told her. "I'll show you when we reach Thebes."

"But I'm not going to Thebes—not yet."

Sheftu's black brows arched. But he said only, "Then you must see it later. It's not difficult to find. The queen has caused a highway to be built—at what cost I wouldn't dare guess—from the river straight across two miles of desert and valley to the temple's first terrace. A great stone avenue it is, lined on each side with sphinxes. And each sphinx has the head of Her Gracious Majesty."

47

By this time Mara was convinced the whole conversation was aimed at Nekonkh. He was staring fixedly, and she thought angrily, into space.

"Is it not unusual," she ventured, "that a queen's image appear on a public monument?"

"It is most unusual," said Sheftu. "But then these are unusual days in the land of Kemt. Do you know the writings of the ancient prophet Neferrohu, Lotus-Eye? He, too, speaks of unusual times. . . ." Sheftu lounged against the gunwale, quoting absently, " 'Behold, that which men dreaded now exists. Foes are in the East, and Asiatics descend into Egypt, and no protector hears. . . . Speech is in men's hearts as a fire; no utterance of the mouth is tolerated. . . .' "

Nekonkh turned suddenly and made a stiff little bow to the young man. "A word with you, friend, when time permits—in my cabin," he jerked out, and walked away abruptly.

Sheftu straightened, satisfaction on his dark face. "Excuse me," he murmured. "I must leave you now."

And he, too, strode toward the cabin. Both men disappeared under its barrel-shaped roof.

So! The captain had at last been goaded into that private conversation. For a moment Mara leaned against the gunwale, drumming absently on it with her finger tips. Then she strolled idly down the deck, yawning and blinking as if overcome by drowsiness, stopping now and then to watch the oarsmen or stare up at the taut curve of the sail. When she reached the bales of wool stacked behind the cabin she paused, then with the ease of long practice melted into the shadows so casually that not a person on deck could have said where she vanished. Stooping low, she moved swiftly between the bales and crouched behind the cabin's rear wall. Within, she could hear the vague murmur of voices. She pressed her ear to the boards.

". . . henchman of the king," came Nekonkh's gruff

mutter. "One of those fools—or heroes—we spoke of on the voyage down. I suspected it then and I'm sure of it now."

"I meant you to suspect," returned Sheftu with a low laugh.

"Then I'm right!"

"Quite right. I'm the leader of the movement, and a close friend of His Most Princely Majesty—though no one knows it but his followers. On the surface I live the life I was born to, that of an arrogant and wealthy lord, devoted to the queen."

Lord Sheftu! thought Mara, tingling with astonishment. Like an echo came Nekonkh's whispered exclamation. "*Lord* Sheftu! Then you must be the son of Lord Menkau, Friend of Pharaoh and the richest man in Egypt—the great Menkau who died only last flood time and was entombed in the Royal Valley itself. . . ."

"Right again. I am in the full confidence of the queen. It's most convenient. Even more convenient is the stream of gold and silver that pours into my hands from the palace treasury. Aye, Her Majesty distributes bribes as lavishly as she does everything else! But my share of them flows in a strange direction."

"To Thutmose?"

"Precisely." Again the low laugh. "Hatshepsut's gold buys her own downfall."

Behind the cabin wall, Mara had to choke down her delight. Oh, lucky chance that had drawn her here to listen! This information would be worth a fabulous amount to that new master of hers! How his granite face would come alive when she mentioned the name of Lord Sheftu—when she told him how the queen's gold was being used! She could almost see the thin smile that would curl those thinner lips. . . .

But suddenly she found herself picturing Sheftu's face instead, and the way the little golden river reflections danced across it, and how his arms had felt about her.

49

Don't play the fool! she warned herself. Nobody matters, nothing matters except freedom and gold! Think you this Sheftu would thank you for holding your tongue? Pah! He'd slice it off quick enough, if he thought it could harm him! Look out for yourself, and let him do likewise!

She pressed closer to the wall.

". . . one of your allies," Nekonkh was urging. "Surely you have need of a ship and a captain you could trust. I'd pledge my life—"

"We must all do that. Our lives, our fortunes, our brains —they're all forfeit if ever we hold back for safety's sake. There's no safety anywhere in the Black Land while Hatshepsut rules it! She's like a dagger pointed at Egypt's heart. We must knock it away whatever the cost in lives and gold."

"I understand, I agree! I wish to be one of you!"

"You *are* one of us, Captain," returned Sheftu smoothly. "Had I not been sure of you, you would never have reached Menfe."

"I—I see," muttered the other.

On the other side of the wall, Mara shivered a little, remembering the coldness of Sheftu's eyes yesterday. The man was a fanatic, and therefore dangerous as a cobra. She felt sympathy for Nekonkh.

"So be it," Nekonkh was saying gruffly. "And the Devourer take me if I ever fail you! What are my orders?"

"There may be some very soon. For the present, I would know your plans for the next few weeks. Name me the voyages you will make."

There was an odd little silence. Mara frowned and leaned closer—then Nekonkh's voice came again. It was louder, but it sounded a little strained.

"Once in Thebes I'll lay over for five days, while a new cargo is making ready. Then I must deliver the shipment to Heliopolis, taking on timber there which I will bring back to Abydos for the reconstruction of the—"

A tiny sound close behind Mara made her whirl around. In an instant she was on her feet, shrinking back against the cabin wall. Not three feet from her, lounging casually against a bale, stood Lord Sheftu.

He smiled, and a little chill ran up between her shoulder blades. "Are you not tired of straining your ears?" he inquired mildly. "Join us inside, you will be able to hear much better."

And to die much faster! thought Mara.

Without answering, she leaped for the open space between two bales. But quick as she was, he was quicker. Without seeming to disturb his lazy pose, his hand shot out, and fingers like iron bands closed over her wrist.

"I repeat, join us inside. We crave your company."

"Indeed!" Mara spoke through her teeth, trying in vain to twist away from him. "I'll wager you do, at that. Let me go!"

"You'd gain naught by that. We're on a ship, you know. Just where could you run to?"

"Over the side!"

He gave a short laugh. "Have you forgotten the crocodiles?"

"Better them, than you!"

Sheftu's eyebrows rose in mock dismay. "Is my company so repellent? I thought you were enjoying my conversation. Otherwise I'd not have let you overhear so much."

"*Let* me? You knew I was listening?"

"Of course. You arrived here at about the moment our good captain was telling me his suspicions. Now I think of it, he's still chatting away to empty air in there. Suppose we go tell him he can stop now."

Sheftu grinned and started out through the bales, Mara's wrist still firm in his grasp. There was nothing to do but follow, as she found after a final struggle. She looked down in despair and real wonder at the hand which held hers. It

51

was lean and shapely—the hand of an aristocrat. Yet it had the sinews of a porter's.

Aaaah, unlucky day that I laid eyes on this Sheftu! she mourned. May misfortune take the *kheft* that led me to this ship, of all ships in Menfe's harbor. . . .

They were free of the stacked bales now, walking the few paces of open deck. Mara gazed hungrily at the sunlight and the green river, the blue, blue sky. Never had they seemed so beautiful. She thought of pharaoh's golden palace, the freedom and luxury which might soon have been hers, the unread scrolls in Zasha's Room of Books; and the dim sweet memory of that other room. Soon even memories would be lost to her.

He is not really cruel, she thought. He will do it quickly.

They stepped inside the cabin door, and the sun was dimmed. There in the shadows sat Nekonkh, still muttering obediently of cargoes and voyages. He leaped to his feet as they entered.

"So! The eavesdropper!" he growled.

"Nay, our guest! How can you be so inhospitable, Captain? Give the maid a stool, she seems pale."

Grimly Nekonkh obeyed, and Mara sank down on the leather cushion, swallowing hard. She had never experienced this sort of ruthlessness—the sort that came sheathed in exquisite charm.

Sheftu settled one hip comfortably on the plank table and began to swing his leg. "This is better," he approved. "I dislike an atmosphere of deceit. It is far better to be frank with one another, don't you agree, Captain?"

"Yes, my lord," said Nekonkh uncertainly.

Sheftu spun around to him. "Never call me lord. I am a scribe, Captain. My life might hang on your remembering that—and yours certainly does! Do you understand?"

The sheath had slipped for a moment. Mara gripped the sides of her stool, and moisture broke out on her forehead. She wished heartily he would kill her and be done with it.

"Aye, I understand," muttered Nekonkh.

"Good. As I was about to say, we will have no secrets among the three of us. You both know who I am, and what master I serve." Sheftu turned again to Mara, smiling. "And I know—as perhaps you do not, Captain—who this Blue-Eyed One is, and what master she serves."

The words were almost casual, but had the ship suddenly stood on end, Mara could not have been more shocked. She was on her feet without knowing she had moved. "Master? I have no master! You're talking nonsense."

"What a liar you are," he said.

Half frantic, Mara went over in her mind every detail of her sudden purchase, the walk through the streets with her new master, the conversation behind carefully secured doors. No one could possibly have overheard, or guess without overhearing. Was this Sheftu a sorcerer?

"You're bluffing!" she spat at him. "You know naught of me before the day I boarded this ship. How could you?"

"Why, it took no particular effort. The knowledge was fairly thrust upon me. I know, I assure you."

"Prove it!"

His smile hardened. "My dear Mara—I don't have to prove it."

Aye, he spoke truth. She was trapped and he'd never dare let her leave this ship alive. Moreover, she was convinced he did know everything. Somewhere, somehow, he had found her out. Her master's cold warning sounded again in her ears: *If anyone should find out, you will die at once.*

"So be it," she said bitterly. "But you need not soil your lordly hands with my death. Others will save you the trouble."

"Nay, I do not hire cutthroats, it is not my way. Though I've no stomach for this day's task, believe me! What a pity, to close forever those lotus-blue eyes. . . . Sit thee down, maid. Thy face is as white as thy dress."

53

She sank down again, barely able to mutter a sarcastic retort. "I thank you for your concern! It comes a little late."

"Nay, perhaps not." He clasped his hands comfortably about his knee. "You find yourself in an unenviable situation, Blue-Eyed One. But I must point out that you were warned. I spoke truth yesterday when I said I'd not decided what I wanted of you. Now I have no choice; I must silence you—or use you. I prefer the latter. But since I don't trust you as far as tomorrow, I must have some weapon to hold over your pretty head. Come, now. You'd best do as I say. There's an ugly punishment for a runaway."

Runaway! thought Mara despairingly. If that were all!

If that were all . . . *was* that all he knew?

Nekonkh was speaking, his voice more gentle than usual. "So that's what she is! I wondered a little at her rags, and that gold chain! No doubt she stole it from her master. Why didn't I guess?"

"Why?" Sheftu laughed shortly. "Look at her, Captain—there's the reason. Has she anything of the slave about her save those rags? If I'd not actually seen her dragged home to a beating by the stupid oaf who owns her . . . Look you, Mara. I'll not send you back to him—on one condition."

"What condition?" she whispered. Her mind was racing. If he thought her merely a runaway—but what of that conversation she had overheard? Would he dare release her with such information? He seemed to be ignoring it altogether. What, in Amon's name, could he have in mind? Why didn't he speak?

"*What* condition?" she repeated.

"That you serve me, instead of Zasha." Sheftu got up and began to pace the tiny room. "But not as a slave, Mara. As an ally. I need someone like you, who is unknown, beyond suspicion—and clever. It is a dangerous task, but you have no choice, as I think I've made clear."

Mara listened in silence, hardly able to believe what he was saying. For the second time in one week she was being

54

threatened with her life, being maneuvered with almost identical phrases into the position of spy and intriguer—and by two who were deadly enemies, fighting in opposing camps, for opposing causes!

It was incredible, but it was true. And suddenly it struck Mara that it was also hilarious.

She stood up so abruptly that the folding stool she had been sitting on overturned and collapsed. She hastened to right it, struggling meanwhile to gain control of herself. She must not laugh, she must not! But she was hard put to it to hide her elation, the sudden return of all her old brash confidence. Sheftu knew nothing that could hurt her; whereas she had him as neatly checkmated as if this were a giant's game of draughts. True, he had found out she was a slave. What matter? He did not know her master. And before he found out—long before that—he would be in chains.

He may be clever, she thought. Well, so am I! He may be a great lord and a ruthless one, but he has yet to find out how ruthless a guttersnipe can be!

She faced him submissively. "I agree to the condition. You're right, I have no choice."

"I'm glad you see that. Our prince needs your courage and your wits. Come, put them to work with mine on this matter. I want you to carry a message to His Highness. To do that you must be introduced somehow into the palace, and I prefer that you stay there if we can possibly arrange it. There will be other messages."

Nekonkh, who had remained in the background, an uneasy spectator to the little drama, stirred finally. "Have you thought of the Canaanite princess, whose ships are now at Abydos? Could not this little one be disguised—"

"As a barbarian?" Sheftu laughed and gestured toward Mara. "This maiden? Every line of her spells Egypt! No, Captain, I thought of it and discarded the idea. It would be perfect, but—"

"Why as a barbarian?" murmured Mara demurely. "I

55

speak Babylonian. Will not the princess need an interpreter?"

"An interpreter!" Sheftu halted his pacing.

Nekonkh objected. "They will have arranged for that already."

"Aye, one is to go aboard at Abydos. But we will change their arrangements! This one is far better—for us—and I believe it can be done. Blue-Eyed One, already you are invaluable! But we need to find you clothing, some woman to dress your hair—"

Mara summoned all her audacity. "Leave that to me. Look you—there is a sandal maker in Abydos, an old man I once befriended. I was bound for his house, because I knew he would hide me, perhaps give me a few *deben* to buy bread and lodging in Thebes. He hates Zasha. I think he would arrange this other, too, perhaps for a price—"

"Aye, for a price." Sheftu's smile twisted a little. "Men will do anything—for a price. Tell me more of this one. Does he know how to keep his tongue in leash?"

"Would I have been willing to trust him myself, if he did not? He has no family, few friends—he's a crusty sort, but he always liked me, and he bears a grudge against Zasha, who cheated him once in trading—"

"Zasha travels to Abydos to buy his sandals?"

Mara came alert sharply. So Sheftu was not swallowing all this without tasting, as she had thought he was. She had best beware that lazy smile. . . . "Zasha once lived in Abydos," she answered. "His wife is the daughter of a priest there."

"Then you, too, lived in the Sacred City. In what street was Zasha's villa located?"

"The same that runs past the Temple of Osiris," said Mara, knowing there must be such a temple, and praying that the street which passed it might also cross the district of finer homes. Evidently it did, for Sheftu made no comment, beyond asking her the old man's name. She invented

56

one hastily, and he nodded as if satisfied, resuming his perch on the table.

"So be it. Buy the garments of him, and buy *him*, too. You must not be in his debt. Here!" His hand went into his girdle, and came out again holding a heavy ring fashioned of electrum, a costly mixture of gold and silver. It was encrusted with tiny garnets and lapis lazuli in a design of lotus flowers. Mara drew a long breath as she took it. Zasha the jewel trader had never handled anything like this.

"Give him that," said Sheftu, "for his help and his silence. But tell him nothing save that you have fled from Zasha."

"I understand." Mara slipped the ring into her own sash, where it nestled against the queen's tiny scarab. Again she struggled with inward mirth.

"The next problem is installing you as interpreter," Sheftu went on. "That is more difficult. I dare not be seen. Who captains the princess' ship, Nekonkh? Is he Egyptian?"

"Aye. One Saankh-Wen. A thick-witted fellow, but—"

"Can he be bought?"

"Doubtless." Nekonkh rubbed his chin. "But would he talk later? He's a garrulous sort, especially in his cups."

Mara was growing impatient, anxious to have done with it. Once the details were settled, she would be far safer from Sheftu's probing mind. As to Saankh-Wen, no problem existed, though she dare not tell them so. Come, use your head! she thought. You must manage this part too. . . .

"Even in his cups," she said, "would a man talk of his own misdeeds? Perhaps a soft glance and a glib tongue would be of more use here than bribery. If a man is bribed, and feels guilty later, he can blame those who bribed him. But if he is led to substitute one interpreter for another because blandishments sound sweet to his ear—whom can he blame later but himself? He would scarce boast of his own foolishness, would he?"

"And all men are fools," added Sheftu blandly.

Not you, my friend! thought Mara. Aloud, she said with

a shrug, "This one might be. The captain says he's thick witted."

"Aye," growled Nekonkh uneasily. "But the idea seems chancy. . . ."

"Perhaps not." Sheftu was studying Mara with amusement. "This maid understands the arts of blandishment, Captain. I witnessed a little encounter of hers with a baker's boy, back in Menfe, that gave me real pleasure. I believe we can risk it. If it fails, there will still be time to try something else. We'll not leave Abydos until she gives the signal."

"Then all's settled?" inquired Mara.

"Aye. Except for the message you are to give the king. Tell him I have—" Sheftu hesitated, and changed the sentence. "Tell him the war hawk is coming."

"The war hawk is coming? But what does it mean?"

Sheftu smiled. "It is the king I wish to enlighten, Blue-Eyed One, not you." He got up from the table. "We'll arrange our signals tomorrow. But now we must separate, or the crew will be marveling at all this tongue wagging." He started for the door, but paused before Mara, still smiling faintly. "Lest you be wondering, it will *not* be feasible to slip away from me in Abydos, to sell my ring, or to do anything at all save what we have planned. Make no mistake about that. If my prince is endangered, I care not what color eyes I close forever."

He moved past her and out of the cabin. Shaken a little in spite of herself, Mara rose to follow, but Nekonkh stopped her with a touch on her arm. She turned to find him gazing down at her with a troubled frown.

"He's a hard master, that one," he whispered, jerking his head toward Sheftu's retreating figure. "I sweated for you, when he sat there swinging his leg and juggling your life about in his two hands. But you should not have eavesdropped!"

"I'm not afraid of him. He'll do me no harm as long as

58

I'm useful to him. But, Captain—how he must hate the queen and love his prince."

"Aye . . . but I think he loves Egypt even more. To my notion that's what makes him throw away his gold and his life like this, and use men as if they were tools. That's why he holds a bludgeon over the head of even a friendless maid like you, little one, and turns your wits to his own purpose, and takes chances that could end in murder. . . ." Nekonkh shook his head. "Aye, he's reckless, and perhaps mad. But —Amon help me—I think I'd follow him to the River of the Dead and back!"

"He may demand it," said Mara slowly.

She left the cabin, drank in the sun-drenched air and the fresh, clean smell of water and canvas sails and wind— miraculously restored to her again—then sought the privacy of her pile of hides.

All is changed now, she reflected. Yet all is still the same.

Tomorrow, when they docked at Abydos, she would proceed with her former plans as if nothing had happened today. But what a difference there was! She now had knowledge that would buy her freedom from her new master in an instant, and perhaps shower her with gold as well. In fact, she had wealth already, in the shape of that jewel-encrusted ring—which of course would never leave her sash. All her dreams were beginning to come true. As for revenge— Osiris! She had that tenfold, a hundredfold. . . .

Then why, she thought, am I not happier?

She moved restlessly on the soft skins, puzzling over the queer flat taste of her triumph. Finally she raised herself on one elbow and frowned out across the green and sparkling river, which was struck with fire where the sun's rays touched it.

Lord Sheftu. A great nobleman, he was—as far from the likes of her as the very sun up yonder. He must have been amusing himself in truth, these seven days!—seeking her

59

company, flaunting his charming manners, even holding her in his arms a moment. But it was clear what he thought of her. Guttersnipe!

At that moment Sheftu walked along the edge of the deck and paused, leaning on the rail. She could not see his expression, for his profile was black against the dazzling sky. But there was weariness in his pose, and he looked lonely, human—far different from the deadly menace who had lounged against that bale. Perhaps it was true, that he had no stomach for this day's work.

Mara turned away angrily, not wanting to look at him, not wanting to think of the fact that the price of her freedom was his destruction.

CHAPTER 6

Frightened Princess

SAANKH-WEN proved to be a squat, middle-aged man with a stupid face and eyes that seemed half-asleep. He barely looked at Mara when she showed him the scarab and asked for instructions.

"Interpreter? Aye, I remember now. You're to find the Inn of the Lotus, it's close by, just yonder where you see the donkey turning into the alley. They've got their orders there—mention my name."

Mara started in the direction he indicated, glancing

about her curiously. The wharfs of Abydos were not so different from those at Menfe, though the traffic had an unfamiliar character. There was less merchandising here, fewer foreign vessels. Instead there were funeral barges. She counted eight in the harbor this moment. Abydos was the most ancient and sacred of all cities; the god Osiris himself was thought to be buried here, and all who could afford it arranged for their funeral processions to make pilgrimage from their own cities to this Gate of the Underworld before the final ceremonies of entombment.

The Inn of the Lotus was easy to locate, since it had a carved wooden flower swinging over its doorway. Mara entered, identified herself to the vacant-faced woman in charge, and was directed up an outside staircase. In the room above, a coal-black slave girl awaited her. Mara discovered almost immediately that she was deaf and dumb.

Thoughtfully she followed the girl into an adjoining bath chamber, where great jars of water stood about the walls and the stone floor sloped to a center drain. The queen's man had made very sure of secrecy in this process of transforming her from a ragged slave into a person "above suspicion." The woman downstairs was vague and stupid, this one was deaf and dumb, and Saankh-Wen himself incurious.

All the better for me, reflected Mara, remembering the menace in Sheftu's voice that morning when he had warned her again against trickery. The *Silver Beetle* was to loiter upriver until noonday, when the barge of the princess should overtake it. After seeing for themselves that Mara was safely on board, Sheftu and Nekonkh would proceed to Thebes, and she would be free—to carry out her own plans.

She frowned. It gave her little pleasure to think about those plans. She turned her attention instead to the enjoyable ministrations of the black slave girl.

The jars of water were poured over her, her hair was

61

cleansed and trimmed and her body rubbed with scented unguents until it glowed. Then, leading her back into the first room, the slave pointed to a little carved chest that stood in one corner. Mara opened its lid, and the last of her uneasy humor vanished. There were piles of snowy linen, leather sandals—she had never owned sandals in her life, even the common sort woven of palm fiber—there were a few pieces of jewelry, colored sashes, a warm white woolen cloak, deeply fringed. There was a whole wardrobe in that chest, even to the pots and vials containing scents and cosmetics. It was not too lavish. It was scaled perfectly to the needs of a priest's daughter, the role Mara was to play. But to her it was unimaginable luxury. And as she shook the garments out one by one and looked at them, she felt again the fierce determination that nothing, nobody must stand in the way of her possessing such things always, freedom and gold and a life worth living—gardens with lotus blooming in the fishpool, roast duck and honey on the table, rows and rows of papyrus scrolls on the shelves in a beautiful room. . . .

So she dreamed, as the black girl dressed her in an ankle-length sheath of white linen, secured the wide straps over her bare brown shoulders and wound a cinnamon-colored sash twice about her waist, looping it in front so that the ends fell luxuriously to her sandals. Her hair was combed to glossy smoothness, scented and delicately oiled; her eyelids were properly painted, with brows and lash line elongated almost to her temples. There were gold bands for arms and ankles, too, and a broad collar formed of cylindrical beads enameled the same deep radiant blue as her eyes.

She put away the little copper mirror at last, with a sigh of content. It had been a long time since she had enjoyed even the near-necessity of eye paint, which all Egyptians, men and women, considered essential to a decent appearance. And the rest was elegance undreamed of. The sandals did pinch a little, of course, where the strap passed up

between her toes, and the high-curling tips would trip her
if she didn't watch out. She was not accustomed to such
grandeur. Never mind, she would grow accustomed to it!
Only a guttersnipe went barefoot.

Followed by the slave, who padded silently behind her
carrying the chest, she returned to the wharf. Saankh-Wen
was now sitting on a folding stool on the deck of the princess' barge, staring apathetically at the cooks moving about
on the attendant kitchen boat, which was moored nearby.
Mara glanced up, shading her eyes.

"Let down a ladder, please."

He turned toward her, then leaned over the gunwale, his
sleepiness gone. "You're the interpreter?" he asked uncertainly.

"Yes."

"The same one?"

"Of course. I identified myself not half an hour since."

"Aye. Aye." His thick lips curled in a smirk. "But you
look different now."

"Indeed?" Mara gave him a perfunctory smile, careful
neither to offend nor encourage him. She did not wish him
to remember her longer than was strictly necessary. "Will
you let down the ladder?" she repeated.

He hastened to obey. When she stood beside him on the
deck, her head held high, her eyes cool, he stopped gaping
and became more respectful. "The princess and her train
will return soon. You're to wait in there. I'll stow your
chest."

"Very well."

As the slave woman walked across the wharf and out of
her life as silently as she had come into it, Mara made her
way to the pillared pavilion which occupied most of the
deck space of the barge. There was space on each side for
twelve oarsmen, but there was neither mast nor sail, and
the captain's cabin had been removed in order to enlarge
the quarters occupied by Inanni and her women. Mara

63

pushed aside one of the hanging carpets that formed the pavilion's walls, and stepped in. The first thing she did was to kick off the unaccustomed sandals. Then, comfortably barefoot, she began to look about her.

Dazzled by the sunlight outside, she could not at first distinguish one object from another in the shadowed interior. But as her eyes grew accustomed to the gloom she began to make out couches and low tables, clothing boxes and all the feminine hodgepodge of trinkets, mirrors, jewelry and scents necessary to an entourage of a dozen women. The better she could see all this, the more astonished she became. She stepped quietly about the place, examining with curiosity and not a little revulsion the strange possessions of these barbarians. How different they were from anything Egyptian! The jewelry was crude and tasteless, the boxes uncarved, and the scattered clothing so vulgar in its gaudy colors that Mara's civilized Egyptian nose wrinkled disdainfully. All clothing should be white. In Egypt, even a slave knew that much.

Except for the furniture, which like the barge had been built in Thebes, there was nothing in the pavilion which looked as if it might have any connection with a high-born princess.

Princess! scoffed Mara inwardly. Probably some shepherd's daughter, whose father bullied a few neighbors into calling him king.

Turning her back on the untidy room, she stretched full length on one of the couches and fell to wondering what life might be like in pharaoh's palace.

She had not long to wait before the cries of a runner, "*Abrek! Abrek!*"—"Take care, take heart to thyself!"— warned her that the train of the princess was approaching. Hastily groping for her sandals, Mara listened as the hubbub reached the water's edge. Saankh-Wen barked an order, evidently for the bearers to set down the litters and allow the women to emerge, for in a moment the air was filled

64

with the sibilant mumble of Babylonian. As the women filed on board, it sounded as if a hundred great bumblebees had been loosed on deck.

Mara rose, and walking to the carpet wall of the pavilion, pushed a hanging aside and stepped out. She found herself face to face with the Canaanite princess.

At first glimpse, Mara could not help smiling. Inanni was overfed and dumpy, with untidy brown curls clinging damply to her forehead and escaping here and there from the long shawl she wore over her head. Half smothered and sweating in her bulky woolen draperies, which swathed her from head to toe and were striped and embroidered all over in garish colors, she looked every inch the gawky barbarian. But her eyes moved Mara to sudden pity. They were enormous, timid, frightened dark eyes, and they stared at the Egyptian girl as they must have stared at countless strange faces and customs that had come up to bewilder her in this foreign land.

"Who are you?" she whispered helplessly.

"Your interpreter, Highness," returned Mara in Babylonian, smiling more sympathetically this time, and dropping briefly to one knee.

Inanni's relief, at hearing a familiar tongue spoken by one of these arrogant Egyptians, was pathetic. She gave a great sigh of pleasure, and turned excitedly to the dozen gaudily clad and perspiring serving-women who huddled behind her. "It is an interpreter! She speaks Babylonian!" she cried, as if they could not hear for themselves. And at that all the plump faces lighted up, and those who understood Babylonian turned to explain the joyful news to those who spoke only their local dialects, and for a while nothing at all could be heard except their excited jabbering.

At last, though, Inanni gestured them to silence and turned eagerly to Mara. "Oh, please," she begged, "find out from that man there, who commands the ship, if we may leave this place soon and row on to Thebes! So long have we

65

been on this river—so many, many tiresome days, and no one explains anything—and a week now we have been in the temple yonder, while the priests mumble strange things over us, and make us wash and wash and wash until we are like to drown! What is it all for? Are we never to leave off traveling and washing?"

"Patience, my princess," soothed Mara, stifling a grin. "I can answer your questions without talking to Saankh-Wen. Any foreigner journeying to pharaoh's palace must undergo the ceremonies of purification. But it is over now. We leave immediately, and before another night and day we will moor in Thebes."

"Ah, thanks be to the beautiful Ishtar! Thanks to Baal in his temple! Come, let us go in out of the sun, I am like to die of heat!"

Still chattering like a congregation of peahens, the women swarmed inside, and safe now from masculine eyes, began to shed their thick shawls and scarves and cloaks, and to fling themselves panting on couches.

"I shall never grow used to this climate!" groaned the princess, running her hand through her sweat-dampened hair. "And I'm told that it is far hotter in the season of flood! How do you live under such a sun?"

"We dress for it," Mara pointed out in amusement. "We, too, would smother and gasp for air in those heavy woolens. We wear wool only at night, when the air is cold. You will find yourself more comfortable, my princess, when you possess an Egyptian wardrobe."

Inanni glanced at Mara's bare shoulders and sheer narrow garment and blushed crimson. "Oh, I could never wear those things!" she gasped. "Shocking! My brothers told me this was a dangerous and wicked land, for all that the temples are paved with silver!"

Mara laughed outright at this. "We are not wicked, only sensible. You may grow wise too, after a summer spent on the Nile!"

66

She refrained from adding that it would also be well for Inanni and her women to grow thinner, both for coolness' and fashion's sake. The vision of these fat Syrians in the narrow Egyptian sheaths filled her with mirth.

Almost at once they could hear Saankh-Wen's bellowed orders and the bustle of casting off. In a short time the barge was maneuvered through the funereal traffic in the harbor, and as they picked up speed on the open river the cool north breeze began to drift through the pavilion. Most of the Syrians went gratefully to sleep, but for some time Inanni kept Mara busy with questions about Egypt, and the king, and the golden palace for which they were headed. Mara gave what answers she knew, and glibly invented the others. But finally the princess, too, dropped into uneasy slumber, and Mara rose and tiptoed out to the open deck. The fragrance of roasted meat from the attendant kitchen boat had warned her that noonday was near.

Standing at the prow shading her eyes against Ra's dazzling beams, she soon located the *Silver Beetle* standing off the west bank. As she watched, the broad sail rose rib by rib, like a gigantic fin, and the vessel moved into the middle of the stream. The closer it came, the faster Mara's heart pounded. She searched its trim decks, so familiar to her and yet somehow different and strange because she stood apart from them now; she spotted Nekonkh bellowing some order up into the rigging, and could almost feel the tug in her own body as the wind filled the sail.

And at last she saw Sheftu, a still, sun-flooded figure with his face in shadow, leaning with that deceptive laziness near the great sweep at the stern. He gave no sign, nor did she, though for a moment they could almost have clasped hands over the narrow stretch of green water between them. Then slowly the distance widened as the *Beetle* gathered speed and drew ahead of the more ponderous barge.

Not until the sail grew small in the distance did Mara turn back to the shadowy pavilion, feeling lonely and unreasonably depressed. Soon she would walk the gleaming pavements of the Golden House, pharaoh's palace—but soon also she must face her second meeting with that new master.

The war hawk is coming. It meant nothing to her, but no doubt it would to the granite-jawed one. Ah, gods of Egypt, what a little time Sheftu had to live!

Part III—The Palace

CHAPTER 7

Royal Summons

THE PRINCESS INANNI was in a sad state. After an entire Egyptian week—ten days—in the Golden House, she was still unable to conquer the awe and terror her new home inspired in her. She awoke, calling nervously for Mara, at the entrance of the first long-eyed Egyptian servant in the morning, and each evening had to be coaxed into the great golden, beast-headed couch that was her bed. The creature's pink-ivory tongue and gleaming teeth terrified her; she could not, *could* not get comfortable on the exquisitely carved ebony headrest which was so much cooler than her hot Syrian pillow. And in-between waking and sleeping there were further ordeals—the cold bath twice daily, senseless torture which Egyptians accepted as a matter of course; the vigorous massaging afterward, the forcing of combs through her tangled, hip-length hair, her vain attempts to master the art of eating with a spoon instead of the fingers.

On top of all this, she had not yet so much as laid eyes on the queen, or on the young king she had traveled so far to marry. Her pride was outraged, she was in tears half a dozen times a day at this cavalier treatment—yet the magnificence of the palace so overawed her that she hardly dared touch the furnishings of her own apartments.

Mara really felt sorry for her.

She herself was drinking in the luxury as parched ground drinks the waters of the Nile. As Inanni's closest companion —for the princess clung to her desperately as the one person who could and would explain away some of the countless bewilderments—she had actually been given a slave of her own, to bathe and dress her. She dined magnificently off roasted waterfowl and incredible pastries, she had shady gardens to walk in and fresh flowers for her hair and neck as many times a day as she desired.

True, she still kicked off those bothersome sandals whenever she had a chance, and had to keep sharp watch over her tongue lest it slip into the vocabulary of the streets. One highly colored phrase would give her away instantly to the palace servants, most of whom were free-born and as far above her in station as she pretended to be above them. Secretly she was a little in awe of them. It took self-control not to show it; it took gall to send them fetching and carrying as if she were some great lady.

But gall Mara had, in plenty, and Inanni's helpless confusion was not hers. She had been a slave in luxurious houses, as Inanni had not; only the scale of this grandeur and her own changed role were new to her. Also, she was a natural mimic blessed with a sense of humor and a cool nerve—which Inanni certainly was not—and her precarious life had made her as adaptable as a chameleon. How often had she stood, ready with comb or fresh linen, beside Zasha's lady's dressing table! Now she was the one who snapped her fingers for others to obey—and she had not forgotten a single haughty gesture. She took mischievous delight in using them all.

Moreover, she had not yet caught a glimpse of her new master, or of Sheftu, either; therefore nothing whatever was required of her save luxurious lounging. Life was so perfect it was in danger of becoming monotonous.

On the eleventh morning after their arrival she was awakened, as usual, by Inanni's frightened call. Smiling through her yawn, Mara slipped from her couch and hurried into the adjoining room.

"Come now, my princess!" she soothed. "It is only the maidservant, to bring thy fruit and greet the day with thee. Cease thy cowering, or she will laugh about thee in the servants' hall!"

Inanni reluctantly loosed her grasp on the bedclothes and sat up, still eyeing the maid with distrust. "She looks sidewise at me, down her nose, as if she were the queen herself!" she complained.

"Nonsense! Her father was likely a stonecutter, or at best a groom in the royal stables. What would thy brothers say?" Mara turned to the servant, who had set down her bowl of fruit and waited now for dismissal. It was true that her painted eyes held an insolent gleam—any Egyptian felt superior to a barbarian.

"Why are your hands at your sides?" inquired Mara coldly.

The servant's eyes met hers and lost their mockery. Hastily her right hand went to her left shoulder.

"Better! It is possible I will not mention your miserable name to Hatshepsut the Glorious—provided you show proper deference to your princess after this."

"Excellency, live forever!" gasped the girl, turning white. "You would not—I never meant—"

"Dismissed," Mara cut her off. The servant prostrated herself and then fled.

Mara was inwardly convulsed. Oh, marvelously done! she thought. Did ever a slave so beautifully subdue a free maid? How she would rage if she knew who it is that plays the great lady!

She turned back to find Inanni regarding her with both gratitude and admiration. "Mara, what did you say to her?"

"Only that you are the Princess Inanni, and must be treated so. Do not think of her, she is as a beetle under your

71

sandal. Come, perfume your mouth with the figs and grapes she has brought you. It will soon be time for the bath."

Inanni's face fell dismally at the prospect. But she climbed down from her high couch, being careful to stay well away from the gleaming teeth of the beasts who supported it. A few minutes later she was hungrily eating a fig, and mourning the skimpiness of Egyptian breakfasts.

"Why, in my homeland we have bread, and good meat. Here, you do not even dignify it by the name of breakfast, but call it 'the perfuming of the mouth!'"

"We do not think of it as a meal," said Mara, smiling. "Lift up your head, Rose of Canaan, perhaps your summons from pharaoh will come today."

"It should have come before! Have they forgotten they sent for me?"

"Nay, of course not! No doubt Her Majesty is allowing you time to recover from your journey. Now do not brood about it, we will do something different this morning. My little slave tells me there are gardens we have not yet visited, also that there is a pavilion on the roof, from which—" She stopped. The tapestry curtaining the doorway into her own bedchamber had stirred noticeably—and there was no draft. "—from which one can see the entire city," she finished evenly. She put down a bunch of grapes, untasted. "Meanwhile, with your highness' leave, I will retire to bathe and dress."

Summoning two of the Syrian women to divert the princess, she walked to the curtained doorway and with a sudden motion pushed aside the hangings. The room was as empty as when she had left it. She stepped inside, letting the tapestry fall behind her. The bedclothes were still in a snarl on the lion-legged couch, the chest and littered dressing table stood, undisturbed, against the wall bright with painted golden butterflies. The doors to both bath chamber and hall were closed and blank.

Yet those hangings had moved.

72

She flung off her night robe, wondering why it had not occurred to her before that a spy might have been set to keep a watch on her. Sheftu had openly admitted that he trusted her no farther than tomorrow, and as for that stony-eyed master of hers . . .

She frowned, realized she had been rapidly putting on her own clothes. *Ast!* Was she trying to reveal herself for what she was? Just as rapidly, she stripped the garments off, put on her night robe again, and clapped her hands for her slave.

The little brown maiden flung open the hall door so promptly that Mara gave her a sharp look. Was she the spy, then? No, surely not. The child was no more than twelve years old, with a face as innocent as a flower. Mara pitied her suddenly, remembering how it felt, at twelve, to stand motionless for hours in some corridor, waiting for the clap of hands.

"Hast been impatient, little Nesi? Go, then, make ready my bath. We'll soon be done here."

When the girl had disappeared into the bath chamber, Mara glanced around once more, uneasily searching for some clue to her uninvited visitor. On a sudden thought she went to the little carved chest and raised its lid. At first she saw nothing amiss. Then she dropped to her knees, lifting with cautious fingers a fold of the topmost garment. Under it lay a common honey cake—the sort sold in the streets of Menfe by the bakers' boys.

She picked it up, frowning. It had not been there before, of that she was certain. She turned it over, scanned it top and bottom, and finally broke it open. There in its flaky middle was a scrap of papyrus. In a trice she was reading the tiny hieroglyphs.

"A princess enjoys the lotus garden in the cool of the evening."

That was all it said. Thoughtfully Mara tore it into a dozen pieces, and after some hesitation, dropped the scraps

73

into a tall alabaster vase that stood in one corner. Even if they were pieced together, they would seem but a fragment from some scribe's copybook. She ate the honey cake, dusted the crumbs from her fingers and went to take her bath.

Very cleverly done, she thought as she lay on the rubbing-table enjoying the ministrations of the capable little Nesi. So there was no spy, only a summons to walk this evening with the princess Inanni in one of the palace gardens—one with a lotus pool. Perhaps she could locate it from that roof pavilion Nesi had mentioned. But which master had sent the summons? It would be like Sheftu to identify himself with the honey cake—he had seen her stealing cakes that day in Menfe. Still, so had the Stone-Faced One. She remembered his acid remark: "Remember, I am no stupid baker's apprentice. Should the chain, and you, disappear somehow between here and the wharfs, it would be—regrettable."

Well, she had not made off with his golden chain, nor had she deceived him in any way. On the contrary, he would have good reason to be pleased with her when they met again. There was no need to be afraid of him. None at all. She had the information he wanted, more than he'd ever hoped to get. . . .

Mara found she was no longer enjoying her massage. Rising abruptly, she led the way back to the bedroom. Should it be not Sheftu but her master awaiting her in the lotus garden tonight, her stay at the palace would be over almost before it began. And that would be regrettable too—especially for Sheftu.

One mention of the cooling north breeze to be found on the roof was enough to arouse Inanni's enthusiasm for a visit there. At midmorning she and Mara, accompanied only by little Nesi, made their way through a maze of halls, up an outside stairway, and out onto the terraced loggia. It was cool and windy, strewn with soft couches and shaded by a

74

great canopy set on beribboned columns. Here and there rose wide-mouthed air scoops which sent the breeze down into the sleeping chambers below. Mara walked to the balustrade and leaned forward upon her elbows. From here, two stories up, one had a wide view of the sunlit labyrinth of courtyards, passages, groves and gardens enclosed by the palace walls. Her strolls with Inanni had showed her only a fraction of them.

"Look, my princess!" she exclaimed. "Your new home."

Inanni looked, trembled, and moved uneasily away. Mara watched her for a moment, half-pitying, half-contemptuous, then turned back to the balustrade. Which garden? There were so many! She made a slow circuit of the roof, almost dismayed at the expanse of the palace grounds and their complexity. Save for the huge guardroom, the entire ground floor of the Golden House was devoted to workshops, kitchens and storerooms. Among and beyond these were walled gardens in bewildering profusion—and every one of them had its lotus pool.

But as she rounded the corner to the north side, she saw what she wanted. It was the largest garden of all, with a pool the very shape of a lotus bud almost overflowing with the blue lilies, and more of them painted along its rim.

Satisfied, she was about to turn away when she chanced to raise her eyes beyond the walls. "Ai, blessed Osiris!" she breathed. "Highness, come to this side if you would see Thebes! There it lies. . . ."

Inanni joined her at the balustrade and together they looked out over the vast spread of the city. The palace stood near the Nile's west bank, within view of the queen's magnificent temple, which stood, low, colonnaded and gleaming white in the dazzling sunlight, far back against the golden cliffs. Mara could see the green incense terraces Nekonkh had helped bring into being; from them the desert descended in two broad benches to the level of the valley, then the Necropolis—a belt of low, dust-colored buildings hous-

75

ing the embalmers, coffin makers, stonecutters, glass blowers, weavers and all other craftsmen whose work was devoted to the tombs—stretched on to join the emerald fields of the flower growers, which in turn extended to the river.

The river divided the city like a silver blade, and was dotted with every size and shape of vessel. Behind the slow-moving sails rose the high east bank and Thebes proper—a maze of white buildings flooded with sun, from whose flagstaffs and massive temple pylons red and white banners waved like beckoning fingers. Every surface sparkled with color and the glint of gold; roofs stretched eastward under the brilliant blue sky as far as the eye could reach.

Mara propped her chin on her hands, drinking it all in. A marvelous city! Grander than Menfe, gayer than Abydos —and even wickeder, it was said, than Bubastis on the lower Nile. It filled her with excitement.

Around the palace itself a small town had grown up, composed largely of the white-walled villas of Egypt's great nobles, and a few of the finest craftsmen's and goldsmiths' studios. Mara stared at the chariots flashing along the stone-paved streets, at the palms thrusting up like plumes from invisible pleasure gardens, and wondered if one of those grand houses belonged to Lord Sheftu.

"Ai, what a life they lead, those great ones! Think, my princess, you are one of them now, and live in the Center of the World. Is it not a glorious city you have come to after all your journeying?"

"I hate it," whispered Inanni.

Startled, Mara swung around. Inanni was gripping the balustrade, her plump face white with misery. Her eyes swerved away from Mara's astonished ones, as though she were frightened to have spoken her mind for once. But she went on recklessly. "It is too big, and too full of buildings! In my homeland there are plains and green pastures, and the tents of the shepherds shine in the sun, and the flocks graze all about. . . . It is not like this in any way! All speak my language there, but here all are strangers to me and know not my ways, and I know not theirs. . . ."

"What does that matter? Think, you are to be the bride of royalty! Of a prince of Egypt!"

"The king has not sent for me."

"But he will!" Mara could not help laughing a little. "Meanwhile, have you not all you could desire? Slaves, and comforts, and a home in the Golden House itself? Take heart! It is not possible you could be homesick!"

"Is it not?" Inanni turned, gathering the folds of her heavy shawl, and made an effort to smile. She had never looked gawkier, or more defenseless, but suddenly she was not funny at all. "I suppose it is not. You have been good to me, Mara, and speak to me in my own tongue and explain things, and try to teach me to be Egyptian. But I fear I am no credit to you. I cannot help longing for the plains of Syria, and the voices of my brothers."

She broke off, tears welling into her eyes, then moved abruptly to the other side of the pavilion. Mara turned away too, no longer amused at a ridiculous barbarian but sorry for a homesick maid, with all her heart.

Suddenly, above the voices of the doves in the palace eaves and the faint, melodious creaking of water wheels in the fields, there came a new sound—far, high, piercing. Mara looked up. There above her in the radiant vault of the sky a great bird soared—Horus, the falcon, the god, the symbol of royalty. As she watched, it closed its powerful wings and dropped like a plummet upon a desert lark just spiraling upward from the meadows. The lark's melody was choked off in mid-trill; again the great wings beat and the falcon wheeled off toward Libya. Its triumphant scream, seven notes on a descending scale, trailed after it like a banner. Mara was still breathless from the beauty and cruelty of its attack when an exclamation from Inanni made her whirl around.

A chamberlain had emerged from the door to the stair-

77

way. He advanced to Inanni with measured tread and bowed stiffly.

"Princess, rejoice. The Glorious One, Daughter of Ra Most High, Horus of Gold and Great God of the Land of the Double Kingdom, commands your presence."

"Mara?" quavered the princess, taking an uncertain step backward.

But Mara was already hurrying to her side. "Quick, Highness! Send little Nesi to summon your women. We must go down at once—it is the audience with the queen!"

CHAPTER 8

Her Majesty, the Pharaoh

A SUDDEN HUSH fell upon the crowd in the huge, colonnaded guardroom, and all heads turned in one direction. Courtiers, priests, glittering ladies and grouchy ambassadors fell back silently to make room for the procession which had entered from the courtyard at the far end of the hall.

The chamberlain, tapping his long beribboned wand, paced first. Inanni followed him, with Mara close by her side and the twelve Syrians at her heels. Slowly they moved down the long aisle of watching faces, past all the supercilious, painted eyes and quirking lips, past the arched brows, the murmurs behind hands, the disdainful shrugs—down the whole shining length of the room.

It was the worst ordeal Inanni had had to face, and this one she met like a princess. Mara, close beside her, could feel the plump arm quaking under its gaudy, thick draperies. But Inanni held her chin high and kept her eyes unwaveringly on the back of the chamberlain's neck. Perhaps she was thinking of her brothers.

There was an antechamber to pass through before they stood in front of the tall, bronze doors. Here the chamberlain faced them and rattled off a list of instructions concerning court etiquette of which Mara translated only the least confusing. Then, at last, the doors swung open; the chamberlain stepped forward and flung himself on his face, intoning: "Behold, the majesty of the Black Land! Horus of Gold, Enduring of Kingship, Splendid of Diadems, Ruler of Lower and Upper Egypt, Enduring-of-form-is-Ra, Makere Hatshepsut! May the god live forever!"

Mara, suddenly trembling from head to foot, advanced beside Inanni until they stood inside the room. There, across a stretch of gleaming pavement, stood a raised dais framed by two exquisitely painted columns. Upon the dais rested a great throne fashioned entirely of shimmering electrum— and on the throne sat a woman so coldly beautiful that it took away the breath to gaze on her.

She sat stiffly, her glittering dark eyes fixed, her hands holding emblems shining with gold and enamel. Fluted linen, fine as a cobweb, enveloped her like mist; she was weighted with jewels. Upon her flawlessly modeled chin was tied the narrow ceremonial beard denoting kingship, and upon her head rested the heavy red and white double crown of the Two Kingdoms, with the golden cobra curving out over her brow.

Woman or not, there sat the awesome majesty of Egypt, the sun god incarnate. The entire procession fell to its knees; fourteen foreheads, Mara's among them, touched the cold tiles of the floor.

"Lift up your head, Princess of Syria," said Hatshepsut. "You may approach my majesty."

Her voice was high and metallic. Mara felt the glittering eyes upon her even before she raised her own, with an effort, to meet them. Pharaoh had not relaxed her godlike rigidity, but she had turned her head, and her scrutiny was so thorough, so impersonal, that it made Mara feel like a bird on a spit.

"You may speak, Interpreter," added the queen impatiently.

Mara tried, and failed. In a panic she swallowed, tried again, and this time managed to inform Inanni that she was to rise and walk forward.

"What shall I say, Mara?" came the princess' frightened whisper as she reluctantly obeyed. "Say it for me, please—"

"May Hatshepsut the Glorious—endure forever," stammered Mara. "The princess Inanni presents her respects to your Radiance."

The queen permitted herself a coldly gracious smile. Then to Mara's infinite relief, the probing eyes were withdrawn from her, and Hatshepsut turned her entire attention to Inanni. There followed conventional questions as to her comfort, congratulations on the successful voyage, assurances that she need only speak to have anything she desired.

Mara was breathing more easily now; the nervous sweat had dried on the palms of her hands, and she had regained the use of her tongue. As she translated the stilted phrases she began to be aware of other people in the room. They were standing all about the walls, motionless as shadows, but here and there the twinkle of gold as a head turned, or the flash of jewels from a lifted hand, gave proof that they were people and not painted images.

"And have you had audience with His Highness, your bridegroom?" inquired Hatshepsut.

Scarcely waiting for Inanni's almost inaudible reply, she spoke with a malicious smile to someone standing to her right and slightly behind her, on the dais itself. "What think you, Count Senmut? Is she not all we expected, and even more?"

So that is Count Senmut! thought Mara. Curiously and with awe she studied the most powerful figure in Egypt—a spare, big-shouldered man wearing a twist of amulets about his throat. The queen seemed ageless, but Senmut's darkly handsome face mirrored all the struggle and scheming of her eighteen years upon the throne. His smile, faint though it was, carved harsh furrows from his flaring nostrils to the corners of his mouth; his eyes were rapacious.

He bent to murmur something to the queen, and she laughed. "Aye, it will be a sight. A pity *she* will not enjoy it. Interpreter, inform the princess that she may expect to meet her bridegroom very soon."

As Mara obeyed, Hatshepsut lifted a slim hand loaded with rings, and beckoned lazily to someone who stood half hidden in the shadows beside the throne. Next instant every word of Babylonian she knew fled from Mara's mind. It was Sheftu who stepped forward, with his leopard's grace—but a far, far different Sheftu from the man who had lounged beside her while the sails slapped and the sun sparkled on the river. This one wore royal linen as casually as the other had worn his simple *shenti;* his dark features were arrogant against a headcloth of woven gold. There was gold on his ankles, his arms, and his long, sinewy fingers, and a blaze of emeralds at his throat. Here was the great noble she had tried, and failed to picture—a lord of creation, as remote from her as pharaoh herself. Only the amulet on his left wrist was unchanged, and its curiously knotted flax threads and familiar beads gave her a feeling akin to homesickness, for he who wore it seemed a stranger.

Then, for just an instant, his eyes met hers, and a delicious warmth stole over her. I was wrong, she thought. This is the same who once held me in his arms, though he would not kiss me . . . the very same, by the beard of Ptah, whose

81

grand rich life I hold in the palm of my guttersnipe's hand this minute!

"Send word to Thutmose today," Hatshepsut was murmuring, "that he must receive this Syrian at once. You yourself, Lord Sheftu, arrange for the marriage as soon as may be, and we will have done with her. How stupid and vulgar she is in her tasteless wrappings! A fit consort for my surly half brother, think you not? *Hai!* How I would like to see that meeting—he will grow red in the face, and hurl vases and ornaments to the floor, and pace up and down in his endless pacings, as he always does." Hatshepsut smiled. "Nevertheless, he will obey me—as he always does."

If her venom enraged Sheftu, he gave no hint of it. His expression was as smoothly controlled as his bow. No more than an inclination of the head was required for his exalted rank, and he bent not a hair lower.

"Pharaoh's name is glorious," he remarked amiably—without specifying, Mara noticed, whether it was Hatshepsut or Thutmose to whom he gave the title. "All shall be as pharaoh desires."

"You are ever trustworthy, Lord Sheftu." Hatshepsut smiled on him, and he smiled winsomely back. "And now, my lord, if you will provide our fat princess with refreshment . . ."

He made a careless gesture; at once lackeys bearing sweetmeats and garlanded jars of wine converged on Inanni, then passed through the ranks of the courtiers, who obediently came to life, clinking their wine cups with the rigidly correct, stilted movements which made court etiquette a sort of elegant ballet. Sheftu turned away and walked—almost sauntered—back to his place, arrogant and assured. Not for him the puppetlike movements of these lesser beings.

Mara, still on her knees behind the princess, watched him and admired his daring. Suddenly her eyes riveted on a half-shadowed figure just beyond him. For the second time she felt the shock of a familiar face, but this time the sensation was distinctly unpleasant. For there, grim-faced as the Devourer himself, stood her mysterious new master.

For a moment the man's cold visage held her fascinated. Did he ever change expression? Just so he had looked when he offered her riches and danger back in Menfe. Just so he would still look while he watched the slow death of that gold-decked young renegade beside him. How would they kill Sheftu, once they knew? He could not hope for the mercy of the strangler—not while Hatshepsut and her wily Architect ruled the Black Land. He would more likely meet the torturer's stake. Or perhaps—Mara had a feeling this would please Count Senmut—perhaps they would bow to Sheftu's ultimate destiny and feed him to the crocodiles; those long, sinister brown-green shapes with their pale mouths wide open, waiting. Just one word from her . . .

I cannot do it! was her first thought. But her second was, Aye, you can do it—since you must.

But was there any need for haste?

The thought calmed her. It would be pleasant to stay at the Golden House a little longer, she told herself. I will not speak quite yet. Later, aye, so be it, but not yet!

At that a new fear struck her. If she delayed, who knew how the cat might jump? It was possible Hatshepsut had met her match in this clever Sheftu. Given a little time, he might bring his plans to maturity and snatch that gleaming throne and give it to his king. Ai! Then what would happen to the queen's favorites and their gold—and the dreams of the princess Inanni's interpreter?

Mara knew only too well. Her only sure safety lay in serving her master. But as she looked from him to the indolently lounging Lord Sheftu, it was hard to choose. . . .

The solution that sprang into her mind next instant was so simple, so obvious, that she all but laughed aloud. She would not choose! Why make a choice between these two when each thought her his ally, his bonded slave? Why not play both ends against the middle—serve both, meanwhile serving only herself? Then, when the cat jumped, she would jump with it! Ah, the opportunities that opened for one who knew how to use her wits!

She started at the sound of the queen's voice. "Dismiss the lackeys, Count Senmut. I think this Syrian does not like our wine." The servants withdrew, and Hatshepsut spoke again, this time to Mara. "Bid the princess farewell. May the gods of Egypt and Syria go with her. And offer her my majesty's felicitations on her coming marriage—which will surely be a joyous one."

The voice dripped mockery, and the beautiful lips twisted in a smile remarkably like the one carving furrows on the dark countenance of Count Senmut, behind her. Mara felt her optimism drain away in spite of all she could do, and the sight of the white mask which was Inanni's face lowered her spirits still further. Friendless, homesick, unfortunate princess! Small wonder she had been unable to swallow the wine.

Inanni managed to stammer out her thanks and farewells, and Mara translated with an effort. Hatshepsut nodded, and her smile grew broader; she began to laugh deep in her throat. The sound grew in volume until the chamber was filled with it. Mara found herself remembering the scream of Horus, the royal falcon, as he plummeted down from the sky that morning to seize the lark. Her flesh was creeping as she rose from her knees at last to back slowly toward the door beside the pallid Inanni.

For the queen, still laughing, had raised her gold-and-enameled scepter. The audience was over.

CHAPTER 9

Lion in a Snare

INANNI'S summons from her intended bridegroom came within the hour. By that time the effect of the queen's laughter had worn off, leaving Mara free of forebodings and once more impudently confident of herself and her wits. And anticipation of the ironic encounter just ahead, in which she herself would become the messenger she had been ordered to discover and betray, fairly intoxicated her. What delicious mischief! It was really too bad there was no one to enjoy it but herself.

But then, she reflected, neither Sheftu nor her granite-jawed master would be likely to see the humor of the situation.

Poor Inanni, having no secret deviltries to buoy her up, was in low spirits indeed. It was all Mara could do to convince her that she must submit to more unreasonable washing and hair combing, and be ready after the noon meal to present herself to the king.

But Mara had a firm way with her, and the food did much to restore the princess' quailing spirits. So when enough water had trickled into the water clock to raise the level to the proper mark, Inanni rose, and accompanied by Mara and two of the Syrian women, followed another chamberlain through gleaming halls wainscoted in gold leaf, through gardens and passages and rooms of state to the apartments of the king.

It was easy to see the position to which Thutmose had

been reduced in this stronghold of his sister. His rooms were lavish and his slaves numerous, but the atmosphere of his apartments was that of a luxurious prison. The guards, one felt, were less to keep intruders out than to keep Thutmose in.

As for the interview itself, it was quite lacking in the ceremonious pomp that had characterized the queen's audience. Thutmose inspired not awe, but sound respect, as Mara found when he strode into the room, attended only by a couple of slaves and a scribe. He was a short, powerfully built man with the nose of a conqueror, vigorous and restless in all his movements. As soon as she saw him Mara began to understand Sheftu's fanatic loyalty, for the fire in those direct brown eyes caught the imagination and held it.

"So this is the barbarian!" he growled, stopping before Inanni and letting his scornful gaze travel over her. "Monstrous! Exactly the bride I would expect my insufferable sister to choose for me—as though I would heed any choice of hers! Pah! Send the wretched creature away!"

He turned and started back toward the room he had just quitted, then changed his mind and swung around to Mara. "Who may you be?" he demanded.

"Mara, the interpreter," breathed the girl in relief. For a moment she had thought the interview already ended, and her chance lost.

"Interpreter? What need of that? I know Babylonian, though I care not for it overmuch. A mumbling language!"

Mara thought fast. Already he was poised to leave again, and he must not!

She bent her head deferentially. "Even Her Most Glorious Majesty must have realized that His Highness would not deign to speak to this lowly Syrian in her own tongue."

The words pleased him. He wrung few enough concessions from his iron-willed sister; even this indirect acknowledgment of his royal status was a victory of sorts. He looked at Mara with more interest.

86

"Hatshepsut is right, for once," he remarked. "However, even with an interpreter at hand, I have naught to say to this—this goatherd's daughter. You might tell her that I have no intention of marrying her, now or ever."

Mara turned reluctantly to Inanni, who was staring miserably at the floor. She had not needed to understand his words to know that Thutmose despised her. His first scornful scrutiny had told her that.

"My princess," began Mara, then found she could not speak the crushing phrases. "His Highness presents his warmest regards," she finished.

She had the satisfaction of seeing Inanni's face come back to life; the great dark eyes lost their look of suffering, and turned hopefully toward the king. Mara turned to him too, well-pleased with her merciful little lie. But one look at his startled face froze the blood in her veins. What a fool she was! Of course, he had understood every word she had said.

"Son of Pharaoh, live forever!" she gasped. "I crave pardon—I could not believe you meant to wound this princess, however lowly—"

"You mean you forgot I could understand," retorted Thutmose.

"By the Feather of Truth, Highness, I meant only to spare this unfortunate maiden, who is homesick and frightened, and who has met only contempt in the land of Egypt. I pity her, and could not tell her that all her journey was in vain— not here, where Your Highness and these others are all watching her. Pray give me leave to do it later, in private."

She broke off, breathing hard. She had been unthinkably bold, she knew that from the horrified expression on the little scribe's face. He stepped up to the king, bristling. "Your Highness! This impertinence is intolerable! With your leave, I shall have this person removed at once, and shall myself see to it that—"

"Be silent," said Thutmose. Without taking his eyes off Mara, he swept the scribe into the background with one powerful arm. "Leave me. Take these others with you."

The room was soon empty of all save the three Syrians, the king and Mara. Thutmose took a step nearer, his eyes still boring into hers. "Now, little one," he said quietly. "Perhaps you will tell me who you really are."

Inanni spoke up. "What does he say, Mara? Why do you not translate?"

Mara managed to control her delight long enough to answer rapidly. "He wishes to know if you are more comfortable with all those others out of the room."

"Why—why—yes, Mara, tell him I am much more comfortable!"

Thutmose ignored her. "Hasten, girl! They will not stay away forever. Who are you?"

"The princess' interpreter, Highness. But also—yours to command."

"At last! I thought as much the instant—" Thutmose broke off, his face tightening. "How do I know this?"

For a moment Mara was at a loss. She had no talisman, no sign, no proof save Sheftu's name itself. "By him who sent me, son of pharaoh," she answered. "By—"

"Name me no names! The very walls are spies. Describe him, if you can."

Inanni was tugging at her sleeve. Mara turned hastily, trying to assemble her thoughts. "My princess, your bridegroom inquires if you have—er—slept well, if your rooms are to your liking."

"Oh, indeed they are. I—it is only the beasts on the couch which . . . No, wait, Mara. Perhaps we should not mention the beasts. I—merely say that the rooms please me very much."

Describe Sheftu? Mara was thinking. As well describe the shape of the wind. Would she describe the gold-hung noble, or the scribe's apprentice she had first seen bending over her on the deck of the *Silver Beetle?* She began hesitantly,

"He is young and tall, Highness, and well favored, with eyes like the night—" But that told nothing of him, true though it was. She pictured again the river lights playing over his face, felt his dangerous charm, remembered with a ▓▓▓▓ ▓▓▓ ▓▓▓▓▓▓'▓ ▓▓▓▓▓ ▓▓ ▓▓▓ ▓▓▓▓▓▓▓ ▓▓▓▓. ▓▓ ▓▓ ▓▓▓ ▓▓ beware. There is a laziness about the way he moves— Ai, I cannot say it as I would! In a crowd he looks the same as other men, but he is not. By the Feather, he is different from any I ever knew! When he smiles—I know not how to tell you of his smile. It is like a magician's potion. . . ."

She stopped in confusion at the amusement on the king's face. "He was not described quite thus by the last messenger—who was elderly and male," said Thutmose drily. "However, I recognize my artful one. Well favored, is he? In truth, he is almost ugly—but no woman ever knows it! Tell me, is he safe?"

"Aye, he is safe," mumbled Mara. So far, she thought vindictively. Why had she made such a fool of herself?

"And well?"

"Translate, Mara!" pleaded Inanni.

"Er—my princess, the son of pharaoh inquires after the health of thy brothers."

Inanni looked wonderingly from her to the king. "Tell him they flourish like the palm. But how long he talked, to say such a simple thing! In truth, Mara, this conversation is exceeding strange! His words speak one thing, and his face another. Look how he scowls! Is it always so with Egyptians?"

"Frequently, Highness. Our language is—is more complex than thine." Mara groped after her scattered wits, wishing the princess at the bottom of the Nile. Between Inanni's questions and the king's irony, she felt like a juggler with too many balls in the air. Now, somehow, she must explain away Thutmose's ill-concealed impatience. Look at him glowering there—in truth, he was small help to her! She invented hastily. "In addition, my princess, His Highness complained of a slight headache, which I forgot to mention. He begs you not to judge his gallantry by his scowl."

"A headache?" Inanni was instantly concerned. "Why, what a pity! No wonder he— Mara, ask him if he has tried a remedy made of the crushed pods of the poppy."

Mara faced the king, wrenching her mind back to the last question he had asked—if Sheftu was well. In Egyptian, she answered it. "Aye, he who sent me is in the bloom of health."

"*Hai!* The gods be praised. Tell me, Blue-Eyed One, where did he find you?"

"On a Nile boat called the *Silver Beetle*. We—we happened to travel together up the river, and met quite by chance."

"By chance, eh? I'll wager nothing was left to chance from then on. He's thorough, that one. I wonder what ax he's found to hold over your pretty head? Perhaps naught but those night-black eyes . . ." Thutmose chuckled, but waved back her retort. "Never mind, I'm sure of him, therefore of you. You may give—" He stopped, jerking his head irritably at Inanni, who was showing signs of impatience. "Proceed with your sweet Babylonian nothings on my behalf, then give me his message."

"What did he say, Mara? Has he tried the poppy pods?"

"No, my princess. He has never heard of such a remedy. He says he will consult the royal physician about it, and is touched by your interest in his welfare."

"Are you sure, Mara? He does not look touched, only angry!"

"Aye, but that is his headache! Indeed, he is not only touched but smitten with Your Highness. He expressed great astonishment that one so comely should also have a warm heart."

Inanni began to glow. "Comely? Did he call me so? Indeed! Then he cannot be angry, after all! I believe he is lonely, Mara. He needs a woman to care for him, that's what it is. None of these cold Egyptian beauties but someone to love and soothe him. . . . Tell him I will prepare the poppy draught with my own hands, and no other shall touch it. How I misjudged him! He is kindness itself, and so handsome—is he not handsome, Mara?"

Murmuring agreement, Mara turned with some nervousness to the startled Thutmose.

"Pray restrain yourself!" he told her. "You will have this fat Syrian in my arms. Come, give me the message, and hasten, our privacy will not last."

"The war hawk is coming."

An instantaneous change came over Thutmose. "Amon be blessed!" he exclaimed. He gnawed his lip a moment, staring at nothing, and Mara could feel herself and Inanni recede into a limbo of unimportance. Suddenly he whirled and began to pace up and down, up and down, until she was reminded of a panther in a cage. Inanni turned to her, bewildered.

"Why does he act so, Mara? What did he say?"

"That he is overjoyed with your offer to prepare the poppy pods. He is now trying to remember whether there are any in the palace storerooms."

"Oh, he need not worry over that! My women brought plenty from the homeland. Tell him the draught will be here within the hour."

Mara hesitated. The king's preoccupied scowl was formidable; she knew he had forgotten their very existence. But Inanni urged her impatiently. "Tell him, Mara!"

"Son of pharaoh," Mara ventured. "I crave pardon, but I must speak lest this maiden grow suspicious—"

"Eh? What?"

"Will Your Highness allow her to prepare this draught . . . ?"

"Aye, aye, let her do what she likes! *The war hawk.*" Thutmose kept on pacing. "That was the exact wording of the message?"

"Aye, Your Highness."

"By Amon, that even my clever one should have such powers of persuasion! I begin to think he is the Great Magician himself—and indeed, he'll have to be. . . . We must have gold, now. Much, and more than much! Tell him that. Ask him . . ." The king halted beside a table, his back to Mara. He picked up a papyrus that lay there, turned it absently in his fingers a moment, then tossed it down again. "Ask him," he went on quietly, "if his magic is indeed a shield and a buckler to him. For he must go on a far journey. There is one, and only one in the land of Egypt who will give gold for my sake—and who has enough."

He paused again, as if reluctant to go on. Mara mechanically invented some fiction or other for Inanni, but her attention remained on the king. A far journey? What was he talking about? There was something strange in his manner, an air of dread coupled with grim resolve that promised no easy task for Sheftu.

Suddenly Thutmose whirled and planted his feet. "Thou of the blue eyes," he said with quiet menace. "Thy life is worth less than nothing should this reach any ears but his. Do you understand that?"

Mara nodded, shrinking back a little. His glare was frightening.

"Then here is the message. Tell him he must journey to the River of Darkness, as we talked of long ago. He must take the treasure of him who sleeps there, even the royal cobra from his brow and the collar of amulets—"

"River of Darkness?" Mara choked on the words.

"Aye. He must take from the dead the gold Egypt must have to live! He must go down into the land of night and bring it forth to me."

There was a cold emptiness in the pit of Mara's stomach. Sheftu's orders were to commit the foulest crime known to Egypt—to rob a pharaoh's tomb. He must break open doors once sealed with prayers and chanting for all eternity, descend into echoing silence, deepest night, creep through rooms and passages and darkest mystery to the farthest chamber, where pharaoh dwelt amid his treasure—and he would die there, trying to wrest it from the *khefts* who guarded it. He will never come back, thought Mara.

Thutmose watched her narrowly a moment as she stood sick and numb with what she had heard. Softly he added, "He knows which door to enter." Then he jerked away to a wine stand at the other side of the room, tore the garlands off the jug and splashed a cup full of the amber liquid. "You may arrange audience for this Syrian whenever you need to see me," he rapped out. "Begone now."

Mara managed to stammer something to the puzzled Inanni, and they withdrew. The king did not acknowledge their farewells. When they left the room he was still standing with his back to them and his head bent, turning the empty wine cup over and over in his hands.

Mara never knew quite how she explained that last few minutes to Inanni's satisfaction, or to what mingling of headache and ardor she attributed the king's behavior. But the words must have convinced Inanni, for the farther she progressed down the halls and passages to her own apartments, the wider she smiled and the faster she walked. Flushed and talkative, she summoned her women as soon as she reached her suite and immediately set them to preparing the poppy-pod headache potion.

"Quickly, Jezra, the finest pods you brought from the homeland, and the little mortar and pestle. Dashtar, fetch a flagon of water and the cup that measures its own contents, for we must know to the width of a hair, lest the draught be too potent. . . . His Highness will find relief soon, I am sure of it! He is so kind, I cannot tell you how thoughtful he was of my comfort! But he is a strange man, nonetheless, scowling and sudden; I was half frightened of him at first. It was his headache that made him so. How he paces! Up and down, up and down. . . ."

The quick, excited voice ran on, the plump fingers worked diligently with the pestle; the room was full of the mumbling hiss of Babylonian comment, exclamation and question. At last Inanni had something to talk about, and something to do. She was happier than at any time since leaving Syria.

Not so Mara. The interview with Thutmose had so disturbed her that she could barely keep up the pretense of listening to the women's chatter. Surely Sheftu would not obey that terrible command! Of all crimes in the land of Kemt, tomb robbing was the most monstrous—a sin against living and dead, gods and man. Even earthly punishment for it was swift and fearful, but what of the vengeance of him who was robbed? Hidden and safe in his secret palace, he lay wrapped in linen and spices, the cobra of Egypt on his forehead and his storerooms filled with the wealth that would sustain him in luxury through his allotted three thousand years in the Land of the West. Would not his *ka* strike Sheftu blind or dumb for daring to enter the Precious Habitation? Would it not creep like a shadow into his body to waste him with illness, to steal away his soul, to bring him down in all his youth to that mooring in the land of silence from whose shore none ever returned?

Nay, it was more than should be asked of any man, even for his king!

Put it out of your mind, Mara told herself fiercely. Sheftu will not obey. If he does, then it is his concern, and none of yours! Look out for yourself, and let others do the same. . . .

But the old formula did not comfort her this time. Nor did the sight of Inanni's joyful face as she labored over the poppy pods and repeated for the admiring Syrians every smallest word of the conversation she believed she had held with the king. A cruel deception that had been, to raise her hopes when there was nothing real to hope for. Mara was not proud of her handiwork. Surely there must have been some other way—but faced with that pacing lion of a man and two conversations to keep up in as many languages, who could have hit on it?

She found she could not bear to hear for the third time how kind and how handsome His Highness was. Pleading a need for rest, she excused herself and went into her own room.

What *kheft* has entered into me? she thought angrily, flinging herself down on her couch. Perhaps too much royalty in one day has given me a fever, that I should fret about a fat barbarian and her feelings! This queen, this king, this princess, this great Lord Sheftu, what have they to do with me and my plans? I must beware of them, that's all. They are strangers, they are enemies. I must never forget it.

Steadied, she sat up and pushed the thick, ebony-black hair away from her face. She would summon little Nesi to dress it, that would be a diversion. She would put on fresh clothes, and have her feet bathed and her eyes bathed, and the long black line of *kohl* painted fresh above her lashes, and demand a blue lotus to wear upon her brow as the great ladies wore them, with its stem trailing down the back of her head.

Soon it would be time for the evening meal, then for that walk in the lotus garden. She must be ready for it.

She rose and clapped her hands for her slave.

CHAPTER 10

The Lotus Garden

A STRANGE MAN my bridegroom is, indeed, thought Inanni as she sank into a chair. From his manner one would take oath he is indifferent—even scornful—yet it is not so. Did he not send those others from the room, that I might be more comfortable? Aye, he is gentle at heart, he must be.

She lay back among her cushions, reaching for a half-finished piece of embroidery that lay on the table beside her. The poppy-pod draught had just been dispatched to the king by one of the chamberlains, and already she was wishing she had not been so hasty in its preparation. Now, again, there was nothing to do, save think about the audience just past and speculate about the next one. Surely he would not behave so oddly next time. . . . She bent over her needlework, shoving out of her mind that first chilling scrutiny, under which she had felt she must sink straight through the gleaming pavements. That was naught but the effect of his headache, and so were the other strange contradictions in his words and manner. They must be. Mara had said so.

Dear Mara. How warm she was, how comforting!

After the marriage it will all come right, Inanni assured herself. The king and I will understand each other, and I will be a good wife to him, and comfort him when his head aches. Perhaps he would even let me go home sometime to see my brothers and the beautiful land of Canaan. . . .

The old hunger started up in her again at the thought of

home. The sheep would be coming in over the green hills right now, their bells sounding faintly on the evening air, their tired shepherd outlined against the sky behind him. Oh, beloved Canaan. . . . Inanni looked up, biting off a scarlet thread, as Mara entered the room from her own chambers. At once the hunger receded a little. She smiled, holding out her hand in welcome.

"I have sent the potion, Mara. Come, sit beside me while I embroider, and talk to me of the king. Do you think he was pleased with me? A little? In spite of his headache?"

"Of course, my princess!" Mara crossed the room with that supple, swinging walk of hers, and sitting down beside Inanni began to chatter reassuringly of Thutmose and the splendid life awaiting his spouse.

How cool she is, how sure of herself! thought Inanni wistfully. I don't believe she is afraid of anything on earth. And she is not unhandsome, though of course she needs more meat on her bones to have a fine figure like my own. In Egypt all women look half-starved. . . . That blue flower is becoming, fastened there just above her forehead. It makes her eyes look like two more blue lilies, down below it. Odd—only a single blossom. For my own part, I would have made a great wreath of them, using dozens of flowers and plenty of ribbons as well, with my hair flowing out all around it. But perhaps that would have been wrong. Mara always knows about these things. . . . Strange, that I should have grown so fond of this Egyptian maiden, whom I did not even know existed three weeks ago! Gentle Ishtar, what would I have done without her in this frightening land! Though I know not what my brothers would say of her. No doubt they would think her glance too bold, for certainly she does not keep her eyes downcast as a maiden should, and has no meekness in her. As for her dress . . .

Inanni blushed and looked away from the narrow garment with its fluted, filmy sleeves, through which the lines of Mara's brown body were quite frankly visible. But that is

97

the way things are done in Egypt, the princess thought
nervously. It is not Mara alone who values coolness above
modesty. The servant maids, that haughty queen herself . . .

Inanni drew her shawl a little closer about her shoulders,
reflecting that, in some ways, it was just as well her brothers
had stayed at home in Canaan. If they had fully realized
the wickedness to which their sheltered young sister would
be exposed, they would have risen up in protest against this
grand and wealthy marriage. Indeed, they would have . . .

To Inanni's relief, the palace servants appeared at that
moment to begin the elaborate ritual of serving the evening
meal. She did not want to go on with her thoughts, to remember that whatever protests her brothers might have
made, she would have journeyed to Egypt just the same. A
Canaanite did not refuse a messenger of pharaoh.

An excellent dinner occupied both her thoughts and ener-
gies for a time. She was just beginning on her third pastry
when Mara, who had finished some time ago, suggested an
after-dinner stroll.

"It is pleasant to walk abroad in the cool of the evening.
And there is a garden with a great pool of lotus which we
must surely visit. I saw it from the roof pavilion this morn
ing."

"Indeed?" murmured Inanni. She found she did not want
the pastry after all. "Of course I—have no objection, Mara.
But—will there be many Egyptians there?"

"In Egypt one must expect Egyptians, my princess," said
Mara with a smile. "But from the roof I saw no one but a
gardener, tending the flower beds. I hardly think it will be
crowded."

"But if it is a large garden . . . ?"

Mara leaned forward on her elbows. "My princess, it is
important that you show yourself. It must not be said that
the king's intended hides like a timid hare in her own apartments."

"No, no, of course not, it would not do, I see that. Let us go at once. I am ready. Dashtar! Jezra!"

I will not be afraid of these Egyptians, Inanni thought. I must not be. Ah, but if only there were not so many of them, all looking at me out of their painted eyes!

Moistening her lips and trying to ignore the tremors of nervousness in the pit of her stomach, she gathered her long robes about her and, with Dashtar and Jezra in reluctant attendance, followed Mara down the hall to the outside stair.

At the bottom they found themselves in the first of a series of walled courts and gardens, through which they passed without encountering anyone more frightening than a few slaves or hurrying servants. Inanni began to relax. She peered curiously at the storerooms and shedlike workshops, catching glimpses of basket makers and glass blowers still at work, of hundreds of stacked wine jars, mountains of baled linen, the neat rows of a kitchen garden. There were vineyards, date groves, curving flower beds in which scarlet sage and larkspur glowed against dark tamarisk trees. As they entered a broad paved area surrounded by weaver's stalls, Inanni gave a start of joy and stopped.

"Mara! Look at that woman yonder," she whispered. "She who cards wool. Why, it is just so that we do it in Syria! I believe she is Syrian herself, I do indeed. . . . Look you, Dashtar, is not that woman from our country?"

Mara said vaguely, "Indeed, she may be. Come, let us go on."

"No, no, wait, I know she is Syrian! Ah, Jezra, do you remember old Ninurta, who taught us to handle the carder when we were children together?"

"Aye, mistress. And this woman resembles her a little, as I trust in Ishtar! The same broad brow, and the little downy moustache on the upper lip!"

"How happy we were then," sighed Inanni.

Mara was fidgeting, saying something about the lotus

99

garden, but Inanni was lost in her homesick dreams. The woman with the carder looked up and smiled, and it was as if a small patch of Canaan opened up suddenly in this alien land, with old Ninurta holding out a hand in welcome.

"I must talk to her!" breathed the princess. She started forward, but Mara caught her elbow.

"Nay, Highness! We must not tarry here!"

"But why not? There are other days to see the lotus garden. Indeed, Mara, I would rather sit awhile with this woman from my homeland than visit a hundred gardens! How kindly she looks at me. . . . Perhaps she will let me ply the carder for a while, and we will talk about Canaan—"

"Nay, wait!" Mara seemed almost alarmed. She recovered herself quickly, drawing Inanni aside. "I fear you forget yourself, Highness. Does a princess speak to a common weaver woman? Indeed, in Egypt this is not done!"

"But—she is—she seems most respectable. . . ."

"She is beneath you! I know not what the son of pharaoh would say if you so demeaned yourself."

Inanni flushed. Ah, I must learn to be Egyptian, she thought. The king will be ashamed of me. She bent her shawled head and moved on in silence across the court.

"It is of course possible," said Mara after a moment, "that you speak to that woman—in another way—in your own apartments, perhaps. Yes, it would be quite proper for your highness to send for her. . . ."

Then why may I not speak to her here? thought Inanni. Mara's tone seemed strangely unconvincing, even distraught. Inanni stole a backward glance across the courtyard at the Syrian woman's broad, kindly face and nimble fingers, away from which she was being led—aye, almost hurried—at a pace hardly suitable to an evening's stroll. What was the matter with Mara? Even now her smile was nervous, as if she were having to force herself to behave normally.

Could it be that *she* was in a hurry, and had feared to be delayed in the Court of the Weavers?

It was a surprising idea, but though Inanni did not see how it could be so, the more she thought of it the more certain it seemed. They passed through the gate, and stepped onto a wide pavement bordered by stone rams, the far end of which was blocked by high, bronze doors and an armed sentry.

"What place is this?" inquired Inanni.

"I believe it is one of the entrances to the palace grounds." Mara stopped, her face quickening with interest. "Aye, it is! Yonder doors pierce the Great Walls themselves, and on the other side is Thebes. *Ai*, Princess, I would love to walk abroad in that city! A place of marvels, it must be—"

"Mara, come! That sentry is—is ogling you!" whispered Inanni, tugging at Mara's sleeve in embarrassment.

Mara's eyes shifted to the sentry, measuring him so coolly that the princess hurried on, scandalized, across the pavement. Mara shrugged and followed. "*Ai*, he is not so handsome as he thinks he is," she commented. "Come, through this wicket now. I think this is the hedge which borders our lotus garden."

Inanni was glad to dodge in anywhere away from the sentry's bold grin. But as they pushed through the last gate he vanished from her mind. Her first impression of the lotus garden was of vast sweeping lawns and the sparkle of water; her second, of a throng of people. She shrank back in dismay, but Mara had already started down a path strewn with powdered lapis lazuli, and there was nothing to do but follow. The place was almost a park, spacious and well watered, dotted with clumps of palms and acacias under which nobles and their ladies lounged. Beside them were low tables laden with beribboned wine jugs and bowls of fruit; behind them slaves waved great plumy fans. Dominating all was the long lotus-shaped sunken pool in the center of the garden, blue as heaven with countless lilies. Their perfume filled the air.

"Is it not beautiful, Highness? Is it not all I said, and more?"

Inanni mumbled assent, hoping she did not appear as gawky and countrified as she felt. The whole court of pharaoh must be gathered here to take the air! Two gossamer-clad ladies sauntered by, their fashionable, blue-wigged heads like heavy flowers on their fragile necks, cones of slowly melting perfume ointment resting atop their curls. The fragrance of myrrh drifted by with them. A coal-black Nubian in a slave's *shenti* crossed the path, carrying a wine jug and a bouquet of golden cups.

"Lift up thy head, Rose of Canaan!" came Mara's low voice. "Do not mind a few stares. Remember, it is not every day these lesser folk may gape at one destined to be the bride of royalty."

Mara's words were reassuring, as always, but her manner was preoccupied. She was scanning every part of the garden, a faint frown between her slanted eyebrows, the very lily on her forehead quivering with tenseness. Again, and stronger, the notion returned to Inanni that her interpreter had business of her own in this place. Was she meeting someone? Perhaps a sweetheart? Why, she could have told me, thought the princess. I would have understood, with all my heart!

Mara turned just then, touching Inanni's arm to guide her into a branching path. Her hand was like ice. Perhaps not a sweetheart! worried the princess. Perhaps someone she fears. . . .

They were making their way to a stone bench under a big acacia tree near the pool's edge. It was in plain sight of the rest of the garden, but some distance from the nearest group of courtiers, to Inanni's relief. She sank down gratefully upon the bench and allowed Jezra to pour her a cup of wine from the flower-wreathed jug nearby. It had been no short walk, and when one possessed a fine, statuesque figure with plenty of curves, one got out of breath easily. It was good to rest.

"Shall I pluck you a lily, my princess?" Mara murmured. Without waiting for permission she moved down the grassy slope and stooped to the froth of blue flowers in the water. Rising, a blossom in her hand, she stood a moment to sweep the garden with yet another searching glance. Inanni found even herself peering this way and that, frowning into clumps of trees, though what or whom she sought she did not know.

At that moment a light step sounded on the path behind her. She turned quickly. A tall figure was approaching through the shadows under a clump of palms. On the slope, Mara stopped short, then with a visible effort continued her unhurried walk back to the bench. She was breathing quickly as she bent over Inanni and offered the lily's fragrance to her nose.

"Here is thy lotus, Princess. Drink of its perfume and forget tomorrow, our sages tell us . . ."

A smooth voice, speaking Egyptian, interrupted her. She straightened, then stepped aside. Inanni found herself looking into the long, impenetrable eyes of a richly dressed young nobleman.

Is this he, then, whom Mara expected? she thought. But he is speaking to me. "Who is he, Mara? What does he say?"

"Highness, may I present His Excellency, Lord Sheftu. He wishes to know if Your Highness finds our country pleasing."

He must be the one, nevertheless, thought Inanni, else Mara would not clasp her hands so tightly. "Tell him it is very beautiful, though far different from my homeland."

Mara spoke, and the young lord listened courteously. He was the same, Inanni realized all at once, who had stepped up to the queen's throne this morning to receive some order. How attractive he was, to be sure—except for his beardless jaw, shaved clean as a baby's after the strange Egyptian custom. Inanni narrowed her eyes, trying to picture him with a luxuriant Syrian beard. The results were exhilarating. Ah, if this were Mara's young man she had reason to breathe quickly! But of course he could not be, after all, since he was a great lord and Mara only a hired interpreter. . . . It was very confusing.

"My lord wishes to inquire if you enjoyed your audience with the king," Mara was saying.

"Oh, yes, indeed. His Highness was very kind."

As Mara turned back to the young Egyptian, Inanni noticed that her tenseness was now pronounced, almost as if she were bracing herself for something she dreaded. Was she in love with this Sheftu, or in mortal fear of him? Inanni could not decide. Evidently what she was trying to tell him was of the gravest consequence, but he would not let her finish, and his voice was stern in spite of his mask of casual interest. Can they really think I believe she is only translating my one little remark? thought Inanni, almost amused.

Of course she might not have suspected, had she not guessed Mara was coming here to meet someone. It did take more time to say a thing in Egyptian, as Mara had explained this afternoon. Think how many words the king had used to make statements that were quite short and simple in Babylonian. A strange man, the king, scowling through his courtesies. . . . But that had been quite different. Mara and this Lord Sheftu were actually talking of their own affairs.

The young Egyptian made a remark, turning graciously to Inanni as he did so. She had opened her mouth to say that she had no objection to their conversing privately, that they need not pretend, when another thought struck her like a blow.

Suppose it had *not* been different, this afternoon? Suppose there were not such dissimilarities in the language?

Suppose—suppose Mara and the king had been pretending too?

"Lord Sheftu inquires," repeated Mara, "if you find the wine to your taste. Will you not answer, Highness?"

"It is very good," said Inanni mechanically. Impossible! she was thinking. There could be no reason . . . But she felt almost numb. This Sheftu was not interested in the wine, he was watching Mara out of the corner of his eye. Just so had it been at the audience—the king's manner bespeaking one thing and his words another. Before Baal, it was so! They were all deceiving her, thinking her too stupid to understand. Aye, and she had been stupid! She had believed, because Mara told her to believe, because she wanted to believe!

"My lord inquires whether you enjoyed your journey, Highness."

"What? Yes—no—"

It doesn't matter what I say, she thought. They're not listening to me, only to each other. I am of no importance. And the king—ah, Mara, why did you deceive me?

That was the part she could scarcely credit yet, that Mara would lie to her so callously. But she must have. It explained everything strange about that audience—the king's scowls and his honeyed words, even his restless pacing. Aye, it was true. Therefore all she had been told was untrue. Thutmose was not kind, he was scornful and arrogant, as his first terrible scrutiny had indicated. He was not pleased with his intended, he despised her.

I want to go home, thought Inanni, closing her eyes. Oh, gentle Ishtar, let me go home to my own land!

Somehow she got through her part of the brief conversation, never knowing what she said. Before long the young man bowed and went away. For some time Inanni sat in silence, slowly, very slowly, accepting the truth.

Mara, in the act of offering a platter of sweetmeats, bent over her in concern. "My princess! Are you ill?"

"No."

"But you are tired. Come, we will go back to the palace. It has been a long day."

Could she be pretending still? thought Inanni as she gathered her shawl about her. No, her voice is warm and sweet. Then why did she do this to me? Perhaps only to be kind, that I might not know my bridegroom scorns me. Bridegroom. Alas, he will never marry me.

They walked slowly up the rise to the main path. The light had faded; a few pale stars showed overhead and the courtiers were drifting out of the garden. The fragrance of lotus came to Inanni's nostrils and the peace of the evening touched her with a gentle hand.

Perhaps, after all, it is just as well, she thought. I could never have learned to be Egyptian, and wear those thin dresses, and look down my nose at humble folk. The king would always have been ashamed of me. Still, if he had let me, I could have been a good wife to him, and comforted him when his head ached. But he does not want that, it was never to be. I wonder why I was brought here, to live in loneliness, to no purpose? I suppose I shall never know. Someday, perhaps, when all their planning and struggling has spent itself, they will forget about me, and then I shall be allowed to go home again, down the long river to Canaan. No one will care, then; they will not even remember.

"You are very quiet, my princess," came Mara's worried voice. "I trust I have not overwearied you."

Inanni smiled at her, shaking her head. Poor Mara, it was she who was weary, with all her scheming and struggling. I will let her think I know nothing of this, thought the princess, and help her with her pretending, that her secrets be not such a burden to her. Doubtless she, too, is caught in a web she cannot escape.

But for Inanni the struggle was over, and the fact brought a queer sense of relief which grew in her as they walked slowly through the dusk toward the gate in the hedge. Even the sidelong, curious glances from painted eyes had lost some of their power to hurt her, she discovered. It did not matter, now, what Egyptians thought of her. She did not have to win a place among them.

Tomorrow, she thought, I will go alone to see the woman carding wool in the Court of the Weavers. It will be good to talk of home.

CHAPTER 11

Night Ride

NOW I HAVE WORN her out, Mara was thinking irritably. Dragging her here and there, denying her even the small comfort of talking to that weaver. But how else could I have done it? I had to reach the garden, I had to. . . .

And now, great Amon, she must wait still another while before she might give Sheftu the king's message. If only she could have got it off her mind at once! But of course he was right, there were too many ears to listen in that place. . . .

She opened the gate and stepped back to let Inanni go through, checking off in her mind the instructions Sheftu had given her. This meeting had been merely to arrange for future meetings, since he dared not be seen with her often on the palace grounds. Tomorrow, he had said, she must contrive some method of slipping out secretly into the town by night, a means of coming and going whenever she chose through the palace walls. Tomorrow evening a guide would await her at the shop of Nefer the goldsmith, just outside the walls, to conduct her to a place where she and Sheftu could talk in safety.

She drew a long breath, following Inanni and her women through the garden gate and between the stone rams that bordered the wide paved drive. One day was a short time in which to make such difficult arrangements. She had no idea how to begin.

As she stepped into the drive she noticed Inanni pulling her shawl over her face, hurrying past the sentry with averted head. She is afraid I will stare the fellow down again, thought Mara with a flicker of amusement. Glancing at the guard, she found him once more obviously admiring her. Suddenly it occurred to her that he might be useful— very useful indeed. She sized him up, reflecting. He was young, well favored enough to be easily flattered (already his pacing had turned to a swagger under her gaze) and he guarded a gate which was apparently little-used by the general traffic to and from the palace. Yes, it was worth a try. Mara gave him a melting glance, allowed a smile to play uncertainly about the corners of her mouth, then strolled after Inanni. Tomorrow evening, when he came on duty again, she would make his acquaintance.

The incident restored her confidence. As they passed rapidly through the deserted Court of the Weavers and the string of little gardens and courts that led back to the stairway, she found her worries fading before a mischievous anticipation of tomorrow and her next encounter with the sentry. It would be amusing to wind him about her finger, exciting to venture for the first time into the streets of Thebes. As for the king's message, that concerned only Sheftu. Play your own game, my girl.

But she had not finished her encounters for today. She

had scarcely bid Inanni good night and retired to her own room when a soft scratching sounded on the door leading to the corridor. Frowning, Mara went to open it. At once a Libyan in a slave's *shenti* pushed into the room and closed the door silently and swiftly behind him.

"You're to come with me," he muttered. "Get a cloak."

Mara's jaw set angrily. She had never seen the man before, but her dislike of him was instantaneous. Everything about him repelled her—his pale foreign skin and colorless hair, the one blind eye which showed milky-blue in his callous face, above all, the insolence with which he ordered her around.

"Which devil's brother are you?" she spat at him.

For answer he reached into his sash and produced something which he held out indifferently on a hand like a chunk of beef. It was a scarab identical to the one Mara's master had given her in Menfe.

Sullenly she turned to fetch a cloak. The Libyan pulled a fold of it half over her face before he motioned her into the hall. A few minutes later they were passing down an outer stair and through a series of unfamiliar starlit courtyards toward what Mara's nose told her were the palace stables. They pushed through a row of acacia bushes and emerged into a stone drive.

"Wait," grunted the Libyan.

It was very quiet after the pad of his sandals died away up the drive. Mara could hear only the light breeze stirring in the acacia leaves, and farther away, the gutturals of the stableboys and the occasional thump of a hoof. The sharp, clean smell of horses came strong to her nostrils, almost obliterating the fainter but ever-present fragrance of lotus that rose on the night air from a hundred palace gardens. It would be nice—it would be lovely, thought Mara, just to stretch out yonder on the grass, with the stars thick up above and the breeze cool, and nothing on my mind. . . .

Suddenly she felt tired all through. Why did he have to send for me tonight? she thought. Tomorrow would have done as well.

The silence was shattered as a chariot clattered into view around a bend in the drive. The horses came to a prancing halt just opposite Mara, and the Libyan motioned her in with an impatient jerk of his head. Reluctantly she stepped up beside him, and took a firm grip on the chariot's curving side.

"Pull the cloak over your face," he ordered.

With a crack of his whip they lurched forward. For the next few minutes Mara had all she could do to keep her footing as they rattled along at a furious pace, swerving presently into a wider drive lined with torches and alive with traffic. Other chariots hurtled past them, the drivers shouting and popping the whips as was the Libyan. Half blinded by her muffling cloak, and jarred to the bone, Mara had little chance to examine her surroundings, but she guessed the chariot was speeding down the great East Avenue toward the main gate.

A moment later they pulled up briefly under a glaring torch, and the Libyan muttered something to a man who stood there—a sentry, Mara imagined, though she caught no more than a glimpse of him. She had barely time to plant her feet and renew her grip on the chariot side when they were off again, whirling out of the palace grounds and through the dark streets of western Thebes.

It was obvious the Libyan was accustomed to driving for great nobles, for he kept the horses at a full gallop, with arrogant disregard of comfort, caution, or the safety of occasional pedestrians, who scattered like birds frightened from their marsh. Mara clung to the rail with aching fingers, banging her ribs against the side at every corner and wishing her master and his surly Libyan at the bottom of the Nile. She was bruised and sore when at last the horses turned through a tall gateway into a dimly lit courtyard.

110

Snorting and tossing their plumed heads, the beasts halted before a door that appeared to lead into the side wing of a large and impressive house. A groom appeared out of nowhere to take the reins, and the Libyan stepped down, pushing Mara before him.

"This way," he said.

She followed, too weary and confused to notice or care where he was leading her. Inside, the halls smelled faintly of wine and expensive ointments; she caught a whiff of baking pastry as they crossed a passageway. Far off, in another part of the house, there were sounds of music and merriment, as if a party were in progress.

"In there," muttered the Libyan, stopping with a jerk of his head before an open door. She stepped into a small tapestry-hung room, and a tall, spare figure rose from a corner to confront her. Involuntarily she fell back a step. Her master's countenance had grown no more winsome in the hours since morning.

"Insolent, show more respect to your betters!" growled the Libyan, nudging her forward again.

She glared at him, but grudgingly moved her right hand to her left shoulder. The thin smile she remembered all too well from Menfe twisted her master's lips as he strolled toward her.

"Docile as ever," he commented. "I see you have struck up a warm friendship with my servant Chadzar. Did you enjoy the ride?"

"Enjoy?" muttered Mara resentfully. "He drives as if the Devourer were after him."

Again the acid smile. "He has other talents too, especially with that whip he carries. It is well you came with him without argument."

Mara preserved a sullen silence, mentally cursing him and his Chadzar and all their relatives, in two languages. She felt wearier than ever. Perhaps he would let her sit down.

Instead he sat down himself, waving an abrupt dismissal to the Libyan. When the door had closed, he stated, "You have had audience with the Pretender."

"Aye."

"What did you learn?"

"Naught of interest."

"And why not?" His voice turned icy.

Take care, my girl, thought Mara. You'd best bestir yourself and dance to his tune. You can be tired later.

"It was no fault of mine, master," she explained in a more conciliatory tone. "Not even the cleverest spy can learn aught from an empty room. His Highness sent everyone away at once, save the princess and me."

"Sent them away! If that is to be his habit, you'll be of small use to me!"

"Nay, wait, it will not always be so—" Really frightened now, Mara groped for an idea. No use to him? If he thought that, he might sell her tomorrow! Her mind full of unpleasantly vivid images—baskets of unironed *shentis,* shelves of forbidden food, the bite of a lash—she put all her persuasiveness into her voice. "Give me a little longer! It will not be thus always, the king cleared the room only because the barbarian was ill at ease. Next time, I promise, no such thing will happen, I'll see to it myself. I can lead that maiden where I will. . . ."

"So you say," he remarked. He was appraising her coldly, and with doubt.

"I swear it. Only let me show you."

He was silent a moment, drumming his finger tips on the arms of his chair. "So they all left the room. Even the scribe?"

"Aye, the scribe too."

"The *khefts* take their souls," he said with a quiet malevolence that chilled Mara's blood. "Hand-picked, every one of them, yet the fools are afraid of him! And someone's bearing messages."

112

They're all spies, then, Mara thought. The guards, the scribe—especially the scribe. I must be careful of him.

Warily she watched her master's granite face. The harsh line of his brow and nose waked a flicker of recognition in her, but she could not place what it reminded her of. Possibly some statue of a devil-god in the temple at Menfe, she thought sardonically. Surely no other human had such a countenance. Who was he, anyhow? Someone who ranked high with the queen, for he had stood close to the throne this morning. Not so close as Sheftu, however. Only Count Senmut himself stood closer than Sheftu. . . .

Her master stirred in his chair. "Perhaps I will give you one more chance. You think you can prevent Thutmose from clearing the room?"

"I will do my best, master. Only try me, I'll—"

"I see little else to do. I will try you." He shot a venomous glance at her. "And I will know if you fail. Now listen. I realize you cannot discover the leaders of this accursed plot. But with any wit you can find their messenger, or some news of where they meet. I'm in haste, as I think I've made clear." Thoughtfully, he added, "And keep me a watch on the scribe."

"With pleasure, master." He will also, she reflected, instruct the scribe to keep a watch on *me*.

"Very well, then we are done. You have your chance; I trust you will make good use of it. It would be unfortunate if you should disappoint me again."

He clapped his hands, and the Libyan appeared at the door. Muffling herself in her cloak, Mara hastened to follow him into the hall and out once more to the waiting chariot. Even the surly Chadzar was better company than that crocodile in there.

On the ride back to the palace the pace was as headlong as before, but Mara had learned better how to brace herself for it. And on this trip something happened that furnished her considerable enlightenment. At the Main Gate of the palace grounds the sentries had been changed, and the new one was apparently skeptical about Chadzar's credentials. There was a muttered argument growing rapidly angrier on both sides; finally Chadzar leaned half out of the chariot, brandishing his whip.

"Fool and idiot! If you do not know the scarab, I'll wager you'll stand aside at my master's name! Nahereh the brother of Senmut! Now hold your tongue about it, but let me pass!"

It was the end of the argument, but Mara scarcely noticed the lurch as they plunged forward once again. So Lord Nahereh was her master! Own brother to Senmut the Architect, he of the deep-etched smile and avaricious eyes who stood nearest Hatshepsut and her throne.

It was easy, now, to place that fleeting resemblance to someone she had noticed in her master's face. It was no stone devil-god but Count Senmut whose nose and brow traced the same harsh angle. In Amon's name, what hornet's nest had she walked into, that day in Menfe? Sheftu, the queen, the king, and now two devils instead of one to scheme with and lie to and walk in fear of—it would have been less complicated to stay a slave and iron *shentis* all her days. At the moment her future did not seem half so pleasant and certain as it had this morning. And tomorrow night was beginning to loom in her mind again. Might it please Amon to make that sentry susceptible to blue eyes!

At least, reflected Mara as at last she climbed the stairs to the welcome solitude of her own room, life was no longer in any danger of becoming monotonous.

Part IV—The Inn

CHAPTER 12

The Sentry at the Gate

IT WAS the next night. The sun had dropped into the hills behind Hatshepsut's temple three hours since, and the late moon had not yet risen. The palace driveway known as the Road of the Rams was shrouded in darkness. Near the tall bronze doors at the end of the drive a torch sputtered and smoked in its bracket, shedding its orange light down upon the sentry who lounged, yawning, below it.

Mara, concealed in the shadowy gateway leading to the Court of the Weavers, had been watching him for some moments. He was the same who had grinned at her last night, when she passed through with Inanni. So far, so good. But had his mood changed? Perhaps tonight he would be surly, if he had lost at his gaming with the stableboys, or been reprimanded by his captain for some mistake or other.

Well, it was a chance she had to take. Glancing behind her once more to make sure the Court of the Weavers was as empty as the drive, she wrapped the folds of her cloak half over her face and began to sob softly.

After a moment the guard became aware of the sound; she could hear the faint clatter of his sword as he straightened, and prayed Amon he was not the type to shout out a challenge. No, over the cloak's edge she saw him frown this way and that into the gloom, then pick up a hand torch and thrust it into the flame of the larger one. As he started down the drive, holding his light aloft, she increased her sobs, leaning against the gateway as if oblivious to all the world. An instant later the torch shone full in her face.

She gasped and opened her eyes wide, letting the cloak fall as if by accident. To her satisfaction, the glowering visage on the other side of the torch relaxed into a grin of surprise.

"Well, by the *ka* of my mother, it's little Blue Eyes! Why do you weep? You were smiling last night. Eh? Weren't you?"

"I—I don't know—Captain."

"Aye, you were, and at me! Now what's the trouble?"

"It's—nothing."

"Then dry your tears!" He picked up the edge of her cloak, and with a man's amused tolerance, dabbed at her eyes with it. She permitted herself a brave little smile. "There, that's better!" he told her. "You're too pretty to be sad."

"You're very kind, Captain," she murmured, trying her best to blush shyly.

The sentry really did blush a little. "Come, maid, I'm no captain. Only second sentry at a gate pharaoh never uses."

"They keep one such as you only second sentry?"

"Aye, they do. Too young for a good duty, they keep telling me! The devil! I'll wager I can thrust a sword as smartly as those mummies at the Main Gate!"

Perfect, thought Mara. Young, naive, bored with his duty and vain of his muscles.

"I'll vow you could, indeed!" she said admiringly. "Why, they are treating you unjustly. Youth only enhances a strong arm and a handsome appearance. No doubt they are jealous, Capt—er . . ."

"Reshed. Son of Setek the stonecutter."

"Reshed," said Mara softly. She gazed up, wide eyed, into his face, then allowed her lashes to sweep down against her cheek.

He swallowed audibly, moving a little closer to her. "Amon! Do you live in the Golden House, Blue Eyes? I never saw you before yesterday. By my *ka*, you're a pretty thing!"

"You speak with a tongue of honey, sentry. *Ai*, but what use to be pretty when I am sore at heart! Oh, Gebu, my poor Gebu!"

She turned aside, sobbing again, one hand palm-down on the top of her head in the attitude of mourning. As she had hoped, he extinguished the glaring torch out of respect for her grief, then stepped even closer.

"Come, what ails thee, little one? Who is this Gebu?"

"Alas, he is my brother, alone and sick unto death in the city out yonder, while I must stay here within these walls. He is all I have in the world, and I cannot even go to nurse him!"

"*Ai*, poor little maid! Who keeps thee prisoner?"

"I serve the Syrian princess, and must stay beside her. But she sleeps like one dead, there is no need for me at all in the night. I could go each night to Gebu if only—if only—"

Her sobs broke out afresh. "If only what?" murmured Reshed. He patted her shoulder; his arm went about her tentatively, casually. Still weeping, she just as casually slipped free.

"If only I could pass through that gate—in secret—no one knowing or being responsible save myself, even the sentry's back would be turned . . ." Now it was she who moved close to him, one hand on his forearm. "It was you I thought of, I confess it. When you smiled at me last night you seemed so—so kind . . ." Her voice added much to the word. "But of course I was wrong, I hoped for too much.

117

You could never let me through the gate, even with your back turned, your captain would be angry and perhaps would be punish you. . . ."

She turned away, but he drew her back, his arm no longer tentative. "Who fears the captain? Not I, pretty one!"

"You mean you would—that it is possible—"

"I mean we might bargain a little. What would you give me if I turned my back?"

"Give you? But I have no gold."

He gave a low laugh, tightening his arms. "I don't want gold, little Blue Eyes."

"Then, indeed, I know not— Nay, let me go!"

She dodged his kiss expertly, wriggling away to shrink against the gate as if in fright. "You are too bold! Nay, come no nearer—please, Reshed—"

He stopped, laughing again. "What's the harm in a kiss?"

"None, perhaps. But such haste is not seemly! Why, I only this evening learned your name!"

"Oh, that's it! Then let us get better acquainted!" His voice held bravado, but was a little uncertain all the same. He reached for her hand and drew her—gently, she noticed —out of the shadows. "Don't be afraid of me," he said awkwardly.

Mother of heaven, how innocent he is! thought Mara. Standing beside him in the roadway, she smiled forgiveness. "I'm not afraid of you now. Perhaps—" She hesitated, then as if overcome by shyness started along the road toward the big bronze doors. He fell in eagerly beside her.

"Perhaps what?"

"Perhaps I was only afraid of—my own feelings."

"Ah, were you? But when we're better acquainted?"

Already he wore the expression of one diving, headlong, into an acre of feathers. She waited until they stood under the torchlight, then faced him, slanting a look at him from under her painted eyelids. "Why, then I might be more afraid than ever. I believe I had better bid you good-by right now."

"Good-by! But you—I thought you—"

"No matter what you thought! I've changed my mind. You're an overbold young man, coaxing a maid with your honeyed words, trying to kiss her the first moment! Nay, touch me not, you wouldn't dare! I'm going back to the palace. . . ."

She whirled to run, but he caught her angrily about the waist. "And what of our bargain? I'll teach you to play with me, my little—"

Mara suddenly stopped struggling and relaxed against him. "Ai, I was only teasing—please, loosen your arm a bit. I'll bargain with you if you promise not to frighten me again, I swear I will. Don't scowl at me, please. . . ."

He stared down at her, tilting her chin up with his knuckle so that the torchlight shone full on her face. "By all the gods, I never met a maid like you!" he muttered in bewilderment. "You make a man's head swim."

"Reshed—sweet Reshed—are you really going to let me through the gate?"

"I shouldn't."

"But you will?"

"Not so fast! I have my price. I must see you again."

"But to be sure! When I go again to visit my brother—"

"I want more than that, you minx. Look you. I'm off duty three evenings each month. Will you meet me . . . ?"

"Perhaps."

"Aye? On my next holiday, seven nights from now?"

"Perhaps . . ." breathed Mara.

He bent suddenly to her lips, but she dodged him by an inch, lifted the great latch on the doors and slipped through into the street beyond. Leaning in again, she lifted one hand and stroked it lingeringly down his cheek.

"My thanks, dear Reshed," she whispered. "I'll rap three times when I come home again."

Leaving him gazing after her, bemused, she hurried away into the darkness.

He was gone from her mind before the doors closed. How black it was, after the glare of the torch! She could barely make out the thin, tall trunks of the palms which lined the avenue, though when she looked straight up, she could see their plumy heads outlined against the stars. She must go east along the palace wall, Sheftu had said, and when the wall curved south, cross the avenue to the shop of Nefer the goldsmith. Someone would be waiting.

Who? she wondered as she sped east on silent sandals. Would she have to identify herself again? And if so, how? The gods be thanked the granite-faced one had no suspicions of her. He could bait a deadly trap for her tonight if only he knew. . . .

Here was the curve of the wall. Mara peered ahead, wrapping a fold of her cloak over her head and the lower part of her face before she slipped across the deserted avenue. Gaining the shelter of a clump of trees, she saw before her the dim front of a building, cut by one black rectangle—a deeply recessed doorway. Just above it she could barely make out the hieroglyph for "Nefer," traced upon the earthen bricks. Cautiously she moved toward it. There was no sign of anyone, no sound, only that waiting black square. And if it were a trap? Anyone, anything, might be concealed yonder.

She hesitated a long, reluctant moment before deciding that there was no way to try the snare save by walking into it. She cast one glance behind her, then darted into the doorway. Darkness closed over her. She stood a moment with beating heart, then began to move forward, gingerly exploring with one outstretched hand the cool rough bricks that formed the wall. There was no sound at all, save her own uneven breathing. Was she alone, then? Expecting at any second to touch the smooth wood of a door, her hand suddenly met air instead, and after a few more paces she realized the passage had opened out into some different place.

She halted uneasily, trying to make out where she was. A breath of night air touched her cheek, accompanied by a whispered rustling overhead. She was perhaps in a courtyard, canopied by a thatch of dried palm leaves; she saw the outlines of the walls now, and here and there around them large rounded objects, almost indistinguishable in the gloom. She was peering warily toward one when a pebble rolled behind her. She whirled.

Someone—something—was standing beside the wall yonder, a shape of denser black among the shadows. In panic, she shrank back toward the passage from which she had come. Then the figure moved too. There was something familiar about that bulky outline, the set of the shoulders. . . .

"Is it you, little one?" came a low rumble.

"Nekonkh!" Almost stumbling with relief, she darted toward him.

"Hist! Not a sound, maid." He materialized beside her, comfortingly solid, and she felt her arm grasped. "This way. We'll talk later."

She had never been so glad to see anyone. She clung to him with a rush of affection that surprised even herself, feeling him an old friend—her only friend in a chancy, friendless world. This was a weary life, for all its splendor, playing with fire day after day, trusting no one, deceiving all, staking everything on the nimbleness of one's wits! For a moment Mara longed to be back in the market place at Menfe, with no more on her mind than snatching a honey cake.

But only for a moment. She hurried after Nekonkh. "What was that place?" she whispered as they emerged into a street. "Those great humped things about the walls . . . ?"

"Humped? Oh, those were the furnaces, where the gold is melted. We were in Nefer's outer workshop. Here, into this alley now."

He led her across the street and into a narrow lane between dark warehouses. Stumbling over invisible rubbish, Mara spat out her annoyance, then laughed under her breath. "Ai! it's good to speak my mind when I feel like it! I've behaved so priggish of late I'm like to smother of my own mincing and mouthing! Captain, where are we going?"

"To Thebes, to a tavern on the waterfront. So you're weary of your fine life already, eh?"

"Not really. It's good to eat all you can hold, and order slaves about. But my tongue's tired of its leash."

"I'll wager it had to wag some to get you outside those walls tonight."

"Nay, not overmuch," she evaded.

They stepped out of the alley into a jumble of low buildings, sheds, and boathouses. "I smell the river," murmured Mara, drawing a long breath of the familiar, heady reek. A moment later they rounded the corner of a deserted fish stall and the Nile lay before her, stars bobbing all along its darkly rippling length. "Do we go across, Nekonkh?"

"Aye. There's a boat waiting yonder."

He led the way southward along a steep embankment —for the river was sinking lower, in its yearly rhythm—and made for a tall stone image some forgotten pharaoh had erected to his glory there on the shore. At the foot of the image, moored irreverently to one granite toe, lay a fishing punt. Nekonkh grunted something into the darkness beside the statue, and a stooped figure emerged, hobbled around to the mooring rope, and silently motioned them into the boat.

"Who is he?" muttered Mara into Nekonkh's ear as the boatman's oars thrust them out into the stream.

"A papyrus cutter called A'ank, who's too old to earn his coppers in the usual way. You can trust him. He'll be here every night, in case you need him."

"And will I need him often?"

"That's up to— Hail I near forgot to warn you. Never

mention our master's name at the Inn of the Falcon. He's known only as Sashai."

So Sheftu wore a disguise even among his followers! Sashai—The Scribe. "Does no one know him save us, then?" Mara asked incredulously.

"Only a few. The rest think him a messenger for some higher-up who's the real leader. He wants it that way, girl. Watch you don't spoil it."

They fell silent as a barge passed near them on its way to a belated mooring. Its torches threw puddles of molten gold on the black water, and the voices of two oarsmen, quarreling sleepily, drifted back on the night air as it slid away downstream. A moment later the fishing punt was bobbing across its wake, angling slightly to the south to avoid the great dark hulk of a vessel standing far out to anchor. Beyond it rode two others, swaying gently in the current. More and more loomed up as the punt neared the wharves, until it was threading its way among hulls close crowded on every side. At last it bumped to a halt against a ladder. The ancient A'ank held it there while Nekonkh and Mara scrambled cautiously along its rocking length and up the water-soaked rungs to the dock.

A few minutes later they were in a street more crooked, dark, and evil-smelling than any in Menfe, lined with cracked walls and murky doorways, from which an occasional cloaked figure emerged to brush past them into the gloom.

"This is Cutthroat's Alley for certain, little one," muttered Nekonkh, whose hand was ready on his dagger. "Take care you keep your wits about you—and a good blade, too —should you pass this way alone. Here we are, through this door now."

He pushed open a creaking door, like all the rest save for the weathered wooden image of a falcon swinging from a bar above it. Within was a small courtyard, dimly lit by a flare bracketed beside another door at its far end. They

123

made their way over rough cobblestones, past a single
scrubby dom palm, to the tavern's entrance. Nekonkh
rapped. and the door swung open.

CHAPTER 13

Conversation at an Inn

A BURST of noise and golden light flowed out around the
bulky figure of a man who blocked the entrance. *"Hai!* It's
you, Captain!" he cried jovially, stepping back to motion
Nekonkh and Mara past him. "Come in, come in! And who
are you, my dear?"

"Her name is Blue Eye," grunted Nekonkh, before Mara
could answer. "A friend of our friend . . . is he here,
Ashor?"

"Aye, aye, he's here." The innkeeper closed the door behind them, his broad face wreathed in smiles. He was a hulk
of a man, vast of girth and guileless of countenance, dressed
in a rumpled *shenti* and huge copper ear hoops. He pat-
tered ahead of them, the earrings bouncing and his paunch
preceding him, through a tiny entryway and into a large
square room which was smoky with torchlight and smelled
of beer and roasting meat.

All around the walls were cubicles, divided from each
other by shoulder-high partitions, but open to the room and

124

the charcoal fire that blazed in its center in a great pottery pan. In the cubicles, kneeling on reed mats before low tables, were Ashor's customers—men, for the most part, with a scattering of women and an occasional bearded foreigner. They were eating, drinking, gambling noisily at "odd and even," or merely talking in low tones over cups of beer or date wine. One group roared drunken approval of the antics of a juggler performing his feats beside their table; at the next, two solemn old men, one fat, one thin, played an absorbed and silent game of hounds and jackals. On the other side of the room a dancing girl swayed and postured to the jingle of her tambourine and the wail of a blind musician's flute.

In the center of all, stirring the contents of a kettle bubbling over the fire pan, stood a tiny, dried-up woman. From her sash hung a metal loop strung with ring coins, copper and silver *deben*. A curious necklace of shells weighted her narrow chest, and she had the brightest, most suspicious eyes Mara had ever seen. Her long spoon motionless, she watched the newcomers all the way across the room.

"My wife, Miphtahyah," puffed Ashor, noting the direction of Mara's glance. "Wonderful woman. Her hand's at the helm here, is it not, Captain? Aye, they'd rob me blind were it not for her. By the Feather, it's true! A babe of innocence, she calls me, trusting anyone, even these rivermen —" With a breathy laugh he dug Nekonkh in the ribs, then detoured around the beribboned dancing girl to head for a table in the farthest corner.

As they passed, Mara glanced at the girl, whose languid movements now concealed, now revealed, the cubbyhole behind her, in which a scribe sat cross-legged before his inkstand, in earnest conversation with a shaven-headed priest. At that moment the scribe looked around, and the firelight fell on his face. It was Sheftu.

Mara caught her breath, hesitating. But his eyes met hers only an instant, then moved calmly back to his writing

125

block. The dancing girl whirled between them again and Mara walked on. Her cheeks burned as she slipped past the innkeeper into the farthest cubicle and sank to her knees upon the woven mat.

"He'll be with you when it suits him, Captain," Ashor was saying. "I'll fetch date wine to cool your throats."

Giving a hitch to his ample *shenti*, he waddled away, and Nekonkh lowered himself beside Mara, settling back on his heels with a grunt. "You saw him, did you?"

"Aye, and he saw us! But little sign he gave of it."

"He's not here to dance attendance on you, little one. He has more on his mind these days than a pair of blue eyes."

The blue eyes glared at him, and he chuckled softly, shaking his head. "*Hai*, I warned you to steer well around him, that day on the *Beetle*. If you've run aground, maid, it's no fault of mine!"

"I've done naught of the sort, and the devil with you! Why did that woman out yonder watch me so?"

"You mean Miphtahyah? Why, it's her business to watch who comes here, and the falcon lends her his eyes for the task. She'd make a fine helmsman. . . . Ho, Ashor. Set the cups here, I'll play the host."

Nekonkh took the wine jug from the perspiring innkeeper, who beamed and paddled off again, his earrings bobbing. With a broad thumbnail Nekonkh broke the seal, and the sharp fragrance of date wine filled Mara's nostrils. She was watching the amber liquid gurgle into a cup when a shadow fell across the table.

"Live forever, honored strangers," Sheftu said smoothly. "You wished my services? A contract written? Perhaps a list of cargo set down accurately?"

He was leaning in the entrance to their cubicle, his inkstand under one arm, two reed pens stuck jauntily behind his ear. Even in the long robe and coarse linen headcloth of a scribe, his pose was as easy, his grace as careless, as in the court of Hatshepsut.

"Nay, no contract," rumbled Nekonkh, getting to his feet. "But this maid here—"

"Ah, a love letter, then. Guaranteed to thaw the coldest heart."

He grinned down at Mara, and her retort died on her lips. As he turned to murmur something to Nekonkh, she struggled to regain her composure. What was it about his smile? Its warmth? Its sudden intimacy? It rushed to the head like strong wine.

She was aware of nothing but him, as he stood there outlined against the noisy, torchlit room. All day she had nerved herself for this meeting, fearing to find him again the curt and glittering stranger he had been in the lotus garden. Now, all in a moment, her fears had vanished. Here was no gold-hung lord, but her companion of the *Beetle*— warm, teasing, dangerous. Her spirits rose like a sail.

With a nod of farewell, Nekonkh moved out of the cubicle and across the room toward a group of rivermen gaming in another corner. Sheftu slid in beside Mara.

"So you accomplished it," he murmured, seating himself cross-legged, in the scribe's manner, and setting his inkstand on the table.

"Aye. But no thanks to you."

"Was it such a task?"

"Task? Why, at first I knew not even where to start! A hard master you are, Sashai. 'Get thee outside the walls,' you say, as if it were nothing! Then away you stroll, with never another thought of it—"

He laughed, handing her the cup Nekonkh had filled, and pouring another for himself. "But why should I think of it? I have every confidence, my Lotus-Eyed One, in your capacity for guile, not to say chicanery—"

"*Ast!* I'll wager I could learn guile from you."

"Nay, pull in your claws. Were you not as you are, you'd be no use to me."

Mara sipped from her cup, feeling a glow that had noth-

127

ing to do with wine. The flutist's sweet wail threaded through the jovial uproar of the tavern; laughter was warm about her; the juggler's balls spun brighter than shooting stars. Even the dreadful message she must deliver slipped like a *kheft* into the farthest outskirts of her mind.

"You've not told me," said Sheftu, "what you think of the Inn of the Falcon."

"Ahh, I like it well! Save for that old woman with the beady eye out there."

"Miphtahyah? Nay, but she's worth all the rest put together. A marvel of a woman."

"So her husband said," remarked Mara skeptically.

Sheftu regarded her with amusement. "Perhaps it is all in the point of view. I'll admit her virtues would be less apparent to one attempting to snatch a loaf or two from under that beady eye."

"I'm done with loaf snatching! But she could watch me no closer were I after her money ring."

"Well, she has reasons. First, you are new here. Second, she is jealous as a she-leopard of every pretty maid who comes anywhere near me."

"Near *you*? But I thought—"

"Aye, Ashor's her husband. But I'm her child, or so she feels. Miphtahyah was my nurse, from infancy."

Sheftu's childhood nurse! The old woman assumed quite a different aspect in Mara's eyes, and her whole idea of the Inn of the Falcon underwent a rapid change. She had thought it a retreat Sheftu had merely chanced upon; now she realized it must exist solely to serve his purposes.

"And Ashor?" she questioned.

"He was head of my father's stables for many years—and my first companion." Sheftu was smiling a little, remembering. "Aye, we were fast friends. Many's the time I've ridden between his knees in my father's chariot, holding the rein ends and pretending to drive. When I did learn, it was he who taught me. I can see him now, jouncing about beside me, clutching his wig and yelling 'Pull left! Pull right!' "

Sheftu laughed outright, and Mara smiled, fascinated by this glimpse of a childhood so different from her own. "And were you never frightened?" she asked him.

"Not I, but I'll wager Ashor was, sometimes We took a spill or two before I learned what I was doing. One of them broke my arm, and I stayed home from school while Miphtahyah coddled me."

"School," echoed Mara. Visions of scroll-filled shelves danced through her mind. "Did you read the ancient writings? Old tales, and poetry? What was it like, your school?"

He gave her an odd look. "Not like other schools, Blue-Eyed One. I fear I learned more politics than poetry." He hesitated, playing with the amulet on his wrist, then went on. "I was educated at the palace nurseries, along with a few other noblemen's sons. It was there I met my—friend."

"So young?" exclaimed Mara. She had supposed Sheftu and the king had met at court, as youths near grown.

"Aye, I was only nine or ten when I first saw him. He was older, of course. But he seemed to—take a fancy to me. As for me, I worshiped him. He was—well, you've seen what he's like."

"Aye, I have!" Mara thought of the caged lion of a man she had met yesterday—restless, brilliant, moody—and tried to imagine him as a princeling. "Did the queen keep guards and spies around him even then?"

Sheftu nodded, turning his wine cup in his hands. "She's always feared him." He hesitated, as if debating whether to go on, then added, "She tried hard to make a priest of him, as I suppose you know."

"A priest!"

He laughed. "The temple of Amon is an excellent place, little one, for burying excess royalty. It would be hard to say how many younger sons of pharaohs have spent their

129

lives tying up offerings and burning incense instead of making things uncomfortable around the palace. However, in this case—"

There was a tiny pause. He covered it with his most engaging smile, and reached for the wine jug. "Let me fill your cup, Blue-Eyed One, and summon the dancing girl. I fear I have bored you."

You mean you fear you have said too much, thought Mara, wondering how to get the rest of the story without appearing to probe for it. Her curiosity was thoroughly aroused. This had all the earmarks of a tale not intended for her ears—therefore she had every intention of hearing it.

"It is the dancing girl who would bore me, Sashai, but I confess I am puzzled by your story. Our friend is certainly no priest now."

"Nay, he is not," agreed Sheftu blandly.

"Strange," murmured Mara. "It is not hard to become a priest, but hard indeed to cease being one. In fact, I know of no way—unless a man disgrace his vows in some fashion—"

"There was no disgrace!"

Mara raised her eyebrows and waited. There was a flicker of wry amusement in Sheftu's eyes but otherwise he made no acknowledgment of having been neatly trapped. As readily as if it were his own idea, he explained. "It was a miracle which released him, little one. A holy miracle, clearly the work of Amon himself."

So that was it! In a rush memory came back to Mara. There had been a time, some years ago, when the market place at Menfe had been alive with whispers of a miracle. She could recall little knots of people gathered around Theban sailors and merchants, and herself, a ragged child, squirming through their legs in an effort to hear the tale. She had heard it, right enough, and had noticed that it grew more marvelous with every telling. Half awed and half disbelieving, she had ended by shrugging the whole thing off as being of less concern to her than her empty stomach.

"Ah, yes, the miracle," she murmured now. "Its fame spread even to Menfe."

"Marvelous are the ways of the gods," said Sheftu piously.

Mara smiled. She was beginning to understand, and what she understood delighted her. "A truly wonderful thing it must have been," she agreed. "It came to pass during a great festival, am I not right? Under the very nose of the queen, with all the populace looking on. The great golden image of Amon had been borne through the streets, then back again to the temple on the shoulders of the priests, while the incense rose in clouds and the people leaped for joy—"

Sheftu examined his wine cup with great interest.

"—and then, as the image of the god neared its sanctuary, behold! it turned aside, stopped before the young prince, and led him through the curtain into the Holy of Holies itself. They say he walked like one spellbound when he came forth, half fainting, to tell that Amon had named him pharaoh. . . . Was that the way of it, Sashai?"

"Aye," he answered solemnly. "The ways of Amon are mysterious."

There was a little pause. "And most convenient," added Mara.

Sheftu put down his cup and turned to face her. His eyes were full of laughter. "Can it be you are skeptical, little one? Surely not! It was a fine miracle—and took only a little help from the priests who carried the image."

I thought as much! Mara said to herself. And still you have told me nothing I did not guess already. By the Feather, you can't elude the net forever, my wily fish! "So after all," she said deliberately, "your Son of the Sun is naught but a clever politician."

The effect was instantaneous. Sheftu's smile vanished without a trace. "Watch thy tongue, girl! He is no politician, but a conqueror, fit to rule Egypt and the world!"

131

"But if he relies on mere tricks—"

"Listen, my pretty skeptic." Sheftu leaned toward her, his eyes intense, his voice low and rapid. Here it came at last; he had forgotten his caution. Mara tensed herself to listen to every word. "Think you the prince was idle, those years in the temple? He spent them forging the whole priesthood into his weapon. They are ready to rise—today, tomorrow—they need only the signal. As for the miracle, it failed to set him on the throne, but he scarce expected it to. Hepusonbe, the high priest, is Hatshepsut's tool, and besides, it takes more than a miracle to move that woman! Nevertheless, our 'trick' was far from wasted!"

"But if no one believed—"

"The people believed! And they remember. Look around you." Sheftu waved a hand toward the crowded room. "These are all rebels, loyal to the king. More than that, it forced Her High and Mightiness into the pretense of the regency. She waited a little too long to take Senmut's counsel and arrange for the prince to die of some 'mysterious' ailment—after the miracle she didn't dare. Instead she summoned him back to the palace and made a royal prisoner of him. Too late, by Amon! While she piles honors on that architect and his cutthroats, she fails to notice that many of the younger nobles are growing uneasy over the state of the Empire." A slow smile curved Sheftu's mouth as he settled back and reached for his cup. "I have seen to it," he added lightly, "that their uneasiness increases—and that they, too, remember that miracle."

I'll wager you have! thought Mara. So that was the story —it all but took her breath away. This was no palace intrigue, but a revolution, involving priesthood, nobility, and the populace—no doubt the Army as well. And the whole complex affair was cupped in the palm of this prince of schemers beside her. She studied him, half in fear, half in admiration, as he drank his wine. Hatshepsut held Thutmose fast prisoner—but no one stood higher in her trust than the smooth-tongued Lord Sheftu, the most dangerous man to her in all Egypt. How had he accomplished it? Shrewd foresight, patience, deceit so sustained and perfect it was a work of art. Aye, a masterpiece, thought Mara, remembering his airy disregard of court etiquette yesterday, his lounging arrogance.

Yet there was a far different Sheftu—the dark and lonely figure she had seen silhouetted against the flaming sky one evening on the *Beetle*. She felt close to him suddenly. For all his insouciance, for all his gold, he lived a life as precarious as her own. And if he obeyed those terrible instructions she must give him tonight—

As he set down his cup, she turned away, pushing the thought hastily from her mind. No need to think of those instructions yet. No need to think of them at all! Remember, Mara, he is your enemy—and have you not bested him at his own game tonight? Take heart, though he conceals it better, he's no more immune to you than Reshed. . . .

His first words served to verify her confidence. "What is it about thee, maid, that loosens my tongue at both ends? By the beard of Ptah, I've done more talking tonight than . . ."

"Do you not talk to others so?"

"Nay, I do not!" He sounded annoyed, to her mischievous delight.

She quoted blandly from an ancient proverb: "'Be not arrogant because of thy knowledge. Goodly discourse is more hidden than the precious green stone, and yet it is found with slave girls over the millstones.'"

"'Silence,'" he quoted back at her drily, "'is more valuable than the *teftef* plant.' See that you watch your own tongue. Scarce a handful even know who I am, and it is better they do not. Oh, a few know the plans, of course— Nefer the goldsmith, the priest I was talking to when you arrived, Ashor, a few nobles, Nekonkh—"

"And I," reminded Mara.

133

"Aye, and now you." He had leaned forward, his profile half-hidden from her by the bulk of his shoulder, and he was toying with one of his reed pens, turning it over and over in his long brown fingers. "I'll wager I live to regret that," he added.

Mara pressed close to him. "Sashai! Do you not trust me?"

He turned, with a half-smile and a glance from his long eyes that made her heart beat faster. "My lovely Mara," he said softly. "I don't trust you as far as tomorrow."

She jerked away, her confidence suddenly in tatters. "Aye! So you have said before! If it is true, you have great faith in the gods!"

"Nay, I have great faith in your reluctance to go back to loaf snatching!"

He was laughing at her now. All in an instant he had retreated behind that façade of charming banter, where neither thrusts nor wiles could reach him. Furious, she struggled for a manner as careless. How had she ever imagined she felt close to this enigma? He had only made a fool of her. Or had he really opened his mind to her, in a moment of earnestness, and then regretted it? One thing was certain —he wished to remind her, and perhaps himself, of their precise relationship. Loaf snatching! Guttersnipe! Very well. So be it.

She had herself in hand by the time he spoke again. "Never mind that. Let us say you are one of the gambles I've dared to take. So far it's naught but exhilarating. . . . Now tell me, how did you swindle your way through those gates tonight?"

She shrugged. "With a languishing glance and a few tears. There's a young sentry who thinks I'm smitten with him. A *handsome* young sentry," she added.

"Indeed! How pleasant for you. But did tears alone convince him he should let you through the gate?"

"He would much rather have kissed me. But I consented to a bargain . . ."

"Oh, very good! And you will dangle this bargain like a sweetmeat until the fellow has served his purpose. Excellent! It might last for months."

"And again, it mightn't" retorted Mara sharply. The conversation was not going as she wished. "Even a sentry's patience may be tried too far, you know. This one's young and ardent. What if his patience ends?"

Sheftu eased one elbow onto the table, rested his cheek in his hand, and regarded her blandly. His long eyes were brimming with amusement. "You'll think of something," he said.

The devil take you! thought Mara. Aloud, she snapped, "Or perhaps I shall simply keep the bargain."

There was a little silence. Sheftu straightened, took a sip of his wine and set the mug down with care. "Not," he said, "unless you wish me to feed him to the crocodiles—bit by bit."

Mara's mouth dropped open. But before she could speak, another voice, soft and persuasive as the flute's tone, slid between them.

"A lover's quarrel, friend Sashai?"

It was the juggler, standing in the entrance to their cubicle. He had a crooked shoulder, Mara noticed, and a smile of curious charm in a twisted, ugly face. His glittering balls were momentarily at rest in the curve of his arm, save for three which traced a shining, stealthy little circle above his right hand, as if they had a life of their own.

"Nay, Sahure," answered Sheftu easily. "We never quarrel, nor are we in love."

The first was a lie, thought Mara. But the second? She was still tingling with surprise over the remark about Reshed and the crocodiles. Glancing impatiently at Sahure, she found her gaze caught and held by a pair of dark, cynical

135

eyes, profoundly old, profoundly weary, as if they had long ago seen everything, and found value in nothing.

"And may I know this enchanting stranger, whom you claim you do not love?" went on the juggler. "If you speak truth, friend Sashai, then your heart must be a mysterious thing, no more flesh and blood than one of my gilded balls here. Is it not so, Blue-Eyed One?"

"I know not, juggler," murmured Mara. She was half attracted, half repelled by this Sahure with his young, beguiling voice and his old, old eyes.

"Nay, call me not juggler, but friend. My heart is no gilded plaything." The balls rose in a golden fountain above his hand, then resumed their steady circling, but his gaze never left Mara's face. "Have you orders for me, master?"

"Not tonight."

"I am desolate. Would there were cause for me to linger in the light of this little one's countenance—where did you say you discovered her?"

"I failed to say," answered Sheftu drily.

Sahure's smile curved beneath his ancient eyes. "Aye, so you did. But she is not of Thebes, for I have seen high and low, princesses and slaves, and who could forget her? She was not among them. Mother Nile has borne her to us from another shore, no doubt, as she bears the gift of mud which makes Egypt great. Will you permit my poor efforts to entertain you, Face of the Lily?"

Sheftu shook his head. "Begone, Sahure. Others crave your talents."

"While you crave to mend the quarrel which was not a quarrel, with this Lovely One who is not beloved . . ." The three balls leaped up, dazzling, and with a subtle twist of his body Sahure brought all the others into play. "In that case I shall leave you, Flower of Grace, though not forever. May thy *ka* endure and thy shadow seek the light . . ."

The soft voice trailed away as he turned, letting his

gaze slide off Mara at last. The golden cataract of balls switched suddenly to a triangle, then to a pattern of brilliant intricacy before resolving once more into a circle. In a frame of moving light the juggler glided away across the floor.

"Mother of the gods!" breathed Mara. "Is he man or *kheft*?"

Sheftu laughed. "Sahure dwells in a dark land, I grant you. But there's no harm in him. I've found him very useful."

"You mean you trust him with your secrets? Great Amon, he'd betray his own *ka*, I believe!"

"Nay, he's loyal. In any case, he knows little—not even who I am. I admit he tries his best to find out. It's just curiosity."

"Perhaps," muttered Mara. She frowned. This talk of loyalty and betrayal had made her aware of much she had forgotten, and would rather have gone on forgetting.

She twirled her wine mug, watching the play of golden balls on the other side of the room. Why had the juggler tried so hard to discover where she came from and who she was? Already, in his poetic babblings of Mother Nile, he had arrived at one answer, very shrewdly. And his cynical eyes had never moved from her. He would know her next time they met, that was certain. Where would it be? Perhaps in the presence of Lord Nahereh?

She shivered, and took a sip of the wine, trying to dismiss the notion as impossible. But her thoughts were restless now, leaping back to that message she had yet to deliver. It was warm and pleasant here, with the good smell of meat and the torchlight flooding the room with smoky gold. But outside the night was waning. There was still the river to cross, the dark alleys and the silent streets to find her way through, the stealthy taps on Reshed's gate. . . .

She set down her cup and spoke in a low voice. "It grows late, Sashai. I must leave. And before that—"

"Before that you must tell me what I must know. Aye, it

137

is time, maid. But not here," he added, with a glance at the trio of Libyan traders noisily taking possession of the next cubicle. "Come."

He rose and drew her to her feet. Picking up her cloak, she followed him out across the room. We are really enemies, she reminded herself. I care naught for what happens to him. . . .

Nekonkh stood up as they passed by him, detached himself from his companions and drifted toward the door. Otherwise no notice was taken of them. The two old men were setting up their board for another game of hounds and jackals, Ashor was hurrying toward the priest's table with a steaming platter, the dancing girl was passing her tambourine among a group of hilarious artisans in the corner. As they reached the fire pan, where the innkeeper's wife was dishing up more meat, Sheftu paused and spoke quietly.

"Miphtahyah."

She straightened. Sheftu handed her a few *deben*, like any man paying for his wine. "This maid is one of us," he murmured. "She is free to come and go here, at any time."

The old woman's eyes moved to Mara. She nodded grudgingly, then slipped the coins onto her money ring and turned back to the fire. In another moment Sheftu was holding open the tavern's outer door.

The moon had risen now, a faded sliver in the vast, dark sky, and the night had grown chill. Mara wrapped her cloak around her as she followed Sheftu into the darkest corner of the courtyard. Yonder by the gate was a dim hulk which must be Nekonkh.

"Now. Tell me." Sheftu had lowered his voice almost to nothing. "Was my pharaoh well?"

"Aye."

"You gave him my message?"

"Aye, I gave it."

"Well, go on. What did he say?"

She roused herself, trying to shake off a feeling of oppression. "He seemed overjoyed. He said you must be the Great Magician himself."

She could feel Sheftu's deep pleasure. "The gods were with me on that venture. I've not been idle since. When you see him next, say to him that two of the immortal ones—he of the fan and he of the feather—have come into our house. Do you have that clear?"

"He of the fan and he of the feather," echoed Mara mechanically. "Aye, I have it."

"Good. Now for my orders." As she hesitated, he frowned impatiently. "Come, speak. We have not all night."

"He says—you must find more gold."

"I know that. I've promised bribes already I cannot pay. But where? Did he— What's amiss, maid?" Sheftu bent closer, scanning her face, then he slowly straightened. "Is it bad, then?"

"Aye, it is bad! It is so dread a thing I dare not speak it! Ahh, I beg thee, Sheftu, disobey this time! Thy prince has no right to demand such a crime of thee, no matter—"

"Hush!" He clapped a hand over her mouth, darting an angry glance about the courtyard. "Would you have all Thebes hear? Now cease thy babbling and tell me."

"Nay, I'll not! Do not ask me, Sheftu, it is better thus, I vow it is better you should never—"

He swept her forcibly against him, doubling her wrist behind her in a grip that made her wince. "You forget yourself," he said in a low, harsh voice. "You are not judge, but messenger. Tell me what pharaoh commands, be quick."

"Wait, I will, but loose me! I—" A slight wrench on her wrist turned the plea into a gasp of pain. She tumbled the words out. "He asks if your magic be a shield and a buckler to you. Amon help you, you must rob the dead—"

"Go on."

"He said—there is one alone in all of Egypt who will give gold gladly for his sake. You must find this one—by the Dark River—you must take what is his, even to the royal

139

cobra and the collar of amulets. *Aiii,* mother of the gods, loose me, Sheftu!"

"This *is* all?"

"Aye, all, I swear it!"

The pressure on her wrist eased. She leaned against him, trying to steady her breathing. After a time his arms dropped, and he moved a few steps away. But when he spoke at last, it was in his usual ironic voice. "Must I always drag my messages out of you by brute force? It promises to be wearing."

She raised her head. In the dim moonlight his features were composed, if a trifle set. "You are not—disturbed—by this one?"

"It was not entirely unexpected."

"I see," she breathed. "Then you intend to obey?"

"Blue-Eyed One, that is none of your affair."

But she knew the answer. "You're a fool!" she whispered. "Ten thousand kinds of a fool, to risk your soul among the *khefts!* They'll steal away your *ka* and leave naught but the shell of you! They'll dwell in your shadow, they'll bring you down to blindness and sickness, they'll deliver you to the Forty Beasts—"

Her voice cracked, and she broke off.

"You tell me nothing I do not know," said Sheftu softly. "Save one thing—why are you so troubled about my fate?"

"I—" She stopped and drew a long breath. "I am not troubled."

"You are close to tears."

Mara turned away from him, rubbing her sore wrist. "Not I! If you choose to be a reckless fool, it's naught to me." As he said nothing, she whirled back defensively. "I speak truth!"

"Do you?"

"Aye! I do!"

He pulled her back into his arms—quite differently this

140

time. "You never spoke truth in your life," he muttered. "But speak it now. Why do you weep for me?"

Mara's heart was beating fast. He was going to kiss her, it was inevitable this time. "Perhaps for the same reason you threatened to feed my poor Reshed to the crocodiles," she whispered. She waited, scarcely breathing. "Sheftu— were you afraid I might keep that bargain?"

His arms loosened suddenly, and the old faintly mocking amusement returned to his voice. "Nay, I was afraid you might lose your entry in and out of the palace," he said lightly. "'Ai, ai, what a lovely hussy you are. This poor Reshed, I pity him! What will become of his illusions when he finds you out?"

Mara jerked away, furious. "Only what should become of them! He must learn sometime not to believe every maid who weeps on his shoulder."

"Aye, so he must," agreed Sheftu drily. "Go now. Nekonkh is waiting."

Without further farewell he turned and strode rapidly toward the inn.

CHAPTER 14

Shadow of the Dead

THERE WAS nothing of the simple scribe about Lord Sheftu as he sat at breakfast next morning on the roof loggia of his villa on the Street of Sycamores in western Thebes. He was clad in a dressing gown of royal linen girdled with scarlet leather, and beside his chair was a table of carved

Lebanon cedar bearing fruit, bread, cheese and a lily-twined flagon of milk. A Kushite slave hovered in the background. Beyond the balustrade stretched the ample groves, gardens and stables of Sheftu's town estate. They were extensive, but not so extensive as his ancestral holdings downriver, where acre upon acre of farmland—vineyards, pastures, orchards, grainfields—poured their riches every year into his storerooms and purse. It was a monthly accounting of those riches that was being read to him now by the old man in an elaborate wig who stood beside the balustrade—Irenamon, major-domo of the entire domain since long before the death of Sheftu's father, Menkau.

"From your lordship's dairies near the village of Nekheb, thirty pounds of cheese, both white and yellow, and twenty beef for slaughter." Irenamon's voice was like the rustling of a dried palm frond. "In addition, a hundred skins of wine have been brought upriver on your lordship's barge *Hour of Sunset*, to be stored in your lordship's warehouses in the city of Thebes. . . ."

But his lordship was not thinking of beef or wineskins, nor was he showing much appetite for the array of dainties on the golden platter beside him.

While his long fingers crumbled the bread and toyed absently with the fruit, his mind was far away, in the desolate wastes of the Valley of the Tombs of the Kings. In one of the barren gullies of that wilderness was a certain pile of red granite boulders. It looked the same as the other piles tumbled here and there through the valley as if at the whim of a destructive giant. But to Sheftu it was not the same. Far below it, in vast and silent chambers hollowed out of the living rock, slept the one whose peace he must destroy, whose wealth he must steal, whose *ka* he must impoverish.

The dread of it had lain like a stone on his mind since he had dragged that message out of a reluctant Mara. Though he had not let her see it, he hated and feared his task with all his heart. But it was not the crime she thought it, nor was it certain the guardian *khefts* would rend his soul or even strike him blind. For there was one thing Mara had not known when she stormed and pled with him, and that was the identity of the royal slumberer. He was Thutmose I, father of the king—and of Hatshepsut. In life, his arrogant daughter had robbed him of his throne when he was ill and feeble. Would he not willingly be robbed once more, in death, if his gold could overthrow her? The prince had vowed he would, and Sheftu believed. He had to believe. Because otherwise . . .

Sheftu shook away that "otherwise," along with the memory of Mara's predictions as she clung to him in fear. Whatever the *khefts* might do, he had no choice but to descend into the tomb and come out laden. This was the last great gamble he and Thutmose had agreed on long ago, and the time had come to try it. Everything else that could be done was done. . . .

". . . therefore if the grain remained in the warehouses until such time as—I fear your lordship is not listening."

Sheftu pulled his attention back to old Irenamon's reproachful voice. "Aye, aye, tell me that last again, please."

"According to the calculations of our river experts, who are never wrong," repeated Irenamon patiently, "this year's inundation will be a small one, resulting in poor crops and a scarcity of grain in the months to come before Mother Nile again sends her gift to Egypt. Therefore, if a portion of your lordship's wheat still in the warehouses were to remain there, it would command a far greater price next summer in the time of hunger—"

"I understand. Save it by all means against the time of hunger, but do not raise the price, Irenamon. The people must eat, whether they can pay or not."

"As your lordship wishes." Irenamon cleared his throat

and rustled the papyrus. "However, we—er—sell much grain to the agents of Her Majesty for the palace kitchens. . . ."

Sheftu shot a glance at the blandly innocent old face, and hid a smile. "Charge what the buyer can pay. I leave it to your discretion."

The old servant bowed and went on with his lists without further comment, but Sheftu knew that a fresh stream of gold from Hatshepsut's treasuries would soon be pouring into his coffers. Unless, indeed, the treasuries belonged to Thutmose by next summer.

He felt a tremor of emotion at the thought. After six long years it was hard to believe that the end of all this was approaching. Yet the plans he and Thutmose had made so long ago were almost complete, the work almost finished. Hatshepsut's elaborate structure of power was now like a house set upon columns of sand. Enlisting Khofra to gain control of the Army had further weakened the foundations. There remained only a few lords still stubbornly loyal to the queen, out of fear for their own fortunes and futures. These must be won over, by persuasion—and by gold, the greatest persuader of them all.

Sheftu smiled grimly, tossing bread to the pigeons strutting along the balustrade. His regard for his fellow man was not what it had been six years ago. He no longer believed, even in his heart, that there lived man or woman gold could not buy. Only their prices differed. These last cautious ones would cost a pharaoh's fortune, and a pharaoh must supply it—he who slept beneath that pile of boulders in the Valley of the Tombs of the Kings. . . .

His thoughts had come full circle, for the twentieth time that morning. Sheftu left his chair abruptly, and the pigeons scattered with a drumming of wings. Irenamon stopped reading, then began to roll up his papyrus.

"My lord wearies of business," he said tactfully. "Indeed, the morning is too fine for it. *Hai*, when I was your age . . .

Shall I have the boat and the throw-sticks readied to divert you?"

"Nay, old friend, I've no time for hunting. But I pray you, let us finish these accounts another time. I must drive to the temple within the hour. Go below and tell the barber to make ready for me."

As the old man turned toward the stairs, Sheftu laid an apologetic hand on his shoulder. "Forgive my inattention, Faithful One. I have much on my mind."

Irenamon's face lighted hopefully. "Indeed! Can it be that— My lord has perhaps met some young lady?"

"Young lady?" With some difficulty Sheftu achieved a careless smile. "Patience, Irenamon. Someday, I promise thee, my mother's long-empty place at table will be filled. But at present—*Ai*, get thee gone, now!"

Young lady!

Turning irritably as the major-domo hobbled down the stairs, Sheftu signaled the slave to pour him a cup of milk. But even the lotus twined about the flagon brought to mind two mocking eyes, blue as enamel under slanted brows. Why, in Amon's name, must he think so continually of that waif! For a waif she was—remember the market place at Menfe, remember her waking on the boat, a smudge on her face and wild defiance in her pose. Yet a dozen times a day he found himself thinking of the fluid way she walked, dwelling, fascinated, on some elusive curve of her cheek or throat, becoming preoccupied with the shape of her mouth. Aye, and remembering—far too vividly—the yielding warmth of her in his arms. . . . Osiris! He had all but made love to her last night in the tavern courtyard, all but forgotten she was an unprincipled little vagabond bound to him only by a threat and a bribe. He must not forget! The maid could worm secrets from the Sphinx himself!

His lordship set the cup down hard and descended the stairs. The devil! He had talked too much last night, why not admit it? He, Sheftu the Discreet. She knew far more than he had ever intended her to know, yet he'd had to fight the urge to keep talking. Have you not learned, he asked himself caustically, not to trust every maid who weeps on your shoulder?

He walked down a corridor and through a richly furnished sitting room, as blind to their sunny, familiar comfort as he was deaf to the greetings of a couple of house slaves who wished him good morning as he passed. How easy it would have been, there in the moonlight, to throw away all caution, to hold her tight in his arms and whisper that she must not fear; no *khefts* would harm one who came only to carry the dead king's gifts to his living son—to tell her even the name of the royal slumberer, and the place where he lay— Sheftu went cold at the thought. Had the maid bewitched him, that he would court destruction merely to dry her tears? He must come to his senses! He was acting as witless as that young—that *handsome* young sentry of hers.

". . . but I fear I misunderstood. Does my lord wish me to return later?"

Sheftu swung around. He was standing in the middle of his own apartments, but had no more recollection of arriving there than he had of the presence of the barber, though the fellow must have spoken before. He collected his wits with some difficulty, cursing Mara and his own befuddled senses.

"Nay, I want you now, Thoth," he muttered, stripping off his dressing gown. "Prepare your razors at once, I'm in haste."

The feel of the cooling salves and the razor sliding over his chin restored a sense of normality to the day, and he was grateful for the barber's silence, which enabled him to compose himself. As the fragrance of sandalwood from the last lotion rose on the air, Sheftu stood up, running a hand over his jaw.

"You are expert as ever, Thoth. Send my dresser in at once, and tell one of the grooms to harness Ebony and Wind-of-Swiftness to my lightest chariot."

146

Ten minutes later Lord Sheftu spun out of the courtyard and down the Street of Sycamores toward the river. Plumes tossed above his horses' sleek black heads, the sunlight flashed from his gold collar and from a thousand bits of colored glass set into the spokes of his chariot wheels. Driving off the ferry into the crowded streets of eastern Thebes, he flung a handful of coppers to the expectant throng of waterfront urchins, then turned into the Avenue of Sphinxes, which bisected the city and brought him straight through the tall bronze gates of the Temple of Amon.

He stepped down, looking for someone to hold the horses. The huge courtyard swarmed with beggars, hurrying priests, white-clad Thebans buying frankincense and temple offerings from the hawkers whose booths lined the walls. Sacrificial fowl squawked and fluttered in their cages, lambs bleated plaintively. The smell of dust, animals and sacred unguents mingled with the fragrance of a mass of fresh lilies on a flower-seller's stall.

"*Haiii!* Rejoice, master!"

An old peddler had spotted him, set down his tray of consecrated bread and hurried forward to catch the horses' reins. Tossing him a few *deben,* Sheftu made his way through the crowd and into the vast, columned corridors of the temple proper.

He found the priest he sought in a tiny anteroom off the Shrine of Hathor. Djedet was a calm, portly man with a face like a moon, wearing the leopard skin of the *sem* rank over his snowy linen robes. He was tying up onions into the hollow, circular bunches proper for the offering table, but at sight of Sheftu he paused.

"Your lordship, rejoice!" He came forward at once, beckoning a subordinate to take over his task. "There is some matter in which I may serve you?"

"Aye. It concerns the mortuary shrine of my father's tomb. I wish to increase the number of loaves and honey jars left for his *ka* each month. And in addition—"

147

"A thousand pardons, my lord. Pray come into more comfortable quarters, that I may offer you refreshment. My private chamber will serve . . ."

Sheftu followed the solid, stately figure out of the anteroom and down a hall lined with columns so massive they made even Djedet seem fragile as a splinter. Once the door of the little room had closed firmly behind them, the priest's impassive manner vanished.

"Is it the signal? Shall I order the—"

"Nay, my friend. The time is not yet. Indeed, the time will never be, unless you and I can perform one last impossibility." Sheftu sighed, the heaviness of his dread settling over him again. "Sit you down, Djedet. I will tell you what we must do."

The priest's round face grew graver and graver as he listened. When Sheftu had finished, the little room was silent. Then Djedet rose ponderously and walked to the table, where he stood staring down at a pile of scrolls. "You have a plan?" he muttered.

"Aye. We will need two diggers—men we can trust to be silent. Ashor can find them. And to ensure their silence, after the task is done I will send them to my farthest estate, to live in luxury—and solitude—until it is safe to loose them. I know a river captain who will arrange all that. As for your part, you must obtain the Royal Seal."

Djedet swung around, eyes bulging. "But I cannot do that! Only the high priest of the City of the Dead—"

"I know. But you must accomplish it somehow. Listen."

Djedet listened, his expression changing slowly. He moved back to his chair and sank into it, his face intent, his voice low as he put a question or two. At last he nodded. "I think it can be done. Unless the guards at the Valley . . ." He chewed his lip a moment, then shrugged heavily. "Ai, the plan is shot through with danger; but what is not, these days? Better we die, my lord, than Egypt." He rose, touch-

148

ing forehead and chest. "I will do my best, and send word. May the gods be with us."

Better we die than Egypt, repeated Sheftu to himself as he walked slowly back down the corridor. His eyes moved to the columns rising close and massive, on either side, stretching up and up until their carvings were lost in the dim reaches far above him. Old beyond memory they were, like Egypt itself, and they would stand unchanged a thousand years more. Aye, and so would Egypt, no matter who had to die! One death alone would be enough, thought Sheftu grimly—that of a bejeweled and willful queen. . . .

He turned a corner and strode along a passage, neither noticing nor caring where it led. A few moments later, roused by the faint, irregular beat of hammers, he stopped and looked around him. Scowling, he realized he had strayed into the North Wing. Not since last summer had he come to this place, and he had sworn then he would never come again.

Slowly he pivoted to his left. There, only a few paces distant, was the entrance to the hall the First Thutmose had built as his kingly gift to the god. Sheftu walked toward it, his face set, the tap-tap of goldsmith's hammers growing louder in his ears. At the tall doorway he stopped, looking into a huge room flooded with sunshine.

There, in the middle of the roofless hall, stood the queen's new obelisks. They were no nightmare, then, but seven hundred tons of solid reality—monstrous needles of stone ninety-seven feet tall, soaring straight up into the brilliant sky. Sheftu's gaze traveled their length, part of which was at the moment obscured by scaffolding upon which gold workers swarmed. Well he remembered the day last summer those shafts came floating down the river from the quarries, on a flotilla of linked barges that seemed to stretch back to Nubia. No man had ever seen their like, for they had been cut from single blocks of granite, without a seam or a joint, and—because the queen was impatient—in only seven months' time. There was an inscription on them swearing to it.

How, in Amon's name, had mortal hands accomplished it? It was all but impossible. So was raising the obelisks here, within the temple itself. But here Hatshepsut wanted them, and here they stood, though it had been necessary to tear out many of her father's beautiful cedar columns and the whole roof of the hall to make room for them. Bitterly Sheftu stared at the wreckage, remembering the crack of the lash and the antlike swarm of men straining on ropes, dropping, dying, being trampled by their fellows as with a shuddering slow movement the great shafts rose into place—monuments to Hatshepsut's pride and malice.

And now—Sheftu's eyes moved to the scaffolding, through which a growing surface of pale yellow glittered in the sun. Furiously he turned and strode back toward the courtyard, the faint tapping of the goldsmiths' hammers following him. Through the sound he could hear again Hatshepsut's voice: "My Majesty is not pleased. The obelisks are mere dull stone and so unworthy of the Daughter of the Sun. I desire that they reflect Ra's beams from every surface. They shall be cased in electrum. . . ."

Extravagance upon extravagance, until the very gods must be outraged! She would bring ruin upon the Black Land. . . .

The temple's dim quiet ended abruptly as Sheftu stepped into the noise and dust and mingled odors of the outer courtyard. It was like plunging into another element, and the shock steadied him and dissipated his wrath.

Fool, anger gets you nowhere, he told himself as he gathered his horses' scarlet reins and popped the whip over their flanks. Let her have her obelisks—she will soon have nothing else. As for the task ahead, think no more of it now. Djedet will arrange all. You have nothing to do but wait.

CHAPTER 15

The Signal

BUT WAITING was hardest. A day dragged by, then another, without word from the priest. Sheftu had spoken to Ashor early; the diggers were arranged for and waiting, though they knew not what their task was to be. Nekonkh was waiting, the *Beetle* provisioned and ready to spirit the men away. The king was waiting for word, Mara waiting to carry it, Sheftu waiting, in a torment of suspense, to act.

For the first time in six years the wheels of his secret life had ground to a dead halt. All plans hinged on one now, and that one hung like an unanswered question on the air, growing hourly more urgent. It was all Sheftu could do to grace the court of Hatshepsut with unchanged serenity, to behave as usual under the eyes of his household. Hardest of all was to hide from Mara the strain he was feeling, to parry her questions and then laugh at her anger. Each night she came to the inn for news, and he could tell her nothing. Their conversations were like duels. Rather than dreading the task which still hung over him, he now began to long for it, that the issue might be settled. Inactivity ached like a tooth.

Soon after noon on the fourth day, restlessness led him down to the barracks of the queen's bodyguard, whose quarters and parade field occupied a large open area to the rear of the palace grounds. He found Khofra sitting on a hard chair in his severe and cell-like quarters, waiting for the bugle which would summon him to his afternoon inspection of the troops.

"Come in, my lord, come in!" the old man greeted him, waving to a second, and even harder, chair. "Sit down, and test the rigors of military life! Though I promise this is luxury compared to what those poor devils on the parade grounds yonder call their own. Ai, well, there's no other way to make soldiers of them. Hard chairs, hard beds, hard fighting."

"And a general as hard as they," suggested Sheftu, sitting down.

Khofra gave his soundless laugh. "Aye, they look up to me, knowing I've slept on rocky ground oftener than they've slept in their couches. They're coming on, Lord Sheftu, they're shaping up. Someday we'll have an army here, instead of a crowd of idlers. But I warn you—" The old general lowered his voice, and his face grew grim. "I've promised them action. Campaigns, foreign battlefields, victories like those we knew in the old days, for the glory of Egypt. Take care you produce them."

"Never fear! There'll be action in plenty once Thutmose takes command. By the Feather, our empire's in a sorry mess, *Haut* Khofra!" Sheftu got up and began to pace. "Every week a new dispatch comes in. There's another uprising in Nubia, a bad one, and an outbreak on the border farther north. Worse yet, the King of Kadesh has stirred up every city king in northern Palestine and Syria—they're banding together to defy us, and the queen does nothing, nothing! Our governors are going frantic, they need more men, more gold—"

"*They* need it! So do I, by Amon! Yet she's even taking what I have."

Sheftu stopped. "She's doing what?"

"Reducing my forces. Cutting down allotments. Refusing to fill my orders for supplies. You didn't know this?"

"By the Devourer, no!"

152

He listened with growing fury as Khofra explained. The bodyguard, normally two thousand troops, had been reduced by a third even before Khofra had assumed command. In the past two weeks a hundred more had been dismissed, and the pay for those remaining was already five days late.

"Then about the helmets," Khofra growled. "A week ago I sent in a requisition for two hundred archer's helmets, of scarlet leather, well padded and quilted, with a good gold fringe. I needed three hundred, but some of the old ones will serve, though they be shabby enough! This morning the requisition came back—refused. Perhaps she means to send the archers into battle bareheaded? Something must be done."

"Something will be done!" snapped Sheftu. "Now. At once. What of the regular Army, those not of the bodyguard? How badly have they dwindled?"

"By more than half. And as for chariots and horses—" Khofra threw up his hands.

"That will be the task of our prince," said Sheftu. "He'll build the regulars up soon enough, once we've set him on his throne. But to set him there we need the bodyguard, full strength and well equipped. And by Amon, we'll have it! Who rules on these requisitions?"

"My Lord Nahereh, Master of Armories and of the White Storehouse for Linen. He of the face like a chip of granite. He doles out the pay, too—when there is any."

"Nahereh," said Sheftu thoughtfully. Brother of the Architect himself—a man to be reckoned with. Sheftu knew him only too well. It was not the first time that stony face had stood between him and his goal. He dropped into a chair. "He's Senmut's right hand, *Haut* Khofra—and Senmut's the queen's. Obviously she needs the gold elsewhere—for some new extravagance."

"Was not her last one folly enough?" snorted Khofra. "I mean the two obelisks. Gods of Egypt! How does the woman

153

conceive these things? Single blocks, unmarred by joints or even chisel marks—"

"That was merely the beginning," remarked Sheftu drily. He mimicked: "'The obelisks are mere dull stone and so unworthy of the Daughter of the Sun. I desire that they reflect—' By my *ka!*" he burst out suddenly. "There's her need for gold! Did you know, *Haut* Khofra, that she is casing the shafts in electrum?"

Khofra's shaggy eyebrows soared. "Those man-made mountains? Impossible!"

"Aye. Our queen is fond of the impossible. Gold and silver over every inch of those monster slabs—I saw them at work on it myself, only a few days ago. By this time, I'll wager, they're working up near the roof and Egypt's treasury's nigh empty."

"Small wonder she needs funds!"

Sheftu was on his feet, stalking about the bare little room. "She'll not steal them from the bodyguard. Look you, my general. It's clear how this came about. The queen fretting for more gold—the Architect as usual scheming out a solution. 'Most Glorious Majesty, why feed and clothe two thousand idle soldiers in time of peace? Riffraff, eating their bellies full at Your Radiance's expense! And it is my brother Nahereh who holds the purse strings. . . .' *Aiii!* He'll wish he'd held his peace!"

Sheftu paused beside his chair, fingers drumming upon its back. A smile was beginning to curve the corners of his mouth.

"But what can you do?" put in Khofra.

"I can see the queen. I can inform her, with the gravest concern, of the bodyguard's condition. I can thank Amon repeatedly, and loudly, that I discovered the situation before it was too late—"

"You mean she doesn't know of it?"

"Of course she knows! But my general, if I behave like one saving her from disaster, she will not admit she knows. She

154

will first try to find out what is so wrong with Senmut's little scheme."

"And what will you tell her?"

Sheftu smiled. "*Haut* Khofra, Her Radiance the Daughter of the Sun fears one thing only—the loss of her throne. Suppose it were suggested to her that Senmut's motives might not be pure—that he might have reasons to wish her bodyguard depleted, her protection undermined. . . ."

"She would never believe it! Not of her precious Architect!"

"No? Do you remember Nehse, who commanded her great expedition to Punt a few years back? Do you remember Thuti, once Lord High Treasurer—and Neb-iry, only recently Grand Overseer of her temple? Whatever happened to those great favorites of hers, *Haut* Khofra? Strange how they have dropped out of sight—forever."

Khofra shot a sidelong glance at him. "I know nothing of such matters, my lord. But I do know these men commanded projects close to her heart. She has never taken a moment's interest in her bodyguard!"

"She is about to begin," retorted Sheftu. "I'll wager you a gold chain, my general, that an hour from now the palace bodyguard will have become the consuming interest of Hatshepsut's life—and Senmut an unhappy man."

Khofra's skeptical old eyes met Sheftu's across the room, and gradually the doubt cleared away from them. He chuckled, and as the shrill blast of a bugle pierced the silence, he rose, buckled on his quilted cuirass and exchanged his square-cut wig for a leather helmet. "I wish you luck with it, my friend," he said. "I'm no magician, as you seem to be. But get me men and I'll give you soldiers—that I can promise."

With a nod of farewell he stepped out the door which opened onto the parade ground, and joined the two aides who awaited him there. For a moment Sheftu stood watching the ranks of copper-skinned foot soldiers file by the old

155

general in the brilliant sunlight. They were few indeed. As the chariots bearing the archers followed, he could spot horses gone lame, damaged wheels, bareheaded men.

Smiling grimly, he strode out of the building, across the barracks yard and into the palace gardens by the nearest gate.

When he emerged, an hour later, it was with the jaunty step of a man whose time has not been wasted. He signaled a groom to fetch his chariot and stood savoring the fresh breeze and the thought of the interview just past, feeling more invigorated than he had for weeks. It was even possible he might enjoy Lord Merab's party on the morrow. . . .

A baldpated little man in the garb of a priest appeared suddenly from nowhere, cast an idle look about him, then stopping a pace or two from Sheftu, stooped to adjust his sandal.

Sheftu's heart gave a leap, and the party fled from his mind. He turned his back to the little man, but edged closer. He was rewarded by a whisper.

"Tomorrow. The hour of the fifth mark."

Baldpate vanished, leaving Sheftu staring casually into the middle distance with everything in him in an uproar. When his chariot arrived he failed to notice it. Turning on his heel, he hurried into the labyrinth of palace gardens, in search of Mara.

"There," murmured Inanni. "That lamb is finished now. Only one more and the shawl will be done. What think you of it, Mara?"

At the other end of the garden bench, Mara interrupted her fascinated study of the ring on her finger to inspect the square of embroidery Inanni held up. She smiled. Inanni had worked a careful picture in colored threads—a green hillside dotted with lambs and a sleeping shepherd, with the square tower of a Syrian temple showing beyond.

"It is beautiful, my princess."

156

"But not so beautiful as the hill in my memory. . . ." Inanni sighed and plucked another skein of white wool from the workbasket.

After a moment Mara rose and strolled down to the pool in the center of the tiny garden, dropped down on the soft grass beside its rim and once more fell to studying the ring. It was the heavy electrum band with the jeweled lotuses, the ring Sheftu had given her on the ship. She knew well it was dangerous folly to wear it, since it was supposed to have left her possession long ago, as a bribe for that "friend" in Abydos. One glimpse of it and Sheftu would merely wait his moment to cut her throat.

But how the eyes of those high-and-mighty palace servants had popped when they noticed it this morning! Mara grinned at the memory. It was worth a little danger to lord it over them occasionally—especially the supercilious butler who looked down his nose at her whenever he caught her slipping her sandals off. He would think twice next time about whom he snubbed!

She turned the ring thoughtfully on her finger, wishing she had given in earlier to the temptation to put that butler in his place. For already she was convinced that the ring bore some potent charm. All morning good luck had followed her, smoothed her way, made easy the most difficult situations. Think of this morning's audience with the king! If that was not luck—

"Mara," said Inanni suddenly. "Someone is coming. It is the young nobleman of the lotus garden! Ah, would he not be handsome with a beard?"

Mara had swung around, spied Sheftu striding up the red graveled path, snatched the ring from her finger and stuffed it into her sash before Inanni had finished speaking. Now she rose, brushed off her skirt with trembling hands, and sauntered forward as nonchalantly as she could.

"A beard?" she murmured. "I—I had never thought of it, Highness."

157

It was all right, he couldn't have noticed that quick motion, and the folds of her sash concealed the hard little lump underneath it. She faced Sheftu composedly as he stopped before them, smiling.

"Princess, rejoice." His long hand moved from his lips to his forehead in a gesture of careless grace. "I bear pharaoh's greetings. Her Radiance inquires after the welfare of the Princess of Canaan."

For the first time in four days his eyes had come alive. Something had happened. Mara translated hastily.

"Tell him I am content," Inanni murmured.

"She is content. What is it, Sheftu? Tell me, for the love of Amon!"

"The signal has come. I have instructions for you. Say something to the princess."

"Highness, his excellency wishes to know if—"

"Mara." Inanni was facing her, an odd, nervous determination in her manner. "I do not want to talk to this young man, nor does he want to talk to me. Please, will you not—relieve me of the burden? I have an errand elsewhere."

"But Highness!"

"Please, Mara." Inanni put a hand on Mara's arm and looked her full in the eyes. "The summerhouse yonder is empty, and no one comes here. You will be quite alone."

She snatched her workbasket from the bench and hurried across the garden and through the gate, leaving Mara staring after her.

"What is this?" demanded Sheftu in a low voice.

"I don't know. Quite often lately she makes some excuse to slip away from me—I think she goes to see a Syrian woman in the Court of the Weavers. But it is strange that she would do that now. . . ." Mara whirled back to him, suddenly excited. "No matter! Should we question when Amon smiles on us? We're free to talk, if you want to risk it. She spoke truth—no one comes here."

Sheftu flashed a quick glance around the garden, then

took Mara's arm and hurried her toward the little summer-house which stood at the far end of the pool in a clump of acacia trees. It was a light wooden structure, little more than a stone platform and a roof, but vines clambered thick over its three latticed walls, and its open front faced a little away from the gate, so that once inside it, they could see without being seen. Mara sat down on a cushioned stool, looking about her with delight. All was cool green here, speckled with moving sunlight—little flakes and pellets of gold which sifted through the vines to dance agitatedly over Sheftu's white robes and her own and the painted floor, whenever the breeze stirred the leaves.

"Amon smiles indeed!" murmured Sheftu, placing another stool where he could watch the gate. "Something is bringing us good fortune."

Mara, aware of the hard little lump of the ring pressing against her waist, was quite sure she knew what that something was. But she said only, "It's been a day of good fortune for me!"

"What else has happened?"

"I've been longing to tell you. Bless Inanni for giving me the chance! We saw the king this morning—at last. As you know, I've been trying for three days."

"Did he not say you could arrange for an audience whenever—"

"Aye, but it isn't as easy as it sounds! One has to find the proper chamberlain, tell him one lie, and Inanni another—"

Sheftu cut her off impatiently, glancing toward the gate. "No matter. Say on, maid—the rest of it."

"The rest was no easy task either! I had to give him your message somehow, with the room full of people. . . . Aye, I know he sent them all away last time, but I suppose he didn't dare to do that twice, for fear of making them suspicious. They're all spies, Sheftu."

"How do you know that?"

"From the way he glares at them." Mara shrugged,

159

skipped nimbly over why the room had not been cleared, a feat which she had herself accomplished with no small difficulty, and hurried on. "Be that as it may, they were all there, and I had to think fast, I promise you! It was Inanni who saved me—she and the sketches."

"Sketches?"

Mara grinned, pausing a moment to enjoy his bewilderment. She was relishing the whole situation—the secluded little arbor, the danger, their lowered voices, and most of all her secret amusement at how different this tale would sound when she told it to her master. "Aye, the sketches. They were all over the table when we came in the room—sheets and scraps of papyrus and a clutter of pens and ink, and they were all drawings of vases."

Sheftu's face cleared. "*Ast!* The vases. They are a pastime of the king's. His hand is skilled with the artist's pen."

"So Inanni was saying when he walked into the room. 'If His Highness has drawn these, Mara, then he is an artist of great talent. They are the most beautiful things I have seen in Egypt.' And behold, there he stood, hearing every word. I know not which was the more surprised. Inanni's cheeks rivaled the hues of her shawls."

Sheftu was grinning. "And was he flattered?"

"By my *ka*, I believe he was. At least it caused him to think of her as a human being, instead of a Syrian cow. For a moment I thought he was going to forget and speak to her in Babylonian, and then alas for Mara! But he stopped in time and bade me ask her which sketch she liked best."

"Did he indeed?"

"Aye, and she picked one, though she was frightened out of her senses, and all her embroideries trembling." Mara pantomimed Inanni's gesture, extending a timidly pointing finger and then jerking it away as if something had bitten it.

"And then?" chuckled Sheftu.

"He laughed, as you might guess, and folded his arms,

after his manner." Mara sat very erect, folded her own arms, and momentarily became the king. " 'Overornate,' he said, 'and a little vulgar. *Ai,* well, being Syrian she cannot help her taste. Tell her I will have it made up in yellow alabaster and delivered to her, with my compliments.' "

"By Amon! It is well no one but myself sees you imitate him thus!" exclaimed Sheftu a little grimly. "You might forfeit that impudent tongue of yours."

"Nay, I mean no impudence. I but tell you how it happened. Indeed, I'd not mock him, Sheftu. I was naught but pleased by what he had done for my poor princess. Her face shone as if someone had lit a torch inside her. It has made her heart light all day, I think."

"You seem fond of this barbarian," observed Sheftu, leaning backward to peer cautiously toward the gate.

"It may be I am. I pity her, she is so lonely and homesick, and so far from home."

Sheftu turned, a mixture of amusement and impatience on his face. "Do we risk our necks here to talk about the Canaanite? I would hear more of this lucky morning of yours."

"Aye, you shall. But I crave a promise of you, Sheftu. When all this is finished, and the king wears his crown—will you send Inanni again to Canaan? Say you will. Her fate can mean naught to you, whether in Egypt or Syria—"

"She shall sail to the end of the world if you like, but proceed with your story! What have the sketches to do with you?"

"I passed your message by means of them." His promise gained, Mara was willing and eager to go on. "*Ai,* that was a fine bit of sleight of hand, though I praise my own wits! Remember the message? 'He of the fan and he of the feather have come into our house.' Of course I know not what it signifies," added Mara innocently, though she had figured out long since that it meant the queen's fanbearer and some other great noble—possibly a judge, whose symbol was the

Feather of Truth—had been persuaded to swear allegiance to the king. "But I wagered His Highness would know well enough. I juggled the conversation with a skill that would have shamed Sahure, until we spoke again of the sketches, then I stepped forward, *ai*, so impulsively, and snatched a pen and drew a little design as a suggestion for some future vase—and lo, it was a fan and a feather, beside a house bearing the king's *cartouche!*"

"Very good indeed," said Sheftu, who had been grinning as he listened. "A fine tale, and told by one who does not believe in ruining things with false modesty. I congratulate you, little one, on your cleverness, your sagacity, your—"

"Oh, hold your tongue! Could you have done better?"

He laughed softly, shaking his head. "Nay, perhaps not as well. I doubt if—" Suddenly his face went stiff with attention as the sound of voices drifted to them from somewhere just beyond the garden wall. He twisted for a quick glance toward the gate, then sprang up silently and pulled Mara with him to the dimmest corner of the summerhouse. As they stood there, flattened against the latticed wall, the voices grew more distinct, and footsteps crunched on the graveled path.

". . . looked like a man who'd just seen a *kheft* face to face," one voice was saying. "I do not jest, my friend. Something's happened between Her Radiance and the Architect."

"He didn't speak to you?"

"Nay, he was in too much haste! He burst out of her chambers as if the Devourer were after him, and went by me without a glance. I heard him snarling for his chariot, outside, but I didn't stay to wave farewell. The climate's not healthy when he's in a rage!"

"*Ai*, I hope he strangles on it," muttered the other. "Last flood season he took five of my vineyards for Crown property—by royal permission. But I note *his* slaves are cultivating them now."

"He'll want the throne next, hark to my words. Ten years from now . . ."

The voices faded as the two went out the other gate. Mara drew a long breath and glanced up at Sheftu, who seemed to have derived a great deal of malicious pleasure from what he had heard. "Who was it?" she whispered.

"Two nobles who love Count Senmut as much as I," returned Sheftu drily. "Count Kha-Kheper, the one who talked about the vineyards. I believe I had best arrange a little conference with him sometime soon. Now look you, Blue-Eyed One, we must be out of here. I'll not be at the inn tonight, so you need not come. But tomorrow night—"

"It is tomorrow that. . ?" Mara did not finish, but searched his face anxiously.

"Aye," he whispered. "Tomorrow at the mark of five, the messenger told me. It should be finished in two hours, if all goes well."

"*If* all goes well!" she repeated bitterly.

He ignored that. "So get thee to the tavern by the mark of seven, or as soon after as you are able. Is your Reshed still well bedazzled?"

"So I hope. He's tugging at his leash."

"*Ai*, you'll have no trouble—one so clever as you, so remarkable, so sagacious—"

"Oh, leave off!" But her scowl faded as he stood there laughing down at her, the sun flecks dancing crazily over his face and headcloth, and glinting into one jewel in his golden collar until it flashed like a star. "I'll be there, by his leave or without it," she murmured. "May the gods grant you will! Sheftu, take care!"

"Little one, I'll do my best." He guided her gently back to her stool. "Sit here now and let the goldfish admire you awhile. Give me about the count of a hundred. Farewell."

He slipped around the edge of the vine-clad wall and was gone. Mara could hear his footsteps on the gravel path, calm and unhurried. She did not look up, fixing her attention instead on the fat, red goldfish drifting lazily in and out between the lotus stems in the depths of the pool. It would never do to think of where he was going, what he must do before she saw him again—if she ever did.

By the time she had counted the goldfish three times over, the garden had been empty for some time. She rose, went out into the glare of afternoon, and walked slowly across the garden toward the palace.

Part V—The Ring

CHAPTER 16

The Gamble

THE SERVANTS were laying the tables in the yellow-paneled dining room of the princess' suite before Inanni returned from her mysterious "errand"—and by that time Mara had thought long and uneasily about her absence. What did she really know of Inanni, save that she was homesick and unhappy? Very little, or the princess' sudden withdrawal this afternoon would not have taken her so by surprise. Mara did not like surprises. The moment had arrived, she reflected, to converse in private with Inanni.

Accordingly, as soon as the meal was over and the Syrian women, still licking honey from their plump fingers, had wandered into the big sitting room to chatter or do needlework, Mara invited the princess to view the sunset with her from the roof pavilion.

A few minutes later they were emerging onto the breeze-swept loggia. Above them the sky flamed with sunset, trailing scarlet banners of cloud and tinging with pink the myriad white walls and buildings of the city spread out below. Even the Nile looked like a river of fire, set between banks of unnaturally vivid green.

"Beautiful!" exclaimed Inanni as they stood at the balustrade looking out upon it all. But there was a note of dismay in her voice, and she soon retreated to a couch under the partial shelter of one of the painted awnings. Mara, who was accustomed to the violent beauty of Egypt, lingered a moment to feast her eyes on it.

"It is very different," she said softly, "from the sunsets of Canaan, I suppose?"

"Aye, everything there seems softer, and the hills thrust up to hide part of the sky, so that it does not seem so huge and fiery, and one does not feel so small. . . . Mara, perhaps it is not wise to talk of Canaan."

"Very well," said Mara firmly, turning around to her. "Then let us talk of something else. My princess, why did you leave me in the garden today?"

"Why, because I—had an errand—" Inanni's great dark eyes met Mara's, and their expression changed. "So be it," she said quietly. "It was because of what I told you, Mara. That young man did not want to talk to me, nor I to him. He was seeking you."

After a moment Mara left the balustrade and sat down on the other end of the couch. "How long have you known this?"

"Since the day I first saw him, in the lotus garden. Mara —I know other things, too. I know the king has no interest in me, nor ever will, and when I have audience with him he does not speak of the things you say he does. There is a great trouble of some sort here, and I have somehow become part of it. Forgive me, I did not even mean to tell you of this, but today I suddenly—it seemed too burdensome to go through again. I should not have spoken of it, though."

"Why not? Why didn't you tell me long ago?"

"Well, it—I felt it would be easier for you if I pretended I knew nothing, so that you would not be troubled about that part of it. But I fear I am very poor at pretending. Forgive me if I have spoiled everything now . . ."

Mara sat silent, wonderingly studying the plump, anxious face before her. "It is you who must forgive me, my

166

princess," she said at last. "You have shown me exactly how clever I have been!" She got up and walked to the balustrade again, but this time she did not see the red sky and the thousand roofs of Thebes. Inanni had been sorry for her —for *her*. It was a strange sensation, entirely new in her experience, and bewildering. She wondered in some astonishment if she were going to cry, then decided that by rights she should be laughing, hard—laughing at herself. She turned to Inanni, and knew suddenly that she wanted to tell her everything, tumble out the whole story, and plead for understanding. To take down the bars just once, and let another human being in . . .

"Do you—want to hear the rest?" she heard herself saying in a small voice.

"If you want to tell me, Mara."

"I do, but it's mad. They'll kill me if they find out."

Inanni's cheeks grew pale, but she spoke quietly. "They will never find out from me, Mara."

"It would matter to no one—save myself," said Mara with bitterness. "I'm naught but a slave. All my fine clothes and my airs are borrowed property. Not four weeks ago I was starching *shentis* and stealing bread from the baker's boys in Menfe." Mara walked back to the couch, kicked off her sandals defiantly, and curled her feet under her. "And getting thrashed for it, as always. The whole thing began, for me, that day. A stranger in a white cloak came into my master's courtyard. . . ."

It was easy, once she started. She talked rapidly, though in a low voice, explaining her sale, the astonishing interview with her master afterward, her meeting with Sheftu on the *Beetle* and all that had happened since. Inanni's dark eyes grew round with wonder, excitement and anxiety as she listened. Beyond them, over Thebes, the wild red banners in the sky faded to murky rose, and the East darkened, but neither of them knew it.

"So it is a—revolution!" whispered Inanni at last.

167

"Aye. And here am I, tangled in both sides of it! At first all seemed simple—I had but to mention Sheftu's name to my master, and he would shower me with gold, give me my freedom. But now—" Mara hesitated, then added reluctantly, "Of course, naught is different now. I could mention it still."

"But you do not want to now," said Inanni softly.

"Nay, I do not want to now. I am a fool, am I not?"

Inanni shook her head. "You are in love with this Lord Sheftu."

Denial sprang to Mara's lips, and died there as her gaze encountered Inanni's. She ended by shrugging wearily, leaning back against the cushions. "Little good it does me. He thinks me a guttersnipe, and says so. And tomorrow he may be—" She stopped. She had not told Inanni about the tomb robbery, nor did she intend to. "He cares only for his king," she finished.

"You do too, Mara. You want the king to be pharaoh."

Mara nodded. "As I say, I'm a fool. Why in Amon's name should I fret over who rules Egypt? There is always a pharaoh, just as there is always a Nile, but such a maid as I could live her whole life without knowing which face it was beneath the double crown, or caring a fig if she did know! Hatshepsut—Thutmose—what does it matter? I've my own worries—" She broke off, adding, "The trouble is, it does matter."

"Perhaps it is because you know him now."

"Perhaps it is," said Mara slowly. "Aye, and because I have watched him, and talked to him, and seen him pacing up and down, like a lion in a cage— *Ai*, he is a conqueror, my princess! Who else would have had the wit to stage that miracle, or go on plotting a revolution with spies all about him—"

"Or spared a moment to be kind to a princess he does not want," said Inanni with a smile.

She meant the vase. Mara was suddenly very happy

about the vase. "Aye, he is kind, too. He is a great man!"
And you, she told herself a moment later, are becoming far
more interested in him than is good for you! Take care, or
you'll fall under his spell like Sheftu, and throw your life
and all your plans away.

She got up angrily, and padded over to the balustrade
again, where she stood watching the last glow over the hills
and curling her bare toes against the cool pavements of the
roof.

"I'm a fool all the same," she remarked as Inanni came up
beside her. "Will Thutmose ever notice or remember that I
served him? Ast! All pharaohs are alike."

"I know little of pharaohs," said Inanni. "But I have seen
the queen—and I have seen the king. And they are not
alike."

"Aye, but they are! Look yonder." Mara pointed westward, where Hatshepsut's graceful temple shimmered in the
blue shadows under the cliff. "Men died by hundreds in the
quarries to cut those stones for her, and others sailed to
the end of the world to bring back the little incense trees.
I know, I have been told of it. Yet tomorrow the king sends
Sheftu—Sheftu, his nearest friend—on a journey far more
terrible. . . ."

"Perhaps there is no one else he can trust."

"And perhaps Sheftu will never come back! More than
perhaps! Then what good is he to the king or anyone else?
Ai, there is a fool for you!—to do that for any pharaoh. I
told him so only last night."

"And what did he say?"

Mara's anger faded into puzzled wonder as she remembered what he had said. "He spoke nonsense. He said, 'I do
not do it for pharaoh, I do it for Egypt.' What does that
mean? Pharaoh is Egypt." She shrugged. "I didn't understand it then nor do I now."

"I understand it, Mara."

Mara looked at her curiously, and found that her whole

169

timid face was shining with eagerness, like a pale, round moon gleaming through the dark clouds of her hair. In the blue light of evening she looked almost beautiful in her shawls and draperies. "You understand?" repeated Mara slowly. "Then tell me. What did he mean?"

"Egypt is not pharaoh, Mara, nor is it this long, green valley with its black mud that is so different from what I know. Egypt is neither the Nile nor the cities—"

"Then what is it?"

"You, Mara."

"I?"

"And all the others—the people, all those you have told me of, and the fishermen yonder on the river, and the potters and carpenters and their like coming out of all those buildings far over there in what you call the City of the Dead—and their friends, and their kin. . . ." Inanni peered into Mara's face and shook her head sadly. "Alas, that means nothing to you, does it? In your life you have had neither friends nor kin."

"Nor have I needed them!" retorted Mara. Pity, like honey, could become too sweet on the tongue. She half turned away from Inanni, her elbows on the balustrade and her eyes—in spite of herself—on the stream of tiny white-clad figures winding through the streets far over yonder, who had suddenly become not mere figures but human beings, with friends and kin and homes to go to.

"Nay, perhaps you have not needed them," said Inanni gently. "But many others do. I will tell you a little story. When my father was a young man there came a great famine over Canaan, over all of Syria, and many flocks perished in the drought, and there were only a few who made harvest that year, and had grain in their storehouses. And my father, who had been king for only a little while then, but who was very wise, called in these men and showed them the poor, starving in the streets. And then he bade them bring their grain to his storehouses and their flocks to his pastures, and they did so, and until the famine passed, rich and poor shared alike from the common store, which my father divided among them. They did not do it for my father, Mara, but that Canaan might live."

"And did it live?"

"Aye. The enemy from the North swept down and conquered many nations that year, when all were weak from the famine. But in Canaan there were strong men to defend the cities."

The white-clad stream had all but disappeared in the blue dusk, and the sky was a vault of purple. Mara sighed and turned away from the balustrade with a shrug.

"It is a touching story, my princess—if they spoke truth. But what has it to do with Egypt? We have no famine, nor can I imagine any rich noble I have met who would share so much as a grain of corn with those tomb workers yonder. Consider my well-beloved master. *Hai!* I can see him dividing his goods with his grooms and servants . . ." Mara broke off, struck by a sudden unpleasant thought. Her last encounter with Lord Nahereh had directly followed an audience with the king. If the Libyan came tonight . . . "My princess, let us go down now," she said hurriedly. "It grows dark. And I, too, have a story to invent—one so convincing it will pass for truth! Come, let us go down, I must think—"

"Very well, Mara," said Inanni softly. "We will go down." She was silent as they hurried down the stairs and along the hall. But at the door to her apartments she stopped, putting a gentle hand on Mara's arm. "Mara, I hope all goes well with you."

"Do not fear for me, my princess. I'll think of something. Stay, I even have a talisman to protect me!" Smiling, she plunged her hand into her sash and triumphantly produced the ring, which she slipped onto her finger.

"It will bring good luck?"

"Provided I do not wear it in the wrong company," said

171

Mara drily. "And now I will tell you something, though I know not if it's wise to do so. . . ." She hesitated, then whispered rapidly, "The ring brought you luck today, as well as me. If all goes well—if all this we have talked of tonight comes to pass, and the king rules Egypt—then you need stay here and be homesick no longer, in this land you hate."

"They will—send me home?" whispered Inanni incredulously.

"I have Sheftu's promise on it. There, do not look so, or everyone will guess what I have told you! It is only an 'if,' you know. You must not hope too hard."

"Ah, Mara, I will try not, thank you, thank you—" Inanni tried to say more, failed, and hiding the radiance of her face beneath one of her many shawls, hurried through the door and into her chambers.

The Syrian women were still at their embroidering and chattering, but Inanni passed through their midst and went directly to her bedroom. I'm glad I told her, thought Mara. Very glad. . . . Wrenching her mind back to her own affairs, she headed for her room. What was she going to tell that crocodile of a Nahereh? She needed time to think. Perhaps, she reflected as she pushed aside the tapestry that curtained her door, I could accuse that spying little scribe of something or other. Say he was acting suspicious, friendly to the king. She grinned as she closed the door behind her and turned into the room. Pompous little donkey! He would not last long if—

Her thoughts broke off with a jolt. Chadzar the Libyan was leaning stolidly against the far wall, waiting for her.

For a moment she felt an overpowering desire to whirl around, dash back through the door and seek safety in that crowd of Syrians until the last one went to bed. A well-developed instinct for self-preservation prevented her. If she betrayed the least sign of panic . . .

She heard her own voice speaking coolly, almost indifferently. "You come very early."

"I come when I'm sent," grunted Chadzar. "Get a cloak."

"But I'm not ready yet. I came only to fetch the board for hounds and jackals. The Syrian expects me to entertain her until bedtime."

"That's none of my affair."

He pushed away from the wall and walked forward, while Mara cast about desperately for some other excuse to delay, to gain time. He scowled at her, switching his whip impatiently against his sandal. "Make haste! Fetch a cloak!"

There was small use arguing with that restless whip and the look in that one eye, which had begun to gleam balefully in the Libyan's pale-skinned, brutal face. Mara found her cloak and flung it about her with trembling fingers. She would have to do her planning on the way.

But there was no time to plan, no time to think. Before she could conquer her confusion she was in the chariot, sweeping through the streets of western Thebes. The ride was as wild as before, but this time Mara wished it had lasted longer. In vain she struggled to make her brain function as she stepped down into the dark courtyard beside her master's house, moved on reluctant feet through the little side door and into the hall. The same scent of wine and perfume drifted to her nostrils, the same faint echoes of merriment to her ears.

"Cease your dawdling!" growled Chadzar, giving her a prod with the whip handle. "Think you he wants to wait forever?"

An instant later she stepped into the small tapestry-hung study and the door closed behind her.

"Well?" came the chilly voice of her master.

Mara's hand closed convulsively over the ring. "Live forever, illustrious one!" she heard herself saying. "May thy shadow seek the light, may thy—"

"Save your pleasantries for those who wish them," he cut in acidly. "What news have you?"

"Honored one, I have the best of news! I was successful

173

in preventing the king from sending away his attendants. As I promised you, every one of them was present during the interview."

Nahereh said nothing, merely settled himself in a chair and waited. Mara hurried on.

"It was no small matter to convince my princess, I assure you. I coaxed and coaxed, and finally had to prod her a little. 'My princess,' I said to her—very severely, master—'My princess, His Highness himself believes it better to allow these menials to be present during the audience. Come, they might suspect you are afraid of them!' Of course she is afraid of them, master, but she does not like to admit it. And that won the game."

It had, indeed, won the game, though not quite in the way Mara implied. It was the king, not Inanni, who had caught the significance of that phrase "They might suspect" —he who had suddenly decided the attendants should stay in the room. Mara saw no reason, however, to mention these things to the granite-faced Son of Set in the chair before her.

Instead she smiled as if expecting his praise, and helped herself to a sweetmeat from his golden bowl. "And so you see, I shall have this trouble no more, and there'll be every chance to watch for that messenger—"

"You have not found him yet?"

"I cannot be sure," she evaded. "However, I kept a watch on the scribe, as you instructed me. He's of small use to you."

"How so?"

"The king knows him for an enemy. What chance have I to observe anything useful with His Highness guarding every syllable, every motion—"

"I thought you said you would have every chance!"

"With the scribe gone, yes. But while he is there—"

"Do I understand," said Nahereh ominously, "that you have come empty-handed again?"

174

She met his eyes and saw quite plainly that no evasion was going to work. Unless she produced some kind of information, and produced it at once, this man would sell her instantly—or do worse. Her mouth went dry with sudden fear. She had nothing to tell him—save the truth. And if she told him that . . .

A wild scheme darted into her mind. Could she tell him a scrap of truth—a mere scrap, convincing yet not really dangerous? If she could control it . . . Nay, it was too reckless, a mere gamble—

"Well?" said her master.

She heard her own quick laugh, her voice speaking. "Nay, I'm far from empty-handed, master."

The wildest gamble! She must not think of it, with the stakes so high. . . . But what of her own stakes in this game? In fifteen minutes she could be back in her rags, dodging some new master's stick, tossed into oblivion like a handful of rubbish. *Look after yourself, Mara, nobody else will.* . . . She threw the dice.

"I have something—but I know not what to make of it. Perhaps you know that His Highness amuses himself by designing vases? Well, dozens of sketches were spread on the table there, this morning. Big ones, little ones, all inscribed and decorated. And there was one of them—" She paused, feeling herself teeter on the brink of a precipice, tingling in every nerve. To cover her dizzy fright, she turned away idly, reaching into the bowl again as she did so.

"Pray have a sweetmeat!" invited Nahereh with heavy irony.

"Thank you!" She forced a mocking grin, and her nerves quieted. She sauntered to a chair and sank down on its arm. "It seemed to me that the inscription on this one vase looked less like decoration than a message—"

"A message!" He was on his feet and standing over her before she could draw breath, jerking her up to face him.

"By Amon, you'll cease this babbling now, and tell me what you mean!"

"I mean it was a message." She pulled free and sat down on the chair arm again. She felt quite cool now, and recklessly sure of herself. The tingling was gone. "It was the name of a tavern. I'll wager it's where the rebels meet."

Nahereh stared at her a moment. Then he whirled, fetched a writing block and reed pen from a box, and beckoned her curtly. "Copy it here."

She took the block, swiftly sketched a vase, and began to draw hieroglyphs in a border around its lip. She could hear Nahereh's heavy breathing as he leaned over her shoulder, then a low sound, ugly with triumph, deep in his throat.

He took the writing block, and he was smiling. "The Inn of the Falcon."

"Nay, you have read it wrong!" gasped Mara. In dismay she stared at the hieroglyphs she had drawn, and though they blurred and swam with her fright, she could still make out that the last one was no falcon. "You have read it wrong," she repeated, trying to steady her voice. "It is an owl, master."

"Aye, but you've set it down wrong, girl, that's the trouble. It was a natural error. No doubt you caught only a glimpse of the original, and it is easy to mistake the falcon symbol for the owl—"

"Nay, I saw it clearly! It was no glimpse, I took care to study it."

He laughed almost amiably. "Then they, too, set it down wrong, perhaps by intention. *Hai!* Small good it did them! They meant the Inn of the Falcon, you may rely upon it. I know the place."

"You know it?" said Mara faintly. The tingling was back— it had become a roar in her ears, as if she had stepped off the precipice and were falling sickeningly through space.

"We've snared them now," he was saying, half to himself. "So the pen is their messenger! Small wonder we've been puzzled. . . . You did well to notice this. Aye, and I did well to buy you! But I'm seldom wrong. I know a clever slave when I see one. Come, choose a sweetmeat."

"It seems hardly—credible—that a great lord like you would know aught of such an inn. I fancy it's a dirty den, jammed with waterfront riffraff—"

"Oh, I've never set foot in the place. But I know of it, aye, I know of it. Stay, I must think . . ."

Mara drew a deep breath and bit into her sweetmeat. He knew, it was too late to wonder how. There he stood rubbing his hands, thinking how he would use his knowledge. She had better help him think—and fast.

"You will set a spy to watch this place?" she began cautiously.

"Aye. It's their leader we want, not a rabble of underlings."

"It will be a hard choice, master."

"Hard?"

"To choose the spy you want."

"Nay, that's no problem. Stop chattering, girl, I must think."

Mara chose another sweetmeat and strolled a little closer. "The innkeeper's the problem. Have you thought of him? I know the breed, and I'll wager he misses little. Especially this one. Osiris! With a plot hatching on the premises? He'll let no stranger by him, that's certain, as long as this leader is anywhere about. He'd throw out that scribe of yours in no time. Even the Libyan. Master, no man could get past him."

Nahereh was listening now; his head had turned toward her. Mara licked her fingers and flashed a glance at him. "But I could," she added.

His chilly face did not change expression, but there was thoughtful calculation in the gaze that ran over her from head to toe. "Could you, indeed?" he said.

"Why don't you try me? I'm weary of the palace and the Canaanite. I can find the inn—I'm used to such places and

177

used to talking my way in and out of them. I promise I'm a match for any innkeeper."

"What of the palace sentries?"

"I've made friends with a few of them already—just to pass the time."

"You need a taste of the whip, Miss Insolence. Who said you might thus make free with my orders?"

"You never forbade me, master. What harm in smiling at a sentry? I think one of them would let me out for a visit to that inn."

Nahereh sank into a chair and drummed his thin fingers on the arm of it. "Nay, that's too chancy. Use my name. I've no doubt you know it by now."

"Aye, Lord Nahereh," said Mara demurely. "Your fame is far too great in Thebes to—"

He silenced her with a gesture. "Can you leave that princess of yours without her knowledge?"

"Easily."

He rose and strode to a chest in the corner, leaving Mara giddy with relief. "Come here," he ordered. He had unrolled a papyrus; as she approached she saw it was marked into squares and rectangles, like the rooms of a great house. "This is a plan of the palace," he told her. "Here is the guardroom, here is your own chamber, near this stair, here are the king's apartments. And here—" he jabbed a finger at a small square off one of the courtyards—"is a study reserved for my own use when I am at the Golden House. Do you think you could find it?"

Mara nodded. "Aye. Down this passage and to the right. It would be the third door?"

"The fourth. Now look you." He rolled up the papyrus and thrust it back into the chest. "Go tomorrow night to the Inn of the Falcon. Go every night. You have only to give the sentry my name. I will send for you in three days, but if you learn aught before that, I want no delay in hearing of it. Go to my study at once if you have news. If I am not there, you will find someone who will bring you to me."

"I hope," remarked Mara, "that this someone drives better than your Libyan."

"It will be the Libyan." He gave her an unpleasant smile. "What you had best hope, Impudent One, is that you can make good those boasts of yours."

"Did you not say yourself that I was clever?"

"Aye. Only take care you do not become too clever for your own good. Now go."

He jerked his head toward the door, and she went, trying to ignore his last remark. She was none too sure she had not already done that very thing. Still, she had won her gamble, she thought as she joined Chadzar in the hall. The margin had been slimmer than she cared to think about, but she had satisfied the stony-faced one, saved her own neck, and saved Sheftu's too by arranging her own appointment as the spy. Moreover, she no longer need worry about Reshed, who had grown increasingly unreasonable lately. She could now walk past any sentry on the grounds by mentioning Nahereh's name. She had planned well. The only thing she had not planned was that Nahereh should ever know the real name of the inn.

She followed Chadzar across a passageway. A servant flung open the door at its end and came hurrying toward them with a tray of empty plates. Attracted by the gust of music and laughter, Mara glanced into the room beyond him, caught a glimpse of blue-wigged ladies and courtiers grouped in a semicircle about a sumptuous table, with great platters of fruit, and a harpist playing—and just before the door swung shut, a figure darted into her range of vision, and there was a flash of golden balls.

She stopped so suddenly that the hurrying servant almost crashed into her. He clutched frantically at his tray, and the Libyan pulled her on down the hall, muttering in annoyance.

179

"Does your master always hire entertainers for his parties?" Mara asked him breathlessly.

"Would I know, Impudent? He doesn't invite me to them. Nor you either, I'll wager. Make haste. I've other things to do tonight than answer empty-headed questions."

Mara scarcely heard him. There were hundreds of jugglers in Thebes, of course. But if the one she had glimpsed was Sahure, then she was baffled no longer by her master's knowledge of the Inn of the Falcon. Sahure did hire himself out whenever a chance offered—"I have seen high and low, princesses and slaves. . . ." He was always boasting about it. Aye, it all fitted—into a pattern that had almost ruined her gambling! Perhaps the ring had saved her once again.

Thoughtfully she stepped into the chariot and braced herself for the bruising ride home. Sahure had not seen her, that was a smile from the gods. So long as Lord Nahereh did not decide to visit the inn himself, all was still safe. But she was glad Sheftu knew nothing of what had happened tonight. She hoped he would never know how fast and loose she had played with the fate of Egypt and his king.

CHAPTER 17

The Mark of Five

RA, THE SUN GOD, had once more sailed his golden
bark across the sky of Egypt. Over the high blue dome and
into the West he had moved, as from time immemorial—unhurried, serene, remote from the anxious scurryings of his
white-clad worshipers below. He left darkness in his wake
as he dropped behind the desert hills and began his night's
slow journey through the Land of the Dead. Now long hours
passed as he sailed the Dark River. At last he climbed into
the East again, heralded by a rosy glow, bringing a burst
of radiance as he crossed the horizon. Incense rose on the
morning air from a thousand altars; cries of thanksgiving
and entreaty came faintly to his ears, and the smoke of
burned offerings assailed his nostrils. He was indifferent.
Aloof, rigid in his perfection, wreathed in everlasting
flames, he sailed slowly to his zenith and down his unchanging path once more into the West.

It was half after the mark of four, and Lord Merab's party
for the governor of Kush was at its height. At each end of
the long reception hall stood tables loaded with refresh-
ments, draped with flowers. Slaves hurried in and out among
the beribboned columns, pouring wine, placing cones of
scented ointment on the heads of guests and replacing necklaces of lotuses with fresh ones. Two bands of musicians
played alternately; dancing girls whirled.

Lord Sheftu stood beside a garland-hung column near

181

the courtyard door, smiling serenely at the long-drawn hunting tale of His Excellency Pesiur, Master of Granaries, and wishing him and his ever-wagging tongue at the end of the earth. A fool at best, Pesiur was a cursed nuisance now, chattering away the precious moments. For Lord Sheftu to be seen at this reception had been important; for Sashai to escape, unnoticed, was becoming more vital every minute. A vision of the water-clock formed in Sheftu's mind, with its level rising nearer and nearer the mark of five, when he must meet Djedet and the others in the City of the Dead. . . .

"Well told, friend Pesiur, and bravely done! I can see your arm hurls a mighty spear. And now if you will excuse me—"

But no, Pesiur was off again, on desert lions this time, then veering to court gossip without a pause for breath. Sheftu gazed across the room, his head aching from the heavy fragrance of wine and perfume, and from his own exasperation. The laughter of women tinkled about him; they lifted jeweled hands to sip their wine or held lotus blossoms to one another's nostrils with gestures of stilted grace, and occasionally cast lingering glances at young Lord Sheftu. The men strolled idly, stopping to exchange flatteries, gathering in little groups to mutter with their heads together, laughing at the antics of the pet gazelle which gamboled in the middle of the room with Lord Merab's naked children.

And yonder, beyond the children, stood Count Kha-Kheper, his handsome leonine head bent in thought. Sheftu would have given his largest storehouse at that moment to know just what the count was thinking. Was he brooding about those vineyards the Architect had stolen from him? Or remembering the days of his youth, when he had been a commander of archers for the old pharaoh? Or reflecting on the plight of those same proud archers now, whose

shrunken ranks and poor equipment Sheftu had only a few
moments earlier been describing to him?

I must find out, thought Sheftu. It is dangerous to leave
it like this.

Yet outside the light was fading, the minutes stealing
away. Osiris! Would this chattering Pesiur never leave off?

". . . most attentive to the Canaanite princess, have you
not, Lord Sheftu?"

Sheftu snapped alert. "I beg your pardon?"

"Ah, now, the truth, man!" Pesiur's wig was slightly askew, his broad face flushed with delight at his own joke.
"Tell me, is it the princess' embroidery that attracts you?
Or could it be the blue eyes of that little interpreter who
goes with her everywhere?"

Fortunately for Sheftu, there was no need to answer. Pesiur was content with his own roar of laughter, and went
on talking immediately. "*Ai*, you're not the first one, I'll
wager, my friend—and it's certain you won't be the last.
She's a well-favored little maid. Where the devil did they
find her?"

"I believe," said Sheftu distantly, "she joined the princess'
suite at Abydos. Look yonder, my lord. They bring the
mummy."

A pair of slaves had appeared from the Hall of Pantries,
carrying between them the wooden image of a mummy,
rigid and deathlike in its painted wrappings. Other slaves,
bearing huge garlanded bowls of wine, followed the Dis-
players of the Rigid One. According to custom, the procession began a circuit of the room, chanting, "Gaze here, drink
and be merry; when you die, such will you be," amid loud
laughter and cries of thirst from the guests. Even Pesiur
surged after the wine carriers, cup aloft, and Sheftu seized
the moment. He walked swiftly around the other end of the
room, where Count Kha-Kheper was already moving toward him.

They met in a half-concealed alcove near one of the refreshment tables. The count was a large, shaggy-browed, handsome man of middle age, and he at once came gruffly to the point. "I have been thinking of what you told me, Lord Sheftu. Can you swear to its truth?"

"Sacred Maat herself would swear to it, Excellency. The troops were in sorry plight, half the archers bareheaded and none of them paid. And the regular Army is worse yet. Should our enemies choose to attack us some fine morning, Egypt would be defenseless."

"Monstrous!" muttered the other. "I knew naught of it. . . ."

"Her Radiance and Count Senmut keep these things a closely guarded secret."

"That scurvy Architect! Yet he is her favorite."

"I have reason to believe his situation is far from stable at the moment. I—took a hand—in this matter of the bodyguard."

"Good!" grunted the count. "If we could be rid of him—"

"Excellency, think further. Would her next favorite be any different?" Sheftu brought his lips close to the other's ear, dropped his voice to a mere breath. "Egypt must be rid of her, too."

Kha-Kheper's heavy brows drew hard together. In a voice equally low, he muttered, "You speak treason, my lord."

"Is it treason to oust thieves, to rid Egypt of enemies? I am not alone, Excellence. Behind me stands an army—nobles, priests, common folk as well as armed soldiers—waiting only my signal. Your future lies with us—not with Hatshepsut. And the time is near."

Kha-Kheper moistened his lips, flashed a look at Sheftu.

"Nobles?" he murmured.

"Aye, nobles in plenty. Those who love Egypt—and know which barrel holds the fish."

The count was silent; he seemed scarcely to breathe. After

184

a long pause, he murmured, "I am a wealthy man, Lord Sheftu."

"You could be wealthier."

Again Sheftu waited, knowing the crucial moment had come.

"How much?" said Kha-Kheper softly.

"By half again."

The heavy brows shot up, and Sheftu straightened, smiling to himself. Another great one had found his price. The count drew a long breath and met his eyes. "I, too, love Egypt. You have my full support against those who prey on her. When you need me, call—and may the gods smile on our cause."

Turning abruptly, he walked away across the room.

Sheftu's satisfaction was not unmixed with irony. It was surprisingly easy, he reflected, to promise a fortune one had not yet got one's hands on. Getting it was going to be a different matter, yet get it he must; he had made half a dozen such promises on the strength of his plans for tonight. And this one had made him late. . . .

A moment later he slipped out the courtyard door, unnoticed, and raced for his chariot.

It was well past the mark of five, and dusk was gathering over the City of the Dead. From the low, palm-thatched buildings workers were merging—stonecutters powdered with granite dust, embalmers bent with weariness and smelling of natron and spices, yawning glass makers, scroll copyists rubbing their eyes, gold artisans, weavers, potters, carpenters, jewelers. Singly and in groups they trickled out of the workshops to the streets, to form a homeward-bound stream which branched in every direction—east toward the Nile and its waiting ferries, north and south and west to scattered cottages among the fields.

In the lee of a deserted carpenter's shop one small group lingered, casting anxious glances now and then toward the distant palace and the clusters of trees and white walls which marked the villas surrounding it. Two of the men wore the garments of *neocori*, servants of the temple; the third was a burly priest, calm and imposing of mien, of obvious importance. Beside them stood a donkey laden with two huge baskets.

"It is a bad omen that he is late," muttered the smaller of the two *neocori*. "A bad omen."

"Think you he is late on purpose?" whispered the other indignantly. "I'll hear no ill spoken of Sashai."

"I spoke none, friend Kaemuas. Perhaps he failed to receive the message."

"Nay, he had it," the priest broke in.

Once more they fell to scanning the crowd in anxious silence. Suddenly a figure in the long robe of a lesser priest moved along the shadow of the next building, and in a moment was beside them, breathing heavily.

"I could not come sooner. Let us start at once. We have a long way to go."

Without further talk the four struck out westward through the crooked streets, past the mud dwellings and the fields and out across the broad stretch of desert that lay beyond. Their white garments turned pink with the sunset as they moved nearer and nearer the dark blue shadow of the western cliffs, and finally they were swallowed, one by one, by a defile in the face of the rock.

The stones of the steep, narrow path pressed sharp through Sheftu's palm-leaf sandals, and he sweated with nervousness under his priest's heavy wig and tentlike cloak. Ahead trod Djedet, his broad back solid and his head erect. Sheftu thanked the gods for that stoic figure; his own composure had been sorely tried by the venture's inauspicious start—his tardiness, the frantic rush to the meetingplace, and the disturbing memory of a certain remark of Pesiur's. He felt confused and harried. But he could rely on Djedet, and on the diggers too, he thought. Loyal Kaemuas, and

Usur the weaver—both good men. He cast an anxious glance over his shoulder at the donkey. Its great side baskets hung heavy, laden with stones under a top layer of innocent funerary offerings. It was well; they must hang heavy indeed now, if they were to appear almost empty when coming out.

When coming out. Would they really be coming out, a few hours hence, with their mission accomplished and the baskets loaded with inestimable treasure? It was too far ahead to think of. Best wonder whether they could even get in! Sharp-eyed guards waited up ahead, at the entrance. The Valley of the Tombs was the most jealously watched area of land in all Egypt.

Nay, do not wonder about any of it, Sheftu counseled himself. Keep cool, deal with each thing as it comes.

But as he pushed the large worries to the back of his mind, Pesiur's jibe about Mara came again to dance like a mocking *kheft* at the front of it. Was it so obvious, then, that Lord Sheftu was taking a peculiar interest in the Canaanite princess? It was too bad those few casual meetings had been noticed; worse, even dangerous, that Mara had been singled out as the real object of them. Worst of all, for Lord Sheftu's pride, was the fact that his own powerful but secret attraction to those lotus-blue eyes was apparently no secret at all, but plain enough for even a fool like Pesiur to notice and comment on. Was he as transparent as a schoolboy in the first stages of puppy love? It was humiliating. However, if the court gossips thought him merely smitten with a pretty maid, perhaps they would inquire no further into his motives . . . perhaps.

The path turned and twisted, winding upward through the cleft in the hills. At last the palm-thatched hut of the guard station showed ahead in the dusk.

Djedet turned to smile at Sheftu. His moon-face was pale and set, but his voice steady. "The delay did not matter. It is the right hour, my friend. We planned well."

187

"Aye." Sheftu returned the smile with stiff lips, then murmured to the diggers, "Speak no word, remember."

Gravely the little procession moved out onto the barren hilltop toward the hut. A guard appeared at the doorway, then stepped out, followed by another. But thanks to Djedet's careful planning, they carried no torches, for it was not yet full dark. Sheftu was profoundly grateful for the semigloom when the guards came forward to peer into their faces.

"You have permits to enter here?" one asked gruffly.

Djedet advanced a step, his bulk imposing, his carriage haughty. "My good man, I am Djedet, priest of the *sem* rank and second official of the Necropolis. I need no permit. Now harken. Have you seen or heard aught suspicious in the valley the past two days?"

"Suspicious? No, er—Excellence." The first guard's tone had become more respectful. But the second was staring at Djedet closely, and did not add the "Excellence." "You mean robbers?" he demanded.

"*I* will ask the questions," said Djedet coldly. "There has been a report that the tomb of His Majesty the First Thutmose has been disturbed. What do you know of it?"

"Nothing, Your Holiness!" gasped the first guard. "I swear by the Feather of Maat the Truthful One, there has been not a—"

"The report is false," grunted the other.

Djedet favored him with an icy stare. "I trust you are right. But naturally, I must find out for myself. Kindly stand aside."

He started forward, but the second guard stayed where he was, his gaze flicking to Sheftu, then to the two diggers, and finally to the laden donkey. "What have you in the baskets?" he demanded.

Sheftu could only thank the gods for Djedet's convincing air of mild exasperation. "Funerary offerings, of course," said the priest. "Would we come empty-handed to the great one's resting place?"

The guard's heavy face did not change expression as he moved out of Djedet's path and sauntered back to the donkey. With a tremendous effort Sheftu refrained from watching him, affecting an attitude of stolid indifference. But his very spine tingled as he heard the creak of a basket lid being raised. It might be merely a routine check. But if the guard had even the glimmer of a real suspicion, he would push aside the offerings and see those stones beneath. . . .

The lid of the basket dropped. Legs trembling with relief, Sheftu moved forward at Djedet's nod, only half hearing the first guard's apologies. They had filed past the hut and actually started down the path into the valley when, behind them, the second guard spoke again.

"Stay!"

Once more they halted, but this time Djedet's burly back was quivering perceptibly. Sheftu, by contrast, felt a wave of anger sweep aside all the confusion that had been hampering him. Suddenly cool and bold, he grasped Djedet's arm reassuringly under the concealing cloak, and faced the guard.

"You show little respect to His Holiness, fellow! What is it this time? And mind you address him properly."

"I mean no disrespect—Excellence," muttered the guard. "But I have my orders, and I'm to let no one pass without a permit. Since you have none, I will have to go with you."

There was an instant's appalled silence. Then Djedet found his voice, jerkily. "Your devotion to duty is commendable. However there is no need for you to leave your post. We—"

"My comrade can stay at the post," interrupted the guard stubbornly. "It's my duty to go with you."

Sheftu thought fast. Further argument would give them away completely; even the first guard was beginning to

189

look doubtful now. With a warning pressure on the priest's arm, Sheftu said carelessly, "As you wish."

He could feel Djedet go rigid, but an instant later the priest shrugged and started down the path again as if indifferent to the whole thing. The guard fell in beside him, somewhat sheepishly, to the accompaniment of his comrade's relieved jeer. "Ai, Suspicious One, it's a long tramp you'll have for nothing. Until tomorrow, then."

"Tomorrow?" remarked Sheftu as they wound downward through the rocks. "Will your friend not be waiting when we return?"

"Nay, our duty is over in half an hour," rumbled the guard, amiable enough now that he had got his way. "Other men watch through the night."

Sheftu allowed himself a moment's grim admiration of the fellow in front of him, plodding along half-embarrassed but still doggedly doing his duty. If there were more like him, the valley would be well guarded. Unfortunately, there would be one less before the night was done. . . .

The last glow of sunset was almost gone when the little procession reached the valley's floor and started out across it. Nuit, the Starry One, had stretched her dark and spangled body across the heavens, shedding a faint glitter over a vast, rugged wasteland of craggy buttes and sand and rocks, completely bare of vegetation. Eroded, sharp-peaked hills and giant boulders loomed here and there, strange-shaped like sleeping monsters, still breathing heat from their sun-baked sides into the cool night air. There was profound, unnatural stillness. Sheftu trod warily, his eyes fixed on the glimmer of the guard's cloak ahead, his ears straining for some sound other than the whisper of the donkey's hoofs on the sand. But in all that desolation no bird called, no small creature scampered—nothing stirred, nothing lived, except themselves.

In and out among the crags they moved, deeper and deeper into the valley's heart. At last Djedet turned aside into a gully which sloped downward between tumbled piles of rock. He was picking his way slowly, waiting, in an agony of suspense, Sheftu knew, for some signal as to the guard. They were very near their destination now.

Sheftu set his jaw, drawing both hands in through the slits in his cloak. When they emerged again they brought his long, stout-woven sash. Stealthily he closed the distance between himself and the guard; grasping an end of the sash in each hand, he crossed his wrists.

Now, whispered a voice inside him.

One swift movement and the sash fell about the guard's neck. Sheftu snapped it tight, at the same time jamming his knee into the small of the man's back. Next instant both had pitched forward to tumble over the rocky ground, Sheftu clinging to his writhing, threshing victim and still tightening the garrote. There was a scramble of footsteps, grunted curses as the diggers flung themselves upon the guard's flailing arms and legs. A moment later they had him pinioned, and Sheftu's muscles knotted for the last strangling jerk—knotted, but never released their energy. Slowly Sheftu relaxed, and as the diggers glanced up in astonishment, he flipped the sash free and used it instead as a gag. Knotting it securely, he stood up.

"You mean to spare him?" whispered Djedet.

In the starlight the priest's face showed pasty white and sweating. "Osiris! What will we do with him?"

"Nothing, for the present," muttered Sheftu. "Take his sash, you men, and tie him well." He turned his back and walked over to Djedet. He knew he had been a fool to let the fellow live. But he had no stomach for murdering a man whose only crime was stubbornness. It was possible this other plan might work. . . . "He'll be safe enough here, Djedet."

"But later, when we return to Thebes?" came the priest's frantic whisper.

"He will return with us. Nekonkh can spirit him away

downriver with the others, and keep him hidden until it's safe to free him."

"What are you saying, my lord? It's the guards at the valley entrance I'm thinking of—the new ones who come on duty with the night. We shall have to explain our baskets all over again, Amon help us! Can we also carry their comrade past them, bound and gagged?"

"He will not be bound. He will walk among us—but with my knife at his back. He will say only what I—"

There was a sharp cry behind them. Sheftu whirled just in time to see Kaemuas double up, groaning, the guard's tunic rip in Usur's clutching hands, and the guard himself dart up the path, free, and tearing at his gag. With a curse Sheftu sprang after him. The guard was stumbling on the treacherous rocks, staggering a little, but he had the gag off now. Sheftu wrenched his dagger from its sheath.

"Thieves! Thieves! Help in the valley! Thieves . . ."

The cry rang out hideously, echoing off the sides of the cleft. But the guard had not strength enough left to both run and shout. With the last "Thieves!" he staggered into a boulder, saw Sheftu close behind him, and drew his short sword. It clashed once against Sheftu's knife, was deflected by a desperate wrench, freed itself, swung up murderously —then fell clattering to the ground as Sheftu's dagger drove home.

"My friend, you die for Egypt," gasped Sheftu. He caught the crumpling body and eased it down beside the boulder. Usur was beside him, and an instant later, Djedet.

"Master, I could not help it," panted the digger. "I was trying to loose his sash, and he kicked Kaemuas as a mule kicks, as a horse kicks—"

"Be silent." Sheftu leaned against the boulder, struggling to catch his breath, straining his ears for any sign that the guard's cries had been heard. All was silent, except for the crunching of pebbles as Kaemuas plodded up the path toward them. Wearily Sheftu leaned over the guard and retrieved his dagger. "Carry him back and put him across the donkey. Get a torch burning, one of you men."

A few minutes later they were making their way by flickering torchlight down the gully, the donkey with its grim burden following behind along the rocky path. On either side, the barren rock rose higher into darkness, the way wound more steeply down. How much farther? Already the Nile and Thebes seemed leagues away. . . .

Sheftu nearly bumped into the priest, who had come to a sudden halt and was pointing. "*Ast!* we have arrived."

Slowly Sheftu extended the torch. There ahead against the side of the gully leaned a pile of red granite boulders— the same which had haunted him for four interminable days. With an effort he dragged his eyes away from it.

"There is the place," he told the diggers. "Beneath the rubble at the left is the door we seek. Dig until you find it."

CHAPTER 18

By the Dark River

IT WAS an hour before the clang of shovels ceased. Sheftu, sitting on a rock some yards away, was aware of eerie silence and raised his head. The torch flared wild and lonely against the night, revealing a gap in the rubble and a stone stairway leading downward into obscurity. At the top stood Djedet and the sweating diggers, their eyes upon him.

Slowly he rose and walked across the sands, taking the torch from the priest. At the bottom of the steps was a plastered-over door, imprinted with the Royal Seal of the Necropolis and the *cartouche* of the First Thutmose. A tremor passed through Sheftu at sight of the familiar hieroglyphs of the old king's name, enclosed in their oval line. He and the prince had stood on this spot long ago, on the day of the entombment, to see that seal pressed into the wet plaster.

His lips parted, but it was moments before he could force himself to speak. *Not even thy prince should demand such a crime. . . .*

"Open it," he said.

The diggers crept past him, down the steps. Under their chisels the plaster crumbled in an irregular crack, gradually outlining the door. At his elbow Djedet was whispering, "Anubis, strike us not! We have plaster to mend it, we bear the Royal Seal. All shall be as it was, when we have gone."

Sheftu found it hard to breathe. The portal which was to have remained closed and inviolate for three thousand years was swinging open before him, with a creak that woke echoes far back in the depths of the tomb. A breath of stale, dry air drifted out and enveloped him. Slowly, every step an act of will, he descended the stairs and passed through the door into the Habitation of the Dead.

He stood in a tiny entry where the stone floor was strewn with flowers. He remembered them—the last offerings of the funeral party returning to the upper world. They looked only a little withered, as if no more than a week had passed since they were dropped here. But when he touched one with his toe it fell into dust so fine there was no trace left. Shivering a little, he raised the torch. Pleading texts from the Book of the Dead leaped at him from the close-carven walls:

"I have not committed iniquity against men! I have not oppressed the poor! I have not starved any man, I have not

194

made any to weep, I have not committed that which is an abomination to the gods! I have not turned back the water in its season, I have not put out the fire in its time! Since I know the names of the gods who are with thee in the Hall of Double Truth, save thou me from them, Osiris! I am pure! I am pure! I am pure! I am pure!"

Before Sheftu, another flight of steps led downward into darkness.

With Djedet pressing at his side and the diggers with their baskets crowding at his heels, he started the long descent. Down, down, down they crept, into night so black the torch was but a moving spark, into silence so deep the ears rang with it. Staler and more oppressive grew the air— the same air left here years ago when the outer door was shut and sealed. Was there enough for four men breathing hard with fear? Sweat masked Sheftu's face only to evaporate instantly in the shriveling dryness of the place, drawing his skin and stiffening his lips. In vain he tried to keep his mind away from the thought of the millions of tons of rock and earth above them. The deeper they went, the more ponderous grew the weight, the more stifling his awareness of it.

The steps ended at last, in the depths of the earth. The men stopped a moment, hearing their own breathing loud in the silence. All were loath to leave the stair, which now seemed known and safe. Sheftu's thoughts flashed back to the guard, lying so still under the stars far above them—and to the guard's comrades at the valley entrance, who might be starting to search for him, wondering why he had not returned. . . .

A sense of urgency possessed Sheftu. They must hasten, or the alarm would be raised and they'd crawl out at last into a trap.

Fighting his reluctance, he led the way out across a stony floor. One pace, then another, then a third, with the light flickering into the black void. Suddenly a vivid figure twice

the height of a man sprang out of the gloom. The trespass-
ers recoiled as at a blow, and a sound that was half grunt,
half moan, broke from the digger Usur. It was some seconds
before Sheftu could bring himself to raise the torch and
discover that the terrifying figure was one of a procession
painted along the walls of what appeared to be a lofty and
spacious corridor.

Sheftu forced himself to steadiness, to memory of this
corridor from the day of the old king's entombment. Then,
gripping the torch, he started down the long hall. More and
more brilliantly painted figures slid past them in the waver-
ing light—a group of women bent in mourning, with di-
sheveled hair; slaves bearing treasure boxes and furniture,
dignitaries pacing behind a canopied sledge on which rested
a great sarcophagus. It was the old pharaoh's funeral procession, depicted faithfully in every detail, climaxed at the
far end of the hall by the last solemn ritual of the Opening
of the Mouth. There, framing the door, rose the painted
figure of a *sem* priest with his mystic tool, while opposite
him the jackal-headed god Anubis supported the mummy.

Djedet began to chant, in a low, unsteady monotone. "In
peace, in peace, unto the Great God. . . . Proceed in
peace, in peace, unto thy tomb in the Necropolis, in peace,
in peace, unto the Land of the West and thy dwelling on
the Dark Nile. . . ." His voice sounded thin and strange in
the heavy stillness.

The torch and its huddled bearers moved between the
towering figures and under the lintel of the door. Before
them lay more stairs, leading down—always downward
and inward, into darker mystery, thicker silence.

"In peace, in peace. . . ."

The priest's voice was a thread of sound, now muffled
against the narrow sides of the stair, now hollow and unreal
across a passage, rippling as the torchlight rippled along the
carven walls. It was as if he could not stop, though the
monotony of it beat like little hammers upon Sheftu's brain.

He himself was concentrating fiercely, racking his memory at every point where the passage branched. The branchings seemed numberless, and only one was right; the others would lead to pitfalls or blind alleys, traps of confusion set by the old king's architects for just such intruders as they. Each time Sheftu forced himself to pause, choose painstakingly, before leading on. He tried to quicken his pace, nagged by the thought of the guard, but the craving to turn back dragged at his feet in spite of him.

"In peace, in peace, unto the Land of the West . . ."

They had come to a doorway. Across its threshold lay the first storeroom—a large chamber crowded beyond the reach of the smoky light with the possessions of the dead. Here were chariots, dismantled and stacked along one wall; there, a great golden couch, an ebony throne; everywhere, carven chairs and tables, stools, headrests, chests and boxes of clothing, all moveless but somehow waiting. The torch flickered in the still, dead air, but when Sheftu slowly extended it the walls came alive with rows of painted servants—copper skinned, white clad, bearing trays of fruit and meat, jars of wine, platters of bread.

Sheftu stared up at them. It was here the House of the King began in earnest; and these were his servants. Sheftu knew well they were no longer the mere painted outlines they had been on that day long ago when he had walked here grieving beside the prince, when the air was still heavy with the funerary myrrh and flowers, the priests still droning. The moment the wine of the last libation had dried upon the floor, and the silent dark closed in, these figures had been transformed, transmuted, quickened with that mysterious other life which called their *kas* out of the paint and plaster to be the wraithlike servants of the dead king. Sheftu shivered. What right had he, the living, to look upon them now?

"Allow us to pass, O *Ka* of the pharaoh," he whispered. "We leave undisturbed your furniture and linen, we leave

197

your slaves to serve you, your chariots to carry you through the Shining Streets."

Djedet's mumbling grew more urgent. "In peace, in peace, unto the Great God. . . . Proceed in peace, unto they tomb in the Necropolis, in peace, in peace . . ."

Through that chamber, and the next, and the next, they moved, while awareness of the dead king grew always stronger as the torchlight shone over more and more of his possessions. His presence was everywhere about them now —in the jars of honey and unguents sealed with his *cartouche*, in the shelves bearing his favorite joints of meat, in the sandals he had worn, the spear he had flung, the tiny boxes that held his eye paint. Every step led them nearer to him. On the walls were his fowlers and herdsmen, his fishermen dragging in their brimming nets, men threshing his grain or pressing out his wine or fashioning his golden collars—all workers laboring ceaselessly for the royal *ka*, all shocked motionless by the desecrating glare of the torch and the footsteps of living men.

Sheftu's lips were parched, his nerves taut as bowstrings. Was the thin air growing harder to breathe or were the angry hands of *khefts* squeezing at his lungs? An eternity must have passed since they left the starry night far, far above.

Djedet touched his arm suddenly. Ahead lay a door—the final door, for golden statues of the goddess Isis guarded it on either side. They shone fiercely yellow in the torchlight as the intruders drew nearer, they blinded the eye with their hot glitter, but they did not strike. Sheftu heard the harsh breathing of Usur, behind him, as they passed under the upraised staffs and across the threshold of the last and holiest chamber—the heart of the tomb.

There they stopped. Even Djedet's chanting ceased at last; profound and utter silence closed over them as they stood amid a still magnificence. The room was filled with treasure. Everywhere coffers, chests, carven boxes spilled it out upon the floor—jewels and satin ebony, ivory, pale electrum, tall alabaster vases hollowed to fragile translucence, but above all gold—yellow gold that winked and gleamed and glinted from every corner of the chamber.

At first Sheftu could see nothing else. Half-dazzled, he dragged his eyes from the glitter. Before him a path had been swept clean through the rich profusion. At its end two life-sized statues of maidens stood, one foot advanced. Their dresses shimmered with silver and carnelian, and they held baskets of foodstuffs in their golden arms. These were the gentle *ushabti,* closest guardians of the king. They were radiant in the light, with their shining brows and their ageless eyes of lapis lazuli. Between them loomed the huge sarcophagus, veiled by a linen pall so sheer the pink granite showed through its folds. On the wall behind it the Great God Osiris himself welcomed the king's soul to paradise, while on the other walls a host of deities in mystic headdresses were lined in overpowering grandeur.

Sheftu sank to his knees, no longer able to withstand his awe. He felt all sense of time and memory fade away, all objects blur except the tranquil faces of the *ushabti* and the sarcophagus they guarded. Here was the ultimate moment, perhaps his last; for he was in the presence of the dead.

A strange rustling sounded in his ears. Was it the *khefts'* dark wings, or the thundering of his own heart? Nay, it was neither. . . .

Sheftu's mind sprang awake, full of the stealthy shuffle of palm-leaf sandals. Usur, the digger, was creeping past him, his profile rigid, his gaze fixed unswerving on the golden statues. He held a rock in his upraised hand. In a flash Sheftu knew his purpose. He meant to smash the eyes of the *ushabti,* so they could not watch what was to come.

Sheftu leaped for him, struggling to wrest the weapon from his hand. The man made no sound, but his strength was terrible. In utter silence the two strained together, while the light flickered and danced crazily upon the walls.

199

Hampered by the torch, Sheftu was already sinking to his knees in the moment it took for Kaemuas and the priest to overpower Usur and pin him fast. Sheftu staggered to his feet and seized the rock, holding it poised over his sweating victim's forehead in a fist that trembled with longing to smash it down.

"Stay thy hand, my lord," came Djedet's low voice. "Not every man can bear his fear."

Slowly Sheftu's arm came down, his fury faded. It was true. He could not have borne his own tonight save for the purpose which so consumed him that he could give heed to nothing else. He shook his head, trying to steady his thoughts. This Usur was a sound enough fellow in the world of daylight, a weaver, well respected and as courageous as the next one. But what man was prepared to defy the very gods? It was not this man, who broke, that was surprising, it was his companion who still held staunch. . . . In wonder, Sheftu turned to Kaemuas, and saw the answer written on his broad and humble face. It was Sashai whom Kaemuas followed, with blind devotion, though he led straight into the Land of Darkness.

Sheftu put a hand on the massive shoulder, then turned to Usur. "Do not touch the *ushabti*. You must not blind the guardians of pharaoh and leave him defenseless against his enemies. We come here not to rob, but to rescue Egypt, do you understand? The gods have not struck us yet, and perhaps they will not."

He motioned Djedet to loose the man, suddenly feeling so weary he could scarcely stand. Much still lay ahead— there was the treasure to sort, their funerary offerings to set out in place of the gold they took, the baskets to fill and carry through all the rooms and along the stairs and passages back to the upper world, then the outer door to plaster over and mark with the Royal Seal. . . . *Ai!* And what of the guard? Before they sealed the door they would have to carry him down into the first little flower-strewn chamber. The ways of the gods were strange; this common guard, distinguished by naught save stubbornness, had exchanged his life for Egypt's and would sleep forever on the doorstep of royalty.

Unless, of course, he had been missed by his comrades. . . .

The thought prodded Sheftu's tired mind once more. "Make haste," he muttered. "Pick out the heaviest gold."

He never knew how long they labored there below the towering images of the gods, weighing the treasure in their palms, packing the massive cups and crowns and chains and collars in the bottom of the baskets, the jewels and necklaces on top. For Sheftu their work took on the unreality of a fevered dream, in which only the cold weight of gold and the sound of labored breathing went on, unchanging.

He was near exhaustion. The struggle with Usur had nearly drained his strength, already taxed by days of strain and a night of unbearable tensions. His anxieties swirled about him—the guard, the passing of time, the uncertainty of getting out of the valley, and above all the deep hatred of what he was doing. Every move he made, every cup and goblet he plucked from its place, did violence to a lifetime of stern teaching. But it is not for ourselves, it is for the king, he told himself. Better we die than Egypt. . . .

Mother of Truth, how hard it was to breathe! Sheftu dragged himself erect, a gold chain dripping from his hand, and frowned toward the stone urn into which he had thrust the torch. The flame burned murky and uneven—was it nearly used up, or had their hungry lungs consumed the air it, too, required to live?

"Kaemuas! Light a fresh torch!" ordered Sheftu.

The big man straightened, stared blankly at the torch, then paled. "Master," he whispered. "We did not bring another."

The room grew painfully still. Every mind was filling with

a new fear, so fundamental that it swallowed all the rest—the fear of the dark. Here below the earth darkness was total, absolute, unnatural. They remembered too well how it had followed and surrounded them through the whole descent, a formless monster held at bay only by their tiny flame. They remembered the black labyrinth awaiting them now, the windings, the echoing halls and stairways, the lonely passages that led nowhere, through which they must journey back.

There was a low moan from Usur. The wildness was coming over him again, and Sheftu lashed his tired will to combat it.

"No matter." His voice sounded strange. He fought to steady it, though his tongue felt thick and numb. "This one will do. But there is little air left here. Hurry."

To his relief the need for haste submerged Usur's panic. They fell upon the gold with redoubled effort. But Sheftu's eyes slid back to the torch. Perhaps it was only air it lacked —perhaps it would burn bright again when they left this chamber where they had worked—and breathed—too long. The baskets were nearly full now. The room, stripped of its glitter, looked stark and somber.

"You must take what is his, even to the royal cobra and the collar of amulets. . . ."

Sheftu's head throbbed; he turned slowly to the sarcophagus, running his tongue over his lips without changing their dryness. Be ruthless, it must be done, he told himself. He beckoned Djedet with a faint jerk of his head; together they hurried down the clean-swept path, past the *ushabti*, to the spreading edge of the pall. Sheftu lifted it grimly, afraid to pause an instant. Avoiding each other's eyes, the two men seized the heavy lid and struggled to turn it diagonally on its base. It would not budge.

"Usur! Kaemuas!" Djedet panted.

The diggers came, laid hold. Nothing mattered now but haste, the dying torch, the dark. Under the straining of

202

eight strong arms the thick slab grated, inched outward with a horrid grinding of stone on stone, and turned at last to lay open a triangular area at its head. The torch was guttering lower and lower; Sheftu did not look upon the dead king's face but plunged his arms blindly into the dark cavity of the coffin. They came out laden with solid gold amulets worth a prince's ransom. He forced himself to grope once more, to find the heavy circlet with its golden cobra that bound the forehead. He drew it forth, shining, cold. . . .

"Now!" he whispered.

Once more the shoulders strained, in frantic haste. The torch sputtered feebly, winked—the lid grated into place. Sheftu flung the pall across it, sprang with the others for the baskets and the torch. They fled, their starved lungs dragging at the air.

Through the doorway, beneath the upraised golden staffs of the twin Isis statues, in and out among the furniture and piles of weapons that littered the floor—on into the next chamber past the painted fishermen, the threshers, the endless shelves of goods, down a passage and up three stairs, and on—

"Nay, wait!" Sheftu halted, panting. He thrust out the torch, staring at the walls ahead of him, the stairs behind. The light shone dully across the opening of a second passage. "This way!"

He swerved into it, all his flesh crawling. It would have been so easy to miss it altogether! He must go more slowly, be sure that every turn was right. But if he lagged, what of the torch? He looked up at it anxiously. The air seemed better now, but still the flame sank. It was not the lack of air, then, the torch itself was all but gone.

Faster, faster, but take care . . .

One of the diggers stumbled on a threshold and his heavy basket lurched sideways, spilling a stream of gold. With a curse Sheftu was on his knees, scooping up chains and amulets, a fragile bracelet, a necklace ornamented with golden bees.

"Leave it!" gasped Djedet, himself snatching up a handful or two and stuffing them into the basket. "Leave the rest! Go on!"

Sheftu groped once more, swept a fortune into a fold of his cloak and left another where it lay as he staggered to his feet. They fled on, past the pile of dismantled chariots and the great couches, away from the mysterious painted presences of the servants on the walls, through a corridor, around a murky bend. . . . The gloom swept closer suddenly, loomed like a monster over them. Sheftu stopped, unable to see the passage at his feet. All eyes went to the torch, just as the last flame sickened and dropped to nothing. A red coal glowed on for a moment, deepened to crimson as the swirling dark closed in, then died.

Blackness engulfed them.

CHAPTER 19

Fatal Mistake

THE BIG Common Room of the Inn of the Falcon blazed with light and resounded to the usual clatter of crockery and conversation. Though it was well past midnight, Ashor was still waddling here and there with platters of stew and mugs of Kede beer, and the juggler's balls wove a glittering pattern in the air before one of the larger and more boisterous cubicles.

Mara sat alone in the booth at the far corner, slowly twisting the ring which winked up at her mockingly from one finger. A cup of wine stood untouched on the low table before her; it was stale, and flecks of dust had gathered on its surface. She had been waiting for Sheftu since the mark of seven—five weary hours.

The torch flames dipped in a gust of air and she started up quickly, glancing toward the entryway door. But it was only Nekonkh who appeared there, for the third time in as many hours. She sank back upon her mat as he lumbered across the floor toward her.

"Seen naught of him yet, I suppose?" he grunted, sagging in the entrance to her booth. She shook her head, and he ran a hand wearily over his stubbly jaw and up under his wig. "By Amon, I'm about at the end of my hawser. He should have been back by—"

"Nekonkh, he'll not come back! Something's happened. I doubt we ever know what, but something's gone wrong."

"You mean to give up, do you?"

"I'll wait a bit longer, but it's folly. You know that."

Nekonkh slapped his wig back into place and scowled down at her. "Perhaps I do, but he bade me stand by to sail sometime tonight, and the night's not done yet. I'll wager he's not either. I've yet to see the snare Sashai can't wriggle out of, one way or another—"

"Nekonkh, do you know where he is this time?"

The captain shook his head uneasily. "Nay, he doesn't tell me everything, maid. I presume it's dangerous."

"Aye. It's dangerous. He was ten thousand kinds of a fool to attempt such a thing, that's how dangerous it is!"

"Aye, well, now don't look so, little one. It may be all will come right yet. . . ." Patting her shoulder abstractedly, Nekonkh glanced toward the door. "I'd best be starting back. If he should come, with me not there to take charge of that cargo . . ."

He hurried away, his big shoulders drooping. The torch flames dipped once again as he went out.

Mara sat on, with her legs cramped and numbing under her, swirling the dusty wine in her cup. Finally she, too, rose, groped for her discarded sandals and slipped them on. Then she flung her cloak about her and wandered slowly across the room. As she passed the fire pan, Miphtahyah's thin, strong fingers reached out to clutch her arm.

"Where is he?" whispered the old woman fiercely. "You know, don't you? Why is he so late?"

"Mistress, I can't tell all I know. But only he knows what's keeping him."

"You could give me some notion, if you would! One word as to when he'll be here—"

"I've told you I know not!" Mara jerked free. "It may be he'll never be here! It may be—"

Something in Miphtahyah's face cut her short—a curious puckering. She realized suddenly that the old woman's eyes were glassy with tears. Mara bit her lip, and moving closer, touched the tense shoulder. "Mistress, my heart is with yours. I'd comfort you if I could."

The unexpected sympathy was almost too much for Miphtahyah; she pressed a skinny hand to her lips, half turning away. For a moment painful to both of them, she struggled visibly to gain control of herself. Then her hand slid from her mouth down to her strange shell necklace, and her face settled stiffly into its usual network of wrinkles. "We will not give up, Blue-Eyed One. He will—come."

"Aye, he will come." The lie tasted bitter on Mara's tongue. Turning abruptly, she went on across the room.

The courtyard was still empty of everything but moonlight, and even that seemed dim and spiritless. Mara stood on the doorstep a moment, with the torch sputtering behind her, then turned back into the inn. She would order a plate of stew, and if he had not come by the time she had eaten it . . .

Fool! she told herself angrily as she settled down again in her cubicle. Why do you keep hoping? He's lost. You'll never even know what happened.

She could not eat the food Ashor brought any more than she could answer the anxious, unspoken question in his face. She sat toying with the big chunks of meat. It mattered little, now, what she told her master. She would tell him everything. Without Sheftu, the king was ruined, no one else could possibly . . . Oh, mother of truth, why had she ever met him? For a moment she longed to turn time back, undo everything, even go back to the fluting irons and Teta's familiar scolding.

She flung the spoon down, then stiffened, as a shadow fell across her. The juggler, Sahure, was leaning in the entrance to the cubicle, smiling his twisted smile. Three gilded balls circled furtively above his hand.

"Live forever, Face of the Lily," he greeted her. "Thou'rt long alone tonight. Where is our friend Sashai?"

"I know not. Begone!" Mara picked up her spoon and started eating.

"Strange," purred Sahure. "Often he comes here when you do not, but never before have I seen you, save at his side."

Mara glared at him, but preserved a stubborn silence.

"The maid of mystery," the juggler went on dreamily. "Invisible to poor mortals save in the hours of darkness, in this one spot. Where do you hide in the daytime, Eye of the Turquoise, that my heart is never gladdened by your countenance, whether in the market place or the villas of the Great Ones?"

"That is none of your affair!" Mara pushed her plate away, seething. "You take my appetite, juggler! Be off with you!"

He only smiled. With an air of pleasant leisure, he shifted

his crooked body, and the balls danced lightly to the other hand.

"Aye, aye, one must be discreet. And you are the very flower of discretion, are you not, Lovely One? Not a word have you said about your troubles tonight, though it's obvious they weigh heavy on you." Suddenly he bent close to her, his breath in her ear. "Where is he? He is late. You may trust me, I'm in his confidence, like you—"

Pushing him away, Mara scrambled to her feet, swatting his golden balls in every direction and spitting a stream of invective which included several Babylonian phrases Inanni could never have heard of. "Get thee gone, I said, you son of forty devils! I'll not listen to your cursed babble! Be off! Be gone!"

She broke off, breathless, aware that every head in the inn had whirled toward her. There was a pause; then Sahure picked up his gilded balls, and with a faint shrug, drifted away across the room.

Mara drew a long breath and eased down upon the mat. Trust that *kheft*-man? As well trust the red-haired Set himself! "It's only curiosity," Sheftu had said. "He's loyal." Aye, perhaps! And perhaps his loyalty was not as freely for sale as onions in the market place, but she doubted it!

Still trembling a little, she watched him coolly begin his juggling again in another corner. Why, she reflected, should I not admire this rogue, instead of hating him? He seeks only to know which barrel holds the fish, and have I not always lived thus? Nevertheless, I do hate him, and what's more, I'm afraid of him. . . . *Ai*, forget him, she told herself wearily. Forget all of it.

Nothing was to be gained by sitting here longer. She reached for her cloak and rose, moved for the last time through the din of tambourine and conversation and the thick smell of meat, into the chill fresh wind of night.

But this time the courtyard was not empty. Even as she left the torch behind and started across the dark pavements, she heard the click of the gate, and saw the tall, cloaked figure just inside it.

She stood one moment in startled disbelief. Then with a cry she darted toward him, stumbling on the uneven ground, reaching out to make sure . . . "Sheftu?" He was no wraith. He had come, he was here. She felt a relief so intense it made her almost dizzy. "Mother of truth, what kept you, what *kept* you? I thought you were dead!"

"So did I, little one," he whispered.

He was leaning against the wall as if too weary to stand. She put out her hand to touch him, but hesitated, awe-struck by where he had been and what he had done since she saw him last.

"Sheftu, are you—well?"

"Aye, I'm well enough."

"But something went amiss?"

"Everything! Mara—our torch burned out."

"Burned out? Before you—"

"As we were leaving the inner chambers."

Mara felt goose flesh crawl up her arms as the full meaning of that came home to her. "Osiris!" she whispered. She drew her cloak about her, shivering.

"We tried every passage—some of them twice, three times. Amon! It seemed years. We ended by stumbling on the right one. Sheer chance."

It was a moment before she could make her mind go on to anything else. Then she lifted her head quickly. "But you were successful? You brought the gold?"

"All we could carry."

"Then it's done! It's finished and over."

"Aye. It's finished."

Mara drew a long, shaky breath. "And you're back safe. Do you swear all's well with you? Sheftu, come where I can see you. It's so dark."

"Dark? This courtyard dark? Merciful Amon! You know nothing of the dark."

"Nay, perhaps I don't. But I can't see you."

He was quiet a moment. Then he spoke in a different tone, very softly. "I can see you. As clear as in the sun." He lifted one hand and touched her cheek, the lotus in her hair. Suddenly he pushed away from the wall and gathered her in his arms. "I believed I would never see you again," he whispered. "For five hours I believed that. Ah, Mara, what a difference five hours can make in the way a man thinks!"

He's going to kiss me, she thought, he can't help it, he must, he must! "Sheftu," she breathed. "It would have been hard, then, never to see me again?"

He twined his fingers in her thick hair and, pulling her head back, looked down into her face. Then, murmuring something under his breath, he set his mouth against hers, hard.

Triumph swept over Mara, giving way immediately to something so much stronger and deeper that every other reality dropped away. She found herself clinging to him fiercely, caught up in an emotion more compelling than any she had known. For once she did not plan or scheme or use her wits, since it was quite impossible. She did not even think.

It was a long time before he released her reluctantly and pulled her head onto his shoulder. The minutes went by, and Mara drifted back slowly to the ordinary Egyptian night, the courtyard—and cold reality. She was a little frightened. What was it that had happened, in the space of one kiss? This was not something she could play with as she chose. Nay, it was quite the opposite. . . .

His arms still held her. She became aware of them as a separate sensation, like the rough linen of his headcloth against her cheek, like the pebble pressing through the sole of her sandal. She stirred, and at once his arms tightened.

"Let me go, Sheftu, this is—"

"I'll never let you go. Never." He turned his head against

hers, brushing his lips over her hair, her ear, across her cheek. "I love you, Mara."

"Oh, Amon, I would that were true!" she whispered.

"It is true."

For a moment of pure happiness she closed her eyes and let herself believe it. Surely he meant it. . . . Aye, he meant it—tonight. He had kissed her, he needed her—tonight. But tomorrow? She knew quite well how these things turned out. She opened her eyes. "Impossible," she said bluntly. "You're a great noble. A lord of Egypt."

"None of that matters. Not after five hours in the dark." He pushed her away enough to look at her, but kept tight hold of her arms. "I'm not speaking lightly, do you understand?"

"By tomorrow morning you'll forget you spoke at all."

His voice roughened. "I'll not forget! I know what I want. Lotus-Eyed One, I'm weary of dueling with you. You'll share my life, as long as it lasts—and such as it is. Is that clear enough?"

"Quite—clear. But you must be mad. Tomorrow—"

He seized her chin between thumb and fingers and twisted her face up to him. "Be quiet," he whispered. He kissed her, at first gently, then again, not at all gently, and she gave herself up to it.

Never mind tomorrow, she thought. Never mind anything. . . . She was building dreams like palaces.

Sheftu loosed her abruptly and dropped both arms to his sides, moving away a step. "Little one, this must stop." He drew a deep, irregular breath. "I still must show myself inside there, lest they begin to mourn me as dead, and you must get back to your boatman."

"Aye," said Mara shakily. The dreams were still there, turret on airy turret. "I hope he waited for me. Did you see Nekonkh?"

"Before I came here. He's already off down the river with

211

his passengers. As to the rest of it—" Sheftu moved closer, lowering his voice. "You must seek audience with the prince tomorrow."

"Aye, Sheftu."

"Tell him all's well. The door's plastered over and sealed as we found it, and the stones rolled back into place. The tomb has a second occupant now, but . . ."

"It has—what?"

He met her eyes in silence, and she shivered. "No matter," he said quietly. "Mention none of that—naught about the torch or any problems. It's done and finished. I want only to forget it. Tell him the gold's hidden—safe at hand to pay our promises when the time comes. Aye, and tell him Count Kha-Kheper is one of us, I talked to him . . . Osiris! It was only this afternoon. It seems a year ago."

"*Ai*, Sheftu, how tired you must be!" She reached out impulsively. "You'll seek your couch soon?"

"Never fear!" He smiled, folding his hand over hers and pressing it tight, then tighter. "Mara," he whispered.

Suddenly his face changed. He opened his hand and looked down at her finger. Too late, she was aware of the hard shape of the ring as if it were a circlet of fire burning into her flesh.

She could no more prevent her involuntary attempt to jerk away than she could break the iron grasp which suddenly held her. She stood paralyzed, as he slowly raised his eyes to hers. It was the dangerous Sheftu of old who stood there now.

"I am touched," he said softly, "that you should treasure this little keepsake for so long."

"You're angry," she breathed. "Oh, Sheftu, I should have told you long ago. The old man in Abydos would take naught for helping me. But I was afraid if I told you, you would make me give it back. . . ." Thanks be to the gods, her voice was reasonably steady, for all she was giddy with fear. "It was stupid of me, perhaps wicked. Here, take it, Sheftu—"

"Nay, please!" He was silent a moment, then gently loosed her hand. "Keep it as a token of my—esteem."

Mara tried to smile. Why did he stand there so still, just looking at her? He was thinking. Thinking what? She could never tell anything from that impenetrable face.

"I will, if you're certain you wish it. . . . It has brought me luck all day. I think it bears a powerful charm. I wore it tonight to bring you back safe, and it may be that—"

"That I owe my life to it?" he finished smoothly. "Aye, perhaps you're right, little one. Perhaps I do." He straightened, deliberately relaxed, and smiled—warmly, intimately, as only he could smile. "I must leave you, Lotus-Eyed One, though tonight I confess I am especially loath to. Be here tomorrow, as soon after nightfall as you are able. It cannot be too soon, for me."

How much of that was irony? He gave her no chance to find out, for he turned quickly, strode across the courtyard and through the inn door.

Mara stood motionless where he had left her. The moon inched imperceptibly higher in the night sky, and a little breeze sprang up to stir a fold of her sleeve. She shivered. Suddenly she tore the ring from her finger and hurled it with all her strength across the courtyard. Whirling, she started blindly for the gate, then slowed, then stopped. After a moment she turned back, searched carefully for the ring, and found it at last. A guttersnipe did not fling away a fortune, even to satisfy the wildest disappointment. Such gestures were for the rich and secure, whose airy palaces were real.

Tucking the ring into her sash, she hurried out of the courtyard and along the dark and evil streets to the river.

I am secure, she told herself. He believed me. Surely all is well. Could he have smiled like that if it were not?

Aye, he could, and she knew it.

Part VI—The Trap

CHAPTER 20

The Bait

THE LITTLE FLAME still burning in Sheftu's bedside lamp flickered orange and transparent in the flood of morning sunlight. Old Irenamon, letting himself into the room at the usual hour with his master's breakfast, halted in astonishment at the sight of it. Setting down the salver of fruit and soft cheese, he hurried around the end of the tall couch where his lordship still lay, and picked up the snuffer which stood on the table beside the lamp. But to his further astonishment, Lord Sheftu sat bolt upright, seized his wrist and snarled, "Leave it! Let be!"

"But your lordship!" protested Irenamon in bewilderment. "I meant only to snuff the lamp here."

Sheftu loosed the old man's wrist and rubbed a hand over his eyes. Daylight fell strong and clear over the tumbled, twisted coverlets and linen sheets. The night was over. "Of course," he said more quietly. "Put it out, Irenamon. I fear I was not quite awake."

"Aye, that's it, still dreaming." Irenamon extinguished the flame and hobbled back around the couch to set out the fruit for the Perfuming of the Mouth. "However, I wonder you slept at all, with a lamp shining in your eyes. I cannot think what careless slave would have—"

"I lighted the lamp, Irenamon," said Sheftu, climbing out of bed.

"You . . . this morning?"

"Nay, during the night sometime. I know not when."

Sheftu belted his dressing gown, and ignoring the old man's troubled eyes, strolled over to the table on which his fruit awaited him. He intended to make no explanation, now or ever, of the lamp Irenamon was going to find burning at his master's bedside every morning from now until the end of his life. There were many nights in a lifetime; it had taken Sheftu only one of them to discover that the gods of the tomb had exacted their tribute after all. He would never again be able to endure a darkened room.

Absently he took his place at the table while the old man served him with fruit and cheese, and set his silver-rimmed goblet in front of him. Sheftu himself reached for the flagon of milk, only to snatch his hand back as if burned. Next instant he had torn the collar of lotuses from the flagon and flung it from him.

"Your lordship!" gasped the old man.

"Have I no other flowers in my gardens, Irenamon?"

"Aye, dozens! They—they but await your pleasure, my lord. There are scarlet sage, and heliotrope and larkspur, and—stay now—mignonette . . . But the lotuses were ever your favorite."

"I have lost my taste for them," said Sheftu savagely.

"A thousand pardons, my lord, if they have offended you." Irenamon hurried to gather up the lilies and hide them from sight in his wide sleeve, every line of him quivering with distress. "May I further serve Your Excellence before I—"

"Nay. Begone."

Irenamon turned disconsolately and padded toward the door. Sheftu leaned forward on his elbows, rubbing his forehead with both hands.

216

"Irenamon," he said. "Please come back." He waited until the old man stood beside him again, then reached for the flagon and poured his goblet full of milk. "I want you to send a slave to the wharf. Bid him discover if a ship called the *Silver Nettle* has docked this morning."

"Yes, Excellency."

"And Irenamon—I spoke in haste, old friend. About the lotuses."

"Pray do not think of it, my lord."

There was a silence. Sheftu raised his eyes and met the sad, concerned ones of his major-domo.

"You have great trouble," said the old man softly.

"Aye. Trouble with a maid."

"A maid? Is that all, my lord?"

"It is quite enough. Irenamon, I fear I have been a fool. I plucked a lily from the gutter, and it has turned to a cobra in my hands."

The old man's nostrils flared a little with his quick intake of breath, and his mouth set hard. "Then you had best destroy it without mercy."

"Never fear! But it may have done for me already. Be not surprised if you do not hear from me for a day or two. I shall be safe—but absent. If anyone inquires here, say that I have gone to Abydos." Sheftu smiled faintly. "Nay, do not look so. Naught's over yet. Go now. Send the barber up in fifteen minutes, and make haste to inquire about that ship."

"Aye, my lord. And may the gods go with you!"

The old servant hurried out, and Lord Sheftu turned at last to his breakfast.

An hour later he was crossing the worn stone wharfs to the *Beetle's* anchorage. Nekonkh hung over the gunwale, his arms propped wide, his shoulders burnished copper in the brilliant sunlight. Every line of him spelled anxiety. Sheftu stepped into the cool shadow of the hull, swung onto

217

the rope ladder and climbed up through the blue-green dancing reflections into the glare of sun on deck. Nekonkh stretched out a big hand to haul him aboard.

"Was it you sent down to see if we had docked yet?" he whispered.

"Aye."

"Naught's amiss, is it? I landed your cargo at four this morning, and was back by sunrise. All's well with my task."

"It's something else. Send your men ashore, I must talk to you."

Nekonkh bellowed an order, waved his hairy arms. As the crew swarmed down the ladder, chattering like monkeys over their unexpected liberty, Sheftu walked to the far side of the deck and stood there, feeling the warm sunshine beat down over his head and shoulders and the backs of his hands where they lay clasped on the rail. The very air smelled of heat and sun and water this morning. A fleet of fishing boats traced in gilt skimmed across Sheftu's line of vision, their sails pure light and their shadows ink puddles. Two barges moved ponderously upstream. Far across the river a hawk flapped up suddenly, curved and soared and dwindled to a speck in the cobalt sky.

Nekonkh came up beside him, wheezing a little. "All's clear, mate. They're gone. Now what's amiss?"

"We've a spy to reckon with, Captain."

"Ha! That's easy." Nekonkh's hand went to his knife. "Only tell me where he'll be tonight—"

"She'll be at the inn, I fancy."

"She?" Nekonkh's voice changed. "Who is it?"

"Mara."

There was a stunned silence. After a moment Nekonkh began to swear bitterly under his breath. "I can't believe that!" he burst out. "Have you proof?"

"Not yet."

"Then how can you—"

"Patience, I'll tell you everything. Do you remember the

218

day in your cabin yonder, when we hatched our plans? I gave her a ring—"

"Aye, aye, to bribe her friend in Abydos."

"There was no friend in Abydos, Nekonkh. She has the ring yet. She forgot, and left it on her hand last night."

"Oh, mother of the gods," said the captain wearily. He rested both forearms on the gunwale, staring out at the river. "And she had no explanation?"

"Oh, indeed she did. Can you picture that maid without an explanation? But she was lying."

"Now how do you know, mate? It may be she found a way to get what she wanted in Abydos without bribing that fellow! I'll wager she never had a trinket of her own, and what a trinket that was, to be sure! It would tempt the most scrupulous of— Aye, you can smile. I know the maid's not overburdened with scruples, but think of the life she's led, by the Sacred Eye! Ill used and half starved, at the mercy of this master and that one—"

"Save your breath, Nekonkh! I used her well enough, and got naught but treachery for thanks. I assure you I've done some thinking about this—though a little late! She kept the ring because she didn't need it as a bribe. Everything was arranged for her already, in Abydos—she was a spy when she boarded this ship."

"Why, she was naught but a little runaway."

"So we believed," said Sheftu grimly. "So I continued to believe until last night, when I came to my senses. She didn't run away at all, Nekonkh. I think she was sold."

He waited, then looked around at his companion. Nekonkh's still face was carved in sunlight, the jutting nose copper, the eyes deep caverns. "To an agent of the queen," Sheftu went on softly. "That changes everything, doesn't it? I'll wager I've no hold over her—not the slightest—and never did have. A comforting thought, is it not, when you remember what she knows, what she could tell?"

"Why hasn't she told, then? For the love of Amon, she

219

could have wrecked our craft four weeks ago! Why, in the name of—"

"That's the question. Why? I was hard pressed to find the answer, I confess."

Nekonkh eyed him thoughtfully. "I'll wager I know the answer now."

"Devotion to me, you think? Captain, pray do not ask me to believe in fairy tales!" Sheftu's voice was savage, and he realized he was gripping the rail so hard his fingers ached. He had suspected Nekonkh would say something like that, sooner or later, but he had not known what it was going to do to him, how vividly the warm touch of Mara's lips would come back to him, even the fragrance of the lotus in her hair.

He jerked his hands from the rail and turned his back to it. "Nay, we've underestimated the maid. She's playing both sides, Captain—that's the answer. She's maneuvered me as neatly as a toy on a string, all the while dangling this master of hers—the queen's man—from another finger. Hai, she's clever, is she not? No matter who loses this game, she means to win."

"I don't believe it! You yourself said you've no proof."

"I said not yet. I mean to obtain proof, and I mean you to help me."

"Now, how can we do that?" roared the captain, slapping his palm down upon the gunwale. "Man, you can't judge a thing like that on the word of another! Give the maid a chance to defend herself! She may have reasons we know naught of, good reasons—"

"She'll have every chance, Captain," said Sheftu softly. "Every chance." He eased around to face Nekonkh. "I am interested in your attitude toward all this, but I confess, a little confused. Perhaps you can enlighten me. Till now, I understood your allegiance to be to myself and the king— and no one else. Was I mistaken?"

Nekonkh's sun-burnished face lost a little of its rich color.

He started to speak, swallowed, then turned to stare out over the river. "What are my orders?" he growled.

"You will not care for them—nor do I. But we shall set a trap. That's fair enough, as I think you'll have to agree. If she's innocent the bait won't even tempt her."

And if she's guilty? If the trap works!"

Sheftu's shrug and cold eyes gave the answer.

"All right!" roared Nekonkh. "Get on with it, can't you? What am I to do?"

"You're to go to the Falcon tonight. I'll be with you, to make sure all's well, but I'll not go in. Give her some message from me—" Sheftu hesitated, then gestured impatiently. "I'll think of one presently. It must reassure her, so she will think I've dismissed the whole matter of the ring as something of no importance. Make certain she feels safe, Nekonkh. If she's seen the king she'll have a message for me —say I've sent you for it. Act a little excited, as if you had heard good news, as if there were plans afoot. In time, you will tell her those plans—they're the bait for our trap. Do you understand thus far?"

"Aye," muttered Nekonkh.

Sheftu fastened his gaze on the purple sail of a temple boat far out across the blinding, dancing water. "Do not tell her alone, however. Wait until there are others present —Nefer the goldsmith, Ashor, Sahure—it matters little who, but no lingering uneasiness about that ring must prevent her reaching for the bait. If others hear what she heard, she will feel she could blame the treachery on any one of them, if she had to. Hark now. Drop your news casually into the midst of this company. Say the leader I represent has obtained almost limitless funds from some wealthy Theban. Say that the gold is to be smuggled away to a place of safety tomorrow night at about the mark of eight, on the vessel— What ships will be loading cargo tomorrow evening, Nekonkh?"

"The *Friend of the Wind* will be. She sails the following dawn."

"That will serve. On the vessel *Friend of the Wind*." Sheftu straightened, drawing a long breath. "If the queen's soldiers raid that ship tomorrow night, Captain, we'll have our proof."

"And if little Blue Eyes does not take your bait?"

"Nay, she knows the time is running out. She could want no better chance to deliver the whole revolution to that master of hers, gold, rebels and all, and be off with her own winnings. She'll take the bait, right enough—unless she's innocent. Now, is there anything I've not thought of?"

"Nay, you would seem to have thought of everything," said Nekonkh bitterly. "Stay, though. You've not told me that message from you. The one that is to reassure her."

"Oh yes. That." Sheftu ran his palm carefully along the gunwale. It was hot from the sun, and the grain of the wood showed clear and beautiful in the strong light. "You may tell her," he said, "that I have not forgotten what I said last night, when I held her in my arms."

Nekonkh regarded him a moment in silence, then turned away. "Gods of Egypt, this is an ugly business!" he snarled.

"Aye, Captain! It's an ugly world." Sheftu pushed away from the rail and started across the glaring decks, the other following. "Remember," he added sharply, "you're but the counter in this game—I choose the gambits. Is all clear now?"

"I think so. Will I meet you at the Falcon?"

"On the wharf yonder. We'll go together."

Nekonkh nodded sourly, scowling at an imperfectly coiled rope lying near the stern sweeps. "*Ast!* Look at that!" he roared suddenly, striding over to kick it into a sprawling pile. "By the Forty Judges, these idiots can't do anything right! Rivermen, they call themselves. *Hai!* Swineherds, more likely—"

Leaving him manhandling the rope and cursing savagely,

Sheftu swung over the side and down the ladder. He knew how Nekonkh felt. The cheerful laughter of a pair of deck-hands on the next ship grated on him like a file on stone as he dropped to the wharf, slung his cloak half over his face, and strode toward the nearest alley.

The tavern courtyard was dark and empty when Sheftu and Nekonkh pushed open the gate that night and cautiously let themselves in. They crossed the yard in silence, and Sheftu melted into the shadow of the dom palm while Nekonkh strode on to the torchlit door and disappeared inside. A moment later he thrust a hand out to signal.

Sheftu left the dom palm and moved swiftly across the paving stones and into the little entry hall, closing the door silently behind him.

"She's here," muttered Nekonkh.

He motioned toward the door to the big common room, which he had half shut to conceal Sheftu's entrance. Stepping to the crack at the hinge, Sheftu peered through it. One glance told him all was well. A second showed him a lithe, familiar figure curled up in the corner booth, waiting for him. She had slipped her sandals off, as usual, and had tucked her feet under her. Her bare, brown shoulders gleamed in the torchlight, looking like carven gold in contrast to the snowy straps of her dress and the ink-black locks which fell over them. As always, she had fastened a lotus in her hair.

A hard, cold core formed inside Sheftu. With a jerk of his head he motioned Nekonkh on into the room.

"Ah! Good evening, Captain! May thy *ka* rejoice. . . ."

It was Ashor's voice, and almost at once his broad back appeared in front of the door crack, cutting off Sheftu's view of the room. By the time the innkeeper moved on, Nekonkh was approaching the corner booth. As he stopped beside it, Mara's head jerked around as if he had pulled a string.

Sheftu found that he was chewing his lip cruelly, and made himself stop. Her first, sharp, wary glance had told him much. It was the same look she had given him that day on the *Beetle*, when he had surprised her out of sleep, and it reminded him of nothing so much as a quick-drawn sword.

She had disguised it at once, this time, and appeared to be questioning Nekonkh as he edged his big body into the booth beside her. Sheftu watched him closely as he answered her. He was making a great to-do about settling himself on the mat, his eyebrows going up and down with elaborate nonchalance as he talked. Nekonkh could shrug his eyebrows as other men shrugged their shoulders. He seemed to be convincing Mara that all was as usual.

Feeling relief as to that, coupled with a restlessness of such prickling intensity that he felt he was being bitten all over by flies, Sheftu left his post and moved distractedly about the tiny entrance hall, then returned to his crack.

Even from across the room, her eyes looked blue. Sheftu leaned against the wall and let the noise and music and clatter of crockery beat against his ears, trying to pick out her quick laughter from the confusion, trying once again to fathom the strange quality of wistfulness which underlay all her swift-changing expressions, even the most sardonic, the most impudent. What was Nekonkh saying to her now? She had grown serious, frowning down at the cup she toyed with, nodding. He spoke again and laughed; and as she raised her vivid eyes to him, her whole provocative, gamin's face lighted in an answering grin.

Suddenly Sheftu could bear no more. He fled silently out of the inn, through the dark courtyard and across the street, where he took up his waiting again in a doorway that smelled evilly of filth and rotting fish.

It seemed hours before the courtyard gate clicked open and Nekonkh emerged. Sheftu took a firm grip on himself and managed to appear casual as he joined him. "Well, Captain?"

"Mate, I did what you told me. That's all you can ask, is it not?"

"Did she seem—did you watch her face when you dropped the bait?"

"No," said Nekonkh woodenly.

After a moment he started down the shadowy street, and Sheftu fell in beside him. They walked in silence through the alleys and byways into the warehouse district edging the wharf. When they came to the customs dock, where their ways separated, Nekonkh faced around doggedly.

"Look you, Sashai. I know as well as you what's at stake in this, and if the maid trips herself up—well, it's her own doing, and I've naught to say for her. But if that vessel's raided tomorrow night, mate, I could whisk her on board the *Beetle* and sail straight for the Delta. She'd be no danger to anyone, you'd never need see her again. But you could still spare her life. . . ."

His voice trailed into silence. Sheftu was slowly shaking his head.

CHAPTER 21

The Quarry

DARKNESS lay thick next night about a certain warehouse on the river front of eastern Thebes. Some distance away from it, at the water's edge, a yellow glow of torchlight spilled across the wharfs from the decks of the *Friend of the*

Wind, which lay close in against the dock to receive her cargo. They were still loading her; figures moved against the light, humpbacked with burdens as they filed up the gangplank and across the deck. There were the usual thumpings and slammings and bellowed orders; above the lighted decks the tall, black mast swayed gently against the stars. Beyond, the dark length of the river wound away southward, splashed with 'gold here and there, wherever a torch burned.

In the gloom beside the warehouse wall, screened by a pile of fish nets and old lumber, Nekonkh heaved a sigh of impatience and tried for the fiftieth time to get comfortable on the coil of damp rope he was sitting on. Sheftu, a dim blur in the shadows beside him, seemed not to have moved for an hour; the captain wondered bitterly if he had fallen asleep. For all the anxiety Lord Sheftu exhibited, one would think he had come here merely for a breath of air.

As for Nekonkh, it had been the longest day he had ever known, and he'd made rough weather of it, alternating between bellowing ill temper and silent worry until by mid-afternoon every man in his crew was keeping a wary eye on him and his own nerves were taut as a straining hawser. He felt even more tense now, lurking here like a *kheft* at the edge of darkness. . . .

The captain eased his shoulders back against the rough wall and tried to make his mind a blank. The reek of fish and hemp and rotting wood rose strong about him; inside the warehouse, he could hear the loud scratching and scrabbling of a rat. Beyond the edge of the pile of nets the burdened figures moved monotonously back and forth in the torchlight from the dock to the *Friend of the Wind*. Nekonkh found himself automatically checking her trim.

"Overloaded on the port side," he muttered with gloomy satisfaction. "Cargo master's a fool."

Sheftu's voice came out of the shadows, cool and ironic. "It scarcely matters, does it?"

226

"Of course it matters! They'll have to shift half of those bales before they're well into the current. What do you mean, it scarcely—"

"I mean they'll likely not be sailing."

Nekonkh abandoned the subject, shifting his position once again and cursing irritably at the prickling roughness of the rope.

"Patience, Captain," soothed the other. "It cannot be long now."

By all the gods, is he even human? thought Nekonkh. "Do you care naught for what happens to the maid?"

He got no answer. But Sheftu's voice was a little less smooth when he spoke again. "You tied the boat where I told you to?"

"Aye. In the papyruses at the far end of the wharf. It's ready."

They were silent again. After a time Nekonkh twisted around to scan the black mouths of the alleys—still quiet and deserted—then squinted up at the stars. "By the beard of Ptah, if it isn't the mark of eight by this time, I'm no riverman!" He stood up, checked the alleys one by one, then sized up the stack of bales on the dock. "Mate, they've all but finished loading. Look yonder. I'll wager a sail to a *shenti* the hour's eight—or past—"

He stood clenching his fists to keep them from trembling. It should happen now, it should have happened already—if it was to happen. He realized Sheftu had risen too, and was standing stiff and erect at his side, scarcely breathing. Still the minutes crept past, the commonplace sounds of loading went on.

By Amon, she's won! thought Nekonkh at last. She didn't take our cursed bait! All's well. He opened his mouth to blurt it out—and felt Sheftu seize his arm.

"Captain! Look!"

A light shone in the mouth of one of the alleys. Nekonkh tried to blink it out of sight, pretend that it was moving the

227

other way, but it came on, brighter and nearer, accompanied by pounding footsteps. A knot of soldiers burst out onto the wharfs, with more at their heels—they were regulars, in green helmets. There was a shout of surprise from the loaders, a roar that answered it: "In the name of the queen!" Next moment the night was alive with running men, with torches and glinting blades and a confusion of yells as the raiders poured across the wharf and up the gangplank of the *Friend of the Wind.*

Nekonkh dug both fists into his forehead to shut out the sight. Name of Amon, she's only a child! he thought. A waif, after all, who's seen naught but ill luck all her life and needs friends and a chance. . . .

"So be it. I've seen enough," said Sheftu quietly.

Nekonkh had seldom in his life been afraid of anyone. But he was afraid, now, of the tall young man who stood beside him. "Mate," he whispered hoarsely. "Let me do it. I'll find her. I'll have her out of Thebes tonight, I swear by—"

"You'll follow orders, Captain!" Sheftu flung him a look that left nothing but obedience in Nekonkh's mind. "Come, to the boat."

He slipped out of their hiding place and Nekonkh followed. They plunged down the lane beside the warehouse, into the next dim street and then along it, parallel to the river, at a pace that left the captain no time to think or even feel. His mind had gone numb, in any case. He knew they were making for the hidden boat, that they would cross the Nile and lie in wait for Mara somewhere on the other side, intercepting her as she was starting for the inn. He knew what was to happen in some dark alley and that he could not prevent its happening. But it all seemed unreal, a nightmare from which he could not wake.

They swerved back toward the river. A few minutes later Nekonkh was dragging the boat from the concealing papyrus stalks, still moving like an automaton.

228

"Cast off the painter. I've a paddle here somewhere."

They pushed off across the black water, and with the familiar rocking motion, the feel of the paddle in his hand, Nekonkh's numbness began to wear off. He pulled harder and more fiercely, so that the boat shot like a live thing through the current, but the exertion failed to stop his thoughts.

"Bear to your left, Captain," said Sheftu at last. "We'll make for that statue on the bank."

The fishing punt was there, moored to the great granite toe as always, and old A'ank dozed nearby. Sheftu nudged him awake, none too gently, flipped him a deben and ordered him home, then hurried up the bank.

She's a cold-blooded little traitor, Nekonkh told himself desperately as he tied their own boat and hurried to follow. Did she give a thought to you when she decided to turn informer? Or even to Sheftu? She's earned what's coming. She'd have run the whole plot aground if she could. Just don't think. Don't look at her. Remember, don't look at her.

"This will serve," said Sheftu coolly. "I believe she's coming."

Nekonkh emerged abruptly from his preoccupation. They stood in an alley; ahead, up its murky, narrow length, he could just make out a slender, cloak-swathed figure hurrying through the shadows. Nekonkh wet his lips and glanced around him, wishing he could stop going hot and cold like a man with the fever. Sheftu had chosen his spot well. The lane was deserted, closed in by buildings that would remain dark and empty until morning. There would be no one to disturb them.

"Walk casually to meet her," murmured Sheftu.

He strolled forward, and Nekonkh trailed after him, wiping his sweaty palms on his thighs. Presently Mara drew close enough to catch sight of them, and he could hear her sharp little intake of breath as she halted. An instant later she recognized them.

"Sheftu!" Her voice was low, but it held only surprise and pleasure—no fear. She moved swiftly to join them, looking from one to the other in amusement. "What is this, pray? An ambush?"

"One might call it so," answered Sheftu silkily. "Come. I want a word with you." He took her arm and guided her to a recessed doorway, while Nekonkh drifted a little apart, where he could watch both ends of the alley. He could hear Mara's uneasy little laugh.

"Have all the words you wish, but why choose this place? At the inn we could—"

"You'll not be going to the inn tonight."

"Why will I not?" She hesitated, and her tone changed. "Sheftu, you're acting—strange. Is aught amiss?"

"Aye. Much is amiss. The vessel *Friend of the Wind* was raided tonight by the queen's soldiers."

She gave a gasp Nekonkh could have sworn was genuine. "Osiris! With all the gold aboard her? *Aiii*—when you traveled the Shores of the Night to bring it back. . . . Nay, they can't, they mustn't! Those—" Her voice broke with fury, and for a moment her language reeked of Menfe's waterfront. "But shall we do naught but wail of it, for the love of Amon? We must do something! *You* must do something, Sheftu, you're the leader—"

"Aye, a brilliant leader!" Sheftu's voice remained quiet, but the whiplash Nekonkh had been dreading came into it now. "I've saved Egypt with one hand and destroyed her with the other—by trusting a maid as faithless as the wind!"

"Mother of the gods!" whispered Mara. "You think—I did it."

"My lovely Mara, no doubt exists."

"But I didn't do it! I didn't, I didn't! There must have been another who listened, I didn't do it! Sheftu—the juggler! *Ai*, that's who it was! He was there—ask Nekonkh!—he heard everything. It was that babbling Sahure, may the

230

Devourer take him, I knew he'd betray us before we'd done with him, did I not tell you, warn you?"

"I was certain you would place the blame elsewhere."

"*Ast!* Sheftu, you're blind! You've ever been blind about that rogue, and look you now—all the gold gone, the plans ruined—"

"Mara," said Sheftu softly. "There was no gold on the ship."

There was a sudden silence. Nekonkh edged toward them without knowing what he did. He was beginning to feel as if he could not breathe. Suppose it were Sahure? It could have been, it was possible, even probable! Then by all the gods!

"Stay away from her, Captain!" ordered Sheftu.

Mara drew a soft, irregular breath. "Why," she whispered, "should the captain stay away from me?"

"Because he has revealed an unfortunate weakness where you're concerned," said Sheftu. He moved closer to her. For the first time he was failing to hide the strain he was under; Nekonkh could see the tension in his shoulders, and his voice had grown harsh and thick. "This affair is between you and me, little one, do you understand? Let me make it quite clear to you. There was no gold on the ship, nor was it our ship. The news was false. It was a trap, Mara. And you walked into it."

"Sheftu, I did not betray you. I swear by my *ka.*"

"*Ast!* Be silent! I know all about you. All! I know you're a slave in the queen's pay, and have been since you took ship with us in Menfe. I know you lied to me then, and have lied to me every day I've known you, and would go on lying until the end of time if it would get you what you want! Your master believed you, didn't he? I know of that, too—how cleverly you've played both sides, waiting, holding back, until last night you thought you'd chosen certain victory. . . ."

231

Mara was slowly, almost imperceptibly, backing away from him, though she seemed scarcely to move or even breathe. Suddenly she whirled to run. Just as suddenly, Sheftu's hand shot out and seized her wrist. In a flash he had doubled her arm behind her and jerked her close to him. He held a gleaming knife in his other hand.

"Not this time, little one," he said softly.

His rough handling had caused the cloak to fall away from her hair, and the fragrance of lotuses now drifted through the alley. Nekonkh, flattened stiffly against the building opposite, tried to look away and couldn't. His eyes were fastened on the knife blade, and he became gradually aware that it was trembling.

"How have you kept *him* satisfied, I wonder?" whispered Sheftu. "That master of yours, whoever he is. What have you told him? How much have you told him?"

Mara, too, was staring at the knife, shrinking away from it as far as his grip would let her. "Sheftu," she breathed. "You can't do it—you can't—"

"Ah, can I not? Who will ever know—or care?"

She looked up at him suddenly. And then Nekonkh witnessed a very strange thing. Instead of shrinking from the knife, she flung herself close against Sheftu, twined her free arm about his neck and kissed him on the mouth.

What happened next was never clear in Nekonkh's mind. He was aware of a strangled oath from Sheftu, the clatter of a knife hitting the gravel, and felt Mara hurtle against him as if she had been thrown. Instinctively Nekonkh wrapped his arms about her and whirled so that his own body shielded her.

"Take her, Captain!" gasped a voice that might have been Lord Sheftu's. "Take her out of Thebes, out of Egypt, anywhere; but let me never see her again!"

Hasty footsteps plunged away up the alley, pounded around a corner, and were gone.

When Nekonkh's head cleared a little, he found that he

was cursing steadily and idiotically, under his breath, still clutching Mara tight in his arms. He stopped, wet his shaking lips, and loosened his hold to peer down at her. She was weeping stormily, he did not know whether in anger or in fright.

"Is all well with you, little one?" he muttered. "He didn't harm you?"

She shook her head, burrowed harder against his chest and continued to sob. He held her uneasily, patting her shoulder now and then and growling vague comfort under his breath. He was not used to weeping maidens and had no idea what one did for them. But he felt dimly that it would be best to let her weep her fill.

Presently the storm subsided a little, and after a moment she stirred and lifted her head. "Nekonkh—where is he?"

"Gone, little one. Likely halfway to the Falcon by this time."

"He'll go there?"

"Aye, I think so. He'll want to make sure all's well, and besides . . ."

"Besides what?"

"Well, little one," said Nekonkh gruffly, "I think he'll be warning them about you."

"Ordering them to murder me on sight, I'll wager," she burst out. "Just on the chance you'll not take me far enough to the ends of the earth—"

"Aye, just on the chance, just on the chance," he soothed. "But we'll not founder on that sand bar until we hit it. I must take you away, little one, you know that, don't you?" She stirred fretfully against him, and he dropped his arms, studying her profile in the gloom. "Look you, maid. How much of that was true—what he accused you of?"

"Oh . . ." Her hand had wandered to the crushed lotus in her hair. She pulled it out, looked at it a moment, and dropped it to the ground. "All of it, Nekonkh. Save about the ship. Sahure told that, he must have, because I never

233

did, I never even meant to! I swear I've told naught—" She broke off, seemed to hold her breath a moment. "At least not much—" She suddenly went on. "As for the rest, can I be blamed for that? I didn't ask to be sold! But mother of truth, it was a chance to be free, perhaps rich! What did I know about the king then? I'd not even met Sheftu! Once I did, then I wished I'd never seen that cursed master of mine, but—Nekonkh, I've told him naught that matters, I've but played hounds and jackals with him. I had to do that, didn't I? If I'd not done it, he'd have thrown me back in the gutter. . . ."

Ai, she's just a child, Nekonkh was thinking. A little waif in a cursed ugly world, and none to befriend her. "No matter, it's past now," he muttered, patting her awkwardly. "We'll have a fine voyage, clean to Crete if you like. Crete's a good land, little one—an island. A mite odd and foreign, but pleasant, and lively enough even for you. They've acrobats there—men and maids both—who dance about under the horns of bulls and leap over their backs so that you've never seen the like. You'll be no slave, either, and I'll wager you could sell that ring of yours for a hundred gold *deben*. . . . *Ai*, come, little Blue Eye, Crete's the place. Let's be out of this dark alley—"

"You're good to me, Nekonkh," whispered Mara. "And I'll come, but—" She hesitated, resisting when he tried to draw her forward.

"What's amiss now, maid?"

"Nekonkh—how do we know he's gone? He might be waiting, just yonder around the corner! Or he might have changed his mind and come back. . . ."

"Nay, don't worry. He's gone."

"*Ai*, how can you be sure?"

"Now, then, if it'll ease your mind, I'll make certain of it. Come, stand in the doorway here. It'll take but a moment."

Guiding her gently into the niche, the captain walked up the alley in the direction Sheftu had taken. He knew he would find no one. Her fears were needless, but he well understood them and meant to humor every one if it would help her. The winds had tossed her craft enough, he thought belligerently, in her seventeen short years. It was time somebody steered a straight course for her.

As he had expected, the street beyond was quite deserted. He examined several dark nooks nearby, so he could tell her he'd done so, then strode back into the alley. The first moonbeams were beginning to sift their way into it now; out in the open, on the river, it would soon be bright enough to navigate with fair accuracy. It would be a good night to sail, Nekonkh decided, though it might not be wise to venture into those currents beyond the sand bars. They'd slip downstream a few miles and tie up until—

The captain halted and frowned about him uncertainly. Was this not the doorway . . . ? He glanced back the way he had come, wondering if he'd misjudged the distance, decided perhaps he had, and started on. Then he stopped abruptly. There in the gravel at his feet the moonlight glittered over the blade of a jeweled knife. And a cubit or two away lay a crumpled lotus.

"Mother of Amon!" whispered the captain.

The doorway was empty. The whole alley was empty. And that knife—or another—would likely be slicing his own throat before morning, if he didn't find that slippery maid and bring her back.

"Mother of Amon and Isis and Osiris and the Sacred Cat of Bast!" he exploded. He scooped up the dagger, clamped his jaw at its fiercest, and started up the alley, running hard.

CHAPTER 22

Disaster

THREE STREETS AWAY, Mara was already dodging out of the passage beside the goldsmith's shop, and running like the desert antelope along the high, curving wall which bounded the palace grounds. There was but one thing to do; and somehow, through the wild disorder of her emotions, she'd had wit enough to see it and cling fast to it. She was still spent from her storm of weeping, sore in body and mind from Sheftu's merciless handling of her, and shaken in every nerve by the audacious—but no less passionate—kiss which had saved her life. Sheftu was lost to her beyond recall, but hardest to bear was the ironic twist that this time she was innocent—the ship's raid was none of her doing. It was Sahure he'd caught in his gold-baited trap. But he'd refused to believe it, and thereby laid himself and the revolution open to the liveliest danger.

Mara alone, though stunned by the abruptness of her own undoing, recognized the extent of that danger. She alone knew that Nahereh knew about the Inn of the Falcon. She alone could guess that in his rage at finding nothing on the ship he might abandon all subtler tactics and storm the tavern, seizing everyone in it and trusting to later luck to find the leader. *Ai*, but he would already have the leader! The moment he set eyes on Sashai, the scribe, he would recognize Lord Sheftu and all would be over.

There was but one thing to do—find Nahereh, learn his plans, and then, if necessary, slip away from him somehow and carry a warning to the inn. On trembling legs Mara was speeding to do it.

The North Gate loomed ahead—Reshed's gate. Mara clutched her ring, praying its charm would work once more, though Amon knew it had brought her anything but luck the last two days. She had not seen Reshed for four nights now, having lately used the Main Gate and the password of her master's name for her passage in and out of the palace grounds. She knew not what temper Reshed would be in, but she had to try him. She might need desperately to get out again, later, and by that time the use of Nahereh's name might be suicidal.

Breathless, she halted before the gate, tried in vain to quiet her pounding heart, and finally rapped three times. Reshed recognized the signal; she could hear the faint, sharp clatter of his sword as he made a startled move. An instant later the gate swung open—just far enough for his body to block the entrance.

"You!" he growled.

"Aye . . . Reshed, I'm in haste, please let me in."

"What are you doing *out*, that's what I want to know! I've seen naught of you tonight, not for four nights running!"

"Why, today I went out much earlier, with my princess— at another gate. And before that—ah, Reshed, I've wanted to come, if only to linger a moment with you and then go back again! But I could never get away from her, not even for a minute."

"Aye, very likely! More likely, you've found some other simpleton to dry your tears, and let you in and out whenever you crook a finger at him!" Reshed reached out furiously and jerked her closer. "Who is it? That swell-headed sergeant at the Main Gate?"

"Nay, it isn't, it isn't, I've done no such thing! Oh, mother of truth, let me in, I can't stand here arguing! I'm in haste, I tell you. My brother's dying and I must get help—"

She twisted violently in his grasp but only succeeded in reversing their positions, so that it was she who stood with her back to the gate, which hung tantalizingly ajar. He still held her arm fast.

"You never had a brother," he said bitterly. "I don't know whom you meet, outside there, but I'll stake my sword he's no sick kinsman! Aye, I've caught on to your game, you little witch, though I've been cursed slow about it. You've made a fool of me, letting me risk my post here night after night so you could—"

"Reshed, I beg you! I swear by my *ka*—" Tears of despair choked off the words and changed to sobs of fury. She began to fight him like a wildcat, kicking, clawing, beating at him, spitting out her rage. "Let go of me, you stupid clod! I've done naught to you, you've got your cursed post still, haven't you? Let me go, you devil!" Suddenly she froze, staring just beyond his shoulder. "Great Amon! Your captain . . ."

He spun around, and for just that instant his fingers loosened. An instant was all Mara needed. In a flash she had wrenched away and darted through the gate, up the Avenue of Rams and into the Court of the Weavers, leaving him cursing bitterly behind her.

Let him curse, she thought as she sped silently along the graveled paths. He can't leave his gate without raising an alarm, and if he does that he'll lose his precious post and maybe his head for his part in this affair . . .

But, oh, Amon, now how was she to get out of the grounds again in case she had to?

She slowed, almost halted, in an agony of hesitation. Should she go back, try to make amends, try to— Nay, the thing was done now, there was no undoing it. Sick with apprehension, she darted on.

She reached the great Court of Storerooms, some distance beyond the stair she ordinarily climbed to the upper corridor and her own chambers. There she stopped, leaned panting against the rough-plastered wall, and tried to picture in her mind the plan of the palace Nahereh had showed her. The little study he had told her of was near this courtyard, she was sure of that. But which passage? That one, to the right. Aye, it must be, for the other led only to the guard-room; it was the one she and Inanni had walked down that day toward the audience with the queen. How long ago that seemed.

She moved quickly into the passage to the right, turned right again into a dimly lighted hall, and counted the doors as she passed them. One, two, three—four. It was that one. Without allowing herself to pause or even wonder what would happen next, she opened the door, slipped through into a torchlit, crowded room, and closed the door behind her.

Lord Nahereh turned from a group of excited soldiers and rivermen, and stared at her.

"You!" he burst out.

Mara leaned back against the door, feeling all at once spent and weary. Everyone, she thought sardonically, seems overjoyed to see me tonight. . . .

"Yes, I!" she said. "I crave your protection, master! The rebels suspect me."

"Do they! By my *ka*, Amon is good, sending you here at this moment. It has saved my Libyan the trouble of finding you." Slowly he eased down upon the table behind him, folded his arms, and studied her, a faint, chill smile touching the corners of his mouth. "Chadzar," he murmured. "Send these men away, we need them no longer."

The Libyan jerked his head at the soldiers and rivermen—crewmen from the *Friend of the Wind*, Mara guessed—and herded them out through another door. There was still one other person in the room—a quiet figure hunched in the shadows of one corner; but Mara did not move her eyes to see who it was. As the Libyan sauntered back to his post, Lord Nahereh spoke again, his voice dripping sarcasm.

"So the rebels suspect you. How unkind of them, to repay your friendship with cruel distrust."

"Friendship? I've pretended friendship, master. Did you not send me there to spy on them, learn their secrets—"

"Aye, quite right, I did. But you were so—tardy—in reporting any of those secrets that this afternoon I decided to set a spy on you, my Clever One. Only a formality, you understand. To my surprise, the man I picked seemed to be an old friend of yours already."

"Indeed," murmured Mara.

Lord Nahereh turned his head. "You, there! Show yourself."

Even before she saw him, Mara knew who was gliding out of his shadowy corner. Sahure looked oddly incomplete without his golden balls, but his twisted, cynical smile was the same as ever, his tongue as oily.

"Live forever, Face of the Lily! May thy *ka* rejoice, may thy—"

"*Ast!* You son of forty devils!"

"Shocking!" murmured Lord Nahereh. "Is that any way to greet a friend?"

"He's no friend of mine! He's a rogue and a serpent, don't trust a word he says, master, he's as slippery as—"

"Then you're two of a kind!" Nahereh's pretense was finished now; his voice lashed like a whip. "Why did you not tell me of that ship tonight?"

"Because I knew it was a trap."

"By Amon! You'd still lie to me?"

"Don't believe her, Excellency," put in Sahure. "She was there. She heard what I heard."

"Yes, I was there, you crocodile, but I had my wits about me, and you did not! The ship was empty, master, was it not? You found no gold aboard it, did you? Nay, you didn't! It was all a hoax, a snare set for me that I had the sense to stay away from. But this fool walked into it! Now they think I did it, and all I've tried to accomplish is

240

wrecked—they'll not even let me in the tavern after this! In fact, I hear they've orders to kill me on sight—"

"Ahhhhh," breathed Lord Nahereh with satisfaction. "And just who told you that?"

Mara bit her lip until she could taste the blood. "An—an old man, who felt sorry for me."

"Indeed. Someone whose acquaintance you made during those other visits to the inn, no doubt. Those *early* visits—the ones *before* I sent you—the ones I knew nothing about until this juggler told me."

Gods of Egypt, I'm caught, thought Mara. I can't wriggle out of this one, there's no way out, no way out. . . . She parted stiff lips, but no words came rushing to her tongue from that mysterious reservoir of last-minute inspiration which had so often saved her. She stood paralyzed, wordless, and the silence drew out until it was far too long, far too late now to say anything at all, and she was lost. It was all over.

Lord Nahereh smiled icily and echoed her thoughts. "The game's over, isn't it? Too bad. You must have enjoyed it while it lasted. Come now! Who was this 'old man' who warned you?"

The silence went on.

"Excellency," murmured Sahure. "I think perhaps it was a *young* man. One called Sashai. He would have warned her."

A faint, bitter amusement touched the edges of Mara's mind. "Not he!" she muttered.

Nahereh ignored her, turning instead to the juggler. "It is sad indeed that I was not aware earlier of your possibilities. You would have been working for me long ago. Before those soldiers came in with their useless prisoners, you were beginning to tell me of those who come regularly to this inn. Suppose you continue. Sashai. 'The Scribe.' Who is this scribe?"

"Excellency, no one knows. It is he who brings orders

241

from the rebel leader—and no one knows him, either. It is said even Sashai has never seen him. But it is clear to all that our scribe is smitten with this Lily-Faced One here, this Flower of Loveliness. . . ." Sahure's world-weary, indifferent eyes rested a moment on Mara—faintly amused, detached—as they might have rested on a stranger, a carven image, a beetle which he had chanced to crush under his sandal. "As for the others, there is a goldsmith—his name is Nefer—Ashor the innkeeper and his wife, a priest called Djedet, a riverman, Nekonkh, a baker and several artisans. . . ."

He did it easily, casually, as if there were nothing here requiring thought or decision. He merely opened his mouth and named them off—her companions, her allies, all Sheftu's trusted followers; those who had laughed with her and counted her one of them, who ate Miphtahyah's stew or whispered with Sashai or played hounds and jackals night after night while they waited for orders—named them, and so murdered them, one by one. Mara stood dry mouthed, sick, and numbing all over, gazing at last into the face of treachery, with which she had been flirting so long. She could not wrench her eyes away from that unbelievable, sinuous figure with its twisted shoulder, its gestures of fluid grace. It seemed as if evil itself were loose in the room.

"Enough, enough," Nahereh was saying absently. "We can net all those when we choose, like a school of fish. It is the scribe who interests me, this mysterious Sashai. There, juggler, is a fish who might be worth catching. In fact—I think we will cast our net . . . Chadzar!"

"Aye, master."

"Call the soldiers back. There'll be another raid—tonight. At once. Stay, send me only their sergeant, I'll give my orders to him."

"What of her?"

Nahereh's cold eyes moved to Mara. "Later. I want plenty of time for that. Plenty of time. Send her to her chambers

and post a guard by her door. Perhaps it had better be you
. . . nay, I want you for this other. Put her under guard.
Find a guard with a whip." He smiled thinly at Mara. "We
will meet again, Too-Clever One."

"Come," muttered the Libyan.

Moving like one in an ugly dream, Mara walked beside
him through the other doorway, waited while he chose a
burly soldier and growled instructions, went on again with
her new guard through the halls, up the outside stair to the
upper corridor, and at last into her own room. He left her
there, standing motionless among the familiar gilded butterflies. A moment later she heard the bolt grate home, then
the creak of wood as her jailor settled back against her door.

It was some moments before she became dimly aware of
the sounds of movement and chatter from the next room. At
first she resisted them vaguely, as one brushes away a buzz-
ing fly. But in spite of herself the numbness began to wear
away, the fog to clear from her mind. That was Inanni and
the Syrian women she heard in there, talking calmly
together as on any other evening, perhaps putting away
their games and embroidery, yawning good night. . . .

There was another door—the one opening onto the hall
from that sitting room.

No use, she thought. It's but a step down the hall, the
guard would see anyone who went in or out. He guards
that one too, or might as well.

Without plan or any hope, she moved across her room
and passed through the tapestry-hung door into the sitting
room. She had been right, the Syrians were in the act of
dispersing to their sleeping chambers. A few of them paused
to look at her in mild surprise; Inanni's face showed a flicker
of swift anxiety.

"Mara! I thought you were . . . Is anything wrong?"

"My princess," said Mara in a voice that sounded strange
even to herself, "could I—speak to you a moment?"

"For as long as you like."

243

Inanni murmured something to Dashtar, waved all of her women out of the room, and hurried over to Mara. "Sit you down. Your face is ashen. Shall I fetch water?"

"Nay—I'm all right—stay with me, please, my princess . . ."

Grasping blindly at Inanni's hand, Mara sank onto a couch and to her own bewilderment, burst into despairing tears.

"Mara! Oh, oh, oh, something terrible has happened, has it not? I felt it the moment you came in here. . . . There, now, you shall tell me about it in a moment, don't try yet, all's well, all's well. . . ."

"Oh, Amon, I've no time for weeping, I must stop this!" Mara brushed the tears angrily from her face, only to be overcome with fresh ones. "Everything's tumbled about my ears, Princess, all's over, all's wrecked, smashed—Sheftu tried to kill me tonight. He couldn't do it—quite—but my master can and means to and will. . . . There's a guard outside my door now. And I must get out! I must warn them."

As coherently as she could, she told the story—the ship, the black moment in the alley, her flight from Nekonkh, then from Reshed—and the terrible scene she had just witnessed. "Ai, Princess, that juggler is the Evil One himself! It was the way he did it—carelessly, without passion—as if lives are of no more value than onions, and naught means anything! Osiris! I knew not what evil thing I played with, I did not know it would be like this, I didn't understand!"

"Mara, Mara . . ." Inanni stroked her hair, trembling. "Is there nothing you can do?"

"Nothing. I can't leave these rooms. Even if I could, I'd never get outside the gates. I'm snared fast as a bird in a net."

Inanni stilled suddenly, then seized Mara's shoulders in both hands. "Wait. Mara, it's possible that—it may be that I can help you to get out."

244

"You what? How? What—"

"Hush, let me tell you. Do you remember Sherimi, the Syrian woman in the Court of the Weavers, the one I—"

"You've been seeing her, I knew that."

"She has a family outside the gates, Mara, in the City of the Dead. Often she goes home to them each night, though if the work presses, here, she stays on until it slackens, and sleeps in a little room off the servants' wing. She is in the palace now, I talked with her this afternoon and she said she would sleep within the walls tonight. But if she were to change her mind, if she were to rise from her couch now and go home to her family outside the gates, taking a young Syrian maid with her . . ."

Mara was on her feet. "Ai, praise and thanksgiving be to— Quick, Princess! Find me Syrian clothes, all the scarves and shawls and thick skirts you can gather— Stay! Do you think—she'll do this for me?"

"She will do it for me, Mara," said Inanni softly. "We have comforted each other, and it is as if I were her daughter, and she my own kin."

Mara stood for one silent moment, searching the simple, tranquil face and glimpsing a world which she had never known—a world of friends and kin, who shared bread and trouble alike, and comforted one another. "And you would do it for me?" she whispered.

"With all my heart. It is not much I do—" Inanni started for her bedchamber, then hesitated. Suddenly she rushed back to seize Mara's hands, her plump face creased with anxiety. "But it is much, and more than much, that you do, Mara! Oh, think carefully! Once outside the walls you could go free. . . . They will kill you if you go to that inn, you said so yourself—"

"I don't care! I don't care! Make haste, the clothes!"

Inanni dropped her hands and flew to the door of her bedchamber.

245

CHAPTER 23

Capture

FIVE MINUTES later two Syrians in gaudy draperies emerged from the Princess Inanni's suite and started for the stair. Down the hall, the guard's sword clattered as he straightened.

"Stay! Who's that?"

Two shawled heads turned inquiringly toward him, and there was a vague, sibilant mumble of Babylonian, a shrugging of shoulders. He hesitated, but then settled back against the door. "*Ai*, never mind, go on, go on . . ."

The Syrians padded to the stair and disappeared.

A few minutes later one of them returned alone, let herself quietly into the room and drew the bolt behind her. At the same moment Mara was walking beside Sherimi the weaver through the Main Gate of the palace grounds, carrying a basket of linen warp on her head and echoing the Syrian's casual good night to the sentry.

"By my *ka*, Sherimi," he remarked in surprise. "You're a little late, are you not? All Thebes is asleep long since. . . . Who's that with you?"

"Only a new apprentice," answered Sherimi. "I must hasten, sentry, my son is ill and already my work has kept me too long from him."

"May the Starry One send him rest," yawned the sentry absently. "Good night."

Out of sight around the curving wall, Mara pressed the woman's hand in silent thanks, then flung off the heavy draperies and stuffed them into the basket. Sherimi took them and went her way, while Mara, feeling fleet as air in her own thin Egyptian sheath, sped toward the goldsmith's shop, across the street to the dark entrance—and straight into the arms of Nekonkh

"*Hai!*" he growled, seizing her as if he never meant to let go. "So I've snared you at last, my bird on the wing, and *this* time I'll wager you'll not slip away from—"

Mara clapped a hand over his mouth. "Nekonkh, you're the very one I want. Oh, Amon, how glad I am to see you! Quick, quick, to the river, we must find a boat, they're going to raid the tavern. Make haste, I tell you!"

"They're what? Who—"

Nekonkh was moving beside her, even while he protested, but he kept a firm grip on her arm. As quickly as she could, Mara explained, meanwhile tugging him on through the dark streets. "I know not when they started, even if they've started, but there's a chance we may get there first. They had soldiers to call together, orders to give—the Devourer take you, will you hurry? Cease your pulling back!"

"I mean to stand still," said Nekonkh bluntly, and did so. "Let me set my teeth into this. Nay, stop tugging at me, it'll do you no good. Now tell me why I should believe a word of this wild tale when not an hour ago—"

"*Ast!* I know I tricked you, Nekonkh, I had to, you'd not have listened if I'd tried to— In the name of Amon, would I be going to the tavern at all if it weren't to warn them? You know well how they feel toward me by this time! Unless you hasten it's *you* who'll betray them, *you* who'll murder them one by one!"

"So be it, hush, hush! No need to shriek at me." Nekonkh was moving now, raking the riverbank with his glance as they ran down the last slope. "Mind you, I don't say I believe you, but I'll take no chance on . . . None of your tricks, though, Miss Blue Eyes! You'll not get out of my sight from now to Crete, do you understand? By Amon, I think

I'll tie a hawser to you, and make certain. . . . Here's a boat. We'll borrow it now and ask leave some other—"

"Nekonkh! Listen!"

Both of them froze, in the act of climbing into the boat. Somewhere back in the dark maze of streets there was a sound of rhythmic footsteps, a barked order, the clank of weapons.

"They're coming!" gasped Mara. "Make haste, make haste —*now* do you believe me?"

For answer Nekonkh shoved her into the boat, tumbled in after her, and pushed off with a stroke of such violent energy that it seemed to take them halfway across the Nile. Grim and silent, he devoted all his attention to keeping the boat moving at a speed Mara would have marveled at any time but now. Now, no matter how fast they went, the boat seemed to crawl. Her gaze was fastened fearfully on the receding riverbank.

"There they are!" she cried. "I can see them, Nekonkh. They'll take that ferry barge, I'll wager, it's the only craft big enough to hold them all. Oh, hurry, hurry—"

The barge was well past the middle of the river when the little boat bumped the wharf on the east bank. Nekonkh tied the painter in an instant, and scrambled up the water-soaked ladder, pulling Mara behind him. Together they plunged into the gloomy alleys of the waterfront district.

"You must tell them, Nekonkh—I daren't go in—" panted Mara as they ran. "They'll believe you—"

"And where will you be?" he snapped. "If I let you slip away again—"

"Oh, what do I matter now? Put your wits to work, Captain! If I live to reach Crete it's more than I hope for anyway. . . ."

Nekonkh flung open the gate, and they halted, breathless. "I'll wait," gasped Mara. "I swear I'll wait. There in the corner."

Nekonkh loosed her arm at last and sprinted for the door.

Stumbling to the farthest, darkest corner of the courtyard, Mara huddled there, trying to catch her breath and listening for the clatter of weapons in the streets beyond. She heard them, all too soon. But before that she heard Nekonkh's voice in the tavern, followed by scrambling activity, then the sound of the rear door banging open and soft, hasty footsteps scattering in all directions. They were still hurrying stealthily by her on the other side of the courtyard wall when the heavy ones, the bold ones, pounded up the street.

Naught holds me here, thought Mara, shrinking against the wall. I could climb up these vines and be over the wall and away. . . .

But she did not move. She had told Nekonkh she would wait, and just once—just once in her life—she meant to do what she said.

She could hear the swords clanking now, and the panting, and see the orange glow of torchlight over the wall yonder, on the buildings across the street.

Nekonkh, come! Nekonkh, *come!* she thought. Make haste. . . .

And there he was at last, in the doorway, beckoning to her. She darted out of her corner—and the first soldiers burst at that moment through the gate.

"In the name of the queen!" a hoarse voice bellowed.

Mara flung herself back; Nekonkh vanished, and the raiders poured into the courtyard.

Gods of Egypt! They are everywhere, Mara was thinking as she flattened herself against the vines. Swarming over the courtyard like angry bees, dashing into the tavern and through it, shouting, cursing—and from the sound of it, breaking every piece of crockery Miphtahyah owned. Some ran out the back, she could hear them beating about the alleys, calling to one another, growling their fury that for the second time that night their prey had eluded them.

Mara found herself laughing silently, clutching the vines

249

in wild excitement. They all went free! She exulted. You sons of crocodiles, they all slid through your claws, every one! Then a light glared in her face.

"Who's that?" cried a voice. "*Ast!* I found one, at least. Come out of there!" A rough hand dragged her forth. "Look you, it's a maid!"

"A maid?" echoed another voice—one she knew.

She twisted about to face Chadzar the Libyan.

"By the Sacred Horns of Hathor!" he exploded. "What *kheft* spirited you out of the palace? With a guard at the door and every sentry warned—"

Mara loosed her held-in laughter; it rang clear and mocking and triumphant through the courtyard and the empty inn.

"You daughter of forty devils!" spat the Libyan, grabbing for his whip. "I'll teach you to laugh at me—"

From long habit, Mara flung an arm over her face, half crouching. The first savage, familiar bite of the lash quenched her laughter. As she gasped under the second, and the third, and the fourth, she knew her thirty short days of freedom were at an end.

When Mara walked into the great audience chamber of the Golden House, weary, sore, with hands bound tight behind her, it seemed a different room from the one she had entered the morning of Inanni's audience with the queen. Now, soldiers instead of courtiers stood in groups about it, and torches blazed on every wall, throwing dancing, dazzling reflections over the dais and the electrum throne which stood tall and empty, awaiting its occupant. Not gentle Inanni but Chadzar stood beside Mara, whip in hand—and no Lord Sheftu lounged with deceptive laziness in the background, ready to throw her a glance of encouragement, devise a way out.

Instead there was Senmut the Architect, hastily summoned from his bed and talking in low tones with his brother Nahereh—and there was no way out.

Count Sehnut's ravaged face showed a fierce elation; he kept looking over his shoulder toward the door leading to the queen's private apartments.

"I made her summons urgent," Mara heard him murmur. "And we'd best wait, she'll want to do the questioning herself. Amon! What luck this is! Now perhaps that cursed affair of the bodyguard will be forgotten. Her Radiance has shown me naught but the edge of her tongue these last few days, I must confess. You say this slave girl's your only capture?"

"Aye, but she's enough, provided she'll speak truth."

Senmut glanced at Mara, his cheeks furrowing with a faint, contemptuous smile. "There are ways to insure that."

Mara heard him as from a great distance. None of this seemed quite believable; disasters had fallen in such a deadly rain that she felt dazed by now. The night seemed to have been going on forever, like a chaotic dream. Only the fresh welts across her shoulders were vividly real; they throbbed without ceasing, each stripe separately, like crisscrossed bands of fire.

I have grown soft, she thought, or else this Libyan's hand is heavier than Zasha's ever was. . . .

There was a sudden stir among those who stood nearest the inner door. "Now, we'll see!" breathed Senmut with satisfaction. He crossed the room quickly; the soldiers effaced themselves against the walls, and the Libyan gave Mara a shove which sent her sprawling on her face, unable to catch herself because of her bound wrists. The whole company dropped to their knees as the door swung open.

"Behold," intoned the chamberlain. "The majesty of the Black Land, Horus of Gold, Enduring of Kingships, Splendid of Diadems, Ruler of Upper and Lower Egypt . . ."

"Enough!" rang Hatshepsut's high, metallic voice, accompanied by the whisper of her sandals across the floor. "I care naught for ceremony in the middle of the night. Count Senmut, what, I pray you, is of such vast importance that I be roused from my couch at this hour . . . ? Move that cursed cushion! I like it not."

Mara lay tensely quiet, intensely aware. Everything was real now—too real. Her shoulders burned with fresh pain from her wrenching fall, and the Architect's soothing tones turned her sick with dread.

"Your Radiance will scarce regret the loss of a little sleep when you hear my news. I have this night—with some help from my esteemed brother Lord Nahereh—struck the death blow at a conspiracy against your Enduring Majesty's throne and person. The very conspiracy, in fact, that we have long suspected to be in progress under the secret direction of your kinsman the Pretender—"

"Fewer words, Count Senmut! Do you say you have caught the leaders? I see them not."

"Majesty, this wretched slave girl you see before you—"

"*She* is the leader? You ask me," said the queen waspishly, "to believe that tale?"

"Shining One, my tale is not yet told!" retorted Senmut. "When you see the face of this wench . . . Pull her up, there!"

Mara felt the Libyan's rough grasp; the next instant she was on her knees, looking straight into the glittering dark eyes of Hatshepsut. The queen's face was as beautiful as before—perhaps more so, for this time its femininity was not mocked by the tied-on ceremonial beard and the massive severity of the double crown. Confined only by a narrow golden circlet bearing the royal cobra, her hair fell loose about her shoulders; and she wore a flowing dressing gown instead of robes of state.

"Blue eyes," she remarked. "Where have I seen this girl before?"

"Daughter of the Sun, she is the Canaanite's interpreter, and one of our own spies."

"By my father the god!" exclaimed the queen, leaning forward. "She's dared deceive us?"

"Exactly, Your Radiance. And if you will allow my tale to proceed . . ."

The queen leaned back, still staring at Mara. "Go on," she ordered.

And so the tale was told, with all the eloquence and subtle emphasis on his own cleverness of which Count Senmut had made himself master through long years of courting the favor of his queen. Mara listened with growing astonishment, scarcely able to recognize the happenings she knew so well. Nahereh was scarcely mentioned; the soldiers and Sahure dismissed with a shrug. It became clear that Count Senmut alone, inspired by his pure and lifelong devotion to the Radiant One, had solved the whole riddle in a flash of genius, conducted the raid singlehanded, and desired naught for reward save the smile of pharaoh. . . . Aye, and pharaoh was beginning to smile.

Prince of serpents! thought Mara, almost in awe. It was this same sly, persuasive tongue which for years had twisted all reports into the shape of what Hatshepsut wished to hear, a hymn to her own glory. It was these fluidly gesturing hands, as much as the slim, beringed ones resting on the arms of the throne, which maneuvered the destiny of Egypt and her helpless thousands. The Black Land might perish under taxes or the sword of an enemy, so long as these two gained their ends.

Behold, that which men dreaded now exists, . . . thought Mara. The old Prophecy of Neferrohu was forming in her mind. *Foes are in the East, and Asiatics descend into Egypt, and no protector hears. The land is diminished, its rulers multiplied. . . . Little is the corn, great the corn measure, yet it must be measured to overflowing.*

"You, slave!" The queen's voice sliced through her thoughts. "You may address my majesty. Have you heard the charges made against you by His Excellency?"

"Aye, Radiant One," whispered Mara.

"Do you deny them?"

"Nay, I do not—deny them."

What am I saying? she thought in sudden panic. I must deny them, somehow—

"You used your position as interpreter to hold private converse with my half brother the Pretender, you bore messages from him to the rabble at this inn, whom he calls his followers—and you were aware as you did this that you were assisting a plot against my sacred majesty and the throne of Egypt?"

"Nay, nay, I knew it not! I knew not what I did. I was bewitched! Your Majesty, it was as in a dream, I knew only that I must go to the inn, but I did not even understand the words I spoke there! I moved as one under a spell, I swear it was so! His Highness your brother bewitched me—"

"Lies!" cut in Nahereh contemptuously. "None could bewitch that maid, she's half *kheft* herself! She knew what she did."

"I've no doubt of it," said Hatshepsut. "Come, girl, this babble will gain you naught. You bore messages and assisted in treason against me. However, it is possible I might spare your life if you show yourself helpful now. Name me the leader of the plot."

The moment had come. Mara's lips parted, and her heart suddenly began to pound against her ribs. "I do not know him, Majesty," she whispered.

"You do not *know* him?" The queen seemed not able to believe what she had heard. Then her eyes narrowed with fury. "Do you dare defy me? Answer at once, before I have your tongue slit! Who is the leader?"

"I do not know him."

There was an incredulous silence. Then Count Senmut

spoke harshly. "Perhaps, Your Majesty, she has forgotten. You, Libyan! Refresh her memory!"

Chadzar scrambled off his knees and plied his whip with a will. One, two, three lashes blazed across Mara's back, already striped with welts

"Who is the leader?" repeated Hatshepsut.

Trying with difficulty to catch her breath, Mara said, "I tell you I know him not."

"*Ast!* It is the daughter of Set himself that you have brought me, Senmut!" breathed the queen, white faced. "Question this slave, I will not speak to her again."

"I hear and obey, Your Radiance." The furrows of his smile carved deep into the Architect's face as he left his place beside the throne and advanced upon Mara. "I advise you," he rapped out, "to answer me while you're able. Who is this leader?"

"I do not know him."

"Double your strokes, Libyan."

Again the crack of the lash sounded in the room—four times, five times, six. Through a blur of pain Mara heard the relentless voice again. "Who is he?"

Slowly, but stubbornly, Mara shook her head. She heard Chadzar swearing at her under his breath, the Architect rapping out, "Double the strokes again."

Mara gasped in protest, then in agony as the lash bit through the linen of her dress and laid open the skin beneath. She felt the linen tear away from her back, heard the whine of the next stroke and tried to brace herself for it. But the lash was living fire now, and each blow tore through her flesh. She could not brace herself. She could only retch helplessly, try to twist away from the remorseless whip, and grow sicker, dizzier.

"Stay a moment!" cried Hatshepsut. "Call off your Libyan ape, Nahereh, he'll kill the girl and we'll be no wiser than before. You, slave! Up on your knees and listen to me. Can you hear what I say?"

The room was whirling, and the voice seemed to whirl, too; but after a moment splashes of light appeared through the hazy darkness, swam into focus, and resolved themselves into the torches. Mara felt herself pulled to her knees; Senmut was repeating the queen's question impatiently. "Can you hear Her Majesty?" Mara nodded, sick with the smell of blood and the taste of it on her lips when she tried to moisten them.

"Listen well, then," ordered Hatshepsut. "I will spare you all further punishment for your crime if you will answer the question. More than that—I will free you from slavery and give you fifty gold *deben* and a silver chain. Think! Only a word or two and you will walk out of this room a free maid, with gold in your sash and your life before you."

Gold and freedom, thought Mara dimly. Once I wanted those things above all else.

"Majesty," she whispered again, "I do not know the leader."

Nahereh's cold voice broke the heavy silence which followed. "Your Radiance, it is barely possible she speaks truth. The informant I discovered and questioned told of a certain scribe who interested me much. It is said he alone knows the leader. I did not believe this, but . . . if I might put a question—"

"Do so!" snapped Hatshepsut.

Nahereh turned to Mara. "Answer me, Insolent One, or I'll call back the Libyan. Do you know this Sashai?"

"Aye, I know him."

"Who is he, then?"

"Sashai. That is the only name I know."

"Liar! You know him well—well indeed, according to that juggler. Was it not he who warned you when his own followers would have killed you? Aye! And was it not he you risked your own neck to save?"

"He, and others."

"What others?"

Mara was silent a moment. Then she said, "Those—like myself."

"And who is so worthless as yourself, pray? What babble is this?"

You would not understand, thought Mara, even if I told you. You do not know those others. But I know them, Son of Set! Nekonkh and Ashor and Miphtahyah and Nefer and the temple priests and the fishermen on the Nile and the goldsmiths and carpenters and potters and stonecutters going home from their work in the City of the Dead, and their friends and kin, *they* are the others.

She understood Inanni's story now. They were her friends and kin, the only ones she had. They were Egypt. I do not do this for the king, she thought in wonder. I do it for Egypt.

"Still silent!" hissed Nahereh furiously. "By Amon, these rebels are madmen, all of them! Chadzar, come forth again—"

Oh, Amon, I cannot stand another lashing now! thought Mara. Not yet—I must have time, a little time—

"Wait!" she choked. "I will tell you—something—all I know. I have heard them say that he is not a scribe, this Sashai, but a sculptor, one who has worked on the great temple under the cliff. But I do not know his name, I swear it!"

"If that is so, I can find him easily enough!" put in Count Senmut. He stepped closer to Mara. "Describe him!"

"He is—short, not much above my own height, with heavy shoulders and a girth it would take two sashes to go around. He wears a—curled wig and has a scar on his chin."

Senmut straightened slowly, his eyelids drooping with disbelief. "I do not recall such a man among my crew of sculptors."

"But I know him well—he is as I say!"

The queen's scornful laughter cut through her protest. "I think it is her fear of the lash that speaks, Senmut, not her memory! Is there no way to test this, without sending to the

257

City of the Dead to rouse all the sculptors in Thebes from their couches and drag them here?"

"I know a way, Your Radiance," said Lord Nahereh. He walked past Mara to the main doors of the room, and muttered something to a soldier, who hurried out. Returning, Nahereh remarked, "It will be but a moment, Your Majesty. As for you, girl, if you've not spoken truth this time, I hope you've made your peace with the gods."

How can he find out, so surely, so soon? thought Mara. He's bluffing, there's no— Then she remembered the juggler.

She sank back on her heels and let her head drop, her raw and aching shoulders turning to a mass of fire in protest against even that slight movement. She was still dizzy with the pain of it when she heard the door behind her open, the sound of someone falling to his knees, then Lord Nahereh's cold voice. "Here's our testing stick, Your Radiance. Come forward, juggler. Pharaoh would question you."

The twisted, strangely graceful body glided past the corner of Mara's eye, the queen's voice rang in her ears.

"You may speak to my majesty, juggler. I want the truth for once! Is the man called Sashai a short man, full of girth, with a curled wig and having a scar on his chin?"

"Sashai?" echoed Sahure, and Mara's aching flesh quivered under the amusement in his tone. "Your Eternal Radiance, I would scarce describe him so, since he is tall, and of a strength like a tree trunk, and without visible blemish. A young man, he is, somewhat homely of countenance, though this bedraggled lily here found him handsome enough, I daresay . . ."

"Amon deliver me from this wretch of a slave!" gasped the queen, almost transformed by her fury. "She has done naught but lie, naught but defy my majesty! You! Libyan!" Hatshepsut rose from her throne, and her voice rose to a shriek. "Come forward and teach this riffraff who it is she defies! Lay on, do you hear me? Beat her! Beat her! Beat her!"

258

Chadzar was obeying already, and his blows grew heavier with every scream of his infuriated pharaoh. But the screams grew dim in Mara's ears; she swam for a few end less moments in a sea of fire, then faded slowly into a sea of black, where there was no pain.

CHAPTER 24

For Egypt

NUIT THE Starry One, goddess of the sky, arched her spangled body over the land of Egypt and gazed down serenely on its sleeping thousands. In palace and villa and hovel they slept, long of eye, with their amulets about their necks, each stiffly pillowed on his headrest of wood or carven ivory or gold. The sailor slept on his vessel on the Nile, the priest in his temple cell, the beggar in his lane. The scent of lotuses and the river and the black earth rose like the very breath of night to delight Nuit's nostrils, and the cat slept, and the waterfowl slept, and the dead slept in their spices and wrappings, deep in the tomb.

But not everyone slept. In Bubastis, in the North, a thief prowled the night; in Abydos three surgeons worked over an old man who moaned in pain; and in Thebes two men argued in tense and urgent whispers in an alley.

The eyes of Nuit rested on these two with mild curiosity. One was young, dressed as a scribe; the other a burly riverman. They seemed agitated and in anxious haste; presently they left their alley and moved swiftly, but with great caution, down another, glancing always from side to side as if searching for someone. Nuit became aware that there were other dark figures scattered throughout the alleys and byways of this particular area, hiding in twos or threes, sometimes venturing forth, also searching, until they found others. The scribe discovered one such group, joined it eagerly and gave whispered orders, then hurried with his companion toward the river.

There was a small papyrus boat bobbing against one of the ladders of the wharf, which Nuit had not deemed worth her notice until the scribe and the riverman dropped into it and paddled in silent haste out across the Nile. The eye of Nuit was distracted; for a time she was engaged in admiring her own starry reflection in the dark mirror of the water; when she remembered the two men, they were already scrambling up the opposite bank and starting at a run through the streets of western Thebes. At a corner within sight of the palace wall, near a clump of acacia trees, they halted, held a brief conference, then separated. The riverman melted into the thick shadows under the acacias; the scribe made his way by lane and back alley into the district of great walled villas to the northwest. He was moving with the utmost caution now, and he grew warier the closer he approached a certain broad street lined with sycamore figs, and an estate of noble proportions which fronted on it. Nuit was pleased; the sycamore was sacred to her, and its glassy leaves mirrored her own beauty, as well as emitting the delicate, sharp scent most welcome to her nostrils. Because of the sycamores, she looked with favor on the estate whose walls the scribe was circling stealthily, and smiled when he scaled the wall by means of its vines, slipped through a corner of the large date grove, and approached the great columned, silent house set in its midst. She watched him until he gained an inner courtyard by the servants' wing, and knocked softly on a door. Then the faint cry of a woman in Menfe reached Nuit's velvet-dark ear, and remembering her duties as protectress of mothers and childbirth—for was she not the mother of great Osiris himself?—she turned her attention to another drama.

"Irenamon!" whispered Sheftu, knocking again, and more insistently, upon the door.

There was the sound of a startled movement within, then the old man's voice. "Who's there, at this hour of the night? Wait, I'm coming . . ."

In a moment the door was opened a cautious crack, then it swung wide, revealing an Irenamon who looked strangely shrunken and fragile, and bald as an egg, without his eye-paint and elaborate wig. "Your lordship!" he gasped. "What is—"

"Hush! Let me in, quickly." Sheftu stepped into the room and silently closed the door, while the old man fumbled to light a lamp. "Irenamon, has anyone been here tonight? Have you been disturbed?"

"Nay, my lord, none but that Midianite trader, earlier this evening, come peddling his wines as he does every—"

"No one else? You have seen no soldiers about?"

"Soldiers? Indeed no! What would soldiers . . . ?" The lamp glowed into brightness now and Irenamon turned to study his master's face by its light. "Your lordship! Is there trouble? Does it mean something is wrong, that no soldiers have been here?"

"Nay, it means all is unbelievably right!—as yet. Oh, Amon, it means I have made a terrible mistake, perhaps a fatal one for a maid who still keeps silent, even at this moment, under I know not what punishment. . . . Quick, Irenamon! Rouse one of the grooms. I want Ebony and the black mare hitched to my chariot within five minutes, and ready in the main courtyard."

Sheftu caught up the lamp from the old man's table, and

261

shielding the flame with his hand, dashed through the servants' wing into the inner garden and up the stairs to the second floor of the main house. Once in his own room, he tore off his coarse scribe's garments and put on fine linen ones, with his costliest jeweled collar and a golden headcloth. By the time he reached the main courtyard, the blacks were harnessed and tossing their silken heads.

Seizing the reins from a sleepy groom, Sheftu leaped into the chariot and snatched the whip from its holder.

"Your lordship, take care!" begged Irenamon in a quaking voice, gripping the side of the chariot with both hands. "I fear for you . . . May I know where you are going?"

"Aye, and you may know as well that I may never come back. I go to the palace, old friend, to stick my head in a noose. Pray to the Shining One that it will not tighten too soon."

Sheftu leaned to grip the old man's hand. Then he popped his whip and the chariot plunged forward amid a clatter of hoofs, spun out of the imposing gates and down the Street of Sycamores toward the palace.

In Menfe, the baby had been born—a tiny man-child yelling lustily in the Egyptian night. Already the mother had tied a protective amulet about his wrist, and the father was hurrying to burn a pinch of incense for Nuit the Great Mother, in gratitude for the safe birth. As its fragrance drifted upward to the nose of the Starry One, she smiled serenely and allowed her lustrous eyes to move again to Thebes.

She could not find the scribe now; in the great villa under the sycamores she saw none but an old man in night clothes, standing alone by the gates with his bald head bowed in his hands. However, there was movement far away down the dark street—swift and reckless movement, and the clamor of hoofs. It was a chariot, driven full tilt by a young noble in a collar that rivaled Nuit's own star-gemmed throat, and his horses were black as her hair. She watched him with interest as he sped through one street and then another, and upon rounding the last corner beside the palace walls, pulled up short beside a clump of acacias she thought she remembered.

Aye, it was the same, for out of its dark shelter darted the river captain, who held a hurried conference with the nobleman, then set off at a lumbering trot around the curve of the palace wall. The other whipped up his horses and drove straight for the main gate. His voice, bold and demanding, floated faintly to Nuit's faraway ear, and in a moment the palace gates swung open. At his barked order the sentry snapped to attention, raising his sword to salute as the chariot flashed past him and whirled down the East Avenue.

The Starry One had seldom encountered a more impetuous young man, and she found herself pleased by him. She wondered where he had sent the riverman, and to what purpose. After a brief search she discovered the captain some distance to the West, pounding heavily at a door of the long barracks which housed the pharaoh's bodyguard. His answer was the flare of a lamp within, then the door swung open. Nuit blinked rapidly at the light, causing a thousand stars to twinkle. To her disappointment, the captain stepped into the lighted room where her night-seeing eyes could no longer follow him.

"General Khofra?" panted Nekonkh.

"I am he. What is it, man?"

"I bring the signal. Lord Sheftu's orders—to be obeyed tonight, at once! He bids you rouse your soldiers. At the mark of four, exactly, they're to march on the palace. Overpower the sentries first, and leave enough archers at the gates to hold off the regulars should they try to bring aid. Then—"

"Stay a moment!" burst out the general incredulously. "Tonight? The revolution's to take place *tonight?*"

263

"At the mark of four, no later! Harken— Once in the palace, you're to send a detachment to the king's apartments, while you storm the throne room. Take plenty of men for that. We think the room's full of regulars. You've just half an hour. Hasten!"

"You must be mad, my friend! I can't do it that fast!"

"The gods willing, you *can!*" bellowed Nekonkh. "By Amon, you must! Lord Sheftu's walked into the lion's jaws, and he'll die like a trapped rat if we don't bring it off! He may anyway." Nekonkh jammed his wig down more firmly onto his head and reached for the door latch.

"What of the other factions?" barked Khofra, who in spite of his protests was hurriedly buckling on his leather tunic. "The priesthood, the nobles who've sworn loyalty, the common folk. Have they been roused?"

"That's where I'm going now, to rouse the nobles. I've comrades across the river doing the rest. By this time the queen's high priest has fallen, if all's gone well, and there'll be a procession out of the temple at dawn, followed by the populace. They'll do their parts, never fear. But without your seasoned troops—"

"They're far from seasoned, Captain!" said the other grimly, seizing his helmet from a chair. "The thing's impossible, but by every god in Egypt, I'll do my best!"

"Luck go with you!" Nekonkh plunged out into the night again as Khofra vanished down the long hall of the barracks to rouse his soldiers.

Nuit did not see the captain emerge, for she was watching the young man in the shining collar. He had abandoned his chariot near the palace stables and set off at a run through a maze of gardens and courts. Ahead, in the direction he was running, lay the north wing of the Golden House, and the great hall where the woman Hatshepsut—she who arrogantly claimed descent from Nuit's own glorious grandfather, Ra the Shining One—was accustomed to hold her audiences. Something was happening in that hall, something ugly. But there was too much torchlight for Nuit's dark-loving eyes to make out what it was. She felt a flicker of apprehension, quite unsuitable to a goddess, when she perceived that her bold young man was making straight for the anteroom that adjoined the hall. He passed into the mist of light that surrounded the portals, then to Nuit's disappointment, he, like the captain, vanished through a torchlit door.

She shrugged her starry shoulders. These scurrying mortals had amused her, but now she would spend what remained of the hours of darkness in admiring her beauty in the mirror of the Nile. She began to do so, but soon the urgent calling of a woman in the Delta recalled to her mind her age-old duties, and she forgot Thebes as she ushered another new Egyptian into the world.

Mara swam up slowly out of her sea of dark oblivion. Someone was splashing cold water into her face, and shaking her roughly.

They will only beat me again, she thought, keeping her eyes shut. I'll pretend . . .

But even as she planned it she gasped and cringed as the hand touched her raw shoulders.

"She's but feigning now," said Nahereh. "Up on your knees, you!"

But it was not his voice which forced her eyes wide open suddenly, jarred her whole mind alert. It was another voice, outside in the anteroom, and a stir among the soldiers who stood nearest the doors.

"Up on your knees, I said!" repeated Nahereh. Then, impatiently, "What is that? Who's outside there?"

"A noble who demands admittance, Excellence," mumbled one of the soldiers. "He seems most—"

"Let him in," commanded Hatshepsut.

Mara raised herself to her knees, disregarding the pain the movement caused her. It couldn't be—it mustn't! But it was. The tall doors swung open and an arrogant, gold-decked figure she had never thought to see again strolled through them and bowed with debonair grace toward the throne.

"Good evening, Radiant One! Excellencies, rejoice!" remarked Lord Sheftu.

He did not glance at Mara, nor did she at him, after her first agonized recognition. Her attention froze on Sahure, whose sudden intent frown showed that it was only a matter of moments until the jeweled collar and golden headcloth would no longer confuse him. Had Sheftu noticed him? He must have, and he must be all but reeling from the shock of it. *Ai,* why did he come! thought Mara. Whatever plan he'd had in mind, it was defeated before it began.

"You might rather say good morning," the queen was remarking irritably. "Have we turned night into day, or is it your habit, Lord Sheftu, to visit the palace at this hour? I supposed this audience was secret."

"Your Radiance, it is difficult to keep anything secret in the city of Thebes, when both servants and rivermen gossip like magpies—often with each other. I felt my place was by Your Majesty's side. However—" the smooth voice took on a note of amusement—"I seem to have overestimated the emergency. Where are the criminals, Daughter of the Sun? Surely my lord Nahereh's adroit and fearless coup netted more than one wretched slave girl!"

"A poor catch indeed, but all we have," returned the queen, frowning at Nahereh, who had gone red with anger. "And the stubborn wench has told us naught!"

"Perhaps she knows naught," suggested Sheftu carelessly. "But whether she be innocent or guilty, Your Majesty has been ill-advised in the manner of questioning her," he added, with a glance at Senmut. "The maid looks half-dead."

"Should she defy pharaoh and go unpunished?" snarled Senmut.

"Nay. But on the other hand, of what value is her corpse?"

Mara listened breathlessly. By Amon! Already he had contrived to make the whole matter seem vaguely ridiculous, and the count and Lord Nahereh a pair of fools. Could it be possible that— Then she glanced at the juggler and her heart sank. His narrowed eyes were gleaming. He had realized the truth. But would he dare accuse so great a lord? He could prove nothing. . . .

"If Your Majesty will allow me," Sheftu was saying easily, "I might soothe the maid a little, tempt her with some small reward—"

"Nay, we've tried that. My majesty offered her both gold and freedom. She scorned them."

"She *scorned* them?" Sheftu was not acting now, and there was a note in his voice that stirred Mara to a deep, unreasonable joy. As if he could not believe what he had heard, he repeated, "She refused a bribe?"

"Aye, she did, the wretch!"

There was a little silence, and when Sheftu spoke again his voice shook almost imperceptibly. "In that case, naught on earth can unseal her lips. Perhaps, after all, she knows nothing. . . ."

"And perhaps she knows much!" It was a new voice— Sahure's. It rang loud and derisive through the room. "But *you* know more—Sashai!"

Every head jerked toward the juggler, still crouched on his knees but now pointing a long, accusing finger at Lord Sheftu.

"How dare you speak without permission?" gasped the queen.

Sheftu went on at once, as if good breeding alone forbade him to notice an outrageous interruption. "And if she knows naught, Your Majesty—"

"Wait!" cried Count Senmut. "Let the juggler speak! Did he say 'Sashai'?"

"I did, Lion of Courage and Wisdom! *That* is Sashai—he who stands before you in fine raiment and gold! He is the scribe of the Falcon—the same, the same!"

The queen rose to her feet. "What is this babble! Do you know of whom you speak, insolent fool? That is Lord Sheftu, son of Menkau the Friend of Kings, and my trusted courtier!"

"He is also Sashai, Your Magnificence! He is the same, I swear it!"

Sheftu's amused voice broke in. "Who is this madman? He intrigues me."

"Of course he's mad!" cried the queen. "He offends my majesty! Take him away, Nahereh."

"Your Radiance, wait!" Count Senmut stepped forward, and the harsh furrows of his smile deepened slowly in his face as he studied Sheftu. "Surely my lord would be even more intrigued if this juggler could prove his claims. That would be amusing, would it not? Speak, juggler! Have you proof?"

"I have, Lion of Wisdom!"

The queen stiffened. Nahereh pulled the juggler toward him, and Mara caught her breath in sharp and sudden fear.

"You can *prove* this accusation?" burst out Nahereh. "Speak, then, quickly!"

"Let his Highest Excellence the Architect look upon the left wrist of the great Lord Sheftu—"

Oh Amon, it's over, it's all over, he's lost! thought Mara, and the fragile bubble of hope that had been growing in her burst, all in an instant.

"What will I find there?" asked Count Senmut, moving toward Sheftu stealthily, like a great cat.

"An amulet of strange design, Highest Excellence. I have not seen it this night, for his wrist is hidden from me, here where I kneel. Nevertheless I will describe it to you, for I know it well, aye, well, from the wrist of Sashai. . . ."

"Describe it, then!" Senmut seized Sheftu's wrist, and hiding it from the juggler with his own body stared down at it.

"It is a twist of flax thread strung with seven green beads, and knotted seven times. There is a flat bead of carnelian in the midst of the seven, inscribed on both sides. Is it not as I say, Excellence?"

Slowly the Architect's eyes climbed up to rest on Sheftu's immobile face. "It is as you say." He flung Sheftu's wrist down. "Here is your traitor, Radiant One—the incorruptible Sheftu!"

"Osiris!" whispered the queen, dropping back upon her throne. "It cannot be! It cannot be!"

For Mara, time itself seemed to halt. Then Sheftu sighed, shrugged and turned to Count Senmut.

"So it is over, comrade," he said. "We had best admit everything, had we not? But it is sad, that in spite of all our precautions—"

"We!" Senmut was staring at him, suddenly ashen.

"Great Amon, what are you saying?" Hatshepsut fairly screamed. "Do you tell me that Count Senmut, too—"

The Architect whirled to her. "Majesty, it is a lie! He but seeks to drag me down with him! Radiant One—you do not believe—"

"Oh come," put in Sheftu coolly. "The game's over. We've been comrades, let us die like men."

"Curse you! You'll die like a rat, here and now—" Senmut sprang upon him savagely, a knife flashed upward, only to clash upon another that seemed to leap of itself into Sheftu's fist. In an instant the room was pandemonium; Nahereh's cloak fanned Mara as he rushed forward, Hatshepsut was on her feet, shrieking orders that brought soldiers flying from every corner of the room. Mara, torn between terror and wild elation, found herself standing erect, hurling defiance at all of them at the top of her voice. Then the knot of soldiers around the two men burst apart, Nahereh staggered back, and there was Sheftu, held fast by two soldiers, with

269

his fine robe torn but his eyes flashing. On the floor at his feet sprawled the body of Count Senmut.

"So!" breathed Hatshepsut. "One is gone—and the other shall follow!" Her voice rose with fury. "You stand condemned of treason and murder, my lord Sheftu! At sunrise you die."

"And my secrets with me," taunted Sheftu.

The queen's features seemed to freeze; for the first time Mara saw a glint of real fear in her eyes. "What mean you? There are others?"

Sheftu laughed softly, and pharaoh rose as if the sound itself drew her to her feet. "Cease this mockery! What secrets?"

"Aye, what? And when is it to happen? And who will do it? Count your hours, Hatshepsut, for there are few left, and you will not enjoy them. Who can you point to now and say with confidence, 'He is my friend'? Your court is full of traitors, and you know them not! But I know them."

He is gambling for time, thought Mara. On what frail hope she could not imagine, he was taking one last chance, playing on the queen's one weakness—her fear for her throne. And he was doing it as skillfully as a harpist plucks his strings. Hatshepsut was standing rigid, with panic in her eyes.

"What traitors?" she cried.

"Their names die with me."

"And their plans as well! Son of the Devourer, what can they do without their leader?"

"My death will be as nothing to them. It will be as a stone thrown into the Nile in the time of inundation! Do the waters stop for a stone? The plans are made, Hatshepsut, and the hour is near. You will know your enemies when they strike."

For an instant Hatshepsut's face was sickening to gaze upon. Then slowly she straightened, and something of her cold beauty returned as she forced herself under control. She sat down slowly, stiffly, and grasped the arms of her throne.

"Lord Sheftu," she said, "let us approach this in a different manner. Why go to your death when you might serve me in Count Senmut's place—when you might own the choice lands that were his, tax free—when you might be the most powerful man in Egypt? All this I could give you, or more—whatever you asked! Surely there is some treasure you crave?"

Sheftu hesitated and a gleam of triumph appeared in Hatshepsut's eyes. At last he said, "Aye, there is, Majesty."

The queen let out her breath slowly and relaxed, leaning back with a faint smile twisting her lips. "Soldiers! Release his lordship," she commanded.

The men loosed their hands and stepped back. Sheftu stood free. At once he turned, strode quickly to Mara and took her in his arms. Mara, in a rapturous confusion at the unexpectedness of it, barely heard the queen's outraged exclamation. But she felt with all her heart the gentleness with which Sheftu held her, taking care not to touch her blood-stained shoulders, and she heard his murmur in her ear.

"Oh, Mara, my beloved Mara, I would I could save thee, but they come not, and it will soon be too late. . . ."

"Who comes?" she whispered.

But the queen's mocking laughter cut in. "*This* is your treasure, Lord Sheftu?"

"Aye. The greatest treasure in Egypt—a maid whose loyalty cannot be bought. Whatever bargain we make, Daughter of the Sun, must include her freedom."

Mara did not see what signal the queen made to the soldiers; but suddenly she and Sheftu were jerked apart and held fast, and Hatshepsut was on her feet, her voice lashing at them.

"We will make no bargain! Nahereh! Bring forth your

271

Libyan and instruct him to beat this maid to death before his lordship's eyes. Unless—did you wish to speak, Lord Sheftu?"

Mara flashed him a terrified glance and saw that Hatshepsut had found her weapon at last. All Sheftu's cool poise had shattered in an instant; he was fighting his captors like a madman—though his lips were shut tight.

"Begin, Libyan," ordered Hatshepsut.

The lash curled through Chadzar's fingers like a lazy black serpent, then struck. The pain was nauseating; through it Mara heard Sheftu's furious voice, and though she could not understand what he said, she screamed out, "Don't speak! Don't speak! It will not last long—"

It would not last long at all, she thought dimly as the lash came down again. Already the blackness was closing in. She had had too much. After the next blow she would feel nothing. . . .

But the next blow never fell. For an instant she could not distinguish the strange new sound she was hearing from the roaring in her own ears. Then she realized this new roar came from outside; men were running, shouting. And suddenly Hatshepsut was crying out orders in a strange, hoarse voice, and Mara felt herself dumped like a discarded burden as the soldiers leaped over her and ran. . . . The big doors burst open.

Mara struggled painfully to rise, staring about her at the wildest confusion. Soldiers were everywhere, pouring into the room in endless streams, clashing in hand-to-hand combat with those ranged around Hatshepsut, who stood screaming orders before her throne. Nahereh fell as Mara watched, and the gnarled old general who had struck him down whirled as the juggler crept past toward the inner door, seized him, flung him bodily into the arms of two archers—

A shadow fell across her. "Mara! Oh, Amon, no hand but mine shall slay that misbegotten Libyan!" Sheftu scooped her up, cursing incoherently, carried her to the far side of the room and thrust her into a pair of strong and sheltering arms she recognized with wonder as Nekonkh's. As Sheftu whirled away again, she heard the captain's comforting growl in her ear. "Now, little one, all's well at last, everything's out of our hands, our task is done. Rest, little Blue Eyes." He flung his cloak about her, and with a deep sigh of gratitude Mara buried her face in the rough folds of his tunic, and shut her ears to the noise of conflict, and shut her eyes. . . .

When she opened them, she knew not how much later, all was strangely quiet. She twisted about in Nekonkh's arms, which instantly loosened, and for a moment had the peculiar sensation that she was back with Inanni, in Hatshepsut's formal court. Once more the big room glittered with the jeweled collars of courtiers. But now the walls behind them were lined thick with soldiers—those wearing the scarlet helmets of pharaoh's bodyguard. The courtiers, headed by Sheftu, stood in two ranks down the length of the room. At one end of the open aisle thus formed was the dais, the great throne, and Hatshepsut standing motionless and stiffly erect, with her black hair falling in a cloud about her cold and beautiful face, and the cobra on her brow.

At the other end, approaching her with the stride of a conqueror, came the long-fettered king.

Thutmose stopped before the throne and spoke. "Come down."

There was a pause, during which not a head moved, not a finger stirred. Then slowly, haughtily, Hatshepsut descended the steps of the dais and stood before him. He reached out and jerked the coronet of Egypt from her head. Then, still without turning his eyes from hers, he beckoned someone in the crowd. A servant stepped forward, bearing a tray on which rested a golden cup full of some dark liquid.

For just a moment Hatshepsut's gaze wavered, as she looked at the cup. Then it returned unflinchingly to Thutmose.

"You show little mercy, half brother," she said bitterly.

"I show much! I grant you leave to die by your own hand, rather than another's. Take the cup and drink."

Hatshepsut was silent, and the mask of youth fell suddenly from her face. "So be it! I will drink, and forget. But you will not forget, nor will these others, though you chisel my *cartouche* from every monument in the Double Kingdom! My works stand, Son of the Lesser Wife, and they will eclipse yours, and your sons', and those of all pharaohs after me, so long as the land of Egypt is watered by the Nile! You cannot kill the name of Hatshepsut the Glorious! Now, give me the cup. But I am pharaoh and I will not drink it here, in the presence of my enemies! Stand aside, that I may pass."

With a sweep of her fragile, flowing robes Hatshepsut turned and bore the golden cup to her private chambers. Thutmose followed her. The door closed quietly behind them.

A sound like a sigh passed through the crowd in the throne room, but no one stirred from his place, though Sheftu turned to seek Mara's eyes across the space that separated them. It seemed a long time before the inner door opened again, and Thutmose stepped forth—alone. At sight of the royal cobra on his brow, the entire company fell to their knees.

But the king walked straight to Sheftu, raised him, and grasped his shoulders in both hands. There was a low conversation unheard by any save themselves, then both turned toward Mara, and Sheftu quickly crossed the space of bloodstained floor and took her hand.

"Beloved—come with me, unless your hurt is too great. . . ."

Conscious of a hundred eyes upon her, Mara followed him painfully but with pounding heart down the double line of kneeling courtiers to the king.

"So," said Thutmose in the gentlest tone she had ever

heard him use. "It is the little interpreter who has saved Egypt and me this night." He was silent a moment, then lifted his hand to touch his lips and forehead in the salute of respect. "Blue-Eyed One, never again shall you cover your shoulders. I declare your scars to be medals of gallantry greater than any I could bestow, and it is my will that all the Black Land look upon them, and learn the nature of courage." Gravely he lifted a massive gold chain from his own neck and placed it around Mara's. "*Count* Sheftu," he added, raising his voice so that it carried to all parts of the room, "I advance your status to Nearest Friend and Advisor of Pharaoh. Your place is at my right hand as long as I rule Egypt. But I charge you now, leave me and find the most skilled physician in Thebes to treat this maid's wounds. Farewell, and the gods go with you."

He turned away from them, and as they moved once more down the long room, they heard his confident and vigorous step advancing toward the throne. A moment later his voice rang out.

"In the name of Ra the Shining One and of my father, whose royal will decreed it, I claim my heritage as pharaoh of the Two Lands and sole ruler of Egypt!"

CHAPTER 25

The Street of Sycamores

OUTSIDE, the night was soft, the air dark and cool and fragrant. Mara walked with Sheftu past the archers guarding the entrance, across the stone drive and through the gate of the lotus garden. There Sheftu stopped at once, and took her with infinite care into his arms. He kissed her lingeringly, in silence, then tilted her chin and looked down into her face.

"Sheftu," she whispered, "it's all over."

"Nay, little one. It's just beginning. Many things are beginning."

With one arm still about her waist, he led her on across the dewy grass, and with every step Mara's heart grew lighter until even the pain in her torn shoulders seemed a thing of the past.

"Where are we going?" she asked presently. "To find the physician?"

"My lovely Mara, the physician about to be lifted above his station in life will come to *you*—and relate to his grandchildren how he did so."

Mara laughed softly, delightedly. "And he must be the best in Thebes—you heard pharaoh's order. Then I suppose we are going to my room with the butterflies, which I never thought to see again. . . . Aye, of course! I must wake my princess and tell her! You will send her home, Sheftu, as you promised? Without her help I could never have—"

"Hush. We'll tell her tomorrow, and she may sail as far as she likes. But we are not going to her now, little one—you're going home with me. For the rest of your life."

"Sheftu! Is it true? I can scarce believe it." Mara stopped walking and looked at him wonderingly. "You're a count now. And I a free maid."

"A free maid—and about to become a countess." Sheftu grinned down at her. "I trust," he added, "that you will remember to keep your sandals on."

"And if I choose not to?" she retorted.

He laughed softly, taking her face between his hands. "Then you shall go barefoot. Who shall dare cross the will of the countess—except the count?" He dropped a kiss on her lips, then his smile faded, and his arms went around her as if never to let her go. "Oh Mara, Mara. . . . Nay, I'm hurting you. We must go on, beloved."

A countess, thought Mara dreamily as they moved across the grass, into the Avenue of Rams, and on toward the palace stables. I shall be a countess and possess anything I like, and eat roasted waterfowl every day, and wear rings on my fingers and have lotuses, always a fresh one, for my hair—all just as I boasted to Teta. Except it will be better than that—oh, much better—for I shall be with Sheftu. . . .

They had reached the stables, and Sheftu was rapping out orders that produced hasty activity among the grooms. Soon a wide door opened and four Nubians hurried out, bearing a canopied litter far grander than those Mara had made way for so often in the streets of Menfe.

"I am glad," she murmured, "that it is not a chariot!"

She was beginning to feel like a countess already as she stepped into the litter and eased her sore shoulders back against its luxurious cushions. *Ai*, surely I was destined for this at birth! she thought, trailing her fingers along the rich carving of the arm rest and crossing her ankles in exquisite imitation of Zasha's lady. If Teta could see me now!

Why, I will soon forget I was ever a slave in my life, and no one else will know. I shall wear royal linen and perhaps a blue wig.

She extended a gracious hand to Sheftu as he sank down beside her, and to her delight he bent over it gallantly.

"And now, Count Sheftu," she inquired, "could you describe me as a guttersnipe?"

"To be sure," he said pleasantly.

She sat bolt upright. "Sheftu!"

He was laughing under his breath as he lifted her hand again to his lips. "A countess-guttersnipe," he amended. "Far more interesting, Lotus-Eyed One, than a lady born— See now, you were too impulsive. You have hurt your shoulders."

He eased her back against the cushions, one arm about her. The chair lifted, moved at a swift but gentle jog down the long avenue, through the tall main gate, and into streets beginning to gray with the first light of morning. For a time Mara was content with silence and blissful comfort. But a thought was stirring in the back of her mind which she could not put away.

"Sheftu," she said, "when I am your countess, may I have anything I want?"

"Anything, little one." He glanced at her, then added, "Within reason."

Mara grinned, savoring again the flavor of their old dueling at the Falcon. "I only want you to buy me a slave."

"A slave?"

"Aye. One called Teta—who was left one day in Menfe with a basket of unironed *shentis* she did not deserve."

"You shall have her, Blue-Eyed One. But my villa is full of slaves. What do you want of another?"

"I want to free her."

Sheftu smiled, took her hand and settled back beside her. "So be it. That is a small matter, to free a slave. Have we not freed a king?" A moment later he dropped her hand to point: "Look, Mara! Ahead there. Those are our gates."

Eagerly Mara sat erect and peered through the swaying curtains. They were moving down a broad street lined with sycamores, toward the imposing gates of a great white wall. Beyond the wall she could see groves and a spreading roof, the plumes of tall palms waving in the breeze. And still beyond, over all, shone the clear, pink sky of morning. . . .

Even as the chair passed under the last sycamore and through the gates, a great procession of chanting, scarlet-robed priests was winding up the East Avenue toward the palace, trailing the fragrance of myrrh. Nuit, the Great Mother, making her stately way westward to the dark of the underworld, paused at the perfume and the joyous noise, and glanced over a starry shoulder. Something unusual was happening in the Black Land; but her duties were over and she was sleepy. She moved away, blinking, as the great doors of the throne room were thrown open and the procession passed inside, followed by a throng of cheering, white-clad Thebans who filled the streets and ferries and wharfs as far back as she could see.

Then the stars went out, for the bark of Ra, in fiery splendor, burst out of the East. Sunshine flooded the wide desert and the long, green valley of the Nile. The night was over; a new day had dawned for the land of Egypt.